ABU

PRAISE FOR *THE CHOOSING*

"The strong female heroine will appeal to teen readers, and adults and teens alike may also enjoy the themes of corruption and religion, absolute human power, and government as God. . . . Dekker's debut is worth choosing."
PUBLISHERS WEEKLY

"The story vacillates between the sweetness of a tender coming-of-age romance and moments that almost resemble a Dean Koontz thriller. . . . At times frightening but often beautiful, this first volume of Carrington's story will leave readers eager for the next book of this new series."
SERENA CHASE, *USA Today*

"This is an amazing debut novel full of heart, drama, and complex believable characters . . . with a detailed plot, and gripping truths that pierced my heart."
THE BOOK CLUB NETWORK INC.

"A swiftly moving plot puts readers in the center of the action, and the well-described setting adds to the experience. Deeper themes of value and worth will appeal to both young adult and adult readers."
ROMANTIC TIMES

"Whatever expectations you have of debut author Rachelle Dekker, go ahead and put them aside. Rachelle, daughter to bestselling author Ted Dekker, is carving out a space of her own. Her debut novel, *The Choosing*, is a rich statement about the author's future and her impact on Christian fiction."

FAMILY FICTION

"Ripe for discussion, [*The Choosing*] may inspire some readers to open up about the social pressures that they feel both in and out of their faith community. Expect it to appeal to dystopian fans of all ages."

FOREWORD REVIEWS

"Readers will find Dekker's storyline somewhat akin to her father's works in terms of action, adventure, and unpredictability. *The Choosing*, though, explores more the inner workings of her characters and how they feel about their lot in life. I look forward to more dystopian titles from Dekker in the near future."

BOOKREPORTER.COM

"*The Choosing* is an inspiring tale that reaches deep into the hearts of men and women, showing both the love and the darkness that can lurk within."

FRESH FICTION

"Marrying the themes of the popular Kiera Cass Selection novels with the action danger of *The Hunger Games*, Dekker asserts a strong imaginative voice that had me gulping down sentences and events as quickly as they were relayed on [the] page."

NOVEL CROSSING

"This book is part adventure, part romance, part mystery, and it works. The writing is wonderful. It flows in such a way that it keeps the reader turning page after page . . . more than likely long into the night to find out what happens!"

RADIANT LIT

"In her stunning debut novel, Rachelle Dekker plunges readers into a unique yet familiar-feeling dystopian society, where one girl's longing for acceptance, identity, and purpose becomes a mind-bending, pulse-pounding journey that'll [leave] you breathless and reeling. A superb story!"

JOSH OLDS, LifeIsStory.com

"A stunning debut, masterfully written and filled with deep questions of the spirit; I could not put it down."

TOSCA LEE, *New York Times* bestselling author

"A powerful tale for anyone who has ever felt worthless, or feared that their true value is an award they'll never be able to earn."

ERIN HEALY, author of *Motherless*

"A true page-turner! Compelling and intriguing, *The Choosing* is a fantastic debut that will have you glued to the pages all the way to the climactic ending!"

SUSAN MAY WARREN, bestselling, Christy Award–winning author

THE CALLING

RACHELLE DEKKER

TYNDALE HOUSE PUBLISHERS, INC., CAROL STREAM, ILLINOIS

Visit Tyndale online at www.tyndale.com.

Visit Rachelle Dekker's website at www.rachelledekker.com.

TYNDALE and Tyndale's quill logo are registered trademarks of Tyndale House Publishers, Inc.

The Calling

Designed by Dean H. Renninger

The Calling is a work of fiction. Where real people, events, establishments, organizations, or locales appear, they are used fictitiously. All other elements of the novel are drawn from the author's imagination.

Library of Congress Cataloging-in-Publication Data
Dekker, Rachelle.
 The calling / Rachelle Dekker.
  pages ; cm. — (A Seer novel)
 ISBN 978-1-4964-0226-4 (hc) — ISBN 978-1-4964-0227-1 (sc)
 I. Title.
  PS3604.E378C35 2016
  813'.6--dc23   2015032289

Printed in the United States of America

22 21   20   19   18   17   16
7   6   5   4   3   2   1

For my only brother, J. T.
Remember, your strength does not come from fighting
your fears but rather learning to let them go.

Fear only exists when I believe.

When I give it a name, a face, a hand to grip me.

For I fear tomorrow and I fear the past.

I fear the hellos and the good-byes. I fear my monsters; I fear myself.

Above all I fear the dark and its power to swallow me whole.

I watch a tiny flame dance before me, which

knows nothing of the darkness it consumes.

It only knows its heat, its light. And the darkness knows it too.

I watch as the red and orange lick the air,

realizing the flame fears nothing.

But I fear the wind, the slight gust that could forever end the flame,

Leaving me with nothing but ashes.

And when it is gone, all my fears come alive.

I am lost in a sea of things I created and

there is no lifeline to be seen.

For when the light is put out the darkness wins. My fear sinks in.

Yet beauty rises from ashes.

KARA DEKKER

CAST OF CHARACTERS

SEERS
Remko Brant
Carrington Hale Brant
Sam Miller
Kate Miller
Graham "Wire" Tollen
Neil Stone
Trig Mullen
Kal Wright
Connor

THE AUTHORITY
Damien Gold, *President*
Enderson Lane, *Minister of Labor and Director of Authority
    Workers; Interim Commander of the CityWatch*
Monroe Austin, *Minister of Health and Wellness*
Clyde Bushfield, *Minister of Citizens' Welfare*
Rains Molinar, *Minister of Projects and Engineering*

Walker Red, *Minister of Education*
Riley Scott, *Minister of Finance*
Riddley Stone, *Minister of Justice*

OTHERS

Aaron
Ian Carson, *Former Authority President*
Lucy and Rayna Carson, *Daughters of Ian Carson*
Selena Carson, *Wife of Ian Carson*
Jesse Cropper
Dr. Roth Reynard, aka "the Scientist"
Dodson Rogue, *Former CityWatch Commander*
Smith, *First Lieutenant and Interim Acting Commander
of the CityWatch*

YEAR
2259

PROLOGUE

Damien Gold sat down beside Roth Reynard, better known as the Scientist, on the hard wooden bench. The sun was high, the wind soft, and the garden around them still. Things were already in motion and change was upon them all.

The Scientist didn't glance over as Damien sat. He kept his eyes forward, squinting through the sun's rays and clearly lost in his own thoughts. They had these meetings sometimes, out here in the Capitol gardens, because the Scientist enjoyed the sun from time to time, and the garden area itself provided isolation.

"Things have begun," the Scientist said.

"Yes, the compound is fully operational," Damien said.

"Results should happen quickly then?"

"Ideally."

"And the rebels?"

"Aaron's movements are impossible to—" Damien started.

"I have told you before, Aaron is not our primary concern. Remko Brant is the one who steers that ship."

"I disagree; Aaron holds the power."

"Aaron is a delusional radical. But Remko possesses training and wit. He has managed to break through our security systems on numerous occasions."

"On Aaron's authority, though."

"Don't be a fool. If we break Remko, we break their will. Remko is the key."

Damien tried to hide his frustration at the man's clear disregard for Damien's insight. But now was not the time to engage in discourse. With so much happening, they needed to be on the same side.

"We are working on an inside man, as you suggested," Damien said.

"Good. How close are we?"

"Close."

"Then the plan to change the world is functioning as we predicted."

Damien smiled and nodded. "You had doubts?"

"I'm a scientist. I always doubt until evidence is laid before me."

"Don't worry; you'll have all the evidence you need soon."

The Scientist turned to Damien and they shared a knowing look before Damien stood and left.

1

Remko sensed panic from the group behind him. It filled the air around his head and pressed against his skull. They were running out of time. He pushed away the pocket of dread threatening to knock his legs from under him. They couldn't afford to run out of time.

Carrington was on his heels, moving quickly as they maneuvered through the underground tunnel. Sam and his younger sister, Kate, followed alongside Wire, all of their faces focused yet terrified. They all knew time was against them, and they all knew what that meant.

Remko could hear Carrington's fear screaming at him, begging him to move faster, to be better, to save them. He was supposed to keep them alive, to lead them against the Authority, to be their hero, their protector. He was failing.

It had been the same song and dance for the last several months. A ticking clock they were fighting against. Each of them hoping for a pause in its constant rhythm so they could stand still and breathe. Each of them desperately needing a moment in which it didn't feel like the world was crushing them from above, where they came out on top, victorious for once. Remko would settle for just a moment.

A large, round steel grate overhead occupied the

majority of the tunnel's top surface. It operated on a mechanical lock system, like most of the exits within the tunnels. Wire easily disabled the lock using the handheld device that never left his side. He called the device Roxy, something Kate mocked him for constantly, which usually inspired a witty response, and the two of them would fill the space with banter. No one said anything today. Their fear kept them quiet and made the silence deafening.

Sam stepped past Remko, the top of his six-foot-four-inch frame brushing the tunnel's ceiling, and yanked the grate open with a labored pull. They ascended one at a time, Sam leading to help pull the others up and Remko coming through last. Once aboveground, the group awaited Remko's lead. They were now at the end of a long alley deep within the Authority City. The walls of the surrounding buildings towered into the sky above. Dark clouds covered the sun and cast a shadow across the city. The smell of rain hung in the air, the street before them already soaked from the morning's storm.

The streets should be empty by now. People would have already gone inside for the viewing. It was mandatory that all executions of criminals be watched—a visual reminder of what happened to those who rebelled against the Authority. It didn't matter your age or status; even the youngest in the society were required to participate. Back when Remko had felt pride in being a part of the Authority's CityWatch Guard, he'd never felt comfortable with the idea of mandatory viewing of executions. But then, he'd only ever experienced one in person: Arianna Carson, eldest daughter of President Ian Carson and loyal follower of Aaron. Her death felt like a lifetime ago, even though only a year and a half had passed.

Now the executions happened monthly. Trials occurred less and less, people sometimes sentenced to death without a single word of defense. All because they followed Aaron, a man Remko increasingly found himself questioning. Many believed he was their saving grace, but Remko couldn't help but wonder if his grand ideas for change were simply the naive ramblings of a madman. All the same, Aaron had called the woman Remko loved out of the city, and the woman had asked Remko to follow, and he had. He would have followed Carrington anywhere. He still would.

She placed her hand on his shoulder, shaking him from his thoughts. There was no time for thinking; they had to move. He caught her eye for a brief moment and her expression made him sick. Yes, there was plenty of worry and fear, but he could see the hope that lay beyond, hope that they could complete their mission, hope that they wouldn't fail, hope in him. Misplaced hope.

Executions were held in the Capitol Building, which stood a couple of blocks to their left and was always sur-rounded by a heavy CityWatch presence. They had never broken into the Capitol Building before. Usually they were helping people flee the city from their homes or workstations. People Aaron had called to join the Seers in the wreckage of earth that lay miles beyond the city walls. Called to a life that would consist of always looking over their shoulders and wondering how long they could actually survive before they were discovered. Before the Authority rained down terror and vengeance on their group for leading the charge against them. For igniting curiosity and inspiring hope.

Usually Remko and the other Seer scouts spirited people out under the cover of darkness, outwitting and outmaneuvering those chasing them. Like magicians using a curtain to disguise the illusion, pulling the white rabbit out of the hat at precisely the right moment, they employed quick sleights of hand and crafty distractions.

In the beginning it had thrilled Remko. It had thrilled them all—the way Wire broke down the Authority's internal programming at lightning speeds before anyone knew a breach in security had been made; the way Kate slithered into secure locations without detection, moving with speed and strength that seemed impossible for her small frame; the way Sam inflicted fear at just the sight of his stature, the quiver you could see in the guards' expressions when they encountered him. And Remko, calling the shots, directing their perfectly assembled plans. Using the talents of his team to fool and confuse the enemy. It had been a rush. A rush that covered their fear and kept them stable.

Moving through the streets now, that rush was gone, replaced with a sense of shame that this had ever felt thrilling. Shame in believing that at some point they could actually win the game they were playing, that they could actually pull off the big end trick. But the real illusion was that they could ever be successful. Behind the curtain the Authority was pulling all the strings. The rest of them were still just puppets, convinced for a brief moment that they could be real boys and girls.

Remko clenched his molars and reset his focus. He could see the grand Capitol Building through the clouds ahead. As suspected, the streets were nearly empty, but the team still clung to the dark alleyways and moved like shadows toward their destination.

A loud mechanical grind echoed around them and sent a shiver through the ground beneath them. Remko knew the sound. They all did.

High above, large steel plates were sliding back to reveal plasma screens that stretched fifteen feet across and stood over nine feet in height. There were six main government buildings surrounding the Capitol Building. They stood twice as high as the Capitol, their walls reaching into the clouds, and every one of them had a large screen attached to its front. Screens easily seen throughout the Authority City and even into the outskirts of the Cattle and Farm Lands.

Remko could remember seeing those screens from the CityWatch barracks. They weren't used often back then—Remko could only remember a couple of times from his childhood—but they were being used more frequently of late. The Authority broadcast every execution; even with a plasma screen occupying a wall in each home throughout the city, these screens were still used. It was an extra twist of cruelty, another reminder that the Seers were losing. The revealing of the screens meant Remko's time was up.

He increased his speed and the others followed. The plan was to drop into an old water main that was out of commission and traverse its length under the Capitol Building and up through an unused service entrance that would pop them out on the eastern side of the structure. The execution room was on the second floor. Wire knew the guards' rotation schedules, so maneuvering through the side hallways and up an ancient staircase would be all about timing. From there it would be a combination of software and electrical distractions so that they could slide into the room, obtain the objective, and leave.

Even running through the plan now in his mind, Remko knew the chances of success were less than favorable, but they couldn't just sit and watch one of their own die without trying a rescue.

They reached the street grate that led them back underground. Remko yanked it open and one by one they dropped below. They didn't pause to collect themselves; they didn't have time for that. Sam was up front now, crouching but still moving quickly. Kate and Wire were right behind him, and Carrington was inches ahead of Remko. He tried not to think about what must be going through her head right now. Would she blame him if they failed? Was she already? How many times would he have

to let her down before she stopped believing in him altogether? Could he survive if she did? Like blows from a
hammer—*pound, pound, pound*—the questions rocked his
stability and threatened his resolve. He swallowed the fear
and pressure as they reached the end of the tunnel.

In one swift movement Sam opened the overhead hatch
and hauled himself up into the service room from which
they would access the building. After a pause to make
sure the room was clear, he signaled for the others to follow. Once all were back aboveground, Remko again took
the lead. Slowly he approached the main door, twisted the
knob, and peered down the narrow corridor that bled out
into the main lobby several feet ahead. It was clear. He
motioned for the group to move on his count.

Wire glanced down at his Roxy device's screen and
softly read off the rotation quadrants where the guards were
currently patrolling. This was going to be tight and needed
to be precise. They could only be in the main lobby for a
couple of counts before they chanced being spotted.

Remko took a deep breath and nodded. They moved
in sync, one step after the other. The main lobby was
darkened from the gray sky, which they could use to their
advantage. Two guards stood several yards away, their
backs to Remko as they surveyed the main entrance to
the Capitol. According to the rotating schedule, two more
guards swept the room every six minutes and were headed
back to do so any moment. There was no time to wait for
the sweep to be completed; they needed to move now.

Another deep breath and Remko started across the lobby, making sure to stay low and quiet. He could feel the others behind him and was grateful he couldn't hear their steps. Their destination was at the end of the room. The back wall was covered with thick streams of red material that billowed to the ground and stretched the entire length of the wall, hiding a second service door that led to a small stairway. Remko glanced over his shoulder and saw the two guards still facing away, unaware of him and the others.

They reached the edge of the hanging material and slowly slipped behind it. The door was only a couple feet beyond and Remko prayed that their movement behind the loose hanging wall coverings wouldn't pull the attention of the guards near the front. He reached the door and softly pulled it open. He let the others move inside first, then followed, closing the door behind him.

Like the room they had come up into from the water main, this hallway was dim and narrow and smelled of mold. It was all wood—the walls, the floor, the low ceiling.

Remko followed as the group moved forward. According to the building plans Wire had accessed, this passageway should lead to a staircase that would escort them to the second floor. From there they could access the HVAC system above the ceiling. They would have to drop down into the execution room; there was no other way to enter without walking right in through the heavily guarded door.

The execution room was set up simply: a square space with two sections. The main and larger part of the room was a viewing area filled with chairs for those invited to watch the execution, which took place on the other side of a large glass wall. The second part of the room, half the size of the first section, sat behind the glass and held the execution chair and materials. Usually the only people in the second section were the prisoner, the administrator, and two CityWatch guards. This was the part of the room that Remko planned to drop down into.

Once they were above the room, Wire would override the locking system on the single door between the execution chamber and the viewing section of the room, preventing anyone from entering or exiting. Then he'd close the metal plate that slid down over the glass, eliminating the possibility of anyone breaking through the glass or even seeing what was happening beyond it. That would leave the prisoner alone with a single doctor and two guards. Wire planned to cut the power to just the second section of the room if possible, without killing power to the entire floor.

If everything went according to plan, maybe they could actually save the prisoner. The problem was hardly anything ever went according to plan anymore.

They found the stairs and slowly ascended, mindful of limiting the creaking of their steps. At the top another hallway stretched for several more feet and ended at a small ladder that ran up the wall.

Sam reached the ladder first but stepped aside for Kate and Wire. Sam would stay here, as his massive frame wouldn't easily move through the ventilation system above.

Carrington was up next and Remko gave Sam a nod before following. Now enclosed in large steel boxes, the four pulled themselves along toward their target. After a couple of turns, they saw the grate that sat above the execution room.

Remko, Carrington, and Wire stayed back a couple of feet as Kate, the smallest of the group, easily scurried toward the grate. She lowered her head to look through the metal strips and survey the room. Remko waited for her to confirm the number of bodies in the room, but when her face lifted, it was marked with confusion.

She dropped her head again and came back up with the same look in her eyes. Her lips parted as if she couldn't find the words and after a moment she spoke. "It's empty."

"Empty?" Carrington said and turned her gaze to Remko. A weight dropped against his chest and he knew what was coming next.

Roxy beeped at Wire's side. He grabbed for the contraption and his eyes filled with fear. "We have massive movement on the heat scanner. At least ten bodies, maybe more, headed this way."

It's a trap. Remko didn't need to say it; they all knew. He twisted as quickly as possible and moved, the others following. The sound of a familiar Authority member's voice crackled to life, and they all paused.

"Let the record now mark the start of execution 267.1a," Enderson Lane said. The sound was too loud to be coming from a human in close proximity, which meant it was coming from the broadcast system. The execution was starting.

"But she isn't here," Carrington said.

Remko couldn't find words to settle the raging panic that filled her voice. "We have to keep moving," was all he could say.

They slid back across the ventilation ducts until they reached the ladder. Remko was the first down, trying to sort through what was happening. Sam's face was puzzled as the group descended empty-handed. They needed a moment to stop and figure out what had happened, but they didn't have it.

"The prisoner has been found guilty of treason against the Authority by crimes committed in the name of Aaron," Enderson said.

His voice rattled the fragile wooden walls in the narrow hallway and made Remko's mind spin. Somehow the Authority had known they'd come and had moved the execution somewhere else, and now who could say what they would find when they tried to leave.

"What is happening?" Sam asked.

"This isn't good," Kate said.

"If she isn't here then where is she?" Carrington asked.

Remko ignored them all. The sound of muffled shouting grabbed his attention. It was coming from the other side of the wall, signaling that soldiers were gathering in the Capitol lobby. Remko imagined the army of CityWatch members waiting for them to emerge, an army they couldn't fight against. They couldn't go back that way, but they couldn't stay here.

He turned to Wire, who was punching away at Roxy vigorously. "Give me something," Remko said.

Wire nodded. "Okay, there's another way out of these service walkways, but they built a wall up over the exit years ago. The materials they used are cheap; we should be able to break it down."

"What's our time?" Remko asked.

"Maybe a minute till they're on us," Wire said. "I don't think—"

"Let's go," Remko said, grabbing Roxy from Wire's hand and following the machine's guidance. Back the way they had come, running at full speed now, none of them caring about the noise they made. Around a corner to the left, then to the right and down to the end of a final hallway that dead-ended in a wooden wall. Sam pushed to the front without having to be asked and he and Remko started pounding away at the slabs.

Voices reached Remko's ears and he knew that CityWatch guards were now somewhere in the service tunnels headed for them. He kicked the wall with brute force. Pain shot up his calf and into his knee, but he ignored it and kicked again, harder. A crack split across the middle of the wall. Sam crouched and used his shoulder to slam the break, splitting the wood in half. A large crack in the wood showed another long path and their only escape.

Remko reached into the crack and gripped a plank, wrenching it backward and away from the wall. The guards' voices grew in volume and Kate joined in the destruction.

After another second the hole was big enough for her to climb through, then Wire, and then Carrington. It took another hard kick to make room for Remko and Sam to barely squeeze through. The path was shrouded in darkness, thick enough to feel suffocating. It smelled like dead rats and spoiled food. The ground mushed under their feet as they ran forward.

Enderson's voice echoed, bouncing around the dark above their heads. "At this time I would like to impress upon the people of this city how essential the law is to our survival."

Remko struggled to block out Enderson's words.

"The idea that you can survive outside the law, following the whims of a rebel group and their maniac leader, will only bring turmoil and destruction to our way of life. Resisting the way of the law only ends in death. The *Veritas* is very clear about this."

Remko could sense Carrington's crazed worry; he could hear it in her breath as they ran, feel it in her steps as they pounded against the floor. He wanted to stop, sweep her up in his arms, beg her for forgiveness, and promise her that he could save them. But he couldn't do that; all he could do was run.

Enderson continued, "Therefore, whoever resists the authorities resists what God has appointed, and those who resist will incur judgment. As God set forth the law, so the law must be obeyed."

Angry shouts followed them down the long corridor, and more splitting of wood commenced. Remko grabbed

Carrington's hand and yanked her forward. She nearly tripped, but he ignored the physical pain he must be causing her. Better to be in pain than dead. The group was tight now; he could hear the others breathing as they all pushed themselves to their limits. Streams of light filtered through the darkness a couple yards in front of them. Another grate, one that led to a false sense of freedom. They weren't actually ever free. They might still escape the imprisonment of the Authority's law, but they would just find themselves confined by their fear.

Sam reached the grate and started to heave. It was bolted to the wall and his efforts alone weren't going to free it. Remko and Wire stepped forward to join him. All three strained at the grate, but it didn't budge.

"Come on, come on," Kate said under her breath.

"You wanna help?" Wire said. "We're pulling as hard as we can."

"Enough," Sam said urgently. "We need to concentrate on just one corner, not the whole thing. Pull together in short bursts."

More shouting came from behind. Closer.

Sam, Wire, and Remko positioned themselves so they were each holding the grate just inches from the upper-left corner. "One, two, *three!*" Sam yelled.

They all yanked. No movement.

"Bring the prisoner forward," another voice boomed over the broadcasting system.

"Again," Sam said. "One, two, *three!*"

Another pull. Remko thought the grate might have moved just a hair.

"Again," Sam said. "Every three seconds. Go!"

They continued pulling in bursts, following Sam's instructions. Carrington and Kate stuck their hands in to join the effort as well. With every pull, the grate moved a little more. Finally, when Remko had nearly given up hope, the bolt popped free from the concrete wall. But the grate was still in place.

The loudspeakers screeched again. "Please state the name of the prisoner for the records." Remko felt Carrington tremble beside him.

"It's enough," Sam said. Another long second passed as Sam shouldered the others aside, positioned himself at the newly freed corner of the grate, and with a labored pull, the veins in his arms pulsing from the effort, ripped the metal from the wall. Sam stumbled backward, knocking Wire and Kate nearly to the ground, but they recovered and didn't wait for apologies before moving out into the light.

"Of course," Enderson said. His voice was louder now that they were free from the service tunnels. It thundered above them and around them, as if it were part of the air itself.

Remko surveyed their surroundings. They were outside of the Capitol Building's perimeter wall, on the opposite side from where they had entered. He wasn't as familiar with this part of the city, but he knew the underground tunnel system ran beneath the majority of the streets. They just needed to find a place to hide so they could regroup and make their next move.

"The prisoner slated for execution 267.1a is Larkin Caulmen," Enderson said.

The world around them stilled for a split moment and Remko saw a single tear slide down Carrington's cheek. Then the world came back into full swing.

"We have to move," Sam said.

Remko nodded, fighting to tear his eyes away from the woman he loved. The woman he had failed. "We need a place to hide, Wire."

"As is required, we will ask the prisoner if she has any last words before her execution," Enderson said.

"I think I have something—a small abandoned shop," Wire said, his eyes glued to Roxy's screen. "There's a back entrance not far from here and it has a basement tunnel grate."

Remko nodded and they moved. Trying to stay out of sight, taking the corners slow so as not to run into unwanted company. The streets were still empty and the threat of rain still hung in the air, but the clouds had shifted and from here they could see the plasma screen where Larkin's execution was being broadcast. She was strapped to a long white chair, reclined so it almost lay flat, tubes connected to her arms, the steady beat of her heart blinking across a monitor and beeping through the air. Her gray Lint uniform was gone, replaced with the thin, brown, shabby dress customary for all female prisoners. Her thick curls spread around her skull, but more than anything Remko saw her eyes. Even from here he could see the calm sense of purpose, the confidence even in the face of death.

Pain racked itself across his heart and rage flooded his bones. He feared Carrington would stop moving at the sight of Larkin, but he could still sense her behind him. They weren't far from the shop now.

Suddenly a sweet sound echoed across the sky. A song, soft and pure. They all stopped and looked to see Larkin singing.

"When peace like a river attendeth my way, when sorrows like sea billows roll . . ."

Remko felt as if the oxygen had been sucked out of his lungs. The air around his head seemed too thin to replace what had been taken. He heard Carrington whimper behind him and it felt like a punch to his gut.

"Whatever my lot, Thou hast taught me to say . . ."

"That's enough," Enderson said.

Larkin was lost within herself, though, and if she'd heard him she showed no sign. Her face filled with peace, her lips nearly turned up in a smile. "It is well; it is well with my soul."

Roxy started beeping in Wire's hand. They had all become too familiar with that sound. The CityWatch guards were getting close; they couldn't stay out here in the open.

The song continued, "It is well . . ."

"I said enough," Enderson said. He nodded to the doctor stationed at Larkin's left. The doctor picked up a syringe from the small medical table beside him and pulled off the cap.

"No, please . . . ," Carrington said, her face drenched in tears.

"With my soul . . ." Larkin's voice remained strong and pure.

"We have to go, Remko," Sam said. Darkness filled his face as he fought to keep the emotion from his voice. Larkin was one of their own, one of the originals. They all felt this moment as if they were being given the poison themselves.

"Carrington," Remko said. She nodded, fighting sorrow that threatened to overcome her. They followed Wire across the street and into the alley that ran behind the shops.

Larkin's voice drifted over them, cutting them with each step. "It is well . . ."

Remko couldn't block out Larkin's voice; it dug at his insides.

"With my soul . . ."

They reached the back of the abandoned shop and one by one they slipped inside.

"It is well . . ."

They took the stairs quickly, descending into the basement to the grate leading to the tunnels. Sam crossed the space in a few large strides and quickly they were inside the tunnel with the grate pulled back down over their heads.

Larkin's voice reached them even here, and her song seemed to grow in power—"It is well with my soul"—her notes stretching out across the city, her strength filling the sky. Carrington pressed her palms and forehead against the tunnel wall. Her shoulders shook, her tears silent. With one final note, Larkin proclaimed her faith, her belief, her undying resolve, and then everything fell quiet.

Silence encapsulated the tunnel, heavy and paralyzing. Carrington's cry broke the stillness and she slid to her knees, covering her mouth to keep her screams from echoing up into the streets and giving away their position. Remko moved and knelt beside her. He pulled her into his arms and silently begged for her forgiveness. His tears fell into her hair and her body trembled in his arms.

Now sorrow, not just fear, would be their prison.

They had exchanged one prison for another.

2 Selena Carson shut her eyes to ward off the tears she felt rising. She remembered a time when her emotions weren't so frazzled and weak. When she could live through uncomfortable moments without fighting back tears. When the world still held warmth and hope. But that time had died with her daughter a year and a half ago. Now everything felt unjust and cruel.

She opened her eyes and saw that the screen before her had gone black. It was over. The young girl's face floated behind Selena's eyes. Its soft round shape surrounded in dark curls, the eyes filled with such peace even until death. It reminded her so much of Arianna. Selena felt another round of tears storming her gates of control and she ground her back teeth. Each new execution brought her back to that day, and now she'd spend the next several days pulling herself out of the dark pit that always swallowed her after a mandatory viewing.

A small hand wrapped itself around her forearm and she nearly jumped. Rayna, her youngest, gazed up at her, fear dancing on her face. Selena forced a smile and pulled the sweet child to her side. The little girl clung tightly to her mother's leg and pressed her cheek to the side of Selena's thigh. Selena reached out for Lucy, Rayna's older sister, who stood to Selena's other side, but the girl pulled away from her touch.

Lucy's face was cold and hard, a permanent state it had taken on since Arianna's death. She wasn't even twelve yet, and for her to be filled with such hate broke Selena's heart. Sometimes Selena thought that losing a child would have been easier if she didn't have two more who needed her. Having them was supposed to ease the pain, people told her. She loved her daughters more than anything, but they constantly reminded her of Arianna, and their pain in losing a sibling only increased her pain from losing a daughter. Being strong for them felt impossible most days, especially as the city around them dipped deeper into darkness.

There had been a time when Selena was proud of the city outside the Capitol Building, where she lived. Though she was the daughter of an esteemed medical advisor, she'd never imagined Ian Carson would actually choose her, but when he had, the first thing she'd thought was how lucky she'd be to sit at the right hand of the man leading their perfect city. How wrong she'd been. The fantasy had been strong and steady through the births of all three of her daughters, and for years afterward. But it had started to change slowly as Arianna approached her Choosing Ceremony year. Ian had begun coming home from Authority Council meetings worked up and stressed. He'd started to sleep less, and when he did join her in bed, he was restless. Whispers of rebellion started, soft at first, then grew into loud chatter that caused such fear in her husband.

Selena had ignored it all. Focused on the lie that everything would work out. Arianna had told her stories of change while Selena kissed her good-night, and Selena had forced down the worry creeping into her soul. Everything would be as it should be; Ian would make sure of it. The blindness was self-imposed, because the reality of the change in Arianna and the city was too frightening to accept.

And then suddenly Selena was ripped out of her imaginary world where everything was fine, as her own husband murdered their daughter. Nothing had been the same since that day. Not Ian, not the Council, not the city. Darkness engulfed them all. In the beginning Ian had begged Selena to see that this was all Aaron's fault. The false prophet who was calling people out of the city, the man who represented the foolish call Arianna had died for. But Aaron wasn't physically around to blame and hate. Ian was. The Council was, and now the cracks in her false perfect view of the city were everywhere.

She thought this must be what hell was like. The ache of pain that begged her to end it all, that promised her it couldn't get worse and would never get better. But even that was a lie, because it did get worse. The same council that had joined her husband in murdering his daughter had overthrown Ian, and Damien Gold had taken his seat.

Selena shuddered as she thought of the Authority's

new president. He was a different kind of monster than Ian. He was handsome and winsome in public, but in her few interactions with him, she had sensed he was filled with more ego and less regard for the happiness of the city. He had started well enough. Even in her grief and shock with her daughter dead and her husband in prison, Selena had almost believed Damien's promises of justice and renewed hope for the future. But within a few weeks, the sorrow over Arianna's death that coated the city quickly turned to fear. The huge screens built into the sides of the city's tallest towers were unveiled almost daily, it seemed. Under Ian's leadership, execution had been rare—a last resort. Under Damien, execution was a regular occurrence as rebels were caught and made examples of, and the giant screens gleefully displayed every one. As if it weren't bad enough for citizens to be forced to view them in their homes, they had to endure the sounds echoing through the streets as well.

Damien claimed to be offended by violence, but it only increased as he served. Dodson Rogue, head of the CityWatch, had been imprisoned on suspicion of helping rebels escape, and Damien had taken charge, adding patrols inside and outside the city and giving soldiers liberty to be cruel to anyone they thought might be involved with the rebels. Boys as young as thirteen were being recruited to join the CityWatch as they prepared for what felt like war. The seasonal Choosing ceremonies continued, but the thrill of the event was shadowed by dread. The religious gatherings that had once held their society together were cut in half and made optional. All that was good and color-ful and happy about living in their once-peaceful society seemed to have evaporated overnight.

Rayna tugged on Selena's sleeve, yanking her from her thoughts. She glanced down at the tiny girl.

"Can we go visit Daddy?" Rayna asked, her voice quiet.

Before Selena could answer, Lucy huffed disgustedly and turned to storm out. Selena watched as Lucy was stopped at the door by a CityWatch guard. "You aren't allowed to leave without an escort, Miss Carson."

Another Damien change that was ruining their lives. Selena felt her mothering instinct rear up in her chest and she stopped herself from yelling at the guard. That would only make things worse.

"I'm just going back to my room," Lucy snapped.

"I'll call for an escort," the guard said. He nodded to the other guard beside him, who spoke into the receiver at his wrist.

"It's in the same hall—I don't need to be walked there!" Lucy said.

"Lucy," Selena warned, and her daughter turned her head. Tears were gathering in the bottom of her daughter's eyes, and Selena's heart broke. She took a step toward her but Lucy dropped her eyes and turned back toward the door. Selena stopped and a long moment of silence lingered before a third guard came to escort Lucy away.

The girl left, and Selena stood frozen in place. Rayna

tugged at her shirt again, but Selena ignored her. All she could think about was finding a way to protect the two daughters she had left, and the only way to do that was to leave this city.

3 The journey back to the Seer camp was silent. A somber sense of defeat had settled over each of them. Images of Larkin's final moments remained etched inside Remko's mind. Her voice echoed in his brain. *"It is well with my soul."* Even in the face of unjust death Larkin had been at ease, as if death had no power over her, as if it couldn't actually snuff out her life. But then it had, and they had failed to stop it.

Carrington hardly said a word as they traveled back through the underground tunnels to the spot a couple miles outside the city walls where they had left their vehicle. Wire had somehow cloaked the transponder so it couldn't be tracked through the city's main grid. He did that with all the mechanical equipment they used. Anything that could be connected wirelessly could be tracked. They forwent many of the comforts of city living to stay hidden, to stay safe.

With the death of each new Seer, it was harder to rationalize their efforts. No matter what they did, Seers were still being caught and taken and executed. The diligent moving of the camp to keep ahead of CityWatch detection, the hours spent hacking into the main server so they could move throughout the city like ghosts, the countless patrols and sleepless nights—it was hard to see whether any of it was worth the sacrifice.

A year and a half ago, when Remko had agreed to accompany Carrington into the ruins of the earth beyond the city walls to follow a man with a message of freedom, he'd been excited by the idea of new adventures and change. To be forever with a woman whom he'd chosen and who had chosen him back. They'd been married quickly after, a small ceremony when the Seer camp had been less than ten strong. It was a day he thought back on when sleeping with one eye open became too much.

The sun had been setting, painting the sky with oranges and pinks. The group had built a large fire in a spot they had found behind a small hill where the smoke wouldn't draw unwanted attention. Sam and Kate had been there, Remko's brother, Ramses, and his wife, Lesley, along with their easily excitable twins, Nina and Kane. And Larkin. She'd asked Carrington if she wanted to wear a white dress, and they'd both shared a knowing smile and laughed. They'd worn white nearly their whole lives, a color that symbolized their place in society, that marked them as not yet chosen but still filled with hope. It was a color they'd both rather never wear again.

Larkin had pressed Carrington for details of what she'd like to wear but Carrington had only smiled, a fire dancing behind her eyes as she told Larkin to surprise her. And she had. The day before the scheduled ceremony, Larkin had showed up to camp with a stunning dress. Long, flowing satin to the floor, fitted through the bodice, lace sleeves, dark sapphire in color. Remko couldn't tell you what Carrington had worn yesterday, but he'd never forget the way she looked in that blue dress.

Carrington had cried when Larkin revealed the gown. Kate had rolled her eyes because it was just a stupid dress. But they had all laughed. They'd listened to Larkin's dramatic tale of sneaking into the city to obtain the dress, and they'd been drunk on joy. The following day Carrington walked down a misshapen aisle. Aaron stood up front to officiate, the rest of the group beaming. Remko remembered being caught off guard by emotion. His bride had worn yellow flowers in her hair—he remembered that too. And her eyes were part excited and nervous and part sultry and daring, a combination Remko had grown to recognize but which still made his heart race.

That moment had been everything. She had become his, and he had become hers. The struggles ahead not yet realized, the dangers they'd already faced left far behind, all that mattered was her in that blue dress with yellow flowers in her hair. And the taste of her lips during their first kiss as man and wife, the way her fingers intertwined with his, the way his hand buzzed on the small of her back while they danced, the elation of sweeping her off her feet to bring her into their new shared tent, laughing into the dark hours of morning, falling asleep together, waking up together.

Those first couple of months he'd soaked up every second, certain he couldn't possibly feel so much emotion again, but he'd been wrong. Remko could hardly contain his worry when Carrington whispered she was pregnant. To give birth to a baby out here in the wreckage they lived in seemed beyond comprehension. Eight months later, only days after yet another Seer execution, she went into labor. The camp, by then numbering nearly forty people, had been a mix of emotions. Many worried that a baby couldn't survive this life; others were excited for a spark of pure happiness; some were filled with hope that a new generation of life was beginning. All Remko was concerned with was the safety of his wife and unborn child. The labor had lasted several hours. To hear Carrington's cries and not be able to do anything was torture.

When the sound of the baby crying echoed through the tent, Remko's whole world changed. In a single moment the world became about more than just surviving and protecting those around him; it became about creating something worthy of the little girl in his arms. A place she could grow and thrive in.

She'd been so small, with a tiny head full of jet-black hair, bright brown eyes, perfect pink skin. She was stunning. Every emotion Remko had ever felt rushed over him like a tidal wave. He'd sacrifice everything, give it all away, spoil her, teach her, adore her, protect her, love her, kill for her. He'd fallen even more in love with Carrington in that moment, as if this baby had allowed him to open a part of his heart he hadn't known was closed.

They called her Elise, and all the doubts and worries

people in the camp were feeling melted when they met her. She re-inspired hope and gave the camp a shot of electricity. And for a time everyone seemed to run on adrenaline. But it faded as another Seer was taken, as they packed up camp to move again, as they failed to stop another execution. Their joy faded nearly as quickly as it had come.

The large, egg-shaped vehicle slid smoothly to a stop. Wire killed the propulsion drive and the team climbed out. They had pulled into the ground level of an old cement factory nearly twenty miles west of the Authority City. Four other repurposed vehicles were parked nearby, the setting sun casting long shadows of their bodies. The building was missing most of its north wall, and the ground-floor windows were shattered, glass lining the concrete floor. The camp was currently set up on the second level and they could hear the faint sound of commotion overhead.

Remko knew people were working to get the camp packed up. Wire had radioed ahead to let them know they were headed back without Larkin. A failed mission meant moving. Again. They couldn't chance the Authority extracting information from the Seers they took captive. They had no way of knowing what Larkin might have told them, so moving was necessary.

Sam, Kate, and Wire headed toward the metal stairs that led up, and Remko hung back to walk beside Carrington. It was dim inside the building, but he could still see how tired her eyes were. He didn't know what he could say to help. He'd learned early on he wasn't very good with words. Even though his stutter was nearly gone, even though Carrington had somehow given him the strength to speak clearly most of the time, he had faced most of his life without needing to use words. So he oftentimes found himself at a loss for what to say.

He reached out and grabbed her hand, lacing his fingers through hers, and he felt her entire body ease. They took the stairs slowly, neither of them ready to face the next journey. The stress and exhaustion of moving, of keeping everyone together. Even now Remko thought back to that perfect blue dress, in search of strength.

The camp came into view as they ascended the final steps. The scene before them was functioning chaos. People moved about in a sort of rambunctious order as the camp closed in on itself, preparing for transport. Fires were extinguished as tents were folded down and stored. Food was being packed into crates and weapons loaded carefully away. Everything was being moved onto a large, flat, square panel of wood connected to a rudimentary pulley system that would lower it all quickly to the ground floor.

Ramses approached through the continuous motion and nodded for Remko to follow him. Remko gave Carrington's hand a final squeeze as she headed off toward their tent and Elise. He wanted to follow her, to make sure she was all right, to see their daughter's bright face, but he was needed elsewhere. Later, when they were alone with only their infant baby watching, would Carrington hold his absences against him? She claimed to understand, to know that his moments away were necessary for the group, but he still feared that deep down she was making check marks each time she felt abandoned. Building up a tally that she could pull out and lay at his feet, proving he was failing her emotionally.

Remko ignored the urge to rush after her and promise to be more present and followed Ramses to a corner of camp that was less occupied. Sam was there, standing in front of an old steel table rusted from loneliness. Large maps were spread out across its surface. Sam lifted his eyes as Ramses and Remko approached.

"We have scouted out most of the surrounding areas and there aren't many places to go that we haven't already been," Sam said. "We could venture out farther, but it appears most of the land is just that—land. It might prove difficult to find shelter."

"I think I may have another option," Wire said, walking up behind Remko. The boy was tall and thin, barely eighteen, his face mouselike, eyes too large, nose too long. His movements were awkward and clumsy, and he was too smart for his own good. When he'd arrived at the Seer camp, Remko had been worried about his ability to survive. But he said Aaron had called him, and Remko had learned better than to argue about someone chosen by Aaron. It hadn't taken long for Wire to become an essential part of their small community, saving their lives more often than they saved his. The way he manipulated and understood the functionality of anything mechanical or software-based had quickly earned him the nickname Wire.

His real name was Graham Tollen. His father was the
Authority's leading mechanical technician, and as Wire
grew and learned the trade himself, he surpassed his father's
ability long before he was old enough to work. Wire
had explained to Remko once that he saw the world in
numbers. Everything could be broken down to a simple
mathematical equation, and if you could understand that
equation and had the right tools, then you could control it.

"It's risky, though," Kate said, standing beside him. She
and her older brother, Sam, were the complete opposite
of Wire. Strong and fast, they moved like trained war-
riors. They had both been with Aaron before Carrington
and Remko had joined. They were the first two original
Seers—and Kate had no problem reminding people of that.
Remko didn't know very much about their lives before they
became Seers, but he did know they didn't have any family
left, and they blamed the Authority for everything negative
they'd ever experienced.

Kate especially. Small, barely five feet tall, with short
blonde hair that swept across one light-blue eye that was
always filled with darkness, Kate moved like she was carrying the weight of the entire world. As if she would
personally see to it that vengeance for every harmful
deed was paid in full. Sam was more gentle, a beast in
size comparatively, but otherwise they looked like twins.
He was the only one who could talk Kate off the ledge if
necessary.

Besides Aaron. Aaron changed the way Kate spoke,

walked, stood. He eased her, and in the moments when Aaron was around, Kate looked like the young teen girl she was supposed to be, not the warrior that stood before them now.

"But it could work," Wire countered.

Silence fell over the group, Wire's eyes on Kate's face as if he was waiting for her permission to continue. It wasn't a mystery to anyone how Wire felt about Kate. He followed her around like a puppy, and though Kate pretended to find him repulsive, they all saw the way she looked at him when she thought no one was watching. Kate rolled her eyes and Wire took that as the go-ahead.

He pulled Roxy from his side. The device was a Wire original, something he'd been working on for his father before leaving the city. He'd taken it with him, even though it hadn't been fully functional yet. Remko couldn't count the number of mornings he'd woken to find that Wire had been up all night tinkering with the contraption. Ramses had become engrossed in helping Wire make it functional, and the two had nearly set the camp on fire twice.

Wire set Roxy faceup on the table and punched the screen. The device sparked and everyone stepped back.

"Seriously," Kate said.

"It's fine, she's just overworked and needs some new wiring," Wire said.

"Whenever you say *she* needs something I have to stop myself from having a visceral reaction and punching you in the face," Kate said.

"Kate," Sam said.

"What—do you remember how many ridiculous and risky runs we had to make to gather the stupid parts he needed for this thing in the first place?"

"Are you going to hold that over Roxy's head forever?" Wire asked. "I would have thought that she had plenty proved herself by now—"

"You have to stop talking about her like she's real; it's creepy," Kate said.

"Enough, both of you," Remko said. "Wire, what were you going to show us?"

Wire threw Kate a final disapproving look, then took a moment to tinker with Roxy's display before proceeding. "There's an old subway system that runs for miles under the city and out into much of the surrounding area."

"Subway system?" Ramses asked.

"It was an underground train transportation avenue back before the Time of Ruin. Most of it has been closed off so it's not viable for entering the city anymore, but a lot of the underground tunnels are still intact," Wire said.

"Have we vetted it?" Remko asked.

"That's the risky part," Kate said. "We've never been down there. We have no idea what we'll find."

"But we can check it for wildlife," Wire said. "And I could do a chemical and environmental check before we enter. I just need to get close enough—"

"And what if we get all these people there and it isn't stable?" Kate asked.

"I could go ahead now and start the readings. I could radio back before morning," Wire said.

"We may not have until morning," Sam said.

"I know it's a risk, but we don't have any other plausible options currently, and I have a strong feeling—"

Kate huffed. "You want us to risk the lives of these people on your *feeling*?"

"Kate," Sam warned again.

"What? Do you want to take that risk?"

Remko looked at the small map on Roxy's screen and tried to imagine the underground train system. If it was built as a mode of transportation, the tunnels must be strong, large, built to withstand time, and out of sight, which was appealing. "Have you identified the fastest route to the most viable entry point?" Remko asked.

Wire grabbed Roxy and viciously typed on her face. "No, but it'll only take me a couple of minutes."

Kate watched over Wire's shoulder and picked at him while he zoomed in and out, muttering about probable road conditions and visibility, but Wire didn't seem to mind and made adjustments based on anything Kate suggested.

Sam studied the maps on the table, looking for another option in case they needed a plan B.

Remko considered slipping away, but before he could, Ramses placed a gentle hand on his shoulder and nodded for him to follow. Remko did and the two left the others to work.

Ramses glanced at Remko as they walked and Remko knew what was coming.

"How are you?" Ramses asked.

Remko didn't know how to answer that question, so he stayed silent. Quiet fell between them.

Ramses led Remko out past the border of the camp's activity, away from listeners. He stopped at the edge of the floor where a guardrail ran the length of the upstairs. He leaned forward against it, arms resting on its top. "I was thinking about how different you've become in the last year," Ramses said.

Remko looked at his brother.

"I was just thinking about where we all were before this. You were all soldier then. Calculated and emotionless, all about what was right according to the law. Now they call you an outlaw." Ramses teasingly nudged Remko's shoulder, and Remko found himself nearly smiling in spite of the sorrow that hung over him.

"Being a soldier is still part of who you are, but it looks different without a law to follow," Ramses said.

"I'm fine, Ramses," Remko said.

"Something that hasn't changed—you're still a terrible liar."

Remko leaned forward to match his brother's position on the rail. "What do you want me to say?"

"Nothing. I just want you to know that I see how different you are. How much emotion you have invested here. How much emotion you have invested in her."

"Are you faulting me for it?" Remko asked. He felt his defenses spike.

"No, Brother. Love is a beautiful thing. But the pressure you are putting yourself under—"

"I can handle it," Remko said.

Ramses nodded and turned his eyes forward. "Something else about you that hasn't changed. You're still as stubborn as Dad ever was. And your loyalty is fierce. You're a good leader for us."

Remko had never asked to be leader, but he kept silent because he knew voicing that would only incite more concern from Ramses.

"I just worry about you taking on too much," Ramses said.

"I have a family to protect. If keeping them safe means taking on more, then it's not too much."

"Fine. Just don't forget that you're not alone in this. We're all protecting family, and you're mine."

Remko let his defenses slip and nodded. Of course Ramses was worried. He worried about Ramses just as often. "I know, Brother; I know." Remko placed his hand on Ramses's shoulder and his brother nodded.

"I should . . . ," Remko began, tilting his head toward the tent he shared with Carrington and Elise.

"Go. Check on her. Come see me afterward. I'll make sure we have a solid plan together."

Remko gave his thanks and left him, walking back toward the moving chaos. People acknowledged him with nods as he passed, their eyes saying more than their mouths. By now everyone in camp knew Larkin was dead. No one would say anything to his face, or even behind his back, but their looks grew more worried with each failure, and Remko knew the blame landed on him.

A few tents still stood, one of them his. He saw Lesley, Ramses's wife, standing outside packing up what was around her. Her face was filled with emotion and she kept her eyes locked on the task at hand. He knew she had grown close with Larkin over the last year, that being out here in this environment, facing the same troubles, had made them like sisters.

Lesley lifted her face at Remko's approach and he saw her reddened eyes still filled with tears. His heart broke as she wiped the tears from her cheeks and shook her head. "Sorry," she said.

Remko stepped forward and placed a comforting hand on her shoulder. A soft sob escaped her lips and she placed the tips of her fingers against her mouth to control herself. She swallowed hard and released a shaky exhale. "I just keep trying to figure out how to tell Nina."

Again Remko's heart ached. Larkin and Nina had become inseparable the last few months and he hadn't even thought about how this news would affect her. She was just a child. How was she supposed to understand death?

"Carrington's inside," Lesley said, pointing toward the tent. "I was just letting her have a moment before—"

Remko leaned forward and placed a kiss on the top of his sister-in-law's head. "Thank you."

She nodded and tried for a small smile before going back to packing.

Remko pulled back the thick material that served as a cover to the entrance of the tent and stepped inside. He couldn't stand all the way up and crouched as the cover fell closed behind him. Carrington knelt at the back of the tent, on the pile of blankets they used as a bed, cradling Elise in her arms, her face identical to Lesley's—drenched in sorrow.

Elise had grown so much in the last three months, but she was still tiny. The baby watched Carrington's face with awe and Remko moved to be close to them. Carrington glanced up as Remko knelt down beside her.

"I was just telling Elise about her aunt Larkin," Carrington said. "About how much she loved her, that she'll never be alone because Aunt Larkin will be watching her. She may not get to meet her—" Emotion choked out Carrington's words. Tears slipped down her face and dripped off her chin. One landed on Elise's head and the baby fussed at the unfamiliarity of it. Carrington wiped her face and then Elise's head, rocking her softly. Remko put his arm around Carrington and his touch broke the barrier holding her sorrow at bay. She dissolved before him, and he reached out to take Elise from her.

Elise safely secured in his right arm, he tucked his wife against the opposite side and felt her warm tears seep through his shirt. He fought back tears himself as the pain of the woman he loved enveloped the air around him. He had done this to her; his failure had caused her this torture. He tried to escape from the blame that was chasing him through the darkest parts of his mind, but with each heart-wrenching cry from Carrington he felt his resolve slip further. He had done this.

He held both girls close and silently prayed for the strength not to fail again.

4 Damien Gold tapped all ten fingers along the grand table at which he sat. Six Authority members joined him at the table, their faces filled with exhaustion. Each looked more aged every time they met. Time had made them soft. They had become accustomed to the ease of ruling a city without rebellion, and none of them had proven equipped to handle the trouble pounding at the gates of their formerly stable control.

The truth was they had never really been in control. They had all just bought into the lie Ian Carson had fed them. Like silly little children, fat on the candy shoved into their faces. Damien had always seen the underlying problem in the city. He'd known this day was approaching, which had made it easy to come in and offer rescue.

The Authority Council had been at an impasse. The betrayal of Isaac Knight hung in the air like a heavy cloud, and the members had been searching for their bearings. Isaac's psychotic break had shattered the ground on which the council stood, but no panic was necessary, because Damien had been fully prepared to restructure their faith.

Not their faith in God, of course; rather their faith in him. As far as Damien was concerned, the idea of God was coming to an end. It needed to, for the betterment of the people. The Authority City, led by the Carson family since the Time of Ruin, may once have needed to believe in God to ensure a sense of security and ease, but Damien knew a new era was upon them. It was a transition that had been slowly maneuvering its way through the cracks over the last couple of years, and now with the fall of their highest religious leader, Damien could feel the floodgates threatening to explode.

Previously, Damien had held the position of High Council Judge, a position with much power and glory but still in the shadow of Riddley Stone, the Minister of Justice, and the nine other Authority members. Damien had used his level of status to wield more influence than most, but if he wanted to really induce effective change, he was at a disadvantage. Some might say God had reached down and created the perfect opportunity for Damien to step onto the Authority Council after God had pushed Isaac over the edge, but since Damien believed God was a myth, he wanted to give the universe and dumb luck a standing ovation.

He still believed in purpose, of course. Purpose was the reason for existence. Even the fly exists so the spider does not go hungry. So Damien existed to bring the people into a higher place of evolution.

His entrance into the Authority had been swift and easy, first sitting in place of Isaac, spouting whatever religious nonsense was necessary to gain the trust of the other members around him and giving him a front-row seat to Ian Carson's implosion.

It hadn't taken Ian long to self-destruct. The death of a child isn't something anyone should have to watch, but to be the source of that child's death had to create darkness inside a person with enough power to destroy any remaining sense of self. After months of failure in his increasingly frantic efforts to obtain members of the rebellion, Ian's leadership abilities had been called into question. And after additional weeks of failure in his decreasingly effective attempts to lead the city out of the turmoil sweeping the streets, it had been obvious to all that Ian was no longer equipped to sit in the president's seat.

Damien had spent this time efficiently, whispering in the ears of those around him, egging on their rising concern over their once-glorious leader, and securing their loyalty. That part was most crucial. He knew that if and when Ian fell from power, the other members would be looking for a leader they could follow without hesitation. One might think each man who sat around the Authority table would covet the president's seat, but Damien discovered most of them were sheep. Powerful sheep, perhaps, with the ability to make decisions, but to truly lead was a different kind of responsibility, one that very few were able to carry. And sheep didn't survive long without a shepherd. Thankfully, Damien wasn't a sheep.

It had been roughly three months since Ian was overthrown, cast out, kindly asked to leave his post, however one might put it, and three months since the council had asked Damien to step in. In the short span of a year and a half, Damien had moved from High Council Judge to Authority President.

Unlike the other members in the room, Damien had not grown up watching his father rule. Damien's father had been in law, just as Damien was, but with an unfathomable sense of contentment that kept him from rising higher than the position given to him. Damien had never understood his father's acceptance of place and duty. Damien had always wanted more. He found contentment disgusting, a sign of weakness. His mother had taught him that. She'd been the compass that steered him forward toward greatness. Now here he sat, not just a royal like the rest, but the king.

"How could you have let them slip through your fingers?" Enderson Lane asked Lieutenant Smith. Smith had been allowed to sit in on the last couple of Authority meetings at Enderson's request. The fall of Dodson Rogue had been another stab at the falsely assumed stability of the city's leadership. To have two of their own betray the ideals they had sworn to uphold within the same time frame made the sheep frantic. Yet the difference between Isaac and Dodson was monumental: Isaac was mentally unstable; Dodson had made a choice.

After Isaac had used his secondary, untraceable chip to kidnap and murder girls throughout the city, Ian had demanded that every other Authority member turn in their secondary chips. Dodson had claimed that when he went to retrieve his, it was missing. Stolen, he assumed, by Remko after the soldier had been told he could never be with the woman he loved. A story that by all accounts had felt plausible and true. It had been easier for the sheep to believe the lie rather than accept that they had yet again been fooled. But there were too many unanswered questions for the claim to sit soundly.

Witnesses remembered Dodson heading into his office with Remko that night. They also recalled Remko leaving alone, Dodson still in his office, but mysteriously, Remko's chip had been found near Dodson's office later. If Remko hadn't been alone in Dodson's office that night, when had he stolen the chip? He could have taken it earlier, of course, but why would he, if the crime had in fact been a reaction to the Authority's decision? Dodson could provide answers for none of these questions. He was clearly complicit in Remko's crime, but without solid proof—which they didn't have—the other Authority members believed taking away his seat was all they could do for the time being.

Many believed Dodson would rejoin the council once a full and detailed investigation of his missing chip had been completed. But Damien knew Dodson had helped Remko escape, had been the cause of all the turmoil that had followed since. The man was probably a follower of Aaron, even though he claimed not to be. And since rescuing the Authority and setting the community on a new path was his duty, Damien had done what any true leader would do—he'd made sure Dodson paid for his crimes.

Damien had found a less-than-upstanding soldier and paid him to claim he'd spoken with Remko that night and that Remko had admitted to Dodson giving him his secondary chip. When the young soldier, Aryers, had come forward with this information, the first question everyone asked was why he'd kept it to himself so long. But Damien had prepared Aryers for that. Aryers claimed that Remko had threatened his family if he said anything. He said he knew he'd been a coward and would pay for his wrongdoings however the Authority saw fit. Then they wanted to know why Remko would say anything to him in the first place. Aryers replied that he and Remko had been very close, like brothers, and when he'd encountered his friend using Dodson's chip to leave the city that night he'd tried to stop him.

He also spoke about the way Dodson had always favored Remko, treating him more like a son than a soldier. That part Aryers didn't even have to fabricate. With a witness's testimony it hadn't been hard for Damien to convince the Authority to imprison Dodson. Aryers had to serve prison time as well, a short sentence that Damien had warned him about but with the promise that when he was released, he and his family would never have to work again. Damien had no intention of following through on this lofty promise, but by the time Aryers was released the world would be a different place. Damien would make sure of it.

"They escaped through a back passage, and we lost visual of them once they were in the streets," Smith said.

"Do you understand what a grave missed opportunity this was?" Enderson asked.

Smith nodded but kept his chin lifted.

Damien liked Smith. He was strong, intelligent, and confident. Even though Enderson was filling the role of commander of the CityWatch until a more long-term solution could be made, Smith was really the one pulling the strings, and Enderson was aware of how necessary Smith was to the cause. "An opportunity we will have again," Damien said.

Enderson and Smith both turned their attention to the head of the table, where Damien sat. The rest of the table followed suit and waited.

"Remember, capturing all of the rebels is only part of the goal," Damien said. "The larger part is reminding the people that being outside the city walls is not to be free, as the rebels have led them to believe."

"But if we could obtain all of the rebels, there would be no need for anyone to flee the city," Monroe Austin said.

"Do you really believe that shutting down this one group will ensure no further rebellion?" Damien asked.

"We lived in peace for decades without rebellion before Aaron and his Seers," Walker Red said.

"A lie you were led to believe, as I have often said. The idea that you can control the human spirit simply by placing it inside rules is to ensure rebellion as an outcome," Damien said.

"Then why execute the rebels so swiftly if it does us no good in the end?" Monroe asked.

"Because it does us good in the present. Both present and future beasts have to be tamed," Damien rejoined. "So while we solve the problem of humanity's need to be free, to be in charge, to think themselves above the pack, to act against their animalistic nature, fear is a powerful sedative for rebellion."

The table grew quiet. Damien had slowly been introducing the idea of drastic change during the three months since he had taken office, and he saw many of the men before him nod in agreement. Softly treading through the minds of men who didn't accept change easily was a delicate process. The switch necessary for a person to truly see the evil of humanity could easily induce panic and depression. Thankfully, Damien already had a solution, a way to save the world from its inherited issues.

"And how exactly do we solve the problem of *humanity*?" Monroe asked.

Damien paused to collect his thoughts. Monroe was among the last of the Authority members to buy into Damien's way of thinking. He'd also been the only one to fight for Ian's seat when the former leader was overthrown, and he remained hopeful regarding Dodson's involvement in the rebel's escape. If it weren't for Monroe's insistence that they have unwavering evidence against the previous CityWatch leader, Damien would have had Dodson executed weeks ago. Not to fear, that time was coming.

"You ask that question as if you believe there is no problem." Damien calmly folded his hands on the table surface.

"Of course there is a problem; I just don't see how the problem is anything other than Aaron and his Seers."

"Aaron and those who follow him are the physical representation of the problem within man itself. We are seeing the same problem, my friend; you are just not allowing yourself to see the whole picture."

Damien stood and began to pace slowly around the grand table. "Man's insistence on clinging to self, to choice—that is our problem. It is man's need for freedom that causes chaos and rebellion. It is the same issue that caused the conceptualization of the Prima Solution back before the Time of Ruin. To live longer, to be better, to have more, to place oneself above the rest of the population, to care solely about one's own well-being. Selfishness, really, is at the root of chaos and rebellion."

Damien watched a familiar agreement settle over most of the table. Even Monroe held his tongue, so he continued. "After the Time of Ruin, Robert Carson did away with man's persistent allegiance to self, making everyone's task to better serve the unit, the whole. And for a time it worked. Using fear and threats to keep people in line, Robert and God controlled the human disease."

"And after doing away with the rebels and Aaron, we can just go back to the way things were before," Monroe said. "The way that has worked for this community for decades."

"And it may work for a while longer, using brute force and thin threats to dispose of those that step out of line.

But then someone else like Aaron will come along and
we will find ourselves right back where we are. Whether
it happens in our lifetimes or in the lifetimes of our children, history has a wicked way of repeating itself," Damien
said. "Would it not be better to create a different future,
ensuring that the cruel history we are reliving now cannot
come back to haunt us? To ensure that when our sons sit
at this table they won't have to deal with executions and
rebellions?"

Several members whispered to those closest to them and
Damien hid a small smile. "We have the opportunity to
change the world, to shape the future. We must do more
than struggle to hold on to control that we will simply
lose. Anything you can obtain can be taken away. This isn't
about forcing people to submit or convincing them with
religion; this is about changing them permanently, doing
away with the human disease altogether. Giving them a
cure. Calling them into a higher level of existence."

Damien paused to gauge his audience's response to
his words. Good, but not quite good enough. Perhaps an
appeal to a higher power would help. He smiled. "We have
been called, by God, to eradicate rebellion once and for
all. We are the high priests, the chosen few, the soldiers
in a larger war against humanity's basest instincts. If we
continue to do the same thing and expect different results,
then we only leave a legacy of insanity."

Damien knew at the end of the day Monroe would not
stand against the collective. The Minister of Health and

Wellness was still just a sheep trying to become a shepherd. Damien could feel the excited energy filling the room. Destiny was upon them; they were ready for the future. They were ready to be led. And as King Damien, he would lead them into a new era. His era.

5 Remko surveyed the old underground transportation tunnel as people moved around him, setting up camp for the night. The floor was concrete except for the two sets of long metal tracks that ran down the middle and disappeared into the distance in both directions. The walls and ceiling were rounded, shaped like the inside of a dome and covered with a lattice of metal and stone and cables that made Remko think of a honeycomb. A dim lighting system ran along the top of the curved ceiling. Wire had gotten the lights working pretty quickly, which was a nice change from some of the places they had been before. Firelight was hard to navigate by.

Tents were going up, and food was being sorted through and logged—but also cooked, which sent a sweet, warm smell through the air. Sam, Wire, and Kate had gone ahead of the group and radioed that it was safe for the rest to join. The three of them were still out, walking the long tunnels to see what they could find, to make sure they were secure.

Ramses and Lesley were helping direct camp setup so things got done efficiently and with as little chaos as possible, and Carrington had jumped in to help make sure people were getting fed and staying hydrated. She should be mourning, alone in her own space, letting the death of her best friend work its way through her system in a healthy way. But there wasn't time for grieving; there wasn't time for working things through, for space.

The camp was well on its way to being home for the night, and Remko decided to travel down the east side of the long underground system to set up his own perimeter. He let Ramses know where he was headed and, after kindly refusing his brother's company, set off into the darkness.

The tunnel was peacefully quiet, the stillness of the air welcoming. He ventured deeper into the darkness, scanning the area around him, checking the walls, the slight openings, anything that might prove to be harmful. He let his mind spin around the events of the last twenty-four hours. He couldn't get the final images of Larkin or Carrington's painful cries out of his mind. He feared he never would. They would be a part of him now, like the execution of Arianna, the murder of his father by an enraged tradesman, the slow death of his mother from a broken heart, the assassination of his friend and fellow CityWatch guard Helms. They would all follow him, attached like warts. Marks of all his imperfections. He couldn't help but wonder why the Seers were still following his lead after all the warts he'd collected.

But they did. They looked to him for guidance, waited on him to make moves, and followed. They believed his military background gave him some sort of authority in matters that he, truthfully, was terrified of. And people assumed that just as Carrington was completely convinced by and devoted to the teaching of Aaron, so was he.

The truth Remko believed was much simpler: he would do anything necessary to protect those he loved. He followed Aaron's way because he had seen the effect it had on Carrington and Larkin. Because of the way Wire spoke about it and because of how it softened Kate's heart and gave Sam strength. Because of the way it was changing Ramses's and Lesley's lives for the better. But Remko himself wasn't sure he was completely convinced.

Remko respected the way Aaron loved and the simple peace he seemed to carry with him, but that love and peace were getting people killed.

"Searching for answers in the dark?" a voice asked.

A moment of panic pulsed in Remko's gut before recognition of the voice filled his senses. His tense shoulders relaxed as he felt Aaron move from out of the shadows and to Remko's side. "I learned long ago that the darkness never answers back," Remko said.

"I wouldn't be so sure about that. Anything is possible with faith," Aaron said.

Remko didn't turn to face the man but kept his stare forward into the deep tunnel. "Even walking on water?"

Aaron chuckled. "So you have been listening."

The man's buoyancy was infectious, and Remko found a layer of cold begin to lift off his chest. But then thoughts of the last twenty-four hours reentered his mind and the cold only deepened. He turned toward Aaron. "We need to leave," he said. "Being this close to the city becomes more dangerous with each passing day."

Remko felt Aaron's energy change.

"I heard her song from across the wilderness," Aaron said. "'It is well, it is well with my soul.'" Silence filled the space around them and Remko heard Larkin's voice softly echoing through his memory.

"Beautiful, beautiful daughter," Aaron said. Nearly a whisper, his eyes closed, his face lifted to the darkness around them. Tears streaming down his cheeks.

"How is Carrington?" Aaron asked at last.

Remko let the silence sit between them for a moment. "Broken."

"The beautiful thing about brokenness is that it heals," Aaron said. "I am so sorry you have to endure such pain, though."

Remko felt the words in his core. "These are the risks we take," he said, working to hide the emotion in his voice.

"I wish I could say taking risks was at an end," Aaron said.

Remko turned his head, surprised, and gave Aaron a worried look. He knew that tone. "You want us to go back into the city?"

"Events are progressing quickly. Circumstances are changing. People are being called."

"Then let them become Sleeper Seers and be our eyes

and ears inside the walls. Is it nec . . . nec . . . necessary that they come here?" Remko dropped his head and bit the inside of his bottom lip. His stutter came so rarely these days that the sound of it brought back a rush of painful emotions. He could feel Aaron's sympathetic gaze and wished he'd turn his eyes elsewhere.

"Does it always return with the fear?" Aaron asked.

Remko hesitated and took a deep breath. He quieted his raging brain and stilled his heart before he spoke. "No; it comes and goes as it wishes."

"You could be free of it all, you know."

Remko ignored Aaron's last statement and changed course. "I need to understand what we are still doing here, so close to those that wish us harm. Why can't we leave, set out to find a place that we can call our own?"

"And you believe that running away will somehow free you of your fear?"

"We would be safe."

"From whom?"

"From our enemies. From the Authority."

Aaron paused. "Is that who you believe the enemy is?"

Remko could feel heat rising to his face. He was responsible for protecting his family, but Aaron was keeping them in a constant state of threat. How was Remko supposed to respond to that? "More will die," he said.

"I never wanted pain for anyone." Aaron's voice was mournful. "I wish I could save them, but I can only lead."

"Then lead us away from here."

"The city needs to be changed, Remko. How can we change it if we leave?"

"So we stay and put our lives at risk until every last person inside those walls is changed?"

"I know it isn't ideal."

"Not ideal? It's madness!"

"Remko, you must have faith. We are called to save not one but all."

That was the problem. Remko didn't believe. He didn't have Aaron's faith, and he wasn't even sure that faith—the faith everyone around him was clinging to—was real. He sighed and closed his eyes. He recalled all the times he'd had this conversation with Aaron. All the times he'd urged Carrington to try and reason with him. Each time the response was the same. And each time Remko followed Aaron's lead, because he'd been assured by many that without Aaron they would all be lost. Though he was less sure of that now. But this was the course, the path he found himself walking.

"Who is it this time?" Remko asked.

"A family, three in total," Aaron said.

"When are they expecting us?"

"In two days."

Remko fought against his anger and the silent fear that was rumbling inside his chest.

"I know you don't agree with these tactics, and I understand your frustration. You enslave yourself with expectations. But freedom is within reach."

Remko had little interest in Aaron's version of freedom right now. He felt the weight of weariness fall over him. "I'm going to head back. Will I see you there?"

Aaron shook his head. "I came only to speak with you for now." With that, he started off into the tunnel's expansive darkness.

Remko called after him. "People need you in camp. Why vanish all the time? Where do you go?"

"Nowhere," Aaron said. "I never really leave."

Remko could feel his frustration envelop him, and he didn't want to say something he would regret. He turned to head for camp before he lost control of his emotions.

"Remko," Aaron called.

Remko hesitantly looked over his shoulder.

"Things are beginning to change inside the city, and they will change within the Seers as well. It will get darker before we see light again. Know that at any point if the load you are carrying becomes too heavy, you can let it go."

Aaron held Remko's gaze for a long breath before he turned and faded into the dark.

/ / /

Damien paced across the small office floor. There was hardly enough space to take four steps in either direction before he was forced to turn around and return the way he had come. The room was overflowing with aged collections of Old America textbooks, pages ripped out and hung for display, taped or pinned to the walls and windows, marked and underlined. A row of floor-to-ceiling bookshelves lined the back wall, stuffed with more written works and a large assortment of plastic models displaying parts of the body—the brain, heart, stomach, liver. All of them completely unnecessary since Authority scientists and medical workers had access to 3-D projected images that gave better insight into the working functionality of the body, so the outdated models sat collecting dust.

A single table stood in the middle of the room, too wide for the space. It was covered with an arrangement of test tubes, measuring beakers, Bunsen burners, volumetric flasks, and microspatulas; all of which hadn't been touched in years. Graphs and charts covered most of the floor, and the single chair that may at one time have been used for sitting was now the resting place of a box filled with rolled paper manuscripts.

The entire place still gave Damien a twitch, but he had spent a significant amount of time learning to ignore his tendency to burn everything useless. He glanced up at the quiet man who stood staring out the small square of uncovered windowpane and waited. Damien could tell the Scientist was deep in thought from the way he slightly nodded his head as he pondered.

Dr. Roth Reynard was one of the most forward-thinking minds of his time. He possessed the unique ability to see past the limitations of reality and envision what could be. Damien's father had warned him that the

Scientist's way of thinking was a danger to the community and a threat to the well-being of the city, but Damien had always been fascinated with the ideas and vision of the mysterious doctor.

As a teen, Damien had gone against his father's direction and secretly spent time under the Scientist's tutelage. Exploring the secrets of the mind in order to gain a better understanding of the functionality of the brain. The Scientist said the brain was the singular area that controlled the entirety of a person's existence. To understand it was to be in control of oneself, and with enough understanding, one could control others.

At first, Damien had met with the Scientist out of rebellion and curiosity. But as their clandestine study sessions continued, he slowly began to appreciate and eventually adopt the man's ideals. In time Damien found himself fully committed to the Scientist's vision for the community. Together they imagined and began to work toward a clear picture of order. The ability to set boundaries around what a person could believe, to control emotional reactions and infuse proper ways of thinking. With Dr. Reynard's mind and Damien's will, the limitations for what they could achieve were nonexistent. And now that Damien's rise to power had been realized, the road ahead was clear. But still the odds stood against them. Constant obstacles, constant persecution. People were afraid of what they didn't understand; their minds were weak. Damien intended to change that. A plan was in motion, but timing was everything.

"The second round of trials showed much better results than expected, but the mind is a tricky little beast," the Scientist said. He turned to face Damien and the light from the sun showed how unkind time had been to him over the last couple of years. Then again, time was an unkind thing. Dr. Reynard's face was losing its proper hold, and age was dragging his skin toward the ground. His hair was white and thin, his eyes less vibrant than Damien had once known them to be. He was becoming as frail as the world saw him, but Damien knew his mind was stronger than ever.

"It's the self-delusional concept of a soul and free will that are tough to navigate," the Scientist said. "The key lies within inhibiting the brain's ability to enlighten the mind."

"Control the source," Damien said.

"Precisely."

"Can it be done?"

The Scientist chuckled and ran his bony fingers along the bookcase within reach. He swept a line of dust off with his touch and Damien watched the old man rub it between his fingers.

"I would have thought by this point you would know the answer to that question."

Damien felt rebuked. The Scientist was like a father to him, more so than his actual father had been, and hearing disapproval in his tone filled Damien with shame. He dropped his eyes. "Of course it can be done."

"All problems can be solved with the right equation, the proper formula. You are never as far off as you believe."

Damien nodded. In all arenas of life, Damien prided himself on having authority. In his work, his sham of a marriage, his social engagements. He held a firm, controlling hand, but in this office he always felt like a child, with his instructor calling out his faults and playing with his shortcomings. He allowed no one else to make him feel inferior, but the Scientist was his mentor, and Damien couldn't ignore the constant need to seek his approval.

"Speaking of problems," the Scientist continued, "how are things with our soft-minded leaders?"

"They are turning in our favor; the Council is beginning to see the light the future holds. It won't be long now," Damien said.

"Good. Things will unfold quickly when the trials are complete. We need their full and undivided cooperation."

"They will be ready."

The Scientist smiled and nodded. "I have no doubt in you."

Damien masked his delight at the Scientist's words and felt his pulse quicken. Everything would happen fast, and change would finally start to take root in the streets. This was a task Damien had committed his life to, and the ultimate fulfillment of all his work could not happen soon enough.

Trial Entry 37 | Patient 11-4 (Maria Talcum)

Age: 23 / **Gender:** Female / **Status:** Authority Worker
Drug administered at 15:34 hours
Time in observation: 11 days

Patient log

Day 1 after administration: I woke up in a strange place.
It smells like lemons and bleach. I'm in a single room, alone.
It's cold, colorless. I'm afraid and no one will tell me where
I am or why I'm here. My head is pounding, and I don't know if
it's from fear or pain. There's a large mark on my left arm. It
was bandaged when I woke, and a man in a white coat came in
a little while ago to remove the dressing. He seemed nice, but
he wouldn't answer any of my questions. He was accompanied
by two CityWatch guards. I didn't recognize them, but I try to
avoid CityWatch guards so that makes sense. If I do as I'm told
hopefully they'll let me go.

Day 4 after administration: I don't know how long I've
been here. The days run into each other. There's no way for
me to know what time of day it is. There aren't any windows,
but there is a large dark glass square on the far right wall.

Whoever brought me here is watching me. I keep praying that someone notices I'm missing, but I know the chances are low.

Day 7 after administration: I feel strange, like my mind is scraping against the inside of my head to get out. I can't tell if I'm happy or sad. Food makes me sick, but I'm starving. They're killing me. I wish somebody would help me. They're killing me.

Day 10 after administration: My skin is on fire, and my face is starting to blister. My mind keeps trying to think of ways to be free of this place, but then sometimes I don't want to be free at all. Most of the time, I just wish for death. Death would be easier.

6 Remko found the camp in full swing when he returned. The tunnel looked as if they had been there for days, as if this had always been their home. People sat around fires, eating, chatting, some even sharing a laugh. Children played, completely unaware of the danger that followed their every move. One could almost forget that death had touched them so deeply only hours before.

He saw Carrington cradling Elise by the farthest fire, sitting with Kate and Lesley, a small smile on her lips as she played with the tiny baby. His shoulders eased at the sight of joy on his wife's face, even if it was slight and possibly forced. He moved to cross the distance toward the fire and felt a body approach.

Remko turned to see Neil Stone headed toward him. Neil had spent fifteen years as a lead construction architect for the Authority City's largest structures. His knowledge of the buildings' foundations and the inner workings of the city had been invaluable to the team. He'd come to the Seers on his own nearly four months ago with his six-year-old son, Corbin. Neil's wife had died during childbirth, and the message of hope that Aaron had delivered to Neil years after he'd given up on being a good father had saved not only his life but also his relationship with his son. But time was cruel and fear real. It was hard to remember the truth in the face of both.

"Hello, Neil," Remko said.

"Remko. Glad to see most of you are back safe," Neil said.

If Neil was trying to hide the bite behind his words, he was failing. Remko tried to keep his face clear of expression and waited for Neil to continue.

"Can I steal you for a moment, before you head down for the night?" Neil asked.

Remko nodded and followed Neil away from the main commotion of camp.

"Is everything all right?" Remko asked.

"I know we've spoken about this before . . . ," Neil began, and before he finished his sentence, Remko knew exactly where he was headed.

"Neil . . ."

"I know you've spoken with him. I just assumed after several months of being with this group that we would have moved away from this place."

"I understand your concern. . . ."

"Do you? You say that, but do you really? We lost another of our own today. Aren't you afraid of the risk you are putting on your daughter by being so close to the city?"

Remko said nothing, but his expression grew dark. Neil saw the change and shook his head.

"I'm sorry, but I have a son too, and I just can't help but think that staying this close is a huge mistake."

Remko still said nothing. Had he not just voiced these same concerns to Aaron moments ago? Had he not struggled to sleep the last couple of weeks with heavy thoughts, wondering what they were all doing this for?

"I'm not the only one who feels this way. There are others in the camp who believe we would be better off packing up and moving as far away from this place as possible."

"Aaron says—" Remko started.

"Have you ever considered that maybe Aaron is wrong?" Neil said.

The question echoed the thoughts already stumbling around in Remko's mind.

"I know it sounds harsh, and I will be forever in debt to him for what he did for me, but he is just a man. He could be wrong."

Remko found it hard to quiet the nagging voice in his head that whispered its agreement.

"I'm not suggesting we do anything drastic, but some of us are starting to question whether Aaron is really fit to lead. I mean, he's hardly ever present, and when he's here, he never wants to discuss strategic maneuvers or the future; he just tells stories and plays with the children." Neil ran his hand across his forehead with frustration. "I have a responsibility to my son, Remko, to keep him safe—as do you to your own family."

Remko felt heat rise up the back of his neck, and he crossed his arms over his chest. He didn't appreciate Neil accusing him of not understanding his responsibility to his family.

"I don't mean anything offensive by that; I just . . . are we sure that our safety is Aaron's top priority?"

Remko knew he needed to stop this line of thought, even if he wasn't far away from it himself. "Neil, I know what you are feeling—I understand the risk better than anyone—but for now we are called to this place. I'm not saying it will be forever, but for now this is where we stay."

Neil didn't look appeased.

"Next time Aaron is here, we will sit down with him and discuss your concerns, but for now you have to trust him, and if not him, then me."

Neil still looked less than pleased, but he nodded.

Remko thought about Neil stirring up contention with others in camp and reached out to place a reassuring hand on his shoulder. "No one feels the loss of our own people more than I do. Losing Larkin was a tragedy, one that nobody is going to forget quickly. I understand the danger you are putting yourself and your son in by remaining with the Seers. And it may seem easier to run, but we need you, Neil. You are vital to this camp. Please understand that following Aaron's lead is our best choice right now."

Neil nodded with more sincerity and gave Remko a weak smile. "All right—I'll pass the message on. For now we stay, but we can't afford to lose any more Seers."

"I know, believe me," Remko said.

With a final nod, Neil left Remko and headed back for the camp.

Once alone, Remko let his guard fall and rubbed the sides of his forehead with his fingers. He wondered who else in the camp shared Neil's concerns? How many were there? Was it a majority? And more important, how was he supposed to convince them that following Aaron's plan was best if he wasn't sure of it himself?

/ / /

Damien stood inside the small space reserved for the head religious official. Beyond the single red curtain behind him waited the fresh gathering of Authority Workers, rejects from the latest Choosing Ceremony. Lints, the name given to them by the city's people. The poor souls who would now face the rest of their days as outcasts, as was mandated by the law. A flawed use of resources, if Damien were to be honest with himself.

He'd never fully understood the long-standing tradition of the Choosing Ceremony. It was a ceremony put into place to respect the will of God, his father had always told him.

The will of God.

And what was a person supposed to do with such a force if one didn't believe there was a God? He had asked his father this once—a mistake Damien had realized too late. His father had never looked at him the same after that day, and had it not been for the protection from his mother, Damien might have found himself cast aside, destined to be a CityWatch guard, as much an outcast as the girls who waited beyond the curtain.

"All rise for Authority President Gold," a voice said from inside the chapel, where the new Authority Workers had gathered.

Damien grabbed the ornate copy of the *Veritas* perched before him and pushed himself through the heavy curtain. The book felt like a weight in his hand, a leather-bound representation of how much change needed to happen to this city in order for it to grow. How he longed to preach a different message from this pulpit. One that offered hope to a gathering of girls no different than he once was. Cast aside from their community because they'd failed to meet the standards set in some ancient text that was scientifically improbable at best and downright ridiculous at worst. How he longed to help rid them of the rules that kept them enslaved like animals and watch as they ascended into a higher existence.

But he couldn't say that, not yet. He was confined too, obligated to play his role still. Which meant going through the motions that grated against his skin.

Damien swept his eyes across the scared faces of the young girls and hid his disgust for such wasted energy.

He opened the *Veritas* and began the required reading. "The *Veritas* reads, 'Let every citizen be subject to the Authority. For there is no true authority except for God, and those who have been appointed have been instituted by God.'" The rest of the passage fell from his lips, the words familiar and sour on his tongue. His mind drifted as his mouth worked like a programmed machine.

He would possess the minds in this room, in time. They would all change. Change was inevitable, necessary, and already happening. Damien clung to that truth when it felt like the fools around him were committed to halting progress.

He wouldn't confess to believing in hope, but if one were to ask him where he put his hope, he'd say it lay within the wasted people of this city. The people no one was looking for anymore. Those people would be the instruments he would use to perfect and bring about change. Whether people were watching for it, or hiding behind their God's law, change would happen. And then all of this would no longer be necessary. Damien had hope in that.

7 Carrington shivered as a rush of early morning air swept through her hair. The sun was hardly up, throwing its first beams on the western hills, and she already had to squint against its harsh light. Sam and Kate walked several feet ahead of her, lost in quiet conversation about the happenings to come. Remko had announced last night to her and the rest of the usual team—Wire, Kate, and Sam—that Aaron needed some of them to head back into the city for another retrieval. The mood had been somber to start, but the news had brought another layer of quiet retreat.

Carrington watched the cracked pavement under her feet as she followed the siblings. Old, worn-down homes sat scattered on either side of the street. Broken windows and open doors, showing the structures empty. It always gave her an eerie sense to travel through what used to be Old American normality. To think about the way life was hundreds of years ago, when people lived in these homes, dying from a vaccine they thought would save them. Those people had traveled these same streets, but how different everything had been then.

She shook off the uneasy feeling and her thoughts returned to her current situation. She remembered when

the Seer camp had housed just a handful, back before the
birth of her daughter, before so many deaths, before the
pain had become heavier than the joy. Back then, whenever
Aaron asked them to move into the city and gather more
Seers, an excited energy had infused them. Now it felt as if
their duty to bring all that were called out of their imprisonment within the city walls electrified them with fear.

Remko especially. Carrington saw sides of him the
others never would. The cracks in his armor. The things
he let slip when he was staring at Elise and didn't think
Carrington was watching. The things he murmured in his
sleep that kept her awake at times. The pain she couldn't
comfort or fix.

She thought back to the last conversation she'd had
with Aaron. It had been a couple weeks ago; he'd walked
with her alone, sensing her anxiety. Her uneasiness. She'd
been worried about Remko; he'd stopped sleeping regularly.
Even when he was with her, a part of him was somewhere
else.

"He will find his way," Aaron had said.

"You keep telling me that, but as the days pass I wonder
if he's only becoming more lost."

"Being lost is part of the journey."

"He's started stuttering again. It's still rare, but it's been
months since he's stuttered at all and now . . ."

"Does it bother you?"

"No, of course not. But it bothers him. It makes him
feel weak, as though he's failed. The pressure he puts on

himself . . . I want to save him from this, but it feels overwhelming sometimes."

"Be careful not to lose yourself in trying to help him find his way. Trust that the path he is on is exactly where he's supposed to be."

Carrington tried to hold on to his words now as her mind drifted to Larkin. Tears stung the insides of her eyelids and she dropped her gaze so that Kate and Sam wouldn't see. She knew grief well, understood time was necessary for freedom from its grip, but she wondered how long it would be before the thought of Larkin didn't threaten to cripple her. Her knees shook and she found catching her breath nearly impossible. She reached out and pressed her fingertips to the tree beside her for stability. If her body failed her, the last thing she wanted was to end up on her knees, out here in the morning sun, weeping.

Sam would insist they take her back if that happened and she needed to be away from camp right now. She'd insisted to Remko that she was well enough to go on this scouting run, and she needed to be right. Carrington had thought for a moment that Remko was going to demand she stay at camp and rest. His body language clearly stated that he didn't agree with her choice, but she could be very stubborn when she wanted to be. And she needed to be doing something other than lying in their tent crying. In a different place, in a different time, maybe spending days, even months, mourning the loss of her best friend would be appropriate, but this was not that time or place.

Everyone else in camp was functioning; so would she. Carrington couldn't collapse now, couldn't allow the sorrow latched to her heart to weigh her down. She took a deep, stabilizing breath and focused on placing one foot in front of the other. Pushing out the worry, the fear, the pain. She pictured the field. The one where her Father had saved her, the Father of Aaron, the one who had brought her a message of truth that had saved her life. She stayed there for a long moment.

Beautiful, beautiful daughter. How quickly you forget.

Carrington let his words fill her brain and focused on all the things she'd heard Aaron talk about throughout the last year. About faith, its power, the way it stood against all opposing forces. How there was nothing strong enough to force it down. Faith was an impenetrable wall, not because it shut the fear out but because it invited the fear in. Carrington could barely wrap her mind around her true sense of self, let alone conceive of any way to use that sense to be fearless.

Such power you possess with just a small amount of faith, yet how quickly you forget.

The words seeped into her soul and warmed the chill inside her bones. How quickly she did forget; how hard it felt to remember the truth in the face of loss and fear.

Remember who you are.

A touch shook her from her inner thoughts and she gasped. Sam and Kate stood in front of her, Sam's hand on her shoulder. "Are you okay?" he asked. She was standing still, and both of them were giving her troubled looks.

She hadn't even realized she'd stopped moving. She gave a small smile. "Sorry—I'm fine."

"Are you sure you don't want to go back?" Sam asked.

Carrington shook her head and Sam nodded.

"We want to scope out the area over those hills," Kate said, pointing to the south where a large grouping of hills stood less than half a mile out. "Wire said he was encountering some weird electrical readings from the other side."

"This far from the city?" Carrington asked. The Authority City loomed to the east behind them. If you stood on a hilltop and strained your eyes, even from their location, more than twenty miles away, you could just make out the thundering walls that encircled the city and marked it as a prison.

"Yeah, that was Wire's thought too," Kate said.

"We move in very carefully and stay close to the trees to keep us covered," Sam said.

Even this far outside the city walls, Carrington knew that the sky above could be a danger. There were always eyes searching for them. They could never be too careful. Two months ago a flying drone had spotted one of their scouting units and they had barely broken camp before the place was plagued with CityWatch soldiers. They'd lost three Seers that day. Two of them, killed during the camp invasion; the third had been taken, never to be heard from since. His name was Mac Tyler. He'd left behind a wife and two small children. His wife had helped Carrington deliver Elise a month before her husband was taken. No one knew

what had happened to him. He had not been executed—
not publicly, at least—and their Sleeper inside the prison
had never reported him being held there either. It was the
not knowing that haunted Mac's wife. She walked around
like a shell most days, doing only what was necessary to
survive. Grief had claimed her as one of its own, and she
couldn't be freed.

Mac was not the first Seer this had happened to. Seers
were taken nearly every time the CityWatch caught up with
them. Usually they were executed. But occasionally raids
were not followed by executions, and the rest of the group
was unable to decipher where the victims had gone. As if
they had been erased from existence. It always left an eerie
mark on camp. Executions were cruel and permanent, but
at least they left evidence of a Seer's life.

The gathering of abandoned homes faded into a
wooded area and Carrington followed as Kate and Sam
moved gracefully through the trees around them. The forest stretched up the sides of the hills they were headed for,
lending a thick overhead cover the entire way. The protection ended near the top of the peak and the three slowed as
they reached the break in the trees. The sun was warm now,
and Carrington felt sweat collecting on her forehead.

"Hopefully it's something functional so we can repurpose
it," Kate said.

"Hopefully it's not heavy," Sam said. "You two stay here."

Kate rolled her eyes but stayed with Carrington as
Sam quickly covered the last few yards to the hilltop and

dropped to his chest to safely peer over. He lay there for a long moment, frozen, his eyes trained forward.

"Wonder what it is?" Carrington said.

"I'm ready to find out," Kate said, and before Carrington could urge her not to, Kate was moving toward her brother. He snapped his head back to her and Carrington watched him mouth something violent, but Kate ignored him and dropped to her belly beside him.

Carrington waited for one of them to motion for her to follow, but they both just lay there and her curiosity got the better of her. She stayed low as she moved up the rest of the hill and could hear Sam's angered growl when she dropped down beside him.

"What part of *stay here* was confusing for you two?" Sam said.

Carrington carefully peered over the ledge to see a deep valley below. In its center sat a large, long, white building shaped like a warehouse. A tall, wired fence circled the rectangular structure; a couple of black CityWatch vehicles sat along the outside of the fence, and Carrington could make out armed men walking the grounds.

"What is this place?" Carrington asked.

"I have no idea—I've never seen it before," Sam said.

Carrington searched for any other detail that might help her understand what she was seeing. A rumble came from the north. In the valley below her, a large CityWatch transport kicked up dust as it made its way toward the huge protected building. Kate, Sam, and Carrington all reacted the same and lowered themselves even closer to the ground as they watched the vehicle pull up to one end of the structure. A handful of CityWatch soldiers appeared from inside the building and walked to the transport. They opened the back double doors and motioned for whoever was inside to exit.

Carrington squinted to see as the people stepped out of the vehicle. All of them wore different colored uniforms. Farm Lands, Lint, Cattle Lands, and even what appeared to be a CityWatch member were hauled out of the transport and into the monstrous structure.

"What the heck?" Kate said.

"They look like they're restrained, but I can't really see anything clearly from here," Sam said.

"Are they prisoners?" Carrington asked.

"We need to get closer," Kate said. She started to move, but Sam grabbed her arm.

"That is not a good idea," he said. Kate tried to yank her arm away but Sam kept his grip firm.

"What if those people are being hurt? We can't just leave them here to be . . ." She trailed off.

"To be what? We don't know what's happening here. And look at that security! There are only three of us. Walking down there is a suicide mission."

"He's right, Kate," Carrington said, even though the thought of what might be happening to those people made her gut roll. "We're on a scouting run, not a retrieval mission; we have no idea what we could be walking into.

Better to take this information back to camp and discuss it with the group."

Kate drilled both of them with a glare, but she had to know that they were right. Finally she nodded and ripped her arm away from Sam. She pulled Roxy from her pocket and used the device to capture several photos. She got at least a dozen before Sam motioned for them to head back to camp.

Once back down the hill and into the cover of trees, Sam cleared his throat. "So, Wire let you take Roxy?"

There was a tease on the edge of his voice and Carrington bit back a smile. It was common knowledge that Wire was smitten with Kate, and even more common knowledge that Kate tried extremely hard to pretend that she didn't feel the same.

"If you say another word I'll drag you back up the hill and push you off the edge," Kate said.

Sam chuckled and Carrington, for a moment, ignored the clawing worry that lived inside her head, the pain that weighed on her shoulders, and the fear that her world was falling apart too fast for her to save it.

/ / /

Damien waited for the guard to unlock the steel security door in front of them. With a soft click, the door popped open and both men stepped across the threshold into a dark brick-walled hallway. The guard turned back to shut and lock the door through which they'd just entered, then quickly moved to the opposite end of the hall, where there was another locked door. The prison's security had been updated since the rebels had defeated its previous safety measures, freeing a Seer during an active daytime shift. It had been an embarrassment for the CityWatch and the Authority.

Escorting Damien through the second door, the guard nodded to the president. He then moved back into the hallway, shutting the door and leaving Damien alone in a small square room.

The entirety of the space was white and two doors occupied the walls, one at each end: the door Damien had just stepped from and the one in front of him. A tiny camera hung above the second door and moved silently as it scanned Damien for approval. After a moment of patience, the second door slid open and Damien moved into the final room.

Bare cinder-block walls outlined the space; heavy metal rods stood close together from the floor to the ceiling across the center of the room, dividing the space into two parts: the part behind the barred wall where the prisoner sat and the part where Damien stood. Black cameras hung in all four corners, their bodies rotating on schedule to cover the entire room.

Damien walked forward and sat in the single metal chair that had been brought in for him, crossing his arms over his chest.

Ian Carson sat on the other side of the barred wall in dark-brown prison clothes, his blue eyes tired and his graying hair long. His face was unshaven and pale. It was hard to believe that the man before him used to be the Authority President. The majesty was gone from his shoulders, the thunder in his voice now nonexistent, as if they had all just imagined that Ian had once been royalty. He was now just as common as the thieves who occupied the other cells throughout the prison, except he was in solitary, away from the general prison population. He was also fed three times a day and was allowed weekly visits from his wife and living daughters.

Damien hadn't been to visit the man once since his incarceration—partly because he didn't see the point and partly because the sight of the once-great Ian Carson, now a shriveled mess lost to his own weakness, was enough to make Damien violent. How many years had he sat in the judge's seat, coveting the power and position that Ian held? How many times had he dreamed of gaining favor from the esteemed president? How often had he wished just to sit at the table and follow his leadership? All to discover that the great leader of Damien's people, his childhood hero, was easily crippled. It was said that those placed on pedestals were oftentimes the ones who disappointed the most in the end. Damien would never carelessly place his faith and affection in an idol again.

But today he had to control his raging disappointments; his plan for humanity couldn't be finished without this fallen king.

"I was surprised to hear I would be seeing you today," Ian said.

"I have come with business. A proposal is a better way of putting it," Damien said.

"How is the Council? The rebels—what of their progress?"

"That information is for Authority members only; it is no longer any of your concern."

"No, I guess it isn't. You made sure of that."

"Resentment won't do you any good in here."

"Resentment is all I have left." Ian paused and shifted his eyes off to the left, staring into empty space. "Did you know that neither of my daughters will come to see me anymore? I suppose that's my punishment for allowing their eldest sister to be executed."

Damien kept his expression stony. "I'm sorry to hear that."

"Don't patronize me."

The cell was quiet for a long while as Damien let Ian feel his manufactured empathy. He picked his next statement carefully. "It's clear that you have some unresolved guilt from the tragic events surrounding the trial and execution of your daughter. What if I offered you a way to be released from your guilt?"

Ian turned his eyes to Damien. "Your business proposal?"

"A chance to right your wrongs as a father and as a president." Damien saw how his words lit a fire behind

Ian's eyes and he treaded carefully. The tests had shown that results were better with the more willing subjects. "I know there are still those who are loyal to you and that they send you word from the city, so I assume you have heard whispers of the new direction we are taking with our rebellion problem."

"Eradicating the human disease."

Damien smiled. "It's good to have spies, no?" Ian didn't respond, and Damien didn't wait for him to. "We are on the edge of a new frontier. Science is making strides within the brain that have previously been thought impossible. Imagine being able to control loyalties and memories. Think of the difference we could make, the chaos we could avoid."

"You say *we* as if I have a choice," Ian said.

"Of course you have a choice. You always have a choice. Your choices are the reason you're here. The two of us can debate all day about the failings or non-failings that surround your presidency, but the Authority had you excommunicated because of the poor choices that led to lack of control in your station, and your family lost trust in you because of your choices leading to lack of control of your daughter."

The fire turned to a boil in Ian's expression, and Damien knew his words had struck a deep chord in Ian's mind. He just needed a final push.

"And if I choose not to participate in your proposal?" Ian asked.

"You are welcome to live out the rest of your days here, imprisoned for your inadequacies, but I can't offer you anything to improve your situation if you choose that path. Alternately, you can help me change the world and redeem yourself from the failings that will otherwise haunt you," Damien said. "That is the choice."

He saw the slight change start in Ian's face, and with a final exhalation, Ian's angry expression lifted to reveal crumpled defeat. He knew Damien was right.

"And the other Authority members that are caged in this brick prison—will you offer them the same chance for redemption?" Ian asked.

Damien paused to admire Ian's loyalty to even those from his table who had fallen from grace. "Yes, well . . . Isaac's mind is too far gone to be helped, but Dodson has been made the same offer."

Ian gave Damien a curious look and without words Damien understood what he was wondering.

"Dodson has no interest in making the world a better place; he sides with the rebellion and will be treated as any other rebel, regardless of the seat he once occupied."

Ian dropped his eyes to the floor and Damien allowed him some time to consider what was being presented to him. Finally, Ian raised his head. "What becomes of my family if I agree?"

"They will always be treated as an Authority family; I give you my word. If all goes well, you will see them again."

Ian nodded. "And if things don't go well?"

Damien felt a twinge of pity touch his chest and he was surprised by the emotion. Maybe his disgust for the man before him had been unwarranted to some measure. It was, after all, his failure that had led to Damien's opportunity to take charge. Maybe he owed the man's weakness more credit. "Then I will make sure that people remember you for more than your failings."

Ian took another moment to consider the offer placed before him. "What happens to me if things go well?"

Damien shifted and gave a half smile. "Then you forget this old life with all your mistakes and pain. You ascend to a truer state of existence."

Ian and Damien locked eyes for a long second before Ian sighed and nodded.

Damien smiled. Part of him had known this would be the outcome all along. There really was no other choice.

le to follow the way of God with self-serving
ns. And he had enforced their law, caused suffering
of their rules.

time he was here, Remko fought his own mind to
h thoughts at bay so he could focus on the task at
oday he had more on his mind than usual.

n Sam, Kate, and Carrington had returned from
rning's security patrol, they had filled him in on
ey'd found. Only miles away from the camp they'd
blished loomed a threat they knew nothing about,
barely had time to process the information before
again. Compartmentalization was necessary for

He placed the new information into a bucket and
t away along with a bucket for his grief over Larkin,
for worry over Carrington and Elise, a bucket for
sure to appease Neil and the others in camp who felt
bout their direction. Plop, plop, plop. He dropped
o buckets and tucked them away. Now he mentally
ff all the emotional distractions and refocused.

lly Aaron communicated the number of people
uld be led out of the city and specified the check-
here they would meet up with a Sleeper. Remko
re of dozens of Sleeper Seers who lived seemingly
lives within the city, and there were seven check-
On each run, the team met with the Sleeper, col-
hotos and names of the individual or individuals
eed, and acquired any other helpful information
ght need to complete their task.

Trial Entry 64 | Patient 03-8 (Stephan Mills)

Age: 34 / Gender: Male / Status: CityWatch guard
Drug administered at 04:11 hours
Time in observation: 12 days

Physician's log
Entry made by attending: Dr. Andrew Phillips
Day 11 after administration: Patient has refused to make further voluntary journal entries, so we are currently uncertain
of his mental state. He has begun to show violence whenever
food is offered and I fear he may be trying to starve himself.
We will be watching him closely.

Day 13 after administration: Patient has presented with a
fever of 101.9 for the last 46 hours and has started to have
night terrors, very similar to the others in his testing group.
We have made a note to decrease the dopamine levels in the current strand to steady heightened brain activity.

Day 20 after administration: Some positive signs today. The
patient seems to have forgotten a list of mandatory CityWatch
protocols that were essential to his position. Awareness of his
failure to retain this knowledge has agitated him further but
shows great progress for the current injection strain.

Day 23 after administration: The combination of our chemical manipulations and the patient's own paranoia have brought about a string of strenuous migraines that, if continued without treatment, could permanently affect his vision. Due to this development, in addition to the lack of proper nutrition because of his refusal to eat, an unacceptable level of stress has been placed on his cardiac muscle. I have therefore made a request that patient 03-8 be moved into Test Group bc:X to see if the new strain of vaccine can yield better results.

8

Remko and the others c[...]
of the northernmost city [...]
high above their heads, [...]
into the air. Cameras an[...]
installed along the top, [...]
team used the undergro[...]
the city, but they knew the CityW[...]
doing tunnel patrols, and they n[...]
enter the city. That meant they w[...]
today.

They couldn't hear the mover[...]
the walls, but Remko could imag[...]
feet of City Workers, store owne[...]
There would be CityWatch guar[...]
ten-minute increments, twice as [...]
he still called himself one.

Truth be told, Remko felt sick[...]
he set foot across the threshold o[...]
Not only because he worried for [...]
cess, but even more because this [...]
poison he'd so willingly drunk. T[...]
bought into. A single group of m[...]
power, sitting inside gold-encrust[...]

the pe[...]
intenti[...]
becaus[...]

Eac[...]
keep s[...]
hand. [...]

Wh[...]
this m[...]
what t[...]
just est[...]
and he[...]
leaving[...]
surviva[...]
tucked[...]
a buck[...]
the pre[...]
unsure[...]
them i[...]
shook [...]

Us[...]
who w[...]
point [...]
was aw[...]
norma[...]
points.[...]
lected[...]
being [...]
they m[...]

This time was no different. Aaron had told Remko that a family of three needed to be rescued. Now it was up to Remko and his team to get inside, locate their Sleeper, acquire the family, and get out.

Remko glanced at Wire, who was tinkering with Roxy in his palm. Wire, Kate, and Sam had been making occasional scouting runs along other sections of the wall to map out its strengths and weaknesses, as well as to collect data so Roxy could infiltrate its technical systems.

"The plan is simple," Wire said. "I have enough access to their defense systems to turn off this section of the wall for thirty seconds at a time. That means going up in pairs."

Sam dropped the bag he had slung over his shoulder and unzipped the top. He pulled out two grappling hooks that were each fastened to the end of a long, thick rope. He tossed one hook to Remko.

"Old-school, I see," Kate said.

"We work with what we have," Sam said.

Sam reached back into the bag and pulled out a small black container the size of a box of playing cards and opened it. Inside lay two thin metal circles. Sam pulled one out and glanced it over. "These had better work."

"They will," Wire said. "Just press one to the ball of your boot; there are microscopic magnets on the surface that will keep it in place. These walls were constructed after the Time of Ruin; they're laced with metal to help reinforce their stability in case of outside attacks."

Kate grabbed the second disk from Sam and held it

up against the light. "And these will magnetize through the stone? They seem a bit small to be as powerful as you described."

"They'll do the job," Wire said.

"Where did you get these again?" Sam asked.

Wire smiled. "I made them."

Kate dropped her hand and shot Wire an annoyed look. "And have you tested them, like with actual humans?"

Wire's face lost some of its prideful zest, and he dropped his eyes back to Roxy. "Don't worry; they'll work. Just place it on your dominant foot and use it as an anchor while you climb."

Kate rolled her eyes. "How come every time we use one of your contraptions, I feel like I'm gonna end up dead?" she said to no one in particular.

Wire ignored her while Sam and Remko moved to the wall. They would only have thirty seconds, and they couldn't toss the grappling hooks until the system was down, because the pressure of the hooks would signal intrusion. Once the hooks had connected, they would have to move quickly.

Remko stood poised to throw his hook with Sam to his right in a similar stance. He glanced at Sam, and Sam nodded that he was ready. He'd already attached the silver disk to his right boot and Kate was ready with the second disk in place on hers. Now they waited for Wire's count.

Blood pounded behind Remko's ears and he focused past his nerves. Up and over—that's all it was. Up and over.

"We move in five," Wire said, and Remko felt everyone's breathing still. He knew his team was trained and qualified. This was nothing they couldn't handle. He forced all hints of panic from his mind. He took a deep breath and waited for the signal.

"Now," Wire said.

Sam and Remko both wound up and tossed the hooks high into the air, aiming for the top ledge of the wall. Remko knew Wire had added magnetic tips to the ends of the hooks so they would be drawn to the metal lining the ledge, but they still had to get them high enough for the magnetics to respond.

Remko felt his hook connect and tugged to ensure it was secure. He stepped aside as Kate's hands wrapped around the rope and heard the zing as her boot fastened to the wall, just as Wire had said. She had to use all her strength to rip her boot off the wall's surface as she ascended. Each step was obviously a struggle, but she would never admit it. Sam was also ascending, his rope pulled tight with his weight.

"Fifteen seconds," Wire said.

Remko could feel sweat gathering at his hairline. Kate and Sam were halfway up the wall, but time was running low. The seconds seemed to compress as each vertical step his team members took pounded inside Remko's chest.

"Eight seconds," Wire said.

Remko glanced to both sides. He wondered how long they would have before guards swarmed this area. Could they get far enough away to have a chance? Maybe they should have risked the tunnels; at least then they wouldn't be out in the open like this.

"Four seconds."

A hook sailed off the wall and hit the ground at Remko's feet with a thud. Remko looked up to see Sam yanking Kate up and over the ledge; a half second later the second hook descended.

Roxy beeped in Wire's hand and Remko let go of the breath he'd been holding. The boy glanced at Remko, and Remko could see the worry in his eyes. Their turn.

Wire wasn't strong enough to sling the hook to the top of the wall, so Remko would have to do both. The two silver magnet disks flew down from above and landed softly at Remko's feet. He grabbed them and handed one to Wire. He gave the boy a reassuring nod and hoped only confidence was visible behind his eyes.

Attaching his disk, Remko grabbed the first rope tightly and once again forced all distractions from his mind. There could be no mistakes here.

"Go," Wire said.

Remko slung the first hook with all his might and felt it connect. With a quick tug he handed off the rope and moved with one fluid step to the second rope. He had barely lifted the hook from the ground when he wound up to throw. The second it took to sail through the air toward the top felt longer than it should, and a fresh hint of worry began to creep into Remko's chest. Then the hook connected and Remko pulled himself up and onto the wall.

With a couple of labored steps he caught up with Wire. Remko could feel the disk under his boot working as an anchor, and he doubled his pace, passing Wire, his eyes fixed on the top. Remko pushed himself to his limits as he approached his target. Then he was up and over the top ledge. He saw Kate and Sam squatting on the roof of the building beneath him. Remko yanked his rope up from the other side of the wall and tossed his hook to Sam. He then moved to Wire's rope and began pulling the kid up as Wire struggled to continue his ascent. There was no way to know what their time was with Roxy tucked safely in Wire's pocket, but the cutoff had to be close.

Remko yanked hard a couple more times and reached to grab Wire's arm. Wire crawled over the top of the wall awkwardly and dropped to the roof next to Kate. Remko quickly collected the second rope and pushed himself off the wall, hitting the roof just as the timer on Roxy began to beep.

Remko paused to breathe as sweat dripped from his nose. He wiped his hand across his face to clear the perspiration and felt Sam's hand on his shoulder. "That could have been worse." Remko couldn't help but smile through the raging of his heart as he stood to join the others.

"I'm tracking the movements of the CityWatch patrols," Wire said, his eyes on Roxy, which was tucked back in his palm. "The patterns of their shifts haven't changed, which gives us an advantage."

Only the sound of breathing filled the rooftop as each member prepared for what was next: down the steel ladder at the left side of the building and into an old alley tucked away from the rest of the city. The distance they needed to travel wasn't long, but the next couple of moves had to be carried out with perfect accuracy.

Sam led as they all descended the ladder. Once in the alley, Remko looked to Wire.

"We have a window coming in ten," Wire said.

Remko closed his eyes and imagined the street ahead of them and their destination on the other side. It was an outside street, less traveled than most, picked precisely because traffic was lighter.

"Five seconds," Wire said.

Remko opened his eyes and moved to the front of the pack as they edged toward the alley's opening.

"Three."

He steadied his heart and slowed his breathing. There was always a chance that they'd run right into a guard or roving inspector. They could never be too careful.

"Now."

And they were moving. Quickly but with precision.

The street was empty, but the sound of the busy city reached them from several blocks away. Their destination stood in the center of a circled gathering of shops selling wood-carving tools, fine fabrics, and baked goods. The space was shared by a small bar, closed till later in the afternoon. Remko noticed the collection of white flowers that occupied the interior windowsills of the fabric shop, tool shop, and bakery. Sleeper Seers. The white flowers signified that the owners of these shops were followers of Aaron and would welcome Remko and his team—or at the very least not report their presence to the Authority.

The bar's windowsills were empty, but since it was still closed, Remko tried not to let any misgivings interfere with his speed. Out of the corner of his eye, he thought he saw unwanted movement behind one of the bar windows, but he told himself to keep moving, that it was his mind creating unnecessary fear.

They crossed the open street toward the back of the first shop and sneaked along the back side of each building. Sam was the first one to the bakery. He moved to a small side entrance, followed closely by Kate and Wire, Remko slowing in order to enter last. Once inside he shut the door and they waited a beat to make sure no one had seen them. Sam peered through the side windowpane to check the street and nodded that it was all clear.

The side entrance brought them into the kitchen at the rear of the shop. The scent of fresh bread filled the air; sweet rolls and plain wheat loaves sat on trays and in lined baskets on the counters, but the kitchen was void of people. Remko knew this section of the city had little foot traffic, which was one of the many reasons they traveled this route. It was unfortunate for the shop owners, though.

A moment later a small, round man entered the kitchen and gave Remko a kind nod. "Upstairs," the man said, and Remko thanked him before taking the narrow steps to his right. The wood creaked under their feet as the team moved forward and up. A door stood at the top of the stairs and Remko pulled it open.

"Remko," Seth Hale said.

Remko moved across the room to greet his father-in-law with a grateful hug. Carrington worried about her parents and younger brother constantly, and seeing Seth alive and healthy meant returning with good news.

Pulling back from Seth's embrace, Remko found himself taken by how much Carrington looked like her father. And how much Elise looked like them both.

Seth cupped his hand at the back of Remko's neck and studied him for a long moment. "You look well. How are my daughter and that beautiful baby of yours?"

"Good; healthy," Remko said.

Sorrow filled Seth's eyes for a moment and he nodded. "Tell Carrington I have been thinking of her more often since Larkin's . . . just tell her I never stop thinking about her."

Remko nodded and Seth released him. Remko thought about urging Seth to leave with them, to come and live with them beyond the city walls, but he knew what Seth's answer would be. Seth would never leave the city without his wife, Vena, and Vena believed Aaron was a heretic.

Even after witnessing the way Isaac Knight, an Authority seat holder, had treated her only daughter, Vena refused to see the Authority for what it really was. It had taken Carrington months to come to terms with the fact that for now she would remain separated from her family. She would have to live with the worry about their safety, knowing the Authority could try to use them as leverage against her.

Remko had watched her let go of the anger she'd held against her mother for so many years. Vena was on her own journey, Carrington explained to Remko; her mother needed to believe that everything she had placed her hope in wasn't a lie. Vena wasn't ready to discover the truth, and that was okay. Everything happened when it was supposed to, and Carrington believed that one day she would reconnect with her mother in a place of truth.

So Seth remained inside the city, keeping his wife and son close and helping to lead the charge against the Authority from inside the walls.

The number of Sleeper Seers had grown quickly after Remko and Carrington had fled the city when Aaron started calling people out into the wilderness. Without intending to, Seth had become the head of the Sleeper Seer community and in turn had become a crucial part of the mission.

The shop owner entered the room with a tray of different baked goods and a pitcher of water. He set it on a small table, and Remko noticed the tremor in his hand and the nervous way his eyes kept running over the group. Seth must have noticed the man's unease also, and he moved to his side. They spoke softly as Sam, Wire, and Kate helped themselves to the food.

The round man gave Seth a shallow smile and left the room without a word. Carrington's father turned back to the team and met Remko's gaze.

Nodding, understanding the question in his son-in-law's eyes, Seth sighed. "People are starting to get very nervous," he said. "Things are happening in the city that have put them on edge, and they worry that helping and supporting Aaron and his followers will get them killed."

"But the threat is no different now than it's always been," Sam said.

"For some, perhaps," Seth countered. "Certainly for those of you living outside the city the danger is no greater now than ever. But with Damien Gold in the president's seat, even loyal citizens face imprisonment and execution simply for being suspected of sympathizing with rebels."

He paused, and Remko felt a fresh wave of appreciation and affection for this man who was risking so much for them.

"And actually, we may be facing a new problem," Seth continued. "It's mostly rumors and hearsay, but people have been . . . disappearing. Men, women, children even. Vanishing for days, sometimes weeks at a time. Some of them come back; some don't."

Remko thought of Mac Tyler and the others who had disappeared from the Seer camp without a trace in recent months, and his unease returned.

"It's been causing a nervous stir among the people," Seth went on. "Some say you can tell which ones have been taken because they're sort of different, changed somehow. Others say those who come back wear a mark."

"A mark? Like a physical mark?" Sam asked.

Seth shrugged. "I can't be sure. Most of the things I've heard could very well be rumors."

"That can't be good," Kate said.

"Like I said, right now it's a lot of nervous people talking. But with Damien Gold running the show, anything is possible."

"Any leads on what is happening to these people or why?" Remko asked.

"Not yet, but I'm working on it. The second I know anything, so will you," Seth said.

"We need to move, Remko," Wire said. "I didn't factor in spending much time here and we have to be conscious of the afternoon patrols outside if we want to get back before dark."

Remko held Seth's gaze a moment longer and hated the queasy feeling that was building in his gut. Rumors of people going missing even inside the city set his teeth on edge. He could hear Aaron's words clear as day: *Things are beginning to change inside the city. . . . It will get darker before we see light again.*

"Remko," Sam said softly.

Remko yanked his mind free from its turmoil and nodded.

"The family you are retrieving will be at the fourth meeting point; J. J. has them there now. We tried to get them closer, but they were extremely difficult to transport," Seth said.

"Why?" Kate asked.

Seth paused and looked a bit worried. "I urge you to hear me out before jumping to conclusions."

Remko could feel the nervous energy of his team rising and felt his own chest tighten.

"I have spoken with this family, the mother specifically, many times. She is committed to change, to seeing the Authority changed—destroyed if necessary. I know that you will be resistant, but just like the rest of us, she was never given a choice before. Now that she has one, I truly believe she is choosing to follow Aaron out of a genuine desire for real freedom. More so than many I have sent with you in the past."

"Who is it?" Remko asked, though he was certain he already knew the answer.

"Selena Carson and her two daughters."

"What?" Sam said.

"Ian Carson's wife, Selena?" Wire said.

"No way," Kate said.

Remko said nothing.

"Are you crazy?" Kate demanded.

"I understand your concern—" Seth tried.

"Clearly not! Otherwise you wouldn't be asking us to possibly surrender to the enemy," Kate said.

Seth's tone remained even and kind in the face of Kate's panic. "Ian has been locked away for months now; he no

longer has any sway within the Authority Council. All
of his power now lies with our new president."

Remko had actually met Damien Gold once. A couple
of years ago Remko had stood guard for a case in which
Damien was the presiding judge. All Remko remembered
was that Damien was smart and cruel.

"Remember that you have a common enemy. The
Authority—including her husband—killed her daughter.
Selena should not be punished for being chosen for her
role as Ian Carson's wife. She had as little choice as any
of us."

"I don't care. It's too risky," Kate said.

"She's right. What if this is all a ploy to get inside the
camp?" Sam asked. "It could be a trap."

"I've spoken with her myself," Seth said.

"No offense, but I'm not sure why that's supposed to
make me feel better," Kate retorted.

"Kate," Remko said. Kate might have a point, but he
would not stand for her speaking to Seth in such a manner.

Kate bit her tongue, but the air around her was filled
with heat.

"Everyone is forgetting something very crucial," Wire
said. The room turned toward the thin boy in the corner.

"What?" Kate snapped.

"Aaron sent us for them."

Remko watched the anger drain from Kate's face as she
dropped her eyes to the ground.

"Let all who come, come," Wire said. "Aaron always says

that. I'm not even sure why we're having this debate." He turned his eyes to Remko, searching for approval.

Remko knew Wire was right. They may not understand his reasoning, but Aaron had sent for Selena and her daughters, and that was reason enough. He looked back toward Seth and nodded. "So what's the extraction plan?"

9 "The fastest route to meeting site four is a combination of aboveground travel and the facility tunnels that run under the main city streets," Sam said, tracing his finger across the map Neil Stone had given them back at camp. "Traveling on the streets is risky, but if we stay in the tunnels the whole way, we won't reach them in time to extract and get back to the escape point. We've used this route before and made it successfully."

"I can't believe we are doing this," Kate said.

"Do you want to go back to camp empty-handed and tell Aaron we didn't extract the target because you were afraid?" Sam asked.

His sister glared at him but got on board. "We should split up aboveground. We'll blend in better as smaller groups," she said.

Seth had given them all brown City Worker uniforms that would help them move through the crowds they were sure to encounter. The uniforms came with hoods that would help shield their faces. Kate was the biggest risk, being a girl, but if they moved quickly and could keep from being detected, she should be able to pull off being a very small man.

"Sam, you go with Kate," Remko said. "Wire, you're with me. What's our time look like?"

Wire was already tapping away on Roxy, calculating distance and speed within the route they had selected. "We need to reach the middle point, where the east and west water veins meet, in the next twelve minutes and forty-three seconds, then across the central vein in under six minutes and fourteen seconds, and up the side of the northern wall to site four with only four minutes and fifty seconds to—"

Kate pushed past Wire, cutting him off. "You could have just said *quickly*," she said. She and Sam already had their cloaks on.

Sam turned to Remko. "We'll take the east side and meet you at the central vein."

Remko nodded. "Be careful."

Kate threw a smile over her shoulder. "Always."

Then the two siblings were off, running down the alley and out into the traffic of the city.

"She never lets me finish," Wire complained.

"Let's go," Remko said and started off toward the opposite end of the alley. Wire followed, yanking up his hood as they moved toward the herd of people already visible on the street ahead.

In order to get to meeting site four, they had to cross directly through the middle of town. Thankfully, it was nearly midday, which meant the streets would be flooded with people. That gave them some protection from onlookers. They could easily just become other faces in the crowd.

Remko tucked his hands inside the pockets that hung

near his waist and traveled swiftly with his head down. Wire had pulled out in front and moved a couple steps ahead. The city was bustling. People meeting up for lunch, others trying to get errands done during the middle of the day, shop owners working to entice people to come inside their stores. Smells from cooking meats, frying potatoes, baking pastries—things the Seers rarely came across in their current humble way of life—reached Remko and made his mind buzz.

He remained focused and pushed forward. They had traveled half the distance to their destination. He could hear CityWatch whistles, the guards' booming commands, the grinding of a nearby CityWatch vehicle. All of them close enough to spot the intruders if they knew what they were looking for. Remko tucked his chin farther and walked faster.

Ahead of him a man carrying a load much too large for him to manage alone knocked Wire's shoulder hard. Wire stumbled sideways and lost his footing, falling to the street. His hood came loose, and Roxy crashed with a thud to the ground beside him. The device tumbled a couple of feet away, and Remko moved quickly to scoop it up and out of sight. A couple of people around them stopped to see what the commotion was, and Remko noticed that the attention of two CityWatch guards standing a few feet away moved to them as well.

Remko yanked Wire off the ground and nodded to the few people who had moved to help.

"He's fine; thank you," Remko said softly, trying not to expose too much of his face. He glanced sideways to see that one of the guards was moving toward them. He felt a string of panic pull inside his chest.

He gave a couple more half smiles and nods to the surrounding City Workers, trying not to seem desperate, but they needed to move.

"Sorry," Wire said.

"We need to go," Remko said. They kept their heads low and pushed forward. Remko glanced back to see the guard still following them. He slid Roxy back into Wire's hand. "We're being followed; give him something else to worry about."

Remko heard Wire swallow. They were still moving—though hopefully fast enough to draw no further attention—and Wire quickly tried to punch Roxy's screen without people around them noticing. Remko could feel the guard getting closer, and sweat gathered at the back of his neck and across his forehead.

"Come on, come on," he said under his breath.

"I'm working on it, but it's hard without being able to properly see what I'm doing."

Remko looked around and saw a butcher's shop only a couple of feet away. Still holding Wire's arm, he tugged him toward the shop and the two stepped into the meat-filled room. Several customers were in line; another few shopped the aisles. Remko yanked Wire behind a large shelving unit that held several varieties of pork, and

Wire pulled Roxy into his full sight. From their position Remko could still see the door, and a second later the guard stepped through.

"We need that distraction now," Remko said.

The guard looked around the shop, searching for them, then began to walk in their direction.

"Got it," Wire said.

Suddenly a loud siren rang out in the central city square. A sound Remko knew immediately. Everyone in the store came to a halt for a moment before a sense of panic, followed by chaos, set in. People scurried toward the exit, leaving their items unpurchased, trying to push past one another to leave.

Remko looked at Wire, whose face was glowing. "Severe weather alarm?"

"You said distraction. I just hacked into the closest mainframe system, and since we are so close to the central weather hub, all I had to do was defeat a set of rudimentary firewalls and recode the alarm to go off on a trigger control that could be wirelessly connected with Roxy here."

"Everyone remain calm and exit single file," the guard shouted at the people shoving through the door. The guard was the last one out, and after a few seconds, Remko moved to see if their exit was clear.

"Impressed?" Wire asked. It was clear from the brash look on his face that he was impressed with himself enough for the both of them.

Remko rolled his eyes and motioned for Wire to follow

as they slipped out of the butcher shop and across the main square, which was now in a complete frenzy.

They easily bypassed the chaos of people, moving onto the side road that led them to their underground entrance. They quickly moved to the large round grate at the end of the short side street, and Remko pulled it open. Wire dropped in first and Remko followed, pulling the grate back into place overhead.

Inside the tunnel, the two shrugged off their brown cloaks and tossed them aside. The interior of this water pipe looked identical to the one they had traveled through earlier, except since it ran unused underneath a larger part of the city, the pipe was wider and thus easier for them to move through with speed. They reached the connecting point and found Sam and Kate waiting.

Sam gave Remko a curious look, and Remko just shook his head. "Let's go," he said, and the rest of his team fell into line behind him.

"Did you have something to do with—?" Kate asked Wire as they ran behind Remko.

"Sure did," he said proudly, and Remko chuckled softly, imagining the disgusted look Kate was surely sending Wire.

"How are we doing on time, Wire?" Sam asked. "And if you could just be general, that would be helpful."

Roxy beeped in Wire's hand. "Roughly nine minutes left."

All four surged forward faster. They still had a little over half a mile to travel before heading back up to the surface.

They ran in silence, the sound of steady breathing accompanying their footsteps.

After several minutes, Remko spotted their escape up. "Here we go—final stretch," he said as he reached the ladder first.

He stepped aside to let the team climb up, none of them even pausing to breathe. One after another they slowed their pace only enough to grab the ladder and start the climb. This brought them to the surface in another alley that ran alongside a large steel factory. Meeting point four was tucked inside the steel factory, which was only half in operation. Since it was so close to the central plaza, the Authority was shutting down the factory one section at a time and transferring the workers to a different facility farther away from the city center. The side on which meeting point four was located hadn't been used for months.

Wire used Roxy to manually override the automated keypad lock, and within seconds they were moving inside the building. It was dark, a pungent burning smell still strong even after months of abandonment. One flight of steel stairs led up to the second level, where a small office served as the meeting location. Remko could see shadows moving inside and he held up his hand for the team to stop.

He was sure the shadows belonged to their Sleeper and the Carsons, but a sliver of caution caused him to take the last few feet alone just to be safe. He moved quietly and pushed through the door to find exactly what he'd expected. He recognized J. J., and relief washed over the young man's face at seeing Remko and the team. He moved to shake Remko's hand and smiled.

"Wow, the rush I felt when I heard your footsteps. Glad to see it's you, my friend," J. J. said. J. J. was a small, kind man who had joined the Sleepers a couple months back after a dear friend had been arrested on suspicion of colluding with Aaron. Before his friend had been executed for his crimes, he'd made J. J. promise that he would continue to fight against the Authority's corruption so that their children might see true freedom one day. Remko couldn't help but fear that day would never come.

Remko shook the man's hand and smiled. Wire, Sam, and Kate had moved to stand behind him and Remko's gaze fell to the Carsons.

He recognized Selena at once. Anyone in the city would know who she was. Jet-black hair that she had pulled back under the hood she wore, her face aged with time and stress but still beautiful and soft. Naturally red lips that made her skin look light and untouched by the sun. Honey-brown eyes that nearly glowed met Remko's gaze and he could see her overwhelming fear.

He stepped past J. J. and extended his hand, smiling. "Mrs. Carson."

She clasped his hand with her own. "Please—Selena. And these are my girls, Lucy and Rayna."

Two small girls moved out from behind their mother. The older one, Lucy, who couldn't have been more than eleven, nodded hello, while the younger girl's eyes filled with fear and tears. They both looked so much like Arianna that a pocket of grief burst in Remko's gut. He knew it would be hard for Carrington to see them every day.

Sam stepped up next to Remko and knelt so that he was eye level with the girls. "Hi, my name is Sam. We are going to have to move pretty quickly, so you two need to stay together the whole time. Can you do that?"

Lucy nodded and grabbed Rayna's hand as the smaller girl started to cry. Before Selena could comfort her, Sam took Rayna's free hand. She looked at him with huge brown eyes but didn't back away. Remko was always impressed by how good Sam was with children.

Sam smiled at her and pulled a long thin chain from his shirt. On it was a small gold pendant that he always wore. It had belonged to his mother and was one of the only things he had left of hers.

"This may look like a normal pendant, but actually it's magic," Sam said. Rayna's eyes fell to the pendant with awe. "You may not believe me, but it makes me invisible to anyone who wants to do me harm. It protects me from the guards and keeps me safe." Sam pulled the chain off his neck and held it in his palm. "Now I don't normally do this, but do you wanna wear it so it can make you invisible?"

Rayna gasped and looked at Sam's face for confirmation. He nodded and placed it around the girl's neck. Her mouth broke into a shy smile as she let go of her sister's hand and touched the pendant carefully.

"I know you're afraid, but I am going to hold this hand, and your sister is going to hold the other. And now you have a magic weapon, so everything is going to be okay. Got it?"

The little girl nodded. Sam stood and Selena placed a hand on his shoulder. She mouthed the words *thank you* and turned to Remko.

"Thank you. I know how much of a risk this is," Selena said.

"Doubtful," Kate said under her breath, but the room was quiet enough that everyone could hear.

Remko shot her a warning look, and she turned to stand guard at the door. It wasn't difficult to understand Kate's frustrations; they were all on edge.

"I'm not sure what to say to ease your suspicions," Selena said. "Just know that I saw Arianna's transformation firsthand. Her words filled our home and touched my heart long before she was monstrously taken from me."

Remko could see the pain that was still fresh behind Selena's eyes, and with a young daughter of his own he could imagine the anger and sorrow that would engulf him if she were ever taken from him. He nodded.

"Damien keeps a very close eye on me. He will know we are missing by now," Selena said.

Remko turned to J. J., who led the group out of the office and down the steps. They would have to leave by a different route, and they were running on a tight timetable.

"Thank you," Remko said to J. J. and turned to Selena.

"We are going to be moving quickly, so as Sam instructed, the three of you are to never leave his side."

Selena nodded, and Remko motioned for Kate and Wire to go ahead. Sam would then move into the middle with the Carsons, and Remko would follow at the rear. He said a quick prayer as the group moved forward through the bottom half of the abandoned factory toward their path out of the city.

10

The move through the city went quickly and without incident. Remko could feel the tension in his shoulders and back releasing. They were close to their vehicle now, moving through the trees that provided shelter from their enemies. The largest and most immediate threat was gone. Behind him, Sam was carrying Rayna on his back, her small arms wrapped around his neck, her tiny giggle spilling through the air as Sam told her tales of Sir Gregory Hoppoliss, a mischievous brown toad who always found his way into trouble.

Selena held Lucy's hand, and the two walked beside Sam, listening intently as Sir Hoppoliss tried to find his way free from the shipping crate he'd gotten himself stuck in for being, once again, much too curious. Wire and Kate walked in front of Remko, quietly discussing Wire's uncanny ability to try to be helpful but instead usually almost get them all killed. Remko noticed the change in Kate's tone. She might constantly rebuke Wire's actions, but the warm, flirtatious tease was hard to miss.

Remko tuned out all the voices around him and set his gaze ahead as the lowering sun pricked through the hanging branches. He could feel the weariness starting to make its way through his bones, and he used the thought of heading home to Carrington and Elise as a shot of energy. He tried to imagine what it might feel like to never have to leave them again. In the stillness of moments like this, when the sun was stretching downward to meet the earth and those he cared about were lost in conversation around him safe from harm, he could almost see the light at the end of the tunnel. A time when they would actually be free of the Authority and its threats. A time when he wouldn't close his eyes and be tormented by his fears. A time when each new morning would present peace and stability and he wouldn't worry for the lives of everyone he loved.

He could almost see it if he focused on it long enough. Through the cracks of uncertainty in his brain, the endless spiral of thoughts that filled him with doubt, if he pushed past all the broken clutter, he could almost imagine a time where such a thing was possible.

Something rustled to his right and re-heightened his senses. He stopped and listened, the rest of the group oblivious. Maybe it was nothing. It wouldn't be the first time he had thought there was danger when there wasn't. He strained to hear another sound, his eyes sweeping the area around them, but nothing came and all he saw were the trees standing firm in the ground as they were supposed to.

Remko lingered in this place of near-panic for another moment before letting it pass and continuing forward. It was hard to believe that the universe itself wasn't against him when it seemed that at every available moment another threat crashed into the small amount of peace he managed to gather, like a wild storm that appeared out of thin air. That's why he couldn't see the light at the end of the tunnel for long. That's why he knew that security and freedom from fear were as much an illusion as the dream of finding a place where he and his family could finally plant roots and be safe.

Out of the corner of his eye he saw a shadow move and he stopped again. He looked at Sam and held his hand up, signaling him to pause. Sam held his tongue as his face turned from playful storyteller to alert warrior; Rayna slid off his back. Kate and Wire turned at the absence of Sam's voice and also paused, waiting for Remko's order.

The group stood like frozen deer, listening and waiting, poised to run like the wind if needed. Nothing came. Remko wondered if he might actually be losing his mind. Could his concern for their safety be causing him to hallucinate?

He released the breath he was holding and shook his head. But before he could motion for the group to move, he saw them.

Two CityWatch guards, their weapons raised, moved out from behind the trees only a couple feet from them. The others saw them too. Selena gasped, yanking Lucy behind her. Kate stepped forward to attack and one of the guards moved his weapon to point directly at her forehead.

"Everyone freeze," he said. Kate stopped in her tracks but kept her glare fixed on the guard's face. The second guard carefully moved toward the group, weapon at the ready. He looked at Selena curiously and stole a quick glance at his partner. His red hair caught the sun's light, making it look bronze. The other one was taller, dark-skinned, with large bright eyes. Remko noticed that they were both breathing hard and looked slightly rattled. They were young, hardly over the minimum age requirement to join the CityWatch. New recruits, he guessed, probably out on a simple patrol run when they stumbled across Remko and the group. Remko made a mental note of the fact that the CityWatch was changing patrol routes again.

"Mrs. Carson, are you harmed?" the redhead asked. Remko noticed the slight shake in his hands.

Selena shook her head and pulled Rayna close to her.

"It's okay, Mrs. Carson. We are going to get you and your girls back safe," the guard said. Rayna started to cry softly at her mother's side, and the guard looked uncomfortable.

"That's how she feels about leaving with you two," Kate said under her breath.

The taller guard stepped forward. "Keep your mouth shut, rebel. All of you move away from the Authority family." He motioned slightly with the tip of his gun.

No one moved.

"Now!" he yelled. "And keep your hands where I can see them."

Remko and Sam moved slowly with Wire and Kate away from Selena and her girls, hands raised. Remko could see the worry and panic that was taking over Selena's face as she clutched her daughters tightly. There was a ten-foot gap between them now, Remko and his team on one side and the Carson women on the other.

"Get down on your knees, hands raised over your heads," the larger guard said. Remko knelt and the others followed. They outnumbered the guards two-to-one, but rushing them was too dangerous with Selena and her girls so close by.

The redhead moved to Selena carefully, lowering his gun as he went. Rayna was still whimpering at her mother's side and the smaller guard tried to flash her a comforting smile. "Don't cry. Everything's going to be all right now."

"No it's not," Lucy said.

Selena gripped her daughter and sent her a warning look.

"We need to call this in," the dark one said. He kept his eyes on Remko, Sam, Wire, and Kate. Especially Kate. From the way sweat was collecting on his forehead, Remko knew that this guard recognized the danger in Kate's face. She was small but not to be underestimated.

The redhead pulled up his arm receiver and spoke. "Patrick, you there?"

A voice loud enough for everyone in the clearing to hear crackled through the redhead's earpiece. "Yep, Seever. What is it?"

"Tate and I have a situation in quadrant sixteen, three miles outside the northeast wall near the far east side."

"What kinda situation?"

"A Delta-67 kind of situation."

There was a long pause. Silence filled the air around all of them as they waited.

"Follow procedure and don't move. Backup is on the way," the earpiece buzzed.

"Copy that." The redhead nodded to his partner, who nodded in return.

"Help me secure them," Tate said.

The redhead looked toward Selena. "More help is on the way. I need you to stay right there while we get these rebels secure, okay?"

Remko could see the urge to run in Selena's posture. He drilled her with a stare until she shifted her eyes toward him for just a moment and he shook his head slightly. She mustn't run—that would only make things worse. He wanted to promise her that she and her girls would make it to the Seer camp; he wanted to reassure her that everything was going to be okay, that she had not made a mistake entrusting her life and the lives of her daughters to him. He and his team would find a way. But even as Remko looked around and tried to formulate a plan, he saw nothing. Backup couldn't be far; even if they could take out these two guards, how could they get away fast enough to avoid being apprehended by the wave coming? What if they were followed to camp? That would put everyone else's life in danger.

Selena held his gaze, then turned back to Seever and nodded. He was eyeing her and Remko curiously but moved to help his partner as he was asked. Remko watched as Tate handcuffed Sam first. Seever had pulled his weapon from its holster and kept it pointed toward the group. Remko was next. He felt Tate viciously yank his raised hands behind his back one at a time and pin them together.

Remko fought to maintain clarity through the growing fear inside his head. Was Aaron's way of freedom worth the lives of the innocent children in front of him? What about the others? It seemed with each new life they brought into camp, his ability to see the purpose of it all dimmed.

The rough plastic from the generic wrist clamps that all CityWatch personnel were required to carry cut against Remko's skin. The clamps were pulled tight, and he knew there was no way anyone was getting out of these. He could almost hear the thoughts of his team, each one trying to come up with a solution to this problem. Remko thought maybe they could overpower the two guards even now if they moved as a group. They were still four to two, but the guards had guns, and Remko didn't even have the use of his hands.

A sense of finality was thundering toward them. All four were now restrained, and Tate was yanking Kate to her feet. "All of you, get up," he said.

Kate pulled against his hold and before he could step away, she threw her head back and connected with his skull. Tate cursed and stumbled back a step, but he didn't lose his grip on Kate. He yanked her around to face him and thrust the back of his hand hard across her face. The blow knocked Kate sideways, and without her hands to help keep her balanced, she fell to the ground.

Sam was moving then, like a bull charging a matador. He rammed his body into Tate, slamming him backward into a large oak. The leaves shook with the pressure of their combined weight, and the sound of cracking bark echoed through the clearing.

Tate recovered from the attack quickly; with Sam's hands still secure at his back, Tate had the advantage. He shoved Sam off, creating enough space to fire several hard punches into Sam's gut. Sam buckled at the waist, and Tate took the opportunity to grab both of Sam's shoulders and force him upright. He then slammed his fist across Sam's face. Once, twice, a third time, until Sam's head fell forward and he dropped to his knees.

Before Sam could recover, Seever was behind him, the muzzle of his weapon grazing the back of Sam's head. He cocked his weapon and the sound halted the entire scene. Sam froze, taking short breaths, his jaw trembling with fury.

"Enough. Nobody move," Seever said. He looked at Tate to make sure he was okay, and Tate nodded. His breath was coming in hard snaps, but that didn't stop him from moving to where Kate lay on the ground and dragging her back to her feet.

Remko saw a thin line of blood trickling down the side of her face from a small gash above her right eye. Kate struggled against Tate's hold but not with as much ferocity as before. Tate followed Seever's lead and pulled his weapon from its place, placing it inches from Kate's temple. She eyed the gun and stilled, but the fire in her eyes only increased.

"You're quite feisty," Tate said to Kate.

She bit her lip, and Remko knew she was struggling to keep her words under control. Her eyes locked on the gun pointed at her brother's back. She wouldn't risk saying anything that might get him shot.

"Nothing to say now?" Tate teased.

"Tate, enough," Seever said.

Tate huffed. "Please, Seever—you think anyone will care how these traitors are treated? They're as good as dead anyway," he said and pressed the end of his weapon against Kate's left temple. "Maybe we should start eliminating them now."

"We were instructed to wait for backup," Seever said.

Tate cocked his weapon, and Remko saw Kate's body shiver. He had to grind his own heels into the dirt to keep from rushing forward. Seever still had his gun cocked and aimed at Sam.

"But she tried to run, Seever, and we couldn't let her get away. We had no choice." The left end of Tate's mouth pulled up into a half grin and Remko could feel the blood under his skin boiling. Sam's body instinctively moved a couple of inches toward his sister, but Seever grabbed Sam's shirt and yanked him backward.

"I said no one move!" Seever yelled.

Selena's girls both whimpered and Remko could feel his resolve to stay still wavering when something zipped through the air over his head. A long, thin object, quick and nearly silent.

Tate cried out in pain and Remko saw an arrow nestled deep in the side of his arm. Tate released his hold on Kate, and before anyone could take another breath, a second arrow flew from the sky and landed in the back of Seever's calf.

Seever buckled and dropped his weapon. Remko moved then, straight for the biggest target. He momentarily worried about more arrows flying out of nowhere, but before he could let himself address the new threat, he needed to attack the first one.

He bent slightly and used his head to ram Tate. The action happened so fast that Tate didn't have time to react. He fell backward onto the ground with a heavy thud and knocked the back of his skull against the dirt. The arrow in his arm caught the side of a tree and snapped in half, sending him into a screaming frenzy.

A shot fired, and Remko turned to see that Seever had fired his weapon in the direction the arrows had come from.

"Lucy, stop!" Selena yelled.

Remko turned again to see Lucy running off into the cover of trees, Selena and Rayna on her heels. A thousand scenarios crashed against the inside of Remko's skull and he felt overwhelmed with uncertainty, but he needed to move.

With Seever's gun no longer pointed at the back of Sam's head, Sam jumped up from his knees with power and turned to attack the CityWatch guard. The boy was small so it didn't take much for Sam to have him on the ground, his weapon now lying far from his reach, fear overwhelming his body. He cried for mercy, shaking like a leaf.

Remko looked back just as Kate was slamming her foot against the side of Tate's face, splitting his lip and knocking him out cold. She squatted, turning her body so that she could use her hands, and found the knife secured in a side pouch at Tate's waist. Quickly she sliced through the restraints holding her wrists and then moved to free Remko.

"Go," she said, cutting him free, "We've got this."

Remko quickly took in the scene. Sam had knocked Seever unconscious and Kate was already moving to free Wire and Sam, Tate's gun tucked into the front of her pants. "Get out of here now," Remko called.

She nodded, and Remko ran after Selena.

He pushed the worry for his team aside and set his mind on finding Selena. They all knew to rendezvous back at their vehicle.

Something shifted in the trees above and Remko slid behind a tree to take cover. He stopped, held his breath, listened, waited. After a minute, he glanced around the trunk back to where he had come from. He could barely make out the CityWatch guards still lying on the ground, but otherwise the area was clear. His team was out.

The world around him had grown still. The wind blew, and it made the leaves rustle slightly, but otherwise the only sound he heard was his own blood pounding in his temples. He searched ahead with his eyes, trying to pick up any movement that might be Selena and her girls, but all he saw were trees.

He took a deep breath and continued moving. They couldn't have gotten too far.

After a couple more minutes of running, Remko paused again to listen and search. He heard a twig snap to his left and turned, waiting for more movement. He saw it then— a small figure rounded the side of a tree too late to avoid being seen.

Remko moved, reaching the tree quickly, and found a small rock overhang big enough to conceal a large person— or three small ones. He approached the structure slowly and knelt down to gaze inside.

Selena's face faded from terror to relief the moment she recognized Remko. Both of the girls were curled beside her, crying, their faces stained with dirt lines, both of them trembling.

Remko reached his hand in for Lucy and she studied his face as if deciding whether she could really trust him. He could only imagine how hard it must be to be old enough to understand what was happening but not old enough to understand why. He nodded toward her and she took his hand. She moved out from the covering with her mother and sister close behind. He took a single moment to make sure they were all right before surveying the land, trying to map out where they were and how they could get to the rendezvous point.

Before he could determine the best course, someone moved out from behind a large nearby tree. A boy, dressed in dark clothes with a hood pulled up over his head, raised a bow and aimed it at Remko.

The girls gasped beside him, and Remko moved to block them from the stranger. Remko raised his hands slowly.

Several things played through Remko's mind all at once. First, the boy couldn't be any older than Wire. He was small, but his face was hard; he wasn't a stranger to trouble. Second, it only made sense that this was the archer who had kept them from all being killed back in the clearing— what were the chances that there were two people out wandering the woods with a bow and arrows—and if that were true, then this stranger had saved them, so why would he hurt them now? And finally, all Remko had was a single knife tucked deep inside his boot, but he'd have to get close to use it effectively. Given the boy's accuracy with his bow, Remko knew getting close would be difficult.

The boy held Remko's stare; he didn't blink, didn't waver. He just stood, bow tight, stance firm, breathing calmly.

And then he spoke. "You can't go back the way you came. There are at least fifteen CityWatch guards there now."

Remko had wondered whether the backup Seever had called for had shown yet. Getting clear was going to be a struggle with that many guards around.

"I heard them call for more, too, so you don't have much time before this place is swarming with them," the archer said.

"Who are you?" Remko asked.

"Does it matter?" the boy replied. He slowly lowered his bow and dropped his hood. He was young, maybe sixteen, with buzzed hair that was dark on his olive skin. Light-brown eyes, strong jaw. He looked much less intimidating without his hood. "I can get you out of here," he said.

Remko studied his face and the boy didn't shy away from Remko's prying eyes. He glanced at Selena, who looked nervous, but he couldn't think of another way out of their predicament. Remko knew these woods, but only certain paths, and from the sound of it they would soon all be trampled with guards. He didn't know if he could trust the archer, but he knew he needed to get Selena and her girls to safety.

"Why would you help us?" Remko asked.

"Because you need it, and because I hate the CityWatch."

Trial Entry 109 | Patient Group bc:X
Age: Various / Gender: Various / Status: Various
Time in observation: 116 days

Physician's log
Entry made by attending: Dr. Mark Harold

—Medical team has encountered another glitch in the current strain of the injection solution. Patient group bc:X has exhibited only portions of the expected neural change. It seems that eradicating certain memory trains is proving more difficult than originally anticipated. The problem lies within the frontal lobe and the steadfast myelin that anchors deep-set memory reactions.

—The Scientist will expect results that I fear we will not be able to demonstrate. Many among the project team are beginning to question whether or not the objective can be obtained. Can the mind be rewired to serve the greater purpose, or will it always fight for its own selfish rights?

—The fear of not being able to produce the results required has some physicians making mistakes, putting the patients at further risk. Although the terminal failure rate has settled, many patients will never recover from a mental standpoint. Their minds are too broken for continued testing; another batch of trial patients will be brought in. We need positive results quickly.

11 The archer quickly led them along the edge of the woods. The forest backed up to a large grouping of buildings surrounded by a parking lot worn from time and overgrown with foliage. The Seers had scouted the buildings once but found the insides filled with small shops too destroyed to be used as refuge.

Remko had placed Selena and the girls between him and the boy with the bow in order to keep an eye on everyone. Remko waited for another ambush, waited for the archer to turn on them, but the farther they traveled the less worried Remko felt. If the archer were the enemy, he would have acted by now.

He was impressed with the way the archer knew the woods, the way he moved the group around obstacles, keeping them covered and out of sight. Remko was starting to believe that maybe this boy actually did want to help. But where had he come from? He said very little, and Remko restrained himself from asking questions that might cause their rescuer to leave. The truth was, until Remko knew where they were and that they were safe, they needed the archer.

Remko kept an eye out for things that were familiar to him. He knew they were headed west because of the location of the sun. He knew they needed to meet up with Sam, Wire, and Kate back at the cave, but he wasn't sure how to proceed now that the archer was with them.

Even if the boy was trying to help, Remko couldn't risk leading him back to their vehicle and then possibly to camp. But he wasn't sure how not to. Options and thin solutions rumbled around inside his head. They were coming to the end of the woods, and Remko knew he needed to think of something quickly.

"Where are you headed?" the archer asked.

Remko said nothing, unsure how to answer.

"Can't tell me; don't worry—I get it."

The archer glanced back at Selena and the Carson girls. "Interesting company to be traveling through the woods with. No wonder the CityWatch is after you."

If the archer recognized Selena, then he had to be from the city. But why was he out here?

"You travel alone mostly?" Remko asked.

The archer nodded. "Never have to worry about anyone but myself."

Remko felt a surge of envy that he shoved aside.

"Must be lonely," Selena said.

The archer shrugged. "I don't have the best track record of choosing good company, so lonely is fine with me." He came to a stop and pointed forward. "That's the edge of the forest there. It spills out at the bottom of the eastern hills—are you familiar with those?"

Remko nodded.

"I'll leave you here then." The archer turned to head back into the trees when something snapped to the left of them. His bow was raised as quickly as Remko could register the sound. They all paused and Remko readied himself for another CityWatch encounter.

A small bunny hopped out from behind a tree and scurried off for protection. The archer lowered his bow and Remko's stance eased. Lucy let out a small laugh and Selena smiled at Remko. "It was probably a really vicious bunny."

Both of her girls softly giggled and Remko couldn't help but smile. The archer did the same and took a couple steps away from the group.

"Thank you," Selena said. She took a step toward the boy and gave him a warm smile. "You saved my daughters' lives; I'm not sure how to repay you for that."

The boy shook his head. "I'm sorry I wasn't there to save your other daughter."

Selena sucked in a painful breath and held the archer's eyes for a long moment. The archer didn't look away or seem uneasy as Selena's eyes searched his face. The ease and confidence with which he carried himself was impressive.

"What's your name?" Selena asked.

The archer again turned to leave but after a short step paused and looked back over his shoulder. "Jesse. Jesse

Cropper." He glanced at Remko, speaking a message with his eyes that Remko understood, then disappeared into the trees.

Keep them safe, the archer had said silently, and Remko intended to.

/ / /

By the time Remko and the Carson women reached the cave where the others were waiting with the transport vehicle, the sun was nearly hidden behind the mountains, the last of its rays dimming in the sky. Kate rushed to meet them as they walked up, punching Remko in the arm and then proceeding to hug him. "We were just about to go searching for your bodies. What took you so long?"

Remko gave her a half grin and walked into the cave, where Wire and Sam looked relieved to see him. "The CityWatch backup showed, so we had to take the long way around."

"The archer helped us, though," Lucy said.

Sam crooked an eyebrow at Remko. "Archer?"

"The one responsible for those friendly arrows, I'm guessing," Kate said.

"His name is Jesse. He was very kind," Selena said.

Kate, Sam, and Wire shared a worried glance.

Remko nodded and tried to ease their concern. "We parted ways miles from here, but we can take an alternate route back to camp. As far as I could tell, he was traveling on foot, so that gives us the advantage."

Sam gave Wire a final look, and Wire flashed Roxy. "I'll keep an eye out for anything strange."

"We need to head back; we're already hours behind schedule. People will start to worry," Remko said. Everyone nodded and climbed into the pod. Remko overheard Rayna telling Sam that a bunny had scared Remko on their trek back, and Remko felt peace in the fact that after everything she had seen in the last couple of hours, the thing she was going to remember most was the bunny.

The ride back to camp was quiet. Lucy and Rayna fell asleep, and Selena was lost in her own thoughts. Kate and Wire passed Roxy back and forth, playing a touch-screen game that Wire had designed in his spare time. Sam kept his eyes on the road ahead as he drove, his window rolled down, the cool night air rustling his hair.

Remko was glad to be headed back to camp with everyone in tow and unharmed. All in all, the day could be marked as a success. He found his mind drifting back to the archer a couple of times. Jesse. He wondered how he'd come to be alone, to use his weapon the way he did, to understand both the woods and the city so well. As children growing up in the city, you were always taught that survival outside the city walls was impossible, that dangers could be found around every turn. But that was just another lie the Authority used to manipulate people into feeling fear so that they would obey. Their power was all based on fear: the fear to disobey, the fear to end up alone, the fear to discover you're worthless. As people living under the Authority, all the decisions you made, you made out of fear.

On the other hand, sometimes it was hard to see much difference in what they were doing now.

The Seers might be free of the Authority's rule, but were they not still basing all their decisions for survival on fear? Wasn't the fear of being captured the resounding echo that drove all of their moves? Could a person ever be devoid of fear, ever move and live in a way that fear wasn't the driving force? Aaron spoke of a path beyond the control of fear, a reality they were fighting to bring to fruition, but was it actually possible?

When they reached the tunnel entrance, Remko was surprised by how quick the trip had felt. After a few more minutes of driving through the dark subway tunnel, the lights of camp came into view. Selena stirred her girls awake as several Seers walked to greet the van, Carrington included. As Remko stepped out of the front passenger seat, he could hear Carrington's sigh of relief.

Remko pulled her into his arms and held her tight. She buried her face in the base of his neck, and the sweet scent of her hair filled his senses. She placed a kiss on his shoulder and pulled back. "Aaron is here, in camp."

Remko could feel the shift in the atmosphere the moment the words left her lips. Kate and Sam, followed closely by Wire and the few Seers that had ventured out to meet the van, headed toward the fire where everyone had gathered.

A smile lit Carrington's face, and her joy seeped into Remko's tired bones. He smiled in response and released his hold from around her waist. She looked over his shoulder and her eyes froze on the three Carson women standing in the shadows.

Remko had totally forgotten that Selena and her daughters would be a surprise to Carrington, and he wished he'd thought to warn her. She moved past Remko toward Selena and extended her hand in greeting.

"Welcome. My name is Carrington. I knew your daughter."

Selena grasped Carrington's hand and just held it. "She spoke of you once; you are just as beautiful as she described." Selena's eyes welled with tears and Carrington, without hesitation, pulled her into an embrace. Selena, shocked for only a moment, embraced Carrington in return.

Remko gave the four girls a moment of privacy and started again toward the fire, keeping them in sight as he did. After a couple of minutes, they started in his direction and soon they were all in the center of camp. Children's laughter filled the subway and Remko knew Aaron must be telling one of his famous tales.

The Seer leader was standing in the center of the crowd with most people seated around him. He preferred to tell stories with his entire being. His arms were stretched high to the sky to emphasize the size of the creature in this particular tale. Wire and Kate were across the crowd, headed for the equipment tent to record the day's happenings. Sam had perched himself on an upside-down crate near the fire and was eating the soup that someone offered him. He saw Rayna and Lucy and motioned them over.

Selena nodded her permission and the two girls moved carefully toward Sam. They caught the eyes of everyone around the fire, as their faces were so recognizable. Looks began to flutter toward Selena as well, but Carrington looped her arm through the cautious woman's, pulling her close. Selena smiled at Carrington's kindness and ignored the curious looks.

Aaron noticed the two Carson girls as they sat beside Sam, and he turned toward them. "That is a beautiful necklace you're wearing," he said, pointing at Sam's pendant still hanging from Rayna's small neck. She was clutching it in her hand and glanced down when Aaron mentioned it.

She paused for a moment, afraid to speak, before looking up at Aaron. "It's magic."

"Magic? What does it do?" Aaron asked.

"Makes me invisible."

"A beautiful girl like you, why would you need to be invisible?"

"So they can't find me."

Every eye in the camp was on the girl and Aaron as they spoke.

"Who?" Aaron asked.

Rayna bit her bottom lip and dropped her eyes to the necklace still nestled in her palm. "The city."

Remko heard Selena inhale sharply beside him and watched Lucy's face register a similar pain. The turmoil these little girls must be facing suddenly fell upon Remko. It was unfair for such a traumatic death to touch their innocence.

"I know a true story about a young boy who was afraid," Aaron said. "He was small—not much bigger than you—and his home and all the people he loved were under attack."

Rayna lifted her chin and watched Aaron with wonder. Lucy was watching as well, along with all of the other children who were inching closer to hear another story.

"See, they were being tormented by a monster, a giant from an enemy kingdom, and this giant was threatening their king, saying he would kill anyone who stood against him. Now, this young boy surely felt fear, but he didn't feel powerless even though everyone else said he was just a small boy, and what could he do against such a monster?

"Now, imagine the army out in the fields trying to decide how to defeat this giant. Imagine the king, worried about what would happen to his people. And then imagine what happened when this young boy showed up, too small for armor or a sword, and marched out onto the grassy plain to face the monster alone."

Rayna's face crumpled with fear. "Did he die?"

Aaron smiled and dropped into a crouch in front of Rayna. "No, he won."

Rayna's eyes grew wide. "How?"

"He had magic too."

She held out her pendant, smiling. "Like mine?"

"A different kind of magic. A kind that lived inside him. See, Rayna, that young boy was already magic in a way. His faith and belief made him powerful, so that he could face the monster and not be defeated."

"Wasn't he afraid?" Lucy asked.

Aaron turned to face the older of the two sisters and nodded. "Of course; fear is a very real thing. But the boy knew the power he possessed was greater than his fear. Because his power came from somewhere much greater than what he was afraid of. It came from his trust in the Father."

"I wish I had power like that," Rayna said under her breath.

"Oh, but you do," Aaron said. "That's why you're here, Rayna; the same kind of magic that helped that boy can help you."

Rayna's eyes lit up with excitement. "And Lucy, too?"

Aaron chuckled. "Yes—all of us."

Lucy shook her head. "It's just a silly story. We are not magic."

Rayna's smile fell and she looked to Aaron to tell Lucy she was wrong.

"Arianna used to tell me about her power, the power that lived inside her, like the magic you talk about, but that didn't save her," Lucy said.

Aaron reached out and took Lucy's hand. She edged backward just a bit but didn't pull her hand away. "Yes, it did. It saved her from her fear. It can save you, too, from the weight you carry. You can be free. You can be magic."

Aaron held Lucy's stare for a long moment and the rest of the camp stayed silent. Tears gathered in Lucy's eyes and she blinked them away. Rayna stood and moved to hold her sister's other hand. "Maybe we could be magic?" she said, in the smallest voice, almost too soft to make out from where Remko stood.

Streams of tears were rolling down Selena's face and tears dotted Carrington's cheeks as well. Lucy gave Rayna a weak smile and nodded. "Maybe."

Before any of them could say another word, Kate called out for Remko from the edge of the crowd. He heard a couple of people gasp as he turned to see Kate standing behind a hooded figure, the figure's arms clasped behind its back and the muzzle of Kate's gun pointed at its head. Several people moved to gather their children and escort them to safety, and Kate shrugged her apology to several glaring onlookers.

Aaron stood from his crouch and moved toward Kate, as did Remko and Carrington.

"I found him snooping around behind the equipment tent," Kate said.

Sam moved to the prisoner and yanked down his hood.

"Jesse," Selena said. She was standing behind Carrington, both of her girls at her sides.

"You know him?" Kate said.

"Kate, meet our archer," Remko said.

"I'd say it was a pleasure to meet you, but . . . ," Jesse said.

Kate placed the end of her weapon at the nape of Jesse's neck.

"How did you find us?" Remko asked.

"He followed us, clearly," Kate said.

"On foot?" Remko said skeptically.

"I don't really open up well at gunpoint," Jesse said.

"Tough," Kate replied.

Remko glanced at Sam and Sam stepped forward and touched Kate's arm.

She looked at him in shock. "You have got to be kidding me. We don't know anything about this punk, and you want me to let him go free in camp?"

"We're all right here," Remko said. "He isn't going anywhere."

Kate huffed in disbelief but after another second dropped her gun and stepped back.

Jesse rolled his shoulders and faced Remko. "Thank you."

"How did you follow us?" Remko asked.

"Actually, you followed me," Jesse said. "I have been living in these subway tunnels for a while."

"Impossible," Wire said. Remko hadn't even noticed his approach. "I scanned these tunnels for miles and got no readings of human life."

"You learn to hide pretty well when you're on your own," Jesse said.

"How long have you known we were here?" Remko asked.

"Since you showed up."

"Why wait till now to turn up?"

Jesse shrugged. "I got curious after today. After seeing her." He nodded toward Selena. "I started to put the pieces together. People tell stories about the rebels, the Seers, and I wanted to see for myself."

"Bad idea," Kate grumbled.

"I don't mean anyone harm. I didn't even bring my bow."

Remko had been wondering where it was. He scanned Jesse's face, looking for signs of falsehood, and found nothing.

"So you are out here on your own?" Aaron asked.

The rest of the group turned at the sound of his voice. Remko had almost forgotten he was there.

"Yep, just the way I like it," Jesse answered. He looked Aaron over and a light went on behind his eyes. "You're not at all what I expected."

"And what did you expect?" Aaron asked.

"I don't know; the way you have the Authority scared, I would have guessed you'd be more intimidating."

Aaron laughed and shook his head. "I am just a teacher."

"Right," Jesse said.

"Come; sit with us around the fire. Would you like something to eat?" Aaron said.

"Aaron, he could be a spy for the Authority. CityWatch guards are probably headed here as we speak," Kate said.

Jesse chuckled and Kate's face filled with fury.

"We should do a perimeter check," Sam said.

Remko nodded. Sam grabbed Wire and the two started off into the tunnels.

Aaron glanced at Jesse. "Are you a spy?"

"No."

"Of course he would say no," Kate said. "He isn't very well going to tell us."

"He saved our lives," Selena said.

"Then you must eat with us," Aaron said.

"No thanks; I should get going," Jesse said.

"You are welcome to stay," Remko said. Kate's face drained of color and a couple of gasps echoed around him. He knew very little about the boy who stood before him, but against reasonable logic, Remko trusted him. There was something in his eyes that put Remko at ease.

"All are welcome to stay," Aaron said.

"No, I'm good on my own," Jesse said.

"Well, then, I will walk you out. I'm headed that way," Aaron said.

"Aaron . . . ," Kate warned.

Aaron walked to Kate and placed both hands on her shoulders. "Daughter of such little faith." Her face flushed and she dropped her eyes to the ground. He placed a kiss on the top of her head and whispered something in her ear that made her nearly smile.

"You don't have to; I'm pretty far—" Jesse started.

"I insist," Aaron said.

Jesse nodded, understanding quickly that there was no way he was leaving alone. He glanced at Remko. "He's not going to take me out into the tunnels and kill me or something, right?"

Aaron laughed, a loud warm sound that filled the air.

Kate stepped up in front of Jesse before he could move and drilled him with a dangerous glare. "He won't, but if you touch him, I will."

Jesse raised his fingers to the right side of his temple and gave Kate a soldier's salute to signal that he understood, and it only made the lines in her face harden. But after a moment, Kate stepped out of the way and Jesse left, following after Aaron as the two disappeared into the dark.

12

Aaron didn't return that night. Remko hadn't expected him to, but his expectations hadn't stopped Kate from staying up most of the night waiting. She'd paced back and forth, leaving a thin trail on the dusty tunnel floor on the outskirts of camp, until well after the sun was up. Sam and Wire had returned not too long after Aaron and Jesse left, happy to announce the perimeter was secure and the readings showed no sign of life for miles in any direction.

Remko turned in for the night with only a couple hours of dark left but woke by habit at the same time the sun was rising out in the aboveground world. He should have made himself go back to sleep, since a few hours barely touched the weariness in his muscles, but he didn't. The camp was pretty quiet, most people still tucked away in slumber.

He made his way to the equipment tent, which doubled as a mission headquarters. The tent was small but tall enough that Remko didn't have to crouch inside. There were two long, wide plastic bins in the middle, both filled with weapons and securely locked. The bins acted as a makeshift table, maps and charts spread across their tops.

Smaller square crates filled with supplies were stacked along the outer edges of the tent. Remko moved to sit on the single empty crate used as a chair near the temporary table. He got to work, recounting events, reviewing CityWatch patrolling schedules, cataloging weapons, and studying maps for different route options.

The tent entrance rustled and Remko looked up to see Neil and another Seer, Trig Mullen, stepping inside.

"Morning," Remko said.

"We need to talk, Remko," Neil said.

Skipping the pleasantries. Remko knew exactly where this conversation was going.

"Neil. I'm not sure this is a good time—"

"We were hoping to get some time with Aaron last night to discuss the big-picture plan here," Neil said, ignoring Remko. "Like you promised."

"The night played out differently. I couldn't control that," Remko said.

"Did you even try? You have pull over Aaron; we need you to keep your promise and set up a sit-down. People have questions and they are making threats. Threats about leaving."

Remko thought again that he should have gotten more sleep as he tried to control the rise of anger filling his body. He was tired of having these conversations, tired of people assuming he could fix all their problems. They were all out here together, facing the same problems together—Remko included. What made them think he was better equipped to handle it?

"Then let them leave," Remko said before Neil could continue.

Neil looked taken aback and glanced at Trig, whose expression was the same.

"Nobody is forcing anyone to stay here and be a part of this community. Anyone is free to leave if they feel the need."

"But they were called here," Neil said.

"Yes, by Aaron, and so we should follow his lead, and currently he wants us here, close to the city," Remko said.

"To what end?"

"I know as much as you do, Neil."

"I doubt that is true. And what of this new intruder? You invited him to stay."

"*Let all who come, come,* Neil; that is what Aaron has always said."

"Yes, *let those who have been called come.* But we know nothing about this boy. He could be a threat."

"He isn't."

"How can you know that? What about our security? Our children sleep here!"

Remko slammed his fist down on the plastic bins and stood. "So does mine!"

Neil's eyes dropped to slits and he leaned in close to Remko's face so that Remko could feel the heat from his breath on his skin. "You are losing control of this situation here," Neil said, "and you are putting our families at risk."

"The situation is fine, but if you continue to stir things up around camp, then we will have discord among our own people," Remko said, trying to remain calm.

"We already have discord."

Remko pushed back from Neil and took a deep breath. "What would you have me do?"

"We want to speak with Aaron," Neil said.

"I don't control him; he doesn't come when I call."

"We want to speak with Aaron and soon." Neil let his words stand in the silence for a moment and held Remko's gaze before turning and leaving, Trig on his heels.

/ / /

The long grass tickles the back of Carrington's arm, but she doesn't mind. In fact, the sensation is comforting and reminds her of how much she loves this field. Laughter bounces through the breeze and she sits up. Someone else is here. The sun is too bright against her gaze, and she uses her hand to shield her eyes. In the distance a shadow is dancing through the gleaming rays, a figure moving toward her with bouncing, twirling steps.

Her heart is racing and she stands to get a better look. Usually in this field Carrington is greeted by Aaron. He comes to give her comfort, to impart wisdom, to be a cool refuge when the rest of the world feels like a desert. Sometimes Aaron doesn't come at all, but the spirit of something else sweeps through the grass like a hurricane. Violent and peaceful and beautiful. The mere touch of its air against her skin is enough to recharge her. Carrington senses it's Aaron's Father, her Father.

But this time is different. The shape is too small to be Aaron. Carrington takes a step forward, ducking around the beams of sunlight to catch a glimpse of the shadow. The figure giggles, closer now, and familiarity seeps into Carrington's mind. She is running full throttle through the tall shards of grass. Tears fill her eyes, then dry against her cheeks in the wind. The figure stops dancing and the sun shifts so Carrington sees her face.

Larkin smiles and laughs as Carrington collides with her. The two girls topple backward into giggles and tears, the tall, thick grass catching them as they fall. Larkin rolls out of Carrington's embrace and onto her back, her arms and legs spread out wide around her like a star. She stares up at the sun, her face full of joy.

Carrington props herself onto her side and keeps her eyes on Larkin's face. She never imagined she would see her friend again, and the thought brings another round of tears.

Larkin glances at Carrington and shakes her head. "Don't cry. It's much too beautiful here to cry."

"I miss you."

"I'm right here. Miss me when I'm gone."

"But you are gone."

Larkin rolls onto her side to match Carrington's posture. "Not really. I'm always here."

"Then I'm never leaving."

Larkin's face changes; seriousness glides across her skin. "He needs you."

"I need you." Silence fills the field and even the wind seems to quiet. "Everything is different now. Things that should be the same feel foreign, as if I've never eaten or slept before. The loss of you is all that is familiar to me."

"Loss is a powerful thing."

"It's more than loss—it's fear, too. Fear that we all are destined for the same fate as you." Tears slide off Carrington's chin. Caught up in her own suffering, she avoids Larkin's eyes. The warmth of the field is lost, the magic of this place hidden beneath her sorrow.

Stillness wraps them both, and the seconds slow. Carrington fears she may be stuck forever in this moment. Then Larkin reaches out and touches her shoulder. The stillness cracks.

"Don't run from your fear. It will just chase you."

"How do I defeat it?"

Larkin smiles. "Stop fighting."

"Let it win?"

"No. Let it go. Accept it and surrender it."

Larkin drops her hand and stands up. She reaches out for Carrington and winks. Carrington can't help but smile and take Larkin's hand. Larkin pulls Carrington from the ground and a chuckle falls from her lips.

"What is it about this field that makes me want to dance?"

A wild wind swirls around them and excitement lights up Larkin's face. "It must be the wind."

With those words, she races off into the field. Spinning and dancing while gusts of wind pull through her hair. Carrington follows, trying to keep up, but Larkin's speed seems unnatural.

Fear clutches at her chest. What if Larkin gets away?

"Slow down," Carrington calls, but her words are lost to the wind. Larkin's laughter fills the space around Carrington even as her figure draws farther away.

"Larkin, stop." Carrington races with all her might, but she feels as if she is running in place.

Larkin is now a spot on the horizon. Carrington again yells for her to return.

And then she is alone again. The wind dies down, and the grass is all that is left with her.

Carrington searches, spins, hopes that maybe Larkin is somewhere close, but all she sees is the open field. Abruptly she falls to her knees, the overwhelming sense of loss pushing her to the ground.

"Come back; please come back."

Suddenly anger replaces her anguish and she balls her hands into fists. The wind took Larkin away; the wind is to blame. Carrington screams out against the air that whips around her. She thrashes her arms against it, trying to push it away. She doesn't want it. She just wants to be free of it.

As if responding to her thoughts, the wind dies out completely. Only the sound of her own heart and ragged breaths fill her ears. And then her cries of sorrow. They crackle against the quiet sky and echo all around her. She pounds her fists into the

*ground and screams. She places her forehead against the dirt
and muddies the ground with her tears.*

"Larkin, please come back. Please!"

A hand shook Carrington's shoulder and she opened her eyes.
Selena Carson hovered overhead, and the shock of seeing her
caused Carrington to shoot up from bed. Selena must have
recognized the surprise on her face, because she took a step
back and waited for Carrington to regain her senses.

She was in her tent, in camp. The space where Remko
slept was vacant, and the misshapen crib at the end of the
bed was empty.

"Elise," Carrington gasped.

"Lesley has her. She was up very early and Lesley
thought it was better to let you sleep," Selena said.

"What time is it?"

"Nearly noon."

Carrington stood and a wave of dizziness broke over
her. Selena moved to assist Carrington as she sat back down
on the bed. She closed her eyes and the dream of Larkin
crashed back against her brain. The threat of tears pounded
in her throat and she swallowed hard to keep them at bay.

Selena handed her a small glass of water and Carrington
thanked her with a forced smile. "I should have been up
hours ago."

"Actually, I think you should probably stay in bed."

Carrington glanced at Selena and couldn't help but see
Arianna in her eyes. She dropped her gaze as more emotion

invaded her senses and drank the water that had been given to her.

Selena sat down on the bed beside Carrington and took her hand. The gesture came as a surprise, but the warmth of Selena's palm was welcome. The tent was quiet for a while, Selena holding Carrington's hand and Carrington avoiding thoughts of Larkin and Arianna.

"You were calling out for her in your sleep," Selena said. "Larkin. I was walking by and heard you calling for her."

Carrington bit her bottom lip and felt a shade of embarrassment heat her cheeks. She tried to think of some way to defend her actions, but Selena spoke before she could.

"It was months before I slept again. I still sometimes wake up calling out Arianna's name."

Carrington could see the pain gathering in Selena's face and wished she had something to say that might offer relief. But all she felt was her own thundering sorrow.

"The pain of loss is . . ." Selena paused and swallowed. "*Overwhelming* seems too mild a description. Death would have been a relief from the agony. It felt like it was the only way to be rid of the pain." She stared forward, her eyes collecting tears.

"I was so blinded by grief that I nearly destroyed my other two daughters. The blame is the hardest part to get through. As parents, we are charged to protect our children, and I let my daughter be murdered."

Selena's bottom lip quivered and Carrington felt a tear slide down her own face.

"The Authority imprisoned my husband shortly after the rebellion started, and I was so alone and controlled by my misery that I nearly left my other children orphaned." Her voice dropped to a whisper. "I can't tell you how often I was tempted to end it all, to give in to the pain and let it own me. To become a slave to the blame that echoed so loudly in my head."

She wiped her face with the back of her free hand and turned her eyes to Carrington. "Did you ever see the Capitol Building's gardens?"

Carrington shook her head.

"They were beautiful. Filled with colorful blooms, full bushes tall enough to hide behind and century-old trees that stood like pillars, shading the perfectly trimmed grass. Arianna always loved the gardens. She told me once that if the trees could still stand after the Time of Ruin and remain the same—beautiful, strong, and free—she should be able to do so as well.

"I knew Arianna saw things differently. She always questioned the Authority, not out of a place of rebellion as people wanted you to believe, but out of a place of wanting to truly know. Know what the world was, and how it worked, and who she was in it.

"I always thought her curiosity was beautiful— inspiring, even. I thought she was going to change the world." Selena laughed and a fresh wave of tears moved down her cheeks. "When she died, I thought all those dreams I'd had for her were for nothing. I'd spend hours in the garden trying to connect with whatever was left of her. Trying to remember anything other than the grief that haunted me. Aaron found me there. Probably in the same place he'd found her."

"He came to you?" Carrington asked.

Selena nodded. "In the middle of the day, in the center of the High-Rise Sector, surrounded by CityWatch on all sides. Or maybe it was all a dream—I don't even know. But he came and at first I was furious. He was the reason she had been killed. I accused him of murder, of being a monster, and he didn't resist my accusation. In fact, he somehow connected with me; he wept with me, suffered with me.

"Then he reminded me of the truths Arianna had told me a hundred times. The truth of my identity and worth. The truths she died for. And, not all at once, but slowly, they took root inside my soul and I discovered that my dreams for Arianna had come true. She had already changed the world. Her belief and her faith in that belief changed my other daughters, you, me."

Carrington smiled and nodded, wiping tears away.

Selena placed her palm on Carrington's cheek and warmth flooded her face. "Grief is real and painful, but it is not the end of us or the ones we've lost. Every day that I change and see change around me, I see Arianna. Larkin will always be with you. Always."

Her gentle words broke any strength Carrington had managed to maintain, and she began to weep.

Selena pulled Carrington's head onto her shoulder and Carrington clung to the woman as tears and painful sobs ravaged her.

/ / /

Remko walked across camp. It was hard to tell what time of day it was inside these tunnels, but he imagined it was late afternoon. Carrington had emerged from their tent a few hours ago looking more exhausted than she had heading to sleep last night. He'd suggested she go back to bed, but she wouldn't hear of it, and he knew there was no point in arguing with her.

He'd sent Kate and Sam on a scouting run to the west, while Wire and Ramses had moved to the north. They would need to find more food soon. Small game was easy enough to come by, but grains, fruits, and vegetables took some searching. Thankfully they had found a close water source, so for the time being they would survive.

He was weary; early mornings paired with lack of sleep and constant thinking and second-guessing were taking their toll. He wondered what would happen if he sneaked off to nap for only a moment. Would the world around him come crashing to an end? Something inside told him trouble was after him and taking time to rest would mean letting his guard down and endangering those around him. Then again, the voices in his head often told him all sorts of things he questioned. *Don't trust Aaron; don't trust yourself; take your family and run; give it up; your efforts are useless.* Maybe listening to his head was the source of his trouble. He really could use some sleep.

Remko had nearly concluded that sleep now was necessary when a figure at the edge of camp caught his attention. His hood was pulled low, his bow was strapped across his back, and he cradled a large sack in his arms. Jesse tentatively walked across the invisible border of the camp. The surrounding Seers stopped what they were doing to watch the newcomer walk by. Worry appeared on many of their faces; curiosity marked others.

Remko moved toward the archer just as Neil Stone and two others stepped out of a nearby tent.

"What do you think you're doing?" Neil asked Jesse.

Jesse stopped but said nothing.

Neil and his two friends formed a wall between Jesse and the rest of camp. Remko jogged the short distance to the confrontation.

"It would be best if you turned around and left," Neil said.

"Neil," Remko said from behind. Neil looked over his shoulder to Remko. His eyes were already shadowed but when he saw Remko the darkness deepened. His whole body seemed to stiffen, as if he was readying himself for another fight. The two men with Neil dropped their heads a bit and slowly moved away, clearly communicating that they didn't want anything to do with a confrontation between Neil and Remko.

Remko held Neil's hard stare for a moment longer

before stepping past him toward Jesse. "I'm surprised to see you," Remko said.

Jesse pulled his hood off and gave a halfhearted grin. He offered the sack he was carrying to Remko, and after a moment's hesitation, Remko took it. He undid the loose string that was holding the top closed and peered inside. Apples—it was filled with red apples.

Remko gave Jesse a questioning look and pulled a piece of fruit from the bag. The people who had gathered, maybe a handful now, were looking on with similar curiosity.

Jesse cleared his throat. "I've been out on my own for a while now. I know how hard fruit is to come by."

"Where did you get these?" Remko asked.

Jesse grinned and Remko knew he wouldn't get the full story in front of this crowd.

"I have my ways," Jesse said.

Someone snatched the apple from Remko's hand. Neil held it out to Jesse with a sneer. "How do we know these are safe?"

"They're just apples, man," Jesse said.

Neil didn't appreciate the archer's lackadaisical comment and turned to Remko. His voice dropped to a hush, but it was still loud enough for most to hear. "He can't be trusted; we know nothing about him."

Remko glanced back at Jesse, who was tracing lines in the ground with his eyes. He was just a boy, hardly old enough to really understand the ways of this world, yet something about the way he carried himself called to Remko. It was a familiarity that rang like a bell inside his brain. A sliver of a mirror that reflected a younger version of himself in the archer's eyes. Remko had been just old enough to join the CityWatch when Dodson Rogue had taken him under his wing. Jesse's exterior was tough, but Remko knew all too well what a person could hide behind a wall.

"Why bring these to us?" Remko asked.

Jesse lifted his chin and shrugged. "You've got kids here. Kids should get apples now and then." He held Remko's eyes and Remko felt another stab of something he understood. Loneliness.

Remko handed the sack back to Jesse, and for a brief second, he thought he saw pain flash across the boy's face. "You should go give them to the kids then," Remko said.

Jesse's eyes brightened and he nodded. He grabbed for the sack as Neil stepped closer. "What are you doing? He can't be trusted near our children."

Remko felt spit land on his cheek and he stepped back. "They are only apples, Neil. When was the last time your son had an apple?"

Neil shook his head, a deepening red taking root in his cheeks. "I won't let him near the children alone."

"Then go with him." Remko placed a hand on Neil's shoulder. "We are in no position to ignore acts of kindness. Let all who come, come."

Neil's jaw twitched and his eyes lightened. He dropped his gaze and moved out from Remko's grip. He turned to Jesse and nearly spit. "Follow me."

Jesse sent Remko a thanks-a-lot glare and Remko felt a smile tug at the corners of his mouth. Several others who stood around watching followed Neil and Jesse, but Remko stayed behind. He would wait until after the gift had been distributed and then find the boy.

"Remko," a voice called from behind him. It was Wire and Ramses, both of them pulling up to a stop and breathing heavy. They had been running, sweat gathering on their foreheads, their cheeks flushed with heat.

The light mood Remko had felt vanished, replaced with the usual worry. "What?"

Wire worked to catch his breath and Ramses, clearly in better shape, spoke. "We intercepted a transmission while we were out. A CityWatch transmission." Ramses took a step closer and dropped the volume of his voice. "About an execution."

Dread filled Remko's brain. "Who?"

Wire and Ramses exchanged pitying looks before Ramses turned back to Remko. "Dodson Rogue."

Trial Entry 174 | Patient 1c-7 (Jaleen Rider)

Age: 19 / Gender: Female / Status: Authority Worker
Drug administered at 11:00 hours
Time in observation: 15 days

Patient log

Day 05 after administration: I could refuse to document my thoughts, I have heard of others doing the same, but I want to remember who I am when they try to erase me. I think that's what they are doing here, erasing us, or at least the parts of us they don't like. I won't forget who I am. I am Jaleen Rider, and I refuse to serve this corrupted Authority any longer.

Day 09 after administration: I'm not sure what happened but I can feel them. All over me and clawing away at the insides of my brain. I woke up with a terrible headache and forgot how I got here, or even where I came from. Water has started to taste like lead, and the lights sting my eyes. I can't get them out of my head, the clawing things. I can't get them out.

Day 11 after administration: I feel as though I may be losing touch with my own mind. The fear has passed and been replaced by a sense of ease that I know should make me uncomfortable but doesn't. I have noticed the way the doctors smile whenever

they are near, as if I have accomplished something I'm not
aware of, but then I'm afraid I've lost all sense of awareness.

Day 14 after administration: I've been asked to document my
mental state and give a recalling of who I am, though I am not
sure why. My name is Jaleen Rider, and I serve the Authority.
I always have; that is the only way. All other roads lead to
extermination of the human race. I am sure of this. My mental
state is clear. I'm not sure there is anything else to say.

13 Damien followed the Scientist down the narrow pathway. Steel rooms, rectangular in shape, cool in color, lined both sides of the hallway as their shoes made soft clicks on the metal floor. Damien fought off a shiver and focused his mind on a warmer place. He always thought the facility was too cold, but the Scientist insisted it was designed purposefully. With him everything was purposeful. That was the beauty of the man's madness.

He heard the mumblings of patients on the other side of the steel doors that sealed the square prisons. Some cried softly; others had started talking to themselves. The drug affected each individual differently. That made the process more difficult. To narrow down the exact biochemical and neurological reactions of the serum so that they could reproduce it effectively and distribute it to anyone was proving to be a challenge. Not that Damien had expected it to be an easy pursuit; in fact, he rather enjoyed the suffering that resulted from failed attempts. Suffering—and witnessing the suffering of others—illuminated a man's weakness so he could strengthen himself. Failure was necessary to any process and this one was no different, even if it could ultimately save their world.

They reached the end of the walkway, where a thick door stood. After a moment, it slid open to reveal a control room. The Scientist and Damien stepped through and the door closed behind them. Damien listened as the door churned, a large steel lock moving into place.

The room before them was white—the walls, the ceiling, the floor, even the coats on the men who sat working. It was a complete contrast to the rest of the facility, which was coated in dark steel and rusted metals.

Square screens filled the far wall from floor to ceiling, each one displaying a different patient in an individual cell. They all wore the same dark-gray patient uniforms, which made it almost impossible to remember what their stations had once been.

In the middle of the control room was a line of five desks, each with a handler. The top of each desk housed a screen that displayed seven patients at a time along with their statistics. It was necessary that all vitals, mental readings, and emotional reactions be monitored and recorded. This room was never left unoccupied, and the desks were never unmanned. This was the entire purpose of the operation: to discover the key combination of elements that would unify every individual reaction. This would enable the serum to ultimately be multiplied and distributed.

A squirrelly man with thinning brown hair and thick-rimmed glasses approached Damien and the Scientist. He was carrying a small handheld device that collected and presented information for optimal viewing. He nodded to both men. Damien noticed the slight shake in his hand as he handed the Scientist the device.

"Dr. Harold," the Scientist said, "I'm hoping you have good news."

Dr. Harold forced a smile. He was, like most men in this room, afraid of the Scientist. Damien didn't blame them; the Scientist was the greatest mind to exist since the Time of Ruin, perhaps even beyond. Everyone longed for his approval, but it was something that was nearly impossible to get. Damien would know. He had been striving for it his entire life.

The Scientist reviewed the data before him, a grim expression on his face. The room was silent except for the ticking of machinery and the clicking of people hard at work. Damien saw a couple of glances from the other men in the room, but none dared to hold their stares for long. If the Scientist caught them watching instead of working, there would be dire consequences.

The Scientist handed the device back to Dr. Harold and cleared his throat. Damien knew that sound very well. Disappointment.

Dr. Harold recognized it as well. And he quickly launched into an explanation. "The serum works through 83.7 percent of the brain currently. The largest struggle we face is the 16.3 percent of the temporal lobe that still seems to reject the idea of a 'pack' versus 'individual' mind-set. The memory agents in this part of the human brain are very strong."

"Do you think I am unaware of this data, as you have just watched me review it?" the Scientist said.

Dr. Harold went silent and Damien felt a twinge of sympathy for the man. He stepped in before the Scientist could verbally fillet him. "What are the plans to combat the strong memory agents that are inhibiting the transition?" he asked.

Dr. Harold swallowed hard and held the device out again. With a couple swipes of his fingers the screen began to run through lines upon lines of numerical data, which Damien would need someone to interpret for him. He glanced at Dr. Harold, who understood and began to explain.

"The issue lies within the strength and advanced reproduction of the myelin highways from neuron to neuron. By the time the serum breaks down the original connection and begins to replace it with our predesigned structure, the original connection begins to rebuild itself. It seems to be a matter of speed."

"And the solution?" Damien asked.

"They don't have one," the Scientist said.

Dr. Harold paused, and Damien knew he was right. Dr. Harold swiped his finger across the screen again. "We are working through a couple of theories that we believe could create a boost, so to speak, in order for the serum to work at a higher—"

"Do whatever you must. We are running out of time," the Scientist said.

Dr. Harold's face went red, as if he had been slapped, but he nodded and returned to work. The Scientist turned to leave and Damien followed, Dr. Harold barking out orders behind them. It was odd to hear such a sheepish man suddenly transform into a tyrant.

The door they had entered through only moments earlier now sealed them out of the room and the two men started down the same hallway they had just trekked. As they approached the opposite end of the hall, the Scientist turned and drilled Damien with a threatening glare.

"Do you understand the gravity of what we are doing here? Or have you forgotten?"

Damien was taken aback. "Of course I understand—"

"I am beginning to wonder if I chose the wrong man to lead this world into a new era."

"You didn't."

The Scientist's stare burrowed into Damien's soul and the chill in the room seemed to intensify. After a long second, the Scientist released Damien from his intense glower and nodded. "Don't ever interrupt me again."

With that the Scientist turned and left.

/ / /

Remko glanced around at the faces gathered in the control tent. Only hours earlier, he and Neil had fought across the large container that served as a table in the center of the room; now they stood side by side, a sense of doom settling around them. Sam, Kate, Wire, Ramses, and Carrington made up the rest of the group. The reason for their meeting was the news Wire and Ramses had discovered about Dodson.

"Do we know any specifics?" Sam asked, breaking the silence.

Ramses ran a shaky hand through his hair. "We have two days. I'm assuming from the usual patterns of execution that it will take place midday."

"But we can't be sure of that. The Authority continues to change their patterns to throw us off," Wire said.

"Why now?" Carrington asked. "They've had Dodson in custody for nearly nine months. Why have him executed now?"

The same question was surely on the tip of everyone's tongue.

"Because it's a trap," Neil said.

"We don't know that for sure," Wire said.

"Of course we do. It's the only thing that makes sense," Neil shot back.

Remko knew Neil was right for once. Just as Larkin's execution had been a trap, Dodson's would be the same, and they would be fools to go after him.

"So you suggest we just sit here and let him die?" Kate said.

"No, I just want us to be aware of the situation," Neil said.

"He's right," Remko said. The tent went quiet. "They will be expecting us to come."

"How could we not?" Carrington said. Remko locked eyes with her across the tent and was thankful for her presence. She was the only Seer aside from Remko who had ever interacted with Dodson, the only person who understood what Dodson meant to Remko and how painful this news was.

"This is different than going after one of our own," Neil said. "I understand he's important to you, but—"

"He *is* one of our own," Ramses said. "We owe that man more than you could possibly understand."

Neil exhaled and shook his head. He was going to lose this battle and everyone in the room knew it.

"Neil is right, though," Sam said. "They will know we are coming, and after barely escaping last time, it will be even harder for us to get in and out."

"The plan will need to be very strategic," Ramses said.

A yell sounded from outside the tent and the atmosphere changed immediately. Remko moved first, the rest close behind.

Through the tent's flap, Remko was met with a startling scene. A couple yards away, a man was swinging a gun, his hands trembling, his face glistening with sweat. Several others stood close by, their hands raised in surrender: two women, a young child, and a couple of men. One of the women was crying; the young boy at her legs was white as a sheet.

The man wielding the gun was named Kal Wright; he'd joined the Seers nearly a month ago. A Sleeper Seer originally, Kal had unexpectedly come and found the camp on his own. With no family, he'd joined the CityWatch as a young man but had sustained an injury that made him unfit for service. He'd then been moved to CityWatch administration, where he'd worked for nearly fifteen years before he'd felt the call to be a Seer.

Kal had always been an incredible asset to their cause—quiet and focused, never harsh or brash. Remko couldn't even think of a time when Kal had raised his voice. Now the man stood only a few feet away, a deep anger clouding his features.

Remko nodded to Sam and Kate to move left and signaled for Ramses and Neil to go right. He held up his hand for Carrington to stay where she was and advanced forward slowly. One of the women's eyes flickered in his direction and Kal turned toward him. Remko paused, as Kal pointed the gun at him.

"Stay back!" Kal yelled.

Remko raised his hands in a familiar pose of surrender. "Okay, Kal."

With Kal's attention now on Remko, Sam quickly moved in and escorted the Seers closest to him into a nearby tent and out of immediate danger. Several others stood watching but kept their distance. Kal didn't seem to notice. All of his focus was now trained on Remko, arm extended and weapon raised.

Remko attempted to take another step closer and Kal viciously shook the gun at him, advancing forward a few steps himself. "I said stay back!"

Remko nodded. "Why don't you put down the gun and we'll talk?"

Kal shook his head too quickly, his shoulders twitching, the place under his arm dark with sweat. He started muttering to himself, something too quiet for Remko to hear. Remko watched the man before him as if he were a stranger. Something was wrong; he appeared mentally broken.

"Kal, what's this about?" Remko asked.

His words snapped Kal out of his rambling murmurs and his face darkened. A look of pure hatred crossed his eyes and Remko feared for a moment that he might pull the trigger. But the storm faded and confusion and pain took its place. Kal gripped the left side of his skull with his free hand and dragged his nails through his hair over and over, mumbling again. His voice grew more frantic, less intelligible.

"Tell me what you want, Kal," Remko tried again.

"I can't remember. . . . I can't . . . *Why can't I remember?*" Kal yelled.

Remko had no idea what that meant. "Kal, just calm down."

Kal shook his head and a soft cry fell from his mouth. Remko thought he saw tears running down the man's face, but it was hard to be certain it wasn't just sweat. He glanced at Neil and Ramses, and Ramses shook his head. Kate and Sam were close too, all of them simply waiting for the signal. But Kal was a good man, a man Remko had trusted many times. His actions weren't his own. Something else had to be happening here.

"It's time," Kal said. "Time for change. 'The pact,' they said. Time for change."

"Tell me about the change," Remko said. "Why don't you come with me and—"

Suddenly Kal cried out, a short plea heavenward, his eyes still trained on Remko, his weapon still raised. He began pounding the side of his head with a balled fist, and Remko stepped forward, fearful the man would knock himself out.

Kal responded to Remko's movement with anger and let loose a single shot through the air. He missed Remko by a mile, but the sound echoed loudly off the tunnel walls and ceiling and caused panic in the camp. People started screaming. Sam didn't wait for Remko's signal. He sped forward, Kate on his heels, and dove for Kal.

The man registered Sam's approach too late and couldn't even swing his gun around before Sam took him to the ground. The gun snapped out of Kal's hand and skidded toward Neil, who swept it up and aimed it at the fallen maniac.

Neil cocked the weapon.

"Neil, hold your fire," Remko called.

"He shot at you," Neil said.

"We don't harm our own," Remko said.

Neil never took his eyes off Kal, who was now crying like a baby, facedown on the ground. His arms had been pulled behind him and strapped together by Sam, who was kneeling next to him. Remko reached Neil and placed his hand on the weapon. Neil moved his gaze and huffed, lowering the gun.

Remko looked at Kal, who was so out of sorts from his

usual manner. Muttering still, snot and tears catching the dirt on the floor and sticking it to his cheeks. "Change, change, change." The words softly echoed from Kal's lips between sobs.

Remko pitied the man and exhaled. "Take him to Connor. Maybe he can help."

"We should be locking him up," Neil said.

"Does this seem normal to you?" Remko said.

"Look around you, Remko—none of this is normal," Neil said. "Survival is our new normal. It's all we have anymore."

"We need people in order to survive," Remko said.

"Not people who threaten us."

"He needs medical attention. Something is wrong with him."

"Something is wrong with a lot of things lately."

Remko could feel the heat rising to his face. He was done fighting with this man. "Do we have a problem, Neil?"

Neil took a step closer so his face was inches from Remko's. "It's hard not to have a problem when every move we take makes me feel like my son would have been safer staying in the Authority City."

Remko's anger flared, but he couldn't ignore the way the man's words stung.

"Dad?" a soft voice whispered.

The group turned to see Corbin, Neil's son, standing outside of the closest tent. The boy looked on with worry and fascination. He was barely six, with full blond hair and crystal eyes. His gaze moved from his father's face to the gun in his father's hand to Kal, still lying facedown on the ground. The only sound was his tender cry.

Neil's body eased. The tension he'd been holding in his shoulders lifted and he tucked the gun into the back of his pants. A small wave of shame flashed across his face before he turned to throw Remko a hard glare and walked over to greet his son.

Remko's eyes followed the man, and he watched as he lifted his small child off his feet and carried him out of sight. Maybe Remko should pity Neil; he was only trying to protect his son. But anger was still the only emotion coursing through Remko's blood. He could feel it working its way to the surface and pricking at the insides of his skin. He understood Neil's concern but couldn't justify his selfishness. He was right to be worried about his son, but Remko needed to be worried about everyone else.

A hand fell on his shoulder and he swung his head around to see Carrington. She gave him a knowing nod and his anger defused slightly. He turned his attention back to Kal, who had gone quiet and still.

"Let's get him to the medical tent," Remko said, bending down to help Sam lift the fallen man.

14

Remko stepped into the medical tent where Kal was sleeping. Connor, their residing medical professional, had given the man something to help him sleep moments after they'd brought him. It had worked beautifully, and Kal had been trapped in dreamland for several hours. Wire was already in the tent standing guard over their crazed madman, even though, with the heavy restraining clamps and the sleep aid, Kal was no longer a threat. Wire looked up as Remko entered. He nodded a silent greeting.

"How are things?" Remko asked.

"Things seem to be back to normal," Connor answered. The doctor was standing beside the bed, a small medical device in his hand recording and delivering data from the wired connections attached to different points on Kal's bare-chested body. "Heart rate, mental waves, blood pressure; all in normal rhythm."

Connor and his family had been with the Seers for a while. They were another group that had come to camp on their own, having heard Aaron speak many times and feeling the need to be a part of the movement against the Authority. Remko had been happy to have Connor's set of skills at their disposal, especially since Carrington had discovered she was pregnant only a couple of months prior to their arrival. It had taken Remko and his team several runs to get all of the medical equipment they had now, but Remko had been motivated by Carrington's impending due date and was relieved to have the proper equipment when she went into labor.

Remko nodded. "You find anything?"

"I just analyzed his blood work and most of it seems very normal," Connor said.

Remko shook his head. There had to be an explanation for all of this. Kal couldn't have simply gone mad.

"But I did find small traces of a chemical that I'm still trying to identify. It seems to have been working its way out of his blood over the last several weeks. From what I can gather—and I can't confirm anything for sure—but based on its apparent path through the bloodstream it may have been deposited in the brain."

"What does that mean?" Remko asked.

"Well, I did a more in-depth brain scan and the results were . . . startling," Connor said. "Are you familiar with the way memory works?"

Remko shook his head.

"Memory is a very complex process that we still barely understand, but to give a simplified explanation, it's the continuous process of neurons firing together in the brain's cortex, the frontal lobe to be precise. Neurons deliver information back and forth through synapse highways that create neural networks. Many believe these networks act as memories. For example, you can arrive at a place and not remember how you got there because you have traveled to that place so many times that your brain is just following a hard, fast memory of the route you always take. A neural network communicates the way without you having to think about where you are going. Your memories just lead you. In fact, many doctors and scientists believe that all our mental capacities are composed of memories. That the actions we take in a given situation come from memories of either what we have done before or of what we think we should do in that situation."

Remko nodded his understanding, and Connor continued.

"Myelin, a sort of shield used to protect the connectors that create neural networks and help them function, is essential to the memory process. Looking at these deep scans of Kal's brain function, it looks like the myelin is being broken down, almost as if something were eating away at the protective barrier."

"What makes you say that?" Wire said, startling Remko. He had forgotten the boy was there with them.

"As far as I can tell, the unidentified chemical is interfering with the myelin before passing through the rest of the body via the circulatory system. If I'm right, it appears to be an intentional attempt to suppress Kal's memories."

"But why do that?" Wire asked.

"I need to research further, but the only benefit I can

see from this process would be to access the core of these neural networks," Connor said.

"I don't understand," Remko said. "For what purpose?"

"Beats me," Connor said simply.

"Is he marked?" Wire asked.

Both Connor and Remko gave Wire a questioning look. "Marked?" Connor asked.

"Seth Hale said that people in the city have been disappearing and coming back different, changed, and marked. Did you find any unusual marks on him?" Wire asked.

Connor nodded slowly. "Funny you should ask. I actually thought it was weird but not unusual enough to bring it up." He moved to the top of Kal's bed and nodded for Remko to help. "Grab his legs, will you? On three we'll turn him on his side."

"Will that wake him?" Wire asked.

Connor smiled grimly. "Not with the stuff he has running through his veins."

Remko did as he was asked and on Connor's count, they hauled the man onto his side. Wire came around the foot of the bed to see what Connor had found. Connor pointed to a perfectly round scar, maybe quarter-size in diameter, near the bottom left side of Kal's back, with a straight line running vertically through the center. It was pale, nearly blending in with Kal's skin, and hardly rose above the surface. Wire ran his fingers along the mark with fascination.

"I just thought maybe this guy had an unusual scar," Connor said.

Wire pulled Roxy from his side and snapped a photo of the mark before Remko and Connor laid the man back down. Wire studied the photo, and Remko could see the wheels turning behind his eyes.

"What are you thinking?" Remko asked.

"People are being taken, marked, changed, some returning with seemingly no recollection of where they've been. I haven't been able to stop thinking about this since Seth mentioned it to us. I've been in communication with a couple of other Sleepers, and they say that the rumored number of missing is near a hundred. The only pattern seems to be that most candidates have little or no family, like Kal. *Why* they are being taken is what everyone is concerned with, but I can't stop thinking about *where.*"

Wire paused for a moment before continuing. "A hundred hostages is a large group, and hiding them in the city would be extremely difficult, especially with all the new Authority security measures. This got me thinking about the structure Sam and Kate discovered outside the city limits to the northwest. They said people from all different stations were being led in there and that the place was surrounded by security. We haven't had time to further investigate, but it can't be a coincidence that this place exists."

Remko had nearly forgotten about the structure. He had been so focused on retrieving Selena and her girls when

Sam had reported it to him that he'd hardly given it a second thought.

"Now with what appears to be evidence of neurological tampering with a man who is clearly marked and presumably was taken at some point when he was a Sleeper Seer, it would be easy to reach the conclusion that someone is orchestrating a systematic effort to take people to this unknown facility and, well . . ."

Wire couldn't finish his thought, but Remko understood where he was headed. It was anyone's guess what might be happening to the people inside those walls.

"I'm sure I'm not the only one thinking this," Connor said, "but the Authority is the only influence large enough to be able to pull a stunt like that off."

Wire glanced at Remko; they both agreed. Could it be possible the Authority was intentionally harming its own people? And for what purpose?

The new threat this presented made Remko's mind spin. They needed more information.

"Connor, continue to run whatever tests you think might give us any indication of what happened to Kal," Remko said.

Connor nodded.

"Wire, you come with me."

Wire waved good-bye to Connor as he and Remko left the tent.

There was one person in camp who might have information, and they needed to speak with him right away.

of you or if I plan to stay long. But I figure for now we all have something in common—none of us want to live under the Authority's rule. So if you all are planning to take them down, then I wanna help."

"Maybe you can," Remko said. He nodded toward Wire, who pulled Roxy from his pocket. He handed it to Jesse, who took it with caution.

"What the heck is this?" Jesse asked.

"Her name's Roxy," Wire said. "Handle her with care."

Jesse flashed a coy grin and cradled Roxy appropriately.

"Have you seen that mark before?" Remko asked.

Jesse studied the photo on Roxy's screen for a moment and shook his head. "Does this have something to do with the man who lost his mind in camp earlier?"

"You know something about that?" Remko asked.

"Not a lot. Just mostly what I've heard."

Remko waited for him to continue.

"A couple weeks ago I was north of the city walls, out in the Old America wreckage. I'd been set up there for a few weeks when a patrol came through. I'm guessing they were searching for your group. Anyways, just a couple of guards, maybe four. I was out of sight, waiting for them to pass, when one of them started acting crazy. Similar to your man in camp today.

"The other guards didn't know what to do. They restrained him and hauled him off, but one of them stepped away to radio it in. I remember thinking it was odd because he put so much distance between himself and the rest, like he definitely didn't want the others to hear what he was saying."

"Did he mention what was happening?" Wire asked.

Jesse shook his head. "Nope, just said the patient hadn't transitioned well. And then something about getting the patient back to ground zero."

Wire turned his attention to Remko. "Maybe that's what they call the structure?"

Remko's mind had already gone there.

"What structure?" Jesse asked.

Remko hesitated. He wasn't sure how much information he wanted to give Jesse, but if he could be of help, then they needed him. "Had you heard of ground zero before?" Remko asked.

"Never. I just assumed it was code for barracks or something," Jesse said.

"It may be something else. Have you been out far west recently, to the gathering of hills?"

"Not that far."

"There's a new active facility hidden in a valley out there, and we think that may be where people are being taken."

"Taken, like the crazy rumors running through the city? You think they have merit?"

Wire jumped in. "A couple of our scouts found the location and saw people being herded inside."

Remko glanced at Wire. "We should discuss this with the others and make a plan. Will you gather them?"

Wire nodded and excused himself. He took a couple of steps to his left and disappeared behind a tent.

Remko turned back to Jesse. "I would appreciate it if you kept this information to yourself."

Jesse dipped his chin in affirmation and Remko moved to leave.

"I could be more useful, you know," Jesse said.

Remko paused and glanced back toward the archer.

"I heard about your friend in the city," Jesse said.

Remko had been pushing back thoughts of Dodson for the last couple of hours while trying to regain control of camp, but he knew their plan of action still needed to be determined. "You seem to hear a lot," Remko said.

Jesse tilted his head to the left and ran his palm across the back of his neck. "I've learned to listen well."

Remko smirked. That was a good skill to have.

"I know the city, and if you're planning to go in after him, I could help," Jesse said.

Remko didn't doubt it, but he knew that wouldn't go over well with the rest of the team. Trust was a hard commodity to come by when you were running for your life. And Remko couldn't blame them. Although he did find himself intrigued by Jesse's skills and presence, there was still much they didn't know about the boy. And his sudden interest in the group and willingness to help pricked at a tiny feeling in Remko's gut that warned against Jesse's intentions.

"It's a dangerous trek; it would mean risking your life," Remko said.

Jesse scoffed with a half smile forming on his face. "I live outside the city and against the wishes of the only form of government we have left. Breathing is a risk."

"Why not live in the city?"

Jesse's expression changed and he dropped his eyes from Remko's face. "That's a long story."

"One I'd like to hear sometime."

Jesse eyed Remko tentatively, but not long enough for Remko to get a good sense of what he was feeling. It was clearly something Jesse wasn't ready to talk about.

"I think for now it's best for you to stay in camp and work with Ramses to learn the way things work around here. That is, if you plan to stay," Remko said.

Jesse shrugged, which was becoming a very common gesture for him, and Remko nodded. "Whatever you decide is fine. I'll send Ramses to find you later."

Remko turned to walk away but after a couple of steps paused. He turned back to tell Jesse he didn't have to be alone anymore, but the boy was gone.

15

Dodson Rogue sat inside his cold cell and stared up at the stone ceiling he'd now committed to memory. Each nick, each bump that protruded from the flat surface bore witness to the time and weather that had left their marks across the stone. The silence was the stone's constant companion and had now become Dodson's only friend.

"Just you and me," Dodson whispered to himself.

In the beginning, the quiet itself had felt like punishment. The dragging hours had swallowed him in stillness. There had been no escape, no place to run or retreat. Dodson wasn't a fool; he'd known what giving Remko his chip would mean. He'd actually been surprised at the length of time he'd remained free. He had imagined that within hours of Remko and Carrington's escape from the city, the CityWatch guards he'd mentored would come for him. Lock him in this very cell and then watch as he was executed.

But time had been cruel, and it had tricked him into believing that maybe he would retain his freedom. Of course, after Ian's demise, Dodson's time had been up. Damien Gold was infinitely crueler than his predecessor, and since the day Dodson had been arrested, he'd waited for death.

Not that he wanted to die. He didn't view death as some kind of morbid final freedom. Death was just death, inevitable for everyone but coming for Dodson sooner than most. He had known prison execution would be in his future. The moment that chip had left his fingers and slipped into Remko's hand, Dodson had prepared himself for this cell. What he hadn't expected was the time.

He'd been in this prison for over eight months, which was eight months longer than he'd expected. He had betrayed his city, the Authority, his calling. Death by execution was the only outcome. Unlike Isaac, who had insanity to fall back on, Dodson had betrayed his station with a clear mind. With more clarity than he'd ever experienced. He'd known, beyond a shadow of a doubt, that handing Remko his chip was the only move he could make.

It was the right move, and Dodson had always been a sucker for what was right. That's why he'd always found great pride in his family's heritage. His father and grandfather had led the CityWatch, just as Dodson had. It was the ultimate position of right and wrong.

Dodson sucked on a dying cigarette that he held between his fingers and watched the smoke rise as he let it slip past his teeth. He'd been wrong—silence wasn't his only friend. A couple of CityWatch guards still felt some sort of loyalty to him, and he was thankful for it every week when a dozen packs of cigarettes showed up with his morning meal.

It wasn't until Dodson had been instated into the Authority that he'd begun to see the evil that lived among the men there. Dodson had always tried to do what was right, but some things had been out of his control. So when Remko had come to him, he'd known the right thing to do was to set the boy free.

Of course, Dodson had no idea that setting Remko free would bring about such a rebellion against the Authority. He felt a smile threatening to surface. The thought that his actions had caused such upheaval initially made him feel very uncomfortable, but now he found the idea revitalizing. Although he hadn't always agreed with the ways of the Authority, he had never enjoyed the idea of a single man disturbing the balance that their ancestors had fought for. He still suspected that Aaron was a danger to their way of life. But Damien was worse. And anything that made the vessels in Damien's head pulse made Dodson smile. He and his original enemy, Aaron, now had a common enemy in Damien, which made them comrades-in-arms.

"Who would have thought—me and that crazed hippie, comrades," Dodson said.

"Crazed hippie?" a man said on the other side of the steel-barred door that locked Dodson in his cage.

Dodson sat up, dropped what remained of his cigarette, and snuffed it out with the heel of his boot. "Who's there?" He strained to see the man who belonged to the voice, but the dark prison shadowed his face.

"I'll admit, I have been called an array of colorful

names, but crazed hippie is new. I like it," the man said and stepped closer to the bars so the small stream of light from the window at the end of the hall stretched across his face.

Dodson's breath caught in his throat at the sight of the famous rebel. In the many months Dodson and the Authority had spent searching for Aaron, Dodson had never actually seen the man. The deep blue of his eyes was overwhelming, and Dodson instantly felt a pull at something that lay dormant inside his chest. *Hope.*

He shoved the odd feeling away and felt his old tactical training take over. This man was the enemy, yet he was standing inside the Authority prison. How had he managed to get past the guards? How did he expect to get away? Dodson should shout out to the guards—he knew they couldn't be too far away—and have this man arrested. Maybe he could trade the capture of the rebels' leader for his own freedom? Dodson knew the thought was preposterous, but then, so was the man standing before him.

"You look worried," Aaron said.

Dodson cleared his face of emotions and silently cursed himself for letting his composure slip. "How did you get in here?"

"I walked."

"You walked?"

"Yes, I enjoy walking. It clears the mind, don't you think?"

"What are you doing here?"

"Now that's the question, isn't it?"

Dodson could feel irritation itching at the insides of his brain. Was all conversation with this man going to be in riddles?

"You really are a fool," Dodson said.

Aaron smiled and nodded. "Perhaps, but I am free."

Dodson angrily huffed. "Not for long. Eventually they'll catch you and lock you up just like the rest of us."

"That may be true, but you misunderstand freedom. Bars won't change my status, just as they don't affect yours."

Dodson stood and crossed his arms over his chest. "So, you're the man Arianna Carson died for?"

Sorrow and pain crossed Aaron's face. His eyes dropped to the stone floor and Dodson felt a stab of regret. Dodson noticed a tear slip down Aaron's cheek and he felt a heavy, uncomfortable silence pass between them.

"A terrible loss. She did not die for me, but for truth," Aaron said.

"Your truth," Dodson replied.

Aaron raised his head and found Dodson's gaze. "Her truth."

Something in the man's words shot through Dodson's chest and once again ignited that forgotten feeling of hope. He fought not to show any reaction and held Aaron's gaze.

"And now you will lead Remko and the others to the same fate?" Dodson questioned.

"Remko will choose his own path, just as all of us do."

"No, he is a soldier, trained to follow orders."

"You're worried about him."

"Of course I'm worried about him! I sent him on this journey."

"He was destined for this journey long before you sent him."

Dodson aggressively spit to the side and grabbed for another cigarette. Why was he even listening to this madman? Again he considered shouting for the guards, but a tiny pocket of curiosity kept him quiet. Besides, what did he owe the Authority? Nothing.

Why were people following this man? It was a question Dodson had been asking himself since the first sightings of Aaron. And why was he here now? He surely knew that Dodson didn't support his way of life. Didn't he recognize the danger he was putting himself in?

Dodson lit the cigarette and inhaled deeply. He turned back to face Aaron and took a step closer to the bars. "Again, what are you doing here? How did you get in here—and don't say you walked! Why come? Why risk it? What's the purpose to all of this anyway? What are you hoping to accomplish?" The questions slipped out one after the other as if through an unplugged dam.

"So many questions," Aaron said.

"I'm trying to figure out who you are."

"I'm the same as you. We are all the same. Brothers and sisters, if not all of one heart and one mind. To understand me, just look for the truth you already possess."

"And what truth is that?"

Aaron smiled. "Do you really want to know?"

The question struck Dodson as odd, and he pondered it for a moment. *Did* he want to know? He hadn't been raised in a society that asked people what they wanted. Citizens were taught as children that certain things were best for them and others were not, and there wasn't much choice in these matters. If he said yes, what would Aaron say? Would he fill his head with lies that would lead him down the wrong path? If he completely abandoned the truths he knew, what would be left? Who would he be?

His mind ran in invisible circles, searching for signs of clarity, but things had already begun to fall into chaos.

If the Authority was all-knowing, then why did he betray them and give Remko the chip?

Because Remko needed to be free.

Why? Were they not all called to follow the Authority's ways?

But the Authority is wrong.

Can truth be wrong?

I don't know.

Maybe the Authority wasn't truth?

Dodson shook his head and took another drag of the smoking tobacco stick between his fingers. This man was known to brainwash his followers; surely that's all this was.

Then why does he call me to hope? The thought penetrated his mind before he could shut it out. With it, he felt a ripple of fear.

"Change can be fearful," Aaron said. His voice pulled Dodson from his thoughts.

"I'm not afraid. I know my days are numbered. Damien has made sure of that," Dodson said.

"Yes, Damien. I haven't had the pleasure of meeting him yet."

Dodson chuckled and looked up at the ceiling before taking another drag. "*Pleasure* isn't the term I'd use." Then he sat up straighter as one thought rose above the rest. He turned his gaze back to Aaron. "Tell Remko not to come for me."

"Remko makes his own choices," Aaron said.

"The Authority will use my execution as a ploy. I'm not worth dying for."

"Your fear and lack of self-worth are what keep you imprisoned. Let them go and you can be free."

"Has anyone ever told you that you sound like a crazy person?"

Aaron laughed and his voice echoed off of the stone walls. The sound warmed the constant chill in Dodson's bones and added another layer of complexity to the man before him. He couldn't tell if Aaron was mad or perfectly sane, but he couldn't deny how much he was beginning to like him. It suddenly didn't seem quite so crazy that people were following him.

The strange man's laughter died out and the seriousness of the situation returned. Dodson was still in prison, he was still sentenced to be executed, and Remko was still going to try and save him, endangering his own life in the process.

As if reading his thoughts, Aaron spoke. "Even if I wanted to stop Remko, I couldn't. He does believe you are worth dying for."

"He's as crazy as you, then."

"Actually, he's much like you."

"Stubborn and grumpy?"

Aaron smiled. "Full of fear and carrying the weight of all those around him."

Dodson took the final drag of his cigarette and flicked it against the ground. "He should be afraid. The Authority will have them all killed if they're caught. Fear will make him sharp."

"No, fear will be his end. It follows him, tortures him, weighs him down. It keeps him imprisoned. It keeps him from freedom."

"He already lives outside the city. Isn't that freedom?"

"That sort of freedom is an illusion. True freedom isn't defined by where we live. It is much deeper than that."

"To be free even in prison."

"Exactly."

Dodson paused and considered his words. "All I want is for that boy to be free." He was speaking more to himself than to Aaron, but his words were true.

"Me too," Aaron said.

Dodson half smiled at the madman and nodded. "Then we are comrades."

Aaron chuckled. "Who would have thought?"

16

Remko could feel the weight of the next couple of hours pushing against his chest. Early that morning, the Seer scouts had split into two groups: Ramses, Carrington, and Neil had gone to try to collect more information on the facility that might be the location of the missing people, while Remko, Kate, Sam, and Wire headed toward the city to rescue Dodson. His execution was scheduled for tomorrow, and they had no time to waste.

They knew the Authority would be expecting them, but the group had decided they couldn't simply stand by and let him die. So they would risk it.

The path before them was familiar because it looked like many they had traveled before, but their approach was foreign. Usually, due to the enhanced security around the prison, their group waited until prisoners were moved for execution before trying to apprehend them. Today, they knew they didn't have time for that; going into the prison was their only chance.

Thankfully they had a Sleeper on the inside, a CityWatch soldier whom Remko had known while serving. The boy was loyal to Dodson and had agreed to help if he could. His assistance would be essential if they were going to be able to pull this off.

The sun was just starting to rise, warming them from the east as they reached the water main that ran underneath the city wall. They had several hours before Dodson would be transported for execution. There were only a couple of tunnels left that remained unguarded, and Remko worried about how much longer they would even have access to these. The Authority had increased its CityWatch recruiting numbers, giving them the manpower they needed to spread out like ants.

Sam moved ahead and yanked back the tunnel's steel covering, dropping through the opening, the others following behind him. Remko entered last, closing them inside before running to catch up. Sam had their way mapped out since this wasn't a usual route they traveled. This tunnel was like all the rest: cold, metallic, and smelling of mold and stale air.

Remko's mind went to the other scout group. They had planned to leave camp at sunrise, as they didn't have as far to go and weren't limited on time. He hated that Carrington had insisted on going. She'd tried to come with them for Dodson, but Remko had fought her on it, which had only made her more stubborn and determined not to be left behind.

He'd tried to explain to her that knowing she was anywhere but safe in camp would only distract him, but she didn't seem concerned with that. She hated feeling helpless.

Ramses and Neil were with her, but still, worrying about her would only open his mind up for mistakes.

He wiped her face from his thoughts and focused on the task at hand. Remko had been trained that fear was a go-to emotion to have in battle because it made you smart and alert. Aaron taught that fear crippled and served as a handicap against seeing truth. Both teachings seemed unimportant when you were trying to fight fear off.

Aaron would tell him not to fight it but to let it go. Remko had done his best. He had tried to see himself as more than what life was blatantly telling him. Tried to find the truth of his identity, the one that could help him let go of his fear. The one Aaron promised would free him from failure and pressure. But each time Remko tried to focus on letting go, his logic reminded him that fear was real. Pressure was real. People did fail, and when they failed, other people died. You couldn't just let go of reality.

Remko tried to keep his mind still as they traveled the length of the tunnels, turning when necessary, the distance feeling longer than it was, the pressure building as they neared their destination. Time stretched, and silence engulfed them except for their heavy breathing and steady footsteps against the steel tunnel floor.

The others slowed ahead of him and Remko knew they had arrived. The tunnel had brought them to an old drainage pipe underneath the prison. The space was too small for most people to fit through, but thankfully they had Kate. The pipe would lead Kate up into a nearby abandoned part of the prison. Once inside, she would make her way to an old boiler room where the larger entrance from the tunnel was located. It was bolted from the other side with a mechanical lock that Remko and his team couldn't access from inside the tunnel and Wire couldn't disable remotely with Roxy. Kate would have to pick the lock, something none of them had ever done, but Wire had researched the old technique and given Kate a tutorial.

Kate moved to the small round opening and placed both of her palms inside the opening to hoist herself up. Wire stepped to her left and she paused. Roxy beeped in his hand softly and an annoyed look flashed across Kate's face.

"Any day, kid," Kate said.

Wire ignored her dig and pulled up the guards' rotating schedule. "According to this, you'll have six minutes to move through the pipe and into the boiler room while the night shift transfers out and the morning shift transfers in."

"Got it," Kate said and yanked herself up.

"That is, if we have the correct information," Wire said.

Kate paused mid-hoist and struggled to regain her strength. Sam moved to help her up and she rolled her eyes at them both for interfering. She shimmied into the tight space and Sam stuck his head in after her.

"Be careful," he called.

"Yeah, yeah," her voice echoed back out into the open space. After a couple of long seconds, her shuffling stopped echoing back to them.

"Let's go," Remko said. They traveled the extra fifty yards to where they were to meet Kate at the larger entrance. It sat directly above them, only a little bigger than the hole Kate had just disappeared through. Remko saw Sam look at the hole apprehensively and knew it was going to be tight.

They waited.

Wire watched Roxy like a hawk, and Remko tried to keep track of time in his head. It felt like it had been longer than six minutes and Remko recognized the worry in Sam's face. Remko distracted himself with thoughts of what came next. Getting inside the prison was the easy part. They had timed it so they would be moving during a shift change, which would help but could not guarantee that they wouldn't meet any unfriendly company.

They weren't completely sure where Dodson was being held, but if the prison system was similar to how it had been when Remko was a CityWatch soldier, then he'd be on the north side, probably in isolation. He may have betrayed the Authority, but he'd still been an Authority member. That would also serve his rescuers' purpose. He'd have a larger cell and be kept away from other prisoners. Their Sleeper friend would be trying to switch rotations with one of the guards scheduled to patrol the north side, so if they ran into any guards, they would only need to worry about overpowering one.

Once they navigated to the cell where hopefully Dodson was being kept, the risky part would then be unlocking his cell door. The locks operated on a distinct software system that changed the code for each individual lock every hour. This was a new improvement since the prison overhaul. Wire could crack the unique code, but it took time, and in their situation, time equaled risk. Wire would have to recode the lock without tripping any alerts inside the system before a guard did a pass through that section of the prison. The other problem was that the north-side cell block was a dead end, so the only way back out was the way they'd come in. If they did get caught, they had no exit strategy. All in all, the plan was as crazy as it sounded, but it was the only chance Dodson had.

Remko was about to ask Wire if he'd given Kate the wrong directions when the grate overhead creaked open and her head popped through. Relief flooded all three of them as Kate threw them a wink and Sam hoisted himself up and through the hole. He fit, but barely.

Wire went up next, and Remko followed. His eyes swept the dark room as he pulled his legs through the opening. The space was larger than he'd imagined, the walls crowded with old artifacts that didn't function any longer, most of which he couldn't even identify. Metal fencing split the area and hid some of the nonworking machinery. A single steel door with a small glass window stood slightly ajar in the far left wall.

"Any trouble?" Sam asked Kate.

"Nothing I couldn't handle," she replied with a sassy spark. Sam didn't look amused and she huffed. "I'm fine.

I had to reroute once because Wire's directions weren't completely accurate."

Wire glanced down at Roxy's screen, a puzzled look in his eyes. "I sent you the exact building schematics. There's no way—"

"Chill," Kate said. "I found it, didn't I?"

Wire swallowed and nodded. Remko could sense Wire didn't like that he had potentially placed Kate in unnecessary trouble.

"Give us a rundown, Wire," Remko said.

Wire refocused on Roxy's screen and tapped quickly as her familiar beeps sang to him. Once he'd rechecked the CityWatch rotation schedule, he pulled up the inner workings of the prison layout. The others gathered around as he pointed out the way.

"The shift transition only gives us relief on the way in. Once we find Dodson, getting him back out is where we run into extra eyes," Wire said.

"We knew that coming in, so we deal with it as we go," Remko said.

"Right. We have a little less than seven minutes before the full force of daily shifts are running."

"Then what are we waiting for?" Kate asked.

Remko gave Sam a quick nod and he took off to the exit first. He glanced out around the open door and signaled back to the rest that the way was clear. He slipped out with Kate, Wire, and Remko right behind.

The hallway was narrow and dark. Little light was

needed since this part of the jail was vacant. After a couple yards, the small hallway bled into the larger stone corridors that were patrolled by guards.

Sam paused and glanced around before stepping out into the main traffic. Again they found the walkway empty, as Wire had predicted, and they moved.

Much like the thin hallway, these walkways were dim; a string of yellowed lights hanging from the ceiling every couple of feet created deep, dark shadows along the path. With quick, synchronized steps they flew down one long passage, taking a left as indicated by Sam, and down another similar stone walkway. This one was well lit, so it was probably usually manned. Remko kept his breathing regulated, trying not to let his nerves get the best of him. He knew at any moment a guard could come around one of these corners and they would have to act fast.

Sam held up his hand for them to pause when they came to the next turn and he flattened himself against the wall, stepping out of the main light. The others followed as they heard a stream of conversation bounce around them.

"I can't even remember the last time I had a full night's sleep. Man, these double shifts are killing me," a male voice said.

"This is my third shift in a row," another voice replied.

Remko pressed himself deeper into the wall and held his breath as two CityWatch guards strode past the hallway they were tucked into. The guards didn't even glance in their direction, both caught up in their conversation and completely oblivious to the imminent threat. Their voices continued to float down the hall and Sam waited until they were gone before risking another glance around the edge to see if the passage was clear. He nodded back to Remko and they moved.

They passed by empty cells and occupied cells. Prisoners glanced at them with puzzled expressions and Remko realized they hadn't considered what the other prisoners might do. Thankfully there were only a few, and by the time they made the last right turn into the north portion of the prison, none of the captives had given away their position.

The north side was slightly different from the rest of the prison. It was exactly as Remko remembered. This was the older section of the original Old Americas building where the pathways weren't quite as straight or smooth. The walls were aged stone and the bars etched with rust. The cells were larger too; only a couple on either side of the walkway. All of them were empty as the Seers traveled forward. Cell after cell sat unoccupied and Remko could feel his heart thundering up into his throat. What if they'd been wrong and Dodson wasn't here? What if he had already been relocated and a string of CityWatch guards was waiting for them around the corner?

Remko was about to suggest that they head back and regroup when Sam signaled for them to stop. He motioned Remko toward the front of the line and pointed to a cell at the end of the left hallway. A person sat inside. The smell of tobacco smoke and body odor floated toward Remko and he almost laughed in relief. He slowly approached the cell and watched as Dodson's head shot up at the sound of shuffling feet. The hard expression that was seared into Remko's memory melted from Dodson's face as he saw Remko's team approach.

Dodson shook his head. "Stupid kid."

Remko shrugged and inspected his former boss. His face was dirty and unshaven. He looked as if he hadn't been eating properly, and his eyes were filled with a strange mixture of sorrow and exhaustion. Anger flared under Remko's skin and he glanced at Wire. The boy was already moving toward the lock.

"The system on those is different," Dodson said.

Wire didn't even glance up. "We know."

Dodson's eyes widened and he chuckled. "Brains and attitude—my favorite two things."

Remko approached the bars and grasped one. "How are you?"

Dodson shrugged and took a draw from the cigarette in his hand. "Can't really complain. I've had a nice, much-needed break from the CityWatch brats, so I could be doing worse."

"Are we seriously risking our necks for a man who is just going to keel over from lung cancer?" Kate asked under her breath. Quiet enough to sound as if she was trying to hide it but intentionally loud enough that everyone still heard her.

"She's right," Dodson said. "You shouldn't be here."

"What did you expect me to do?" Remko asked.

"I expected you to take my chip and get as far away from this hellhole as possible. But instead you keep showing back up. Makes me wonder what the point was."

Remko said nothing. How could he explain that he wasn't sure himself why he was still around? That leaving was exactly what he thought he and Carrington would be doing but that plans had changed and somehow he'd ended up trapped in a role he felt he was fighting against. How could he explain that he had no idea what he was doing anymore and that each day was just another battle for survival?

Dodson flicked the butt of his cigarette onto the floor and its smoke rose into the air. He stood and walked to meet Remko face-to-face. Closer up, Remko could see the lines of sleepless nights carved into Dodson's skin.

"Take your friends and get outta here," Dodson said, "before a gang of guards walks around that corner."

Remko ignored him. "Wire?"

"Almost there; this configuration is tougher than I thought," Wire said.

"That's an order, soldier," Dodson said.

Remko couldn't keep the smile from his face. "That doesn't really work anymore."

Dodson's face flushed red and Remko could almost feel the heat drifting off his skin. Clearly time in solitary hadn't calmed his temper.

"They'll kill you if you're caught," Dodson said. "Don't be more ignorant than you've already been."

"Your appreciation for what we're risking here is overwhelming," Kate said.

"I don't usually applaud stupidity. Remko, please, I am not worth all your lives."

"I'm not going to let them kill you because of me," Remko said. "End of discussion."

Dodson looked a bit startled, and then his eyes softened. "What I did is on me. It was my call. You are not responsible for me."

Remko ignored him and stepped toward Wire and glanced over his shoulder. "Come on, Wire."

"This is a complicated process; I'm working as quickly as possible."

"He was right," Dodson said.

Remko glanced back at the man and saw that he was shaking his head.

"Go figure, that crazed hippie would be right," Dodson said.

"What do you mean?" Remko asked, but he knew exactly whom Dodson was talking about. "You spoke with Aaron?"

Dodson didn't answer right away, and a long moment of silence engulfed the cell.

"Done," Wire said, and the lock on Dodson's prison cell popped open. Remko stepped forward and yanked the gate open with a screech.

"We need to move," Sam said.

Remko met Dodson's eyes. The weary man just stood

there as if he wasn't going to come, and then something jarred him to life and he stepped out. They headed back into the maze of the north side, taking the turns quickly. Sam was leading the charge and took them down the long hallway that they had planned to use to circle back to the boiler room.

The group was halfway down the hall when two guards rounded the corner at the opposite end. Everyone froze, and before Remko's team could react, both guards raised their weapons. Remko didn't recognize either of them, but he hoped one of them was their Sleeper.

"Hands up," one of them said, stepping forward, and the group did as they were told.

Before anyone could make another move, a third guard turned the corner and a pit of dread opened up in Remko's gut. It was Lieutenant Smith. The senior officer's face grew dark as his eyes landed on Remko and Dodson. He set his jaw like a rock and stepped past the other two guards.

Smith held Remko's gaze and said nothing. The sound of breathing filled the small space. Remko knew there was no escape behind them; the only way out was through the CityWatch barricade ahead. Remko and Smith had never been mortal enemies, but they had never been friends either. Of all the CityWatch soldiers Remko had interacted with, Smith had been one of the most loyal to the Authority, and now that he was serving as interim acting commander, Remko feared his loyalty had only grown.

Looking into his eyes now, Remko knew he'd kill them all where they stood if he needed to.

"Arrest them," Smith said. The two guards moved to obey, slipping past their commander and taking the hallway slowly as they moved toward Remko and his team. The one on the left caught Remko's eye and gave an ever-so-slight nod. Remko didn't dare look at Sam to see if he had caught the same message for fear of alerting Smith.

Smith spoke softly into the chip at his wrist and Remko knew he was calling for backup. They had no more time.

"Keep your hands where we can see them," the guard on the right said.

Once the two guards were only a couple of feet away, Remko moved. He charged straight for the guard on the right and took him to the ground. Simultaneously the Sleeper on the left fired a bullet that ricocheted off the stone wall. Remko scrambled with the guard on the floor, knocking his weapon away and landing several hard punches across his jaw.

He rolled off and back up onto his feet, leaving the guard he'd attacked still moaning on the ground. The others were gone, back the way they'd come. He saw the back of Smith's head disappear around the corner as the guard ran after them. Remko raced to catch up. When he rounded the corner, he saw Sam, Kate, Wire, and Dodson charging forward with Smith screaming on their heels. Then their exit was cut off as another pair of guards emerged ahead of them, and Sam yanked the group down a side hallway as shots rang out. Smith followed them down the hallway and out of sight.

Another shot fired, this one from behind Remko. He ducked to avoid the bullet and saw that the Sleeper guard was positioned with his gun raised. The two new guards' faces filled with shock over being fired at by one of their own, but it faded quickly as they advanced on Remko and the CityWatch traitor.

Remko grabbed the Sleeper and moved after Sam and the others down the side hallway, the sound of boots heavy behind them. More shouts echoed around them, and Remko feared more men had joined the pursuit. He tried to stay in the shadows as they rushed down the path while shouts from ahead and behind collided, making it hard to follow the voices he recognized.

Kate's voice bounced near his ear and he knew he was closing the distance between him and his group. He pushed himself to move faster, nearly dragging the Sleeper beside him now. After a couple of long strides, he was back in the thick of the moving chaos. Smith had caught them and was fighting with Sam, the two evenly matched in size and strength, while Kate looked on helplessly. Wire was trying to yank Dodson farther down the hallway, but he was resisting and finally broke free, rushing back into the action. Remko turned to see that at least four more guards were quickly approaching. They needed to get to the boiler room.

Sam cried out and Remko glanced over to see him

stumble backward, gripping his arm. He fell, giving Smith the opportunity to reach for his weapon and raise it toward Sam, hate pulsing from his veins.

"Smith," a voice challenged, and Remko saw Dodson advancing on the lieutenant.

The scene seemed to freeze then, as if the movements couldn't be stopped but couldn't be sped up either. Smith turned his aim toward Dodson, and without taking a breath he pulled the trigger. A deafening shot exploded through the dark walkway and the bullet met its target with deadly accuracy. Dodson's head snapped backward and his body crashed to the floor.

The hallway paused—even Smith—as the realization of what had happened seeped into their minds. Something snapped in Remko's brain and he felt a bloodcurdling scream spring from his chest. He was moving before he could register action, his body smashing into Smith. It happened before Smith could prepare himself and Remko took him to the ground.

The hallway moved back into motion, but Remko hardly noticed. He only had one thought.

Kill.

He placed himself over Smith, a knee on either side to pin the man to the ground, and started attacking his face. Punch after punch extended from his arm and mashed against flesh and bone. Smith struggled against Remko's hold, but Remko only held more tightly and focused on the rage pouring from his skin. Smith's eyes rolled into the back of his head and his body stopped fighting, but that didn't slow Remko's anger.

"Remko! Remko," a voice called through the dull pulsing of blood in Remko's ears. He felt dizzy with fury as he looked toward the sound of his name. The scene around him was grim. The hallway was filled with moving bodies. Wire, Kate, and Sam were outnumbered and tangled up in combat with CityWatch guards on all sides. The floor was darkening with blood that pooled around Dodson's head and spread out like fingers along the cracks in the stone floor. Other bodies lay strewed around, whether dead or unconscious Remko didn't know.

He looked down at the motionless man clasped between his knees. Smith's face was bloodied and already starting to swell, as struggling breaths expanded his chest. Remko stood up from the damage he'd caused and felt a shake start in his fingers. His knuckles were covered with his opponent's blood and he brushed them against the sides of his shirt.

"Remko!" Sam yelled again. Remko was jarred out of his zombie-like state and knew they had to move if any of them wanted to live. He saw that Kate had managed to overcome the guard she'd been fighting and was helping Wire, while Sam was struggling against three soldiers at once.

Remko moved to join the fight when another shot rang out across the small space and Kate yelped in pain. She stumbled forward and hit the ground on her hands and knees. Remko could see blood draining from the back of her calf. She'd been hit.

Ahead of them, another wave of guards was storming toward them. Sam cried out and Remko watched as the three guards got the better of him. He glanced up at Remko. "Get my sister out of here."

Understanding crashed against Remko's skull as he realized what Sam was asking. He wanted them to leave him behind. That wasn't an option, but Remko knew if those guards reached them they would all surely die. He had to get Kate and Wire somewhere safe.

Remko's training took over then, pushing away the pain still ripping at his heart so he could focus. He rushed to Kate as Wire managed to knock the single guard he'd been fighting to the ground. Remko swept Kate up into his arms and Wire moved to help.

"We have to get out of here," Remko said.

"What about Sam?" Wire asked.

Kate was moaning, but she was lucid enough to understand what Remko was suggesting. "We can't leave him!"

"We'll come back for him," Remko said as he took off with Kate in his arms toward the boiler room, Wire on his heels.

Kate thrashed in his arms with what little strength she had left. "No! Remko, no. Stop. Put me down. Sam!" Her voice echoed off the stone walls as they traveled. Remko knew they were still a couple of hallways and turns away from their destination. From somewhere behind them, Remko heard a guard yell, "Follow them!" and he knew it wouldn't be long before they had company. He surged forward, trying not to think about Dodson's dead corpse bleeding in the hallway behind him, trying not to think about the near-dead man with Remko's fist marks across his face, trying not to think about Sam.

Kate was weakening in his arms and he knew he couldn't let her pass out. They needed to patch her wound, but they couldn't stop until they were safe. With a final dig into his reserves of survival energy, Remko turned into the dark hallway that led to the boiler room. His arms ached from Kate's weight, his legs stung from the continuous sprint, but he felt a surge of power when he saw the boiler door.

Wire, who had somehow managed to keep up, followed Remko inside the room and rushed over to open the escape hatch. Angry voices drifted into the room and Remko knew they were out of time. He searched the room, seeing a large contraption he didn't recognize, and laid Kate on the floor. He moved to the contraption and gave a shove. It was incredibly heavy.

"Wire," he called. Wire slammed the boiler room door shut and moved to help. With several labored huffs, they managed to push the steel monster from its place against the wall to sit in front of the door. Remko knew that wouldn't hold for long, but it would give them a head start. He also knew that sealing themselves in here meant leaving Sam behind indefinitely. Remko had no choice but to ignore the screaming in his mind. "Let's go," he said.

"But—" Wire started.

"What choice do we have?" Remko could see the

understanding melt across Wire's face, but he couldn't wait for him to process this. "Now, Wire!"

Remko dropped down into the underground tunnel system and extended his arms as Wire lowered Kate. Once she was fully through, Wire dropped inside and yanked the overhead grate shut. Then they were running again, through the dark tunnel. Remko's mind was yelling that he couldn't leave Sam, that they would kill Sam just as they had killed Larkin, just as they had killed Dodson, but he knew going back would be suicide. He'd never make it to Sam before he himself was killed. His legs shook with pain and his mind throbbed with cruel reality.

This rescue mission he'd brought them on had been a complete failure. He'd only gotten Dodson killed, and now probably Sam. His hands shook, covered in Smith's blood. His shoulders were tense with the effort of carrying Kate, and his whole body ached with grief. His mind tortured him with images of Dodson lying on the floor and Sam ending up the same way.

The mission had failed. He had failed.

17

Carrington stared down into the valley below. The ground was dotted with groupings of trees and foliage, and small hills rolled on all sides, hiding the building from being spotted by anyone who might be casually passing by. Neil and Ramses stood close, both of them surveying the strange facility for the first time. The three of them had left camp at sunrise and made the trek quickly with little discussion of what they'd do once they got there. They had scant information about what they would find. That was their mission—discovery. They needed to know more about this new potential threat.

The building below was large, longer than it was wide. Dozens of windows lined the sides of the structure, but only a handful of them appeared to be in use. Oddly, most of the windows had been covered—perhaps painted—from the inside.

Guards were scattered around the base of the building. They didn't seem to be arrayed in any pattern; most were clustered together to chat and pass the time. Carrington scanned the roof and found it empty. There was a sense of laziness in the stances and motions of the guards. They clearly weren't expecting any intruders, and Carrington hoped she and her partners could use that to their advantage.

Carrington, Ramses, and Neil were not looking for any trouble; in fact, they were hoping to avoid it at all costs. They only wanted information. In order to acquire that, they would need to get inside. But they were moving blind. Thanks to Neil and Wire, they had access to blueprints and other plans for most of the structures in the Authority City, but they had no schematics for this building. It was foreign to them. However, Neil had been a leading city architect and understood a building's structure better than most.

Carrington watched Neil assess what was before them. He nodded to their left and started to move. They followed quickly, wondering what he was thinking. They moved several yards before Neil stopped and nodded toward the back of the building.

"That will be the best place to enter," Neil said.

"Are you sure?" Carrington asked.

"I haven't seen the inner workings of the structure, but it's a twenty-first-century model."

"It's an Old America building?" Ramses asked.

"Definitely. The outer layer that's plastered over the walls isn't something we would have chosen had this building been recently built. The materials used in this structure are too outdated for it to have been constructed within the last fifty or a hundred years."

"What does that mean for us?" Carrington asked.

"It means that it may have a similar interior layout to buildings I've seen inside the Authority City. There is an old structure in the Cattle Lands that favors this one. I've been inside that building before. If this one is the same, then entering through the back exit should bring us into a small hallway designed for emergency exiting only."

"But there's no way to know that the inside of this building is the same as the one in the Cattle Lands," Ramses said.

"Like I said, it's going to be a risk either way," Neil replied.

Carrington watched as a single guard paced from corner to corner of the back wall. He would walk back and forth a couple times before rounding the corner to joke with another guard stationed along the north side of the building. Even if the interior was what Neil predicted, and even if they could get to the back entrance without being spotted, they would still have to get inside. From here it looked impossible.

"Let's say we get past the guards—will the back door be unlocked for us to use?" Ramses asked.

"Doubtful," someone said from behind.

Neil spun, already yanking his weapon from his belt, Carrington and Ramses following suit. Jesse stepped out from the shade of a tall tree and yanked his hood down from his head.

"What are you doing here?" Neil demanded. He aimed his gun at the archer.

Jesse didn't appear afraid of the weapon pointed at him. He kept his arms hanging loosely at his sides and didn't bother to look in Neil's direction. He focused his attention instead on Carrington. She noticed how warm his brown eyes were. The way his hair lifted with the wind, the youthfulness of his face. In this light he looked like a boy, even though she suspected he was probably not much younger than she. Her mothering instincts took over and she felt an unexpected ache in her chest at the thought of his past. Had he always been alone? Had he ever been cared for and loved, watched over so he could just be a child? Or had he always been struggling to survive on his own?

Carrington saw something else in his eyes that she recognized in nearly all the faces of people who joined the Seer camp: a sense of searching. He was looking for his way, for truth. For something that he could grab hold of and call his own. If he was willing, Carrington knew he could find what he was looking for through the words of Aaron.

"You followed us," she said rather than asked.

Jesse nodded. "I know I can help."

"We don't need your help," Neil said.

"Neil," Ramses said, placing his fingers on the side of the weapon in Neil's hand. Neil threw Ramses an irritated glance and lowered the gun, but he didn't put it away.

"How?" Carrington asked.

Jesse moved closer to the group and pointed toward the structure. "There is no way you're going to be able to get to that back door without being seen. You need a diversion that pulls the two guards on the ground and the one on the roof away from the door."

The roof, Carrington realized. She'd thought it was empty. She strained her eyes and found that Jesse was right. There was slight movement, a guard's head twisting back and forth. He would spot them from afar.

"And you think you can create a diversion?" Ramses asked.

"What if you get caught?" Carrington asked.

"Then this would be our lucky day," Neil said under his breath. He was watching Jesse like a hawk, his face filled with malice.

Jesse ignored his comment. "I won't," he said, responding to Carrington's concern.

"Are you two seriously considering trusting this stranger?" Neil demanded.

"I'm just trying to help," Jesse said.

"Why do I have such a hard time believing that?" Neil said, crossing his arms over his chest.

Jesse shrugged, but Carrington noticed his jaw tighten. "Not sure, but it sounds like a personal problem."

The two were squared off, and Carrington feared one wrong move might send them at each other's throats.

"Jesse does make a good point, Neil. How do you suggest we get in there otherwise?" Carrington asked.

Neil spoke to Carrington but never took his eyes off of Jesse. "Have you considered that maybe this is a trap? Don't you think it's convenient that this archer shows up now and insists on helping us into a building we know nothing about? For all we know, the second we open that door a dozen CityWatch guards could be waiting for us."

His words were filled with anger and Carrington wondered what had made the man's heart so hateful. When Neil had first joined the Seers, he had been one of the kindest men Carrington had ever met. Eager to help, eager to be a part of what they were doing. Eager to hear Aaron, to sit at his feet and learn. Somewhere along the way Neil had lost the spark that kept him warm, and now even his glance was cold.

She had noticed this happening with others in camp as well. They had been called from the Authority City to follow a different kind of truth. A truth that taught love above all else, that spoke of true worth and an identity in something bigger than this world. Aaron spoke about faith and trust, about forgiveness through surrender, not violence or grudges or desperate survival. But that's what some of them had become—desperate. Struggle and suffering had made them mistrusting and full of anger. They had been called to live above the laws of the Authority, but when push came to shove, they had reverted back to hate. How had they fallen so far?

"Isn't that a possibility either way?" Ramses said. "We don't know what waits inside, but we won't find out unless we get in."

"He's right," Carrington said, then turned to Jesse. "What did you have in mind?"

"I'll stir up trouble at the northern front corner of the building. That should cause all of the guards to move forward, which will leave the back clear long enough for you to get in."

Carrington glanced at Ramses, who nodded, and then turned her attention to Neil. He held her gaze for a moment before exhaling and holstering his weapon. "Fine, but I want you to know that I still think this is a mistake."

Carrington nodded and looked to Jesse. "Be careful."

Jesse gave a small smile and headed toward his intended target. Carrington watched him move. Like a stealthy shadow he melded into the thicket of trees and out of sight. She shook off her worry and settled in to wait.

The sun was high in the sky, transitioning into the afternoon. Its rays were warm and the air around her was glad for it. The breeze swirled lightly, as if playing a friendly game of chase. Neil and Ramses were both lost in their own thoughts, so silence engulfed the time.

It felt as if they had waited for too long when activity below pulled the three from their stillness.

The guards began shouting and moving together toward the north corner just as Jesse had foreseen. The guards near the back rushed forward to help and Neil was up over the peak of the hill that hid them, with Ramses and Carrington right behind. They hurried down the hill, moving between clusters of trees, trying to keep out of sight.

They reached the last stand of foliage that stood between them and the facility. The building was only a few yards away now, and they paused to make sure the coast was still clear.

"See the panel along the side of the door?" Neil said, pointing. "That's going to be a problem."

"Hopefully not," Ramses said. He yanked a small rectangular contraption from his pocket and punched it on. "Wire has been showing me a couple of tricks."

"Do you know how to work that thing?" Neil asked.

"Kind of."

"Perfect," Neil said.

His sarcasm wasn't lost on Ramses and he glared at Neil. "Only one way to find out."

Ramses left their protective covering first, Carrington following and Neil bringing up the rear. Out from the cover of the trees, Carrington could feel her nerves rippling beneath her skin. They were so exposed and she couldn't stop her mind from fearing the worst. Then they reached the back door and Ramses set to work. Carrington and Neil pressed themselves against the facility's walls and waited.

The seconds seemed to stretch as Ramses worked, and Carrington could see the sweat droplets sliding down the side of the man's face.

"Come on, Ramses," Neil said.

"One minute," Ramses said.

"We don't have one minute."

The lock popped and a huge smile of relief spread across Ramses's face. Neil stepped between Ramses and the door, pausing to take a single deep breath. Carrington prayed Neil was wrong, that when he opened the door nothing would be there but the hallway, that Jesse wasn't what Neil suspected.

Neil peered inside and gave an encouraging nod to the others as he disappeared through the crack. Carrington followed with Ramses right behind. He closed the door, sealing them inside, and they took a minute while their eyes adjusted to the dark.

They were in an empty hallway, silent and unused. The floor was cement, the walls stone. Large lights hung from the ceiling but were turned off. The rest of the space was empty, no foreign machinery or furniture. Just open space and a single steel-framed staircase at the end of the hall.

They moved forward and up the stairs. The door at the top was unlocked and Neil carefully opened it enough to peer through. Then he pushed the door farther and Carrington could see a wider hallway. The walls were large white panels, the ceiling filled with light that made the space almost painfully bright. The floor was white as well and shone enough for Carrington to catch a blurry reflection of herself. The contrast between the dingy hallway they were leaving and this one was drastic.

Neil led them across the brightness toward another door. This one had a pane of glass in it, allowing them to see through to the other side. Neil glanced through and confusion lit his face. He opened the door and let the others in.

It looked the same as the hallway behind them but was lined with big glass panels on both sides. They were dim against the white walls, and Carrington slowly moved to look through one. It was a window, but somehow no light from the hallway seemed to pass through it. The room on the other side of the glass was all gray. It looked cold and hard, a box without any light except for the dim bulb panel that hung from the center of the ceiling. A bed lay in the corner, a side table to its left. A chair and table stood in the opposite corner; all of the furniture was bolted to the walls and floor like in a prison cell, which was essentially what this room appeared to be.

A section of the far wall slid open and Carrington jumped away from the window. She waited a moment as her breathing calmed, then slowly peeked back around the window's edge. A small girl was standing inside the room, the panel in the wall sliding shut behind her. The girl was in a gray uniform that Carrington recognized all too well. She was a Lint worker, thin—almost gaunt—and too young to have been in her position for long. Carrington noticed the girl's hands trembling at her sides. She couldn't see the girl's face, but she imagined it was probably stained with tears. Carrington moved forward so the girl could see her, but the girl didn't react.

"She can't see you," Neil said.

Carrington was startled by his voice.

"These are blackout windows. We can see them, but they can't see us."

"Them?"

"All these rooms are holding people," Ramses said. "People from all over the city."

Carrington moved from window to window and saw men who looked like they were from the Cattle Lands and the Farm Lands, more Lint women, shop owners, High-Rise Sector workers, even CityWatch guards locked away in the rooms.

She stepped up to the last cell and her stomach tensed. Ian Carson lay on the single thin mattress, his face ashen and eyes glazed. She had spent so much time fearing this man, so much time wanting to please him and the other Authority members, to be perfectly what society required of her. Looking at him here, she couldn't imagine how she had ever feared the once-proud man, now reduced to a shriveled reflection of his previous self.

"What is going on here?" Carrington asked. Her heart broke at the sight of these people stowed away in solitude, the terrified expressions on their faces—or worse, like Ian, the lack of any expression at all.

"I think you should come see this," Ramses said. He was standing above them. Carrington noticed for the first time that a steel bridge was secured along the left side of the room, above the windowed wall. At the end of the hall a steep staircase led up to where Ramses was. Neil and Carrington made their way to the top.

The bridged walkway trembled beneath their weight as Carrington and Neil moved toward the end where Ramses stood staring through another long windowed section of the wall. Carrington looked down as they walked, and her stomach turned over. Though they were only twelve or thirteen feet up, she had never been a fan of heights. She was relieved to reach Ramses and grabbed his arm for support. He was fiddling with the device Wire had given him, pointing it toward another door to his left side with a paneled lock.

She looked through the glass before her and saw what appeared to be an old laboratory of some kind. It was dark, but the light from the hallway bled through enough that she could make out the edges of the room. This was not blackout glass, apparently. The lab was small, containing only several long steel tables with different medical equipment on them.

A soft click indicated that Ramses had successfully unlocked the door and he, Carrington, and Neil carefully made their way inside. The floor was much sturdier than the walking bridge they'd just stepped off and Carrington was glad for it. She moved forward to one of the closest rectangular tables and touched a microscope that sat on its end. Dust caked her fingers and black splotches appeared on the device where she had touched it. Clearly it had been a while since anyone had used this room.

The light overhead buzzed to life and she turned to see that it was Ramses who had found the switch. She scanned the illuminated room scattered with medical testing supplies, petri dishes, syringes, and test tubes. Two large refrigeration compartments stood against the farthest wall, while the table closest to her held beakers, Bunsen burners, and several centrifuges. The rest of the items Carrington didn't recognize, but she assumed they were other tools that performed medical and research functions. Everything was covered in a heavy layer of dust, and the air was musty and stale from lack of circulation.

Ramses and Neil slowly moved about the room. No one said anything. What could they say? It was clearly a very old medical laboratory, and below them people were caged like animals waiting to be tested. The question was why? And who was responsible? Neil opened one of the refrigerator doors and a cool whiff of air spread across the room.

"Interesting that the coolers were left on when the rest of the space is clearly out of use," Ramses said. He moved to stand next to Neil and reached inside the unit. He retrieved several different tubes, capped and filled with liquid.

"It seems keeping these cool is important. Let's find out why," he said, carefully placing the tubes in his pocket.

A voice drifted up from below and all three of them froze. It came again, louder, and Neil moved to shut off the light. They stood still in the dark, hardly breathing. The creak of heavy steel ripped across the air, and the voices were loud enough to make out.

"Bow and arrow, I swear," one voice said. Footsteps mixed with the voice and echoed up into the small laboratory. They all dropped into crouches below the windows, out of sight from outside the lab.

"I heard he was pretty good with it," the other voice echoed.

"I'll say," the first voice came again. Both voices were male and close by.

Neil peered around the window's edge and motioned that there were two of them. He made a *CW* with his fingers—CityWatch.

Carrington wondered if the door they had entered through was the only way out of this room and had a sinking feeling that they may have trapped themselves in. If the guards came up the stairs and onto the steel bridge, they would surely discover the infiltrators hiding in the lab.

The guards continued to chitchat. One of them was worried about his sick mother, the other concerned about getting transferred to High-Rise Sector security. They had stopped walking, as if they were just using the hallway below as a place to escape from their duties. Carrington controlled her breathing, fighting off thoughts of peril. What if they didn't leave? What if they came up the stairs? What if more guards came?

Finally, after a handful of long minutes, the footsteps began again and their voices seemed to move down the hall, away from the laboratory. Another loud creak sounded as the voices muffled further and then a thick layer of steel banged behind them. They had left. In one door and out the other.

Neil stood slowly, checking to make sure they were alone again, and nodded that it was safe for Carrington and Ramses to move. The three exited the laboratory and descended the stairs quietly. Neil moved with cautious steps toward the door they had entered through and cursed under his breath. He shook his head and Carrington knew they couldn't exit that way. The guards must have posted up outside the door, which meant their only remaining option was venturing farther into the facility and trying to find another way out. She wondered if they could simply wait for the guards to move on, but she knew that would risk more guards coming and trapping them in this hallway. They had to move on.

Ramses led the charge, slowly slipping through the door at the opposite end of the hall.

This wasn't a hallway but rather a square room with four walls and four doors, each door holding a tiny glass window. The room was the same stark white as the hallway they had just left. They each went up to a door and reported what they saw. Ramses and Neil said their doors led to more hallways with more window-filled walls, more human cages. Carrington's door led to what looked like a medical suite with a long gurney stretched out in the center. Wires and tubes hung limp near the chair, and Carrington struggled not to think about what happened in that room. It reminded her of the execution room in the Authority City, and she fought through a ball of pain that was forming in her gut.

She wanted to rush back the way they'd come and smash through the darkened glass that held these people captive. How was she supposed to leave this place when people were being treated like animals?

A soft whistle yanked her back to reality and she saw Ramses and Neil had chosen one of the doors that led into another hallway. With a nauseated swallow, she followed.

Down the hallway, forcing herself not to see the people imprisoned on either side of her, she followed the men as they passed through another door at the end. This time it opened into a large open space that looked more like a storage area than a medical facility. The huge room was filled with wooden crates, making it hard to see what was waiting at the other side. They moved along the side wall, trying to keep behind the boxes.

Neil stopped and nodded to another large door. Light leaked through the cracks and Carrington knew the rays were too bright to be artificial. Fresh air and sunlight lay on the other side of that door.

But what else was beyond it? For all they knew they'd walk right into a gathering of guards. But what other choice did they have? Ramses and Carrington silently assured Neil they were ready to move and Neil stepped out from behind a crate to head toward the door.

"Hey—you can't be in here," a voice rang out.

Carrington turned to see a CityWatch guard standing across the room, surprise and confusion on his face. They stood opposed, each waiting for the other to make a move. The expression on the guard's face changed and he paled. Ramses grabbed Carrington's arm, and they took off.

"Stop!" the guard yelled.

They rushed behind another tall stack of crates and out of sight.

"I need backup in sector H, possible Delta-67," the guard reported into his walkie-talkie. A voice answered back and Carrington knew that more guards would be here quickly. Neil was ahead of them, racing toward the exit as Ramses yanked Carrington along behind. The door had felt closer without the threat of the CityWatch closing in. Sweat collected at Carrington's hairline, and her chest heaved as they ran.

Neil reached the door and yanked. It was locked. Several more shouts echoed through the warehouse and Neil cursed.

Carrington scanned the space around the crates. They were stacked too high to see over and blocked their view of their enemies as well as any opportunity of finding another exit. They were going in blind once again.

They left the door that they'd hoped would lead them to safety and went back into the maze of wooden boxes. They rounded a corner and saw a guard racing toward them. Neil spun around, nearly crashing into Carrington and Ramses, and shouted for them to go back. They backtracked several long strides and turned down a different aisle. It felt impossible to know if they were headed back the way they'd come or into new territory. Everything looked the same, each aisle and clearing filled with crates.

Carrington moved her gaze upward as they ran and was struck with a thought. The boxes were stacked to different heights; if they could climb up them, they'd be able to see and maybe escape.

"Ramses," she said, pulling out of his hold. He turned his head, and Carrington was already pulling herself up onto a lower stack of crates.

"What are you doing?" Ramses asked.

"Getting us out of here," Carrington replied.

Ramses whistled for Neil to stop. Carrington heard Ramses behind her but kept her gaze upward. She scaled the stacks carefully. The crates were sturdy, most of them large enough for even Neil to climb. They held steady as Carrington moved across them. She approached the top layer and slowly raised her head to look around the room. She guessed she was maybe twenty feet above the concrete floor. From here she could make out the entire room. Behind her to her left was a single door; she assumed that was the door they'd already tried. Two guards hurried past it, talking to each other and into their wrist comms.

In front of Carrington lay what was most likely the front wall of the warehouse. It housed two large cargo doors that were closed and sealed. Beside them was another door, standing ajar with the sun streaming in through its opening. That had to be the main entrance. Leaving that way would surely lead them right into more trouble.

She heard more voices and saw a group of three soldiers walking the aisles in search of the intruders. That made at least five CityWatch guards looking for them.

They needed a way out. Ramses tapped her arm and pointed down at a window. It was probably ten feet lower than where they were; it looked accessible from a nearby stack of crates and was half-open. She glanced at Neil and Ramses and nodded. It was their best option.

Ramses took the lead, carefully maneuvering from crate to crate as they descended toward their escape. Reaching the window, Ramses slowly opened it the rest of the way and glanced down.

"It's gonna be a drop; be careful," he said before heaving himself onto the sill. Using the window's edges and his strength, he managed to sit so that he could slide his feet out first and drop to the ground. Carrington watched him disappear over the edge. Neil went next, and Carrington followed. She was balancing on the ledge, glancing down and hoping she wouldn't break an ankle from the drop, when someone called out behind her.

"There," the voice shouted. "Up there."

She had been seen. She held her breath and dropped down. She fell awkwardly and felt pain shoot up the back of her right calf. Neil pulled her from the ground and more pain exploded through her kneecap.

"Hurry," Ramses called. They raced for the covering of trees. More voices called behind them as they ran.

Carrington felt tears collecting as pain pulsed through her leg, but she pushed on. Boots pounded the ground behind her and she pleaded with her body to move faster. Ramses and Neil were both quite a bit ahead of her. She didn't dare glance behind, but she could feel the guards getting closer.

An arrow whizzed by her head and she heard it hit its target. A painful cry erupted behind her and then another arrow sailed by, followed by a third. She saw Jesse standing at the top of the hill she was scaling with his bow raised and eyes fixed past her. With a final push, Carrington raced up the remainder of the hill and over the top into the trees.

Ramses moved to her side and assisted her as they continued to run, Neil in front and Jesse behind with his back to them, his bow still raised. They moved through the trees, several guards still following them, but Jesse kept them at bay. After at least a mile of running for their lives, the coast seemed clear.

Carrington heaved to a stop and closed her eyes, forcing the vomit nestled in her throat back down. She clenched her fists at the raging pain in her leg and tried to breathe deeply.

"We need to keep moving," Neil said.

"Give her a minute," Jesse said.

Carrington turned and gave Jesse an appreciative look. "Thank you."

He shrugged, but a smile was pulling at the corners of his mouth.

She took another deep breath and looked at Neil. "I'm fine; let's go."

He nodded and again they were on the move. The sun was moving toward the western mountains, and Carrington focused her mind on getting back to camp. Getting back to Remko and Elise. She let their faces defuse the overwhelming ache in her body, praying all the while that Remko was safe and would be there when she returned.

18

Remko halted and placed his palm against the tunnel wall for support. He didn't know how long they'd been running, but it had been a long time since they'd heard any footsteps besides their own. They'd been forced to take a longer way than usual to lose their pursuing enemies, which would add at least an hour to their journey back to camp.

Kate had passed out once during the run. Remko and Wire had stopped to wake her and bandage what they could so she wouldn't bleed out. The bullet was lodged deep, and healing her was way beyond Remko's medical skills. They needed to get her to Connor as quickly as possible. She'd started off fighting against Remko and Wire as they tried to move her to safety. She'd refused to leave without Sam, crying that Remko was letting her brother die, but at some point she'd gotten too weak to fight, and Remko had been grateful for it.

Her accusing words still bored into his insides. She was right—he had probably gotten Sam killed. Wire had stayed very quiet the entire journey and even now, as they took a moment to breathe, he kept his eyes on Kate and away from Remko. Remko could only imagine what the boy was thinking, and it tore at his chest.

Remko set Kate down on the tunnel floor and she moaned as he slipped his arms out from underneath her. Her eyes fluttered open, then closed, and each time they did, Remko worried that she was fading again. Wire bent to help Kate drink what water he had left and Remko tried to breathe past the racing of his mind.

Powerful emotions rocked him and he turned to lean against the wall beside Kate. He closed his eyes and fought the tears collecting behind them. He saw Dodson lying on the stone, blood creating a halo around his head, eyes open and still, an image he knew would always haunt him.

Logic sharpened his guilt. He should have known this would happen. He was building a track record of failing; why had he imagined this time would be different? How could he have been foolish enough to think he could fight against the system? Why were they still fighting? Like stones shot from a sling, one after the other, projectiles of uncertainty crashed inside his brain.

Surrender.

The voice seemed to come out of thin air and Remko glanced at Wire to see if he reacted. But of course he didn't and Remko already knew he wouldn't. This voice was in his head. He'd heard it before. More than heard it, he'd felt it.

But Remko couldn't deal with it now. The voice that told him to just have faith, to just believe in the call. The voice that told him to trust, to surrender his fear. The voice that tried to remind him who he was, as if it knew more about him than he did. Where was the man that voice belonged to now? Where was he when the people Remko loved were being murdered? How could surrender help him win the war he was fighting when he had lost sight of what they were even fighting for?

Or maybe he'd never really known.

The thought rattled inside his being like a caged animal. Could it be true that he was fighting for a faith and calling that wasn't his own?

Stop fighting. Surrender.

He shook his head and ignored the sentiment. He was fighting for Carrington, for love. He couldn't afford to lose sight of that.

Love is surrender.

Remko stood from his place against the wall and Wire jumped. Remko gave him an apologetic look. "We should keep moving," Remko said. "How is she?"

Wire didn't look at Remko when he answered. He kept his eyes on the girl slouched in pain against the wall. "Not good."

"We can't leave him behind," Kate whispered. She wasn't talking to them but rather letting the thoughts that consumed her mind even in her delirious state slip out.

"We need to get her back to camp," Wire said.

Remko agreed. He bent down to pick Kate back up and cringed at the small cry that left her lips.

Wire finally raised his eyes to Remko's face and Remko

could see the red blotches that dotted the boy's face. Blotches from tears, from anger, from grief. "They knew we were coming," Wire said.

Remko nodded. "We knew the risk—"

"No, they knew we were going to be there when we were."

Remko was confused and Wire saw it in his eyes.

"There were four times as many guards in that prison today than we've ever recorded. Why? Why today?"

Remko's mind couldn't seem to wrap itself around what Wire was suggesting.

"They knew, Remko."

The boy turned away from Remko and started off, back toward camp.

/ / /

Camp was beginning to settle down for the day when Remko, Wire, and Kate finally arrived. Ramses and Neil were standing on the outskirts of camp, waiting for them, and Remko saw confusion rush into their eyes at their missing team member. He kept his eyes trained on the ground and headed straight for Connor's tent.

People around gasped and speculated at the sight of Kate, blood soaking through the pitiful bandage that wrapped her leg, as Remko carried her through camp.

He could hear the whispered questions.

"What happened?"

"Where is Sam?"

"Is she breathing?"

"Weren't they supposed to bring back a prisoner?"

He ignored them and crossed the distance to the medical tent with Wire, Neil, and Ramses right behind him. He stepped into the tent and laid Kate on the long table, since Kal was still occupying the only bed.

"What happened?" Connor asked, sidestepping Remko and immediately attending to Kate's wounds.

"She was shot in her calf," Remko answered.

"Shot?" Ramses asked.

"Looks like it's been a couple of hours; infection may already be spreading," Connor said.

"How can I help?" Wire asked, moving to the doctor's side. The two worked quickly, Connor giving Wire orders and Wire following without a second thought.

Remko stepped back and gave the two space but stayed in the tent, not ready to face the rush of people outside. There was quiet except for the shuffling of healing hands, and Remko took the moment to breathe.

"Where's Sam?"

Remko glanced up and saw Neil standing inside the tent, arms crossed, face angry. Remko hadn't even noticed him enter. Remko shook his head, unable to say the words.

"Dead?" Neil asked.

Kate whimpered on the table and tried to sit up, but Wire held her down. Sweat beads decorated her pale face.

Connor looked over at them and Remko knew they needed to leave. He turned and headed out first, Neil right on his heels.

"So the mission was a failure? I don't see Dodson with you, and now we are missing one of our key fighters in this war," Neil said.

People were starting to gather around the medical tent to try and decipher what had happened to Kate. Remko avoided eye contact with them as he pushed through the small crowd and aimed for his tent. Neil was still only inches behind him, but Remko didn't turn to face him. He didn't slow or stop to explain. How could he? He didn't know how, wasn't sure what to say.

"Remko," Neil said, and yanked on Remko's shoulder to pull him around. Remko slapped Neil's hand away and the two found themselves nose to nose. Heat flared off Neil's face and Remko could feel his own anger threatening to take over. Through his core it rose, eating away the pain and guilt until it was all that remained. Anger was easier to carry than shame.

Before either man could say a thing Ramses was there, putting distance between them. "Everyone needs to stay calm," Ramses said.

"Calm? Every time I turn around he is getting another one of us killed," Neil yelled. His words burrowed into Remko's gut, but his anger violently crushed the pocket of guilt Neil's words threatened to expose. The crowd gathered behind Neil near the medical tent had turned their attention to the confrontation, and Neil's voice had brought others from the surrounding tents.

Remko was aware of their stares, but he hardly cared anymore. His anger wouldn't let him. "And you think you could do better?" he demanded. "When have you offered to go into the city and risk your life for anyone, Neil?"

"I completed my mission today; I got my team into the facility and brought back samples. Connor is running tests on them right now. You're the one who failed and came back one man short."

Remko tried to step forward, but Ramses wouldn't let him get any closer. "Your mission to capture information? What risk is there in that? You never volunteer yourself for actual risk."

"I have a son!"

"And I have a daughter! Look around you, Neil; we all have just as much to lose!"

Neil swallowed hard, his face bulging with fury. "But I don't get people killed."

"Sam isn't dead," Remko said. He could feel his anger starting to lose its strength as his guilt and pain began to rise up and build in power.

"And Dodson—where is he?" Neil asked.

The mention of Dodson gave Remko's shame the last ounce of power it needed to overcome his anger. His rage deflated completely and with it his false sense of confidence. The watching eyes abruptly felt piercing, the look on Ramses's face further disarming. For the first time his eyes found Carrington, standing near the back of the surrounding group, Elise cradled in her arms. Her eyes were filled with pity and he broke.

Remko dropped his eyes away from his wife's gaze and felt his anger start to battle back. All the eyes looking at him, the bodies standing around, the way they whispered their disapproval. The way they expected him to be their rescuer instead of offering to rescue themselves. Because of their weakness and fear, he was carrying blame for deaths that none of them could have prevented. Who did they think he was? God?

Aaron. If anyone was to blame for all this death and suffering, it was the man who had led them to this miserable wilderness with promises of freedom. If anyone should have to pay for the sin of murder, it should be Aaron. He was to blame.

"You!" a voice called out, rocking Remko from his renewed fuming.

He looked up to see Wire moving through the collected crowd, his gaze fixed behind Remko. His face was filled with rage, something that looked foreign on the boy who was known to be more logical than emotional. Remko glanced over his shoulder and saw that Jesse had moved to the front of the crowd. The archer seemed puzzled by Wire's outburst and looked around to make sure Wire wasn't referring to someone else.

Before anyone could react, Wire was running at full speed. His target was clear but unprepared for the impact.

Wire met Jesse with propelled force and both boys toppled to the ground. People nearby shrieked and scurried out of the way as they rolled. Jesse cursed as Wire yelled accusations into the archer's face and swung his fists. Wire managed to roll out on top, his face flooded with heat, his knees clutching Jesse's sides.

"Get off me!" Jesse yelled.

"You almost got her killed! Traitor!" Wire screamed.

Ramses and Remko moved to yank the skinny boy off of the fallen archer. Wire elbowed Ramses in the gut and clawed at Jesse's face. Ramses recovered, and with Remko on the other side, they managed to rip Wire free of his victim. He still fought their hold as Jesse pushed himself quickly to his feet.

"What is wrong with you!" Jesse shouted.

"He told them; he told them we were coming. He works for them!" Wire yelled.

"What are you talking about?" Ramses asked.

Remko suddenly understood what was happening before him and whirled Wire around to face him. Wire turned and yanked his arms free of Remko's hold. He was breathing heavily, his glasses barely hanging on to the end of his nose, cheeks flushed, forehead glistening. His eyes were dark.

"Remko, it has to be him. They knew we were coming! They took Sam; they almost killed Kate," Wire said.

"You're crazy," Jesse said, using the back of his hand to wipe the blood seeping from the small cut on his bottom lip.

"Wire, we don't know anything for sure—" Remko started.

"You have to be kidding me. Who else could it be?" Wire started toward Jesse again and Remko and Ramses moved to hold the boy back. "I swear if she dies I will kill you," Wire threatened.

"I didn't do anything!" Jesse said.

"He was with us," Carrington said.

Wire stopped struggling and looked over to where Carrington had stepped into the circle. "He went with us to the facility today."

"So? That doesn't mean anything," Wire said, again pulling himself free of Remko and Ramses.

"He saved my life," Carrington said.

Remko looked at Carrington, worry breaking through the rest of the chaos around him. "What happened?"

"It's nothing," Carrington said, sending Remko a reassuring smile.

"I'm with Wire; this kid can't be trusted," Neil said, speaking up.

Carrington turned to Neil, confusion on her face. "You saw what he did for us today. Why would he help us if he was working with the Authority?"

"It's a trick," Wire said.

"Probably all part of his plan," Neil said.

"What do I have to gain from any of this?" Jesse asked.

"Only the guilty defend themselves," Wire said.

"Enough," Remko said.

Jesse's eyes dropped to slits and he clenched his jaw. He and Wire locked eyes for a long moment before Jesse shook his head. "Whatever," he said, and stormed off.

"Jesse," Carrington called after him, but Jesse didn't pause.

Remko watched after the archer. He didn't want to believe anything Wire was saying. He could barely deal with the problems currently cascading around him. The last thing they needed was a traitor as well. Could it have been a mere coincidence that the prison had been stacked with more guards than usual? Maybe Wire was just reacting to the stress, creating a problem that wasn't there? Or maybe he was right, and letting Jesse stay would only result in more reasons to blame Remko.

Wire stomped back toward the medical tent. People had started to trickle away, and Carrington moved to stand beside Remko. Neil still stood close by as well but Remko could hardly look at him. The two men stood looking in different directions, both too proud to admit their actions had been unnecessary.

"The Authority knew you were coming?" Carrington asked, breaking the silence.

"Wire seems to think so, but we can't prove that," Remko said.

Carrington again glanced at Neil. "He could have left us today, and if he had, we wouldn't have made it out of that complex. Yet you still question him?"

Neil said nothing and kept his eyes on the ground.

Carrington exhaled. "Well, I trust Jesse."

"I do too," Ramses said, stepping closer to them.

"Guess it doesn't matter what I think, then," Neil said.

Remko caught Neil's eyes as they lifted, and for a split second he saw something that resonated with him.

Exhaustion.

The two men had their issues, but at the end of the day they were still fighting the same war. A war they both at some point may have felt called to but currently found themselves questioning. They were the same, he and Neil, both soldiers in an impossible war. In Aaron's war.

Neil turned and walked off, the sound of his boots echoing across the pavement.

Ramses placed his hand on Remko's shoulder, bringing him back from his introspection. Remko turned to see the concern in his brother's eyes and wanted to escape from the questions that were coming. The gathering of people was dispersing, and Remko just wanted to be alone.

"Brother—" Ramses started.

"I'm fine, Ramses," Remko said, starting toward his tent.

Ramses followed. "Carrying all this weight isn't doing you any good."

"What would you have me do? Place it on someone else?"

"Yes. You are not in this alone."

Remko paused and turned back to face his brother. "Are you qu . . . questioning whether or not I'm equipped as w . . . well?" He struggled to get the words out without stuttering and bit his tongue.

Ramses shook his head. "No. I just don't want this to destroy you."

"We're at war, Ramses. Wa . . . war isn't easy."

Pity filled Ramses's face at Remko's verbal missteps and Remko could feel his fury bubbling.

"I said I am fine; stop badgering me," Remko said, then turned and left his brother and his wife standing alone.

19

Remko yanked open the flap to his tent and stomped inside. His mind raced through the events that had just transpired. Neil making a public fool of him, Wire trying to kill Jesse, the theory of a spy living among them, Ramses questioning his ability. Not to mention the events of his failed mission plaguing him as if the disease called memory had invaded his entire being. All he could do was remember. Dodson, Sam, Kate. An endless cycle of torture he couldn't shut off.

He hadn't checked on Kate since the altercation between Wire and Jesse. He hadn't sat down with Neil and Ramses to discuss going back for Sam. He hadn't followed after Jesse to try to make amends. He couldn't manage any of that right now. All he could do was walk to his tent and secure himself inside.

He was remotely aware of Carrington entering behind him and softly placing Elise inside her makeshift crib. He sat on the edge of their bed and propped his arms on his knees. He didn't want Carrington to worry about him; that was the last thing she needed, so he resisted the urge to drop his head into his hands. If he did that, he knew there was no guarantee he could keep his emotions under control.

Carrington sat on the bed beside him but didn't touch him. Her presence was enough to make him want to cave. To give in to the raging sea of sorrow crashing against his strength. But he managed not to.

"Do you want to tell me what happened?" Carrington asked.

He closed his eyes and exhaled slowly. Yes, he wanted to, but he wasn't sure how to maintain control while doing so.

She let the silence linger between them. "Is Dodson dead?" she finally asked, her voice small and quivering.

"Yes," Remko answered. Another moment of silence filled their tent.

"They got Sam?" she asked.

"Yes."

"And shot Kate."

Remko nodded.

The pauses between questions were so long it felt as if the world itself were coming to a stop.

"It's not your fault," Carrington whispered.

Remko let out a short breath. "You're the only one who believes that."

"The only one who needs to believe it is you."

Remko knew where this conversation was heading, and he wasn't sure he could muster any more energy for that kind of interaction. "I have no idea what I believe."

"You used to believe in what we were doing here," Carrington said.

Remko turned his head to look at her. "Did I? And what exactly are we doing here?"

"Following the call."

"No, Carrington; I came following you."

Her eyes registered worry. "Remko—"

"And now I'm stuck fighting a war and I don't even know what for."

Carrington looked away and Remko knew his words had hurt her.

"Stuck? Here with me."

Remko finally gave in and let his head hang. "That's not what I meant."

Another pause separated them.

"We can't lose faith," Carrington said, and Remko let out a huff that caused her to trip over her next words, but she recovered. "We can't let our fear dictate our actions."

He looked up at her. "So if a bear chases me, I shouldn't run for fear of being eaten?"

Carrington looked exasperated. "I don't know. Aaron would say—"

"That I should stop resisting the bear. I know—I'll ask the bear over for lunch. Then he'll eat a sandwich instead of me."

Carrington rolled her eyes. "Remko—"

Remko stood from the bed. "No, please, Carrington. Tell me how I am supposed to stop resisting the fear of death when they are executing our people!"

"I'm not saying we should walk into the Authority City and let them hang us all, but we can't run away."

"Who says we can't?"

Carrington stood too, a foot shorter than Remko but with just as much pride. "How can we change the city if we run away?"

"Why do we have to change the city? Why can't we just start over and make our own city?"

"Because that isn't the call!"

"And what if this isn't my call?"

Pain registered on Carrington's face and Remko was aware of the anger monster growing inside him and working its way into his tone.

"So you just want to leave, make our own city," she pressed. "And then what?"

"Live! Be safe and breathe."

"Is that what living is for you? Breathing? We'll just end up right back where we started. Living isn't about flesh and bone and breathing. It's about faith. Faith that surpasses fear. Faith in something bigger than yourself. That's what we're doing here, showing people how to live!"

Remko paused and turned away from Carrington. He wanted to believe, wanted to feel the passion he saw in his wife's eyes, but all he felt was turmoil. Collecting, swirling, spreading. Anger taking over his fear, taking over him.

"You sound just like him," Remko said.

Carrington didn't respond. Elise whimpered from her crib, and for a moment there was just stillness and her soft cries. Finally Carrington broke from the motionlessness and moved to pick Elise up from her bed. Remko could feel her anger, her unease, and a part of him wanted to just tell her what she wanted to hear. But the larger part of him needed space.

"I'm going for a walk," he said. He started toward the exit when Carrington's hand fell on his shoulder. He stopped, her touch threatening to defuse his anger.

"I see who you really are," she said. "I just wish you did."

Again her words so resembled Aaron's that whatever warmth he'd felt from her touch froze. He didn't glance back over his shoulder as he left their tent.

/ / /

Remko hadn't been walking long when he came upon the archer. Jesse was sitting alone on an old subway bench caked in age. It was plastic and the back held a faded picture of women standing in front of palm trees on a sandy white beach. The tagline written across the picture was lost to time, but Remko gathered that convincing people to travel to this destination was the goal. He couldn't help but long for a place that looked as heavenly and peaceful as the one pictured.

Remko approached Jesse with hesitation. The boy was messing with his bow and Remko knew he could easily bury one of those arrows into his leg. Jesse raised his head at the sound of shuffling feet, and as quickly and smoothly as he lifted his arm, the bow was aimed at Remko's chest.

Jesse held the bow steady for only a moment before releasing Remko. The boy moved his belongings, which were next to him on the bench, and made room for Remko to sit.

Neither of them said anything for a long time. Remko stared out across the old subway, counting the stones on the opposite wall and the cross ties linking the strips of metal that made up the tracks ahead. Jesse fiddled with the sharp points of his arrows and cleaned the bow lying across his lap. The quiet wasn't uncomfortable between them. It felt natural, welcome even.

Finally Remko spoke. "I'm sorry about today."

"Not your fault. I get it. Like I said before, I wouldn't trust me either."

"And thank you for helping Carrington today."

Jesse nodded. "She's one of the only people to be kind to me in a long time. That's no small thing for me."

Remko peered at the boy's face and again found himself reflected in him.

"I'm sorry about Sam and your friend that was in prison," Jesse said.

A quiet beat pulsed between them. "Where did you learn to shoot?" Remko asked.

Jesse placed his collection of arrows back inside the sack beneath the bench. "My grandfather."

Remko waited for the boy to elaborate.

"He was a hunter in the Cattle Lands. He worked for a butcher there, but his skill with a bow made him valuable enough that he was granted permission to hunt for himself as well. He used to take me when he could."

"Did your dad hunt too?"

Jesse let out a sharp laugh and Remko registered his distaste. "My father didn't do much of anything besides drink."

"Is that why you left?"

"It was bearable when my grandfather was still alive, but after he died a couple of years ago, I just couldn't handle it anymore."

"But why leave the city entirely?"

Jesse paused and placed his bow beside his bag of arrows. He seemed to be working through how to answer. "The Authority had my grandfather killed. They said it was a hunting accident, a run-in with a wild boar—as if a boar could take out my grandfather. That man wasn't afraid of anything. He didn't have *accidents*. He was too skilled for that. No, he was murdered, at the Authority's hands."

"What makes you think that?"

"He'd go missing for days at a time, got fired once or twice for missing too many days of work. He wasn't exactly an Authority supporter. He believed people were better off fending for themselves. He could survive out here without the Authority or the CityWatch, and I think that made a couple of people uncomfortable."

"That doesn't seem like enough to have a man killed."

"He had a pretty big mouth to go along with his attitude. He started telling some guys that he knew of a place over the western mountains, another livable society."

"Yeah, they call it the Trylin Myth City; some of the soldiers I used to patrol with would talk about it."

"Well, my grandfather was convinced it was real. He told people he was leaving the Authority City in search of it. He ended up dead before he could."

"The Authority gets antsy when they suspect any kind of threat from the outside world."

Jesse stared forward and fell silent.

"I'm sorry."

Jesse nodded, and once again they were surrounded by comfortable silence. Long minutes passed, both of them lost in their own thoughts.

"You ever think it's real?" Jesse asked as if reading Remko's mind.

"I guess nothing's impossible. Seems unlikely, though. I would imagine the Authority would have discovered something like that by now."

"Who says they haven't? Maybe they're just keeping it from us."

Remko's mind drifted to images of what could be. Maybe white beaches and palm trees lay on the other side of those distant mountains. Like the ones in the picture behind his back, a place free from the threat and fear of being hunted. It felt almost unfair that a place like that might actually exist while they suffered like rats, forced to hide in tunnels and run for their lives.

"We could find it, you know," Jesse said. "If it exists, we could get there. My grandfather talked about it enough that I at least have a general idea of where he was convinced it was. I could show you on a map. You guys have enough supplies and manpower that we actually could get there."

The idea was so appealing that Remko didn't know how to respond. If Jesse had showed up a couple of months ago and suggested leaving this place behind, Remko would never have entertained the idea, but now it was impossible not to.

"Imagine it—our own city. Free from the Authority's rules and twisted religion. Just people learning to live together, starting over and rebuilding the world. It could be good," Jesse said.

A thought occurred to Remko. "Is that why you've been hanging around? Because you hoped you could convince us to go with you?"

Jesse dropped his eyes to the concrete floor and fiddled with his fingers. "I just thought with all the troubles you've faced recently, maybe you were looking for a change. I can't imagine why you'd want to stay here forever," he said, motioning to the tunnel around him. "And I probably can't make the journey on my own."

"So you need us?" Remko teased.

Jesse leaned back against the bench and smirked. "I'll deny that if anyone asks."

Again Remko found himself caught up in the idea of leaving. What would it be like to live in a place where he could watch his daughter grow up free? To be able to make her own choices, without the constant fear of pursuit. How would she be different? Who would she choose to be?

"Why do you stay so close to the city?" Jesse asked. "I've been trying to figure it out."

Remko sighed. "Honestly, I've been trying to figure it out too."

"It has something to do with Aaron, right?"

Remko didn't reply. He wasn't sure what to say, but he could feel his anger stirring at the mere mention of the man.

"That guy seems a bit crazy. I mean, talking about saving the city and all through a higher power. You ask me, that city can't be saved—not by any power."

Remko smiled. "People need hope; they need something to believe in."

"I get it. Hope is hard to come by," Jesse said. He was staring straight ahead again, seemingly lost in thought. "So you don't believe in all this?"

Remko didn't look at Jesse. How was he supposed to answer? With the truth? What *was* the truth? "Right now I'm just trying to figure out how to keep people alive."

Jesse nodded. "I will admit, though, there is something about Aaron. Something different."

Remko recognized the awe in Jesse's voice and again felt anger snaking up the back of his neck. Everyone around him was enamored by the thought of Aaron, all of them so willing to follow him into danger. Even Neil had spent time sitting at the man's feet. For a moment, hearing Jesse talk about leaving this place, about heading toward a mythical city that probably didn't even exist, had released Remko from the constant struggle that roared inside. But now the interest behind Jesse's words reminded him that this prison he was living in was real . . . and suffocating.

"I know Trylin is a long shot, but you could at least think about it," Jesse said. "I understand the hope Aaron makes people feel, but we could make our own hope."

Remko knew he should quash the kid's thoughts about the Seers finding a better place. He should tell him that this was where they were going to stay. Like he had told so many others. Like he just recently told Neil. But the words were getting harder and harder to produce. Instead Remko just nodded and Jesse seemed satisfied.

"I should head back to camp," Remko said. "You wanna walk with me?"

"I'm not sure I'm really that welcome."

"Don't worry about Wire; he's probably cooled off by now."

"*Probably* isn't really good enough for me. That kid is scrappier than he looks. I'll take my chances out here."

"You sure?"

"Yeah, I'm good on my own."

"Don't go too far. I may need you and your bow skills." Remko turned to walk off and heard Jesse chuckle behind him.

"Guess I need to start charging for my services," Jesse said.

Remko smiled and started the trek back toward camp, his mind running with impossible thoughts of Trylin and freedom. True freedom—freedom he could make himself and not wait for someone to give him.

20

When Remko arrived back at camp, the calm of sleep was settling on the tents around him. Thoughts of leaving and finding their own way of life still spun through his mind with each step he put between himself and Jesse. The thought was foolish but intoxicating, and he couldn't chase it away.

He wasn't quite ready to face Carrington yet. She would still be frustrated, and he would say something he didn't mean or talk about Trylin as if it were an actual option, which would only make her more upset. So he decided to check on Kate and talk with Connor. The doctor hardly slept; Remko was pretty sure he suffered from insomnia, but in situations like this, insomnia could be helpful.

He remembered Neil mentioning that he and Ramses and Carrington had recovered some samples from the facility earlier and that Connor had been running tests on them. As expected, the medical tent was still lit, whereas most of the surrounding tents had already gone dark. Remko wasn't exactly sure of the time, but it was late enough for most of the world to be asleep. He pictured Carrington lying awake in bed, waiting for her husband to return, unable to sleep as his painful words bounced around in her head. He pushed the thought out of his mind as he ducked inside the medical tent.

Connor was sitting at a table assembled from stacked crates since Kate was currently laid out asleep on his worktable. Her leg was bandaged nicely and the color had returned to her face. She was breathing deeply, her chest rising and falling in steady rhythm. Remko was glad to see she was doing better.

Connor's head shot up from his microscope and he nodded toward Remko. "Burning the midnight oil?"

"Something like that," Remko said. He walked across the tent to stand beside Connor and peered over the man's shoulder. "Anything useful yet?"

"Well, we can be sure of one thing. These are two different serums, and one of them matches the traces I found in Kal's blood."

"So Kal was at the facility?"

"Appears that way, and if Ramses's descriptions of what he saw there are accurate, he was likely held and tested like an animal."

Remko paused, trying to imagine the horrible things his wife and brother had seen earlier today. With everything that had happened when he first arrived back at camp, he hadn't had a chance to talk to either of them about their trip to the facility yet. If Kal had indeed been imprisoned and tested, it could help explain the man's mental breakdown. His anger was stirred once more as he considered it.

But he wasn't shocked; the Authority was capable of anything. "Any idea why?" he asked.

"I'm working on it; these combinations of fluids are vast and complicated. It may be beyond my abilities."

Remko placed his hand on Connor's shoulder. "Keep trying."

Connor nodded.

"Is she going to be okay?" Remko asked, tilting his head toward Kate.

"Oh yeah. Close call, but she's a fighter. She'll be fine in a couple days. She was lucky the bullet missed all of her main arteries."

Remko knew he'd run out of excuses to delay going back to his tent. It was time to face reality. He gave Connor's shoulder another friendly pat. "Try to get some sleep."

"That's not really my thing," Connor said.

Remko left the man working away and stepped out into the dark tunnel air. He could barely make out his tent's outline a couple of yards ahead and took a deep breath before closing the distance.

Carefully he moved into the tent and paused, expecting Carrington to stir. To his surprise she was fast asleep, her breathing steady and peaceful. Remko moved slowly around to the opposite side of the bed and softly laid himself down into the empty space beside her.

He held his breath, making sure not to wake her as he made himself comfortable, and then stared off into the darkness overhead. His body was weary, his mind exhausted, but he knew he wasn't going to find any rest. Even if he managed to drift off, nightmares would chase him awake. They would remind him where he was, of his prison masked in the lie of freedom, and of the costs of following Aaron.

/ / /

Morning came with aches in Remko's bones. He stirred awake, feeling as though he had just drifted off to sleep, and found his tent empty. Sounds of activity came from outside, signaling that the day was already in full swing.

He sat up, moaning at the soreness in his shoulders and back. Connor would tell him that's where he carried his stress and that the only remedy was relaxation and sleep, which was ironic coming from a man with insomnia.

He swung his legs free of the thin covers and stood. If it wasn't enough that his thoughts had tormented him while he was sleeping, they didn't give him a single moment to collect himself before they launched their frontal attack again now that he was vertical. Sam was still imprisoned by the Authority, a strange serum was affecting people's sanity, human experiments were happening at a heavily guarded facility, Wire was convinced there was a traitor living among them, Carrington was angry with him, and in general, Remko was struggling just to convince himself to leave the solace of his tent. Worse still was that behind it all, the idea of leaving as Jesse had suggested played like a soft melody tempting him to abandon all else. Could he not just take his family and go? Could he ever convince Carrington to follow him as he had followed her?

The anger monster that had latched itself to his chest hadn't dissolved in the night, and Remko felt it lingering as he pulled on his boots. It clouded his mind and interfered with his ability to control his emotions. He knew he was a walking fuse, on edge, simply waiting for the spark that would set him off. When he was young and couldn't find his words, his father used to tell him it was better to use his frustration to induce deeper focus. He had advised his son to let the pain be fuel—better to use it than to fight it. So that's what he would do. Release the anger spreading through his blood and use it as an extra dose of adrenaline to propel him forward.

Remko stepped out of his tent and caught the attention of several nearby Seers. They glanced up at him slyly and then turned back to each other, their faces filled with suspicion and anxiety. He knew the second he was out of earshot they would be whispering about him. His failures, his inability to lead, his encounter with Neil in the middle of camp the evening before.

Good, his anger scoffed. *Let them talk while they hide like children under their mothers' skirts. Wonder how long they'd survive alone out here with the pressure of the world breathing down their necks.*

"Remko," someone called.

He turned to see Ramses jogging toward him, Connor on his heels. Both of them looked rattled and Remko muted his anger. They nodded, signaling Remko to step out of plain sight and beyond the range of any lingering ears.

Once safely tucked between two tents, Ramses spoke. "Kate is missing."

"What?" Remko said.

"She's not in the medical tent this morning, and we can't find her anywhere."

"How is that possible?" Remko asked, turning to Connor. "She was shot yesterday."

"Well, like I said, the bullet missed any main arteries and she's on some very heavy painkillers. She probably feels invincible, actually. Wherever she went, she took several days' worth of medical supplies with her—bandages and the rest of the painkillers and antibiotics I had. It looks like she plans to be gone for a while."

Remko cursed under his breath. "She went after Sam."

"She didn't go alone. Wire's gone too," Ramses said.

"The medical supplies will only mask so much; if they get into any serious trouble, or if she puts too much pressure on her injury, she will be in big trouble," Connor said.

"What's going on here?" Neil asked, walking up from behind Ramses and Connor.

"Kate and Wire went after Sam," Ramses said.

Neil cursed and placed his hands on his hips. "Now why do you suppose they would do that?"

"Apparently Kate's faith in me to get her brother back was hazy through all those painkillers," Remko said. He waited for Neil to make some smart remark, but he didn't.

"We have to go after them," Ramses said.

"What? No way; we can't risk that," Neil said.

"Kate had a bullet in her leg less than ten hours ago and most of the CityWatch guards could break Wire in half. We can't just let them walk into the city," Ramses said.

"They made this choice; let them live with the consequences," Neil said.

Before Ramses could further his argument, Neil continued. "I know they're our own, but we have other threats here we need to deal with. I'm sorry—I think both of those kids are great, but we can't ignore our responsibilities here and chase after them because they made a terrible judgment call!"

"They could die, Neil," Ramses said.

"We could all die! Isn't that what you said?" Neil pointed at Remko.

Remko hated to admit how much sense Neil was making. He could feel his anger rearing its head. If he did go after them, he would once again be putting himself at risk to save those who couldn't save themselves. Maybe it would be better for them to have to fend for themselves, see how well they could get along without his rescue.

"Remko," Ramses said.

His brother's voice snapped Remko back to reality and he nodded.

"You can't seriously be considering going after them?" Neil asked.

"We've lost too many, Neil; we have to at least try," Remko said.

"Yeah, because you've got a great track record with—"

"Enough!" Ramses snapped. He got right in Neil's face and Neil stepped back. "No one is asking you to volunteer."

Neil paused and looked from Connor, who was standing very quietly, to Remko and back to Ramses. He shook his head. "Say what you want, but I'm not risking my neck for them."

It was Ramses's turn to shake his head. "No one thought you would."

Neil huffed and with a final sneer walked away.

"I'll go with you," Ramses said to Remko.

"No, Ramses. I want you to stay here, watch over camp, and help Connor with testing those samples."

"You can't go alone," Ramses said.

"I'm not going to. I know someone who might be willing to help."

/ / /

Damien sat in the large office he was still getting used to. Most of the time he found himself more at home in the Scientist's cluttered space across the city, but it was essential that he be present at the Capitol Building to assure people that he was, in fact, in control of this city.

The incident in the prison had sparked controversy among the members of the Authority. It was hard to keep them focused and on track when the rebels continued to serve as a distraction. They were like birds, the Authority members; something shimmering somewhere and their attention was yanked from the actual task at hand. Damien wished they would recognize that the rebels were merely a diversion placed in their path to test their will, not an actual threat worth fretting about. The real threat lay within the minds of the people walking the city streets. It was much bigger than silly lost sheep led by an outlaw.

Though Damien had to admit the outlaw himself was of interest to him. It wouldn't be long before the rebels discovered what Damien was trying to accomplish. There had been a break-in at the facility, which Damien had known was bound to happen, but he wasn't worried. In fact, he felt a sort of thrill at the prospect of the mysterious Aaron coming to terms with reality. How would he react when he learned that Damien would soon steal the people's belief in a greater power? Damien wished he could be a fly on the wall to revel in his victory. For the time being, however, it seemed that babysitting the Authority members while the Scientist and his team perfected the serum was the mundane task he'd been cursed with.

A knock sounded at his office door, and a small smile played its way across his lips. Thankfully, playing babysitter came with occasional perks. "Come in," he called.

The door opened smoothly, and two CityWatch guards led a prisoner in. He was a beast of a man, youthful but hardened by circumstances. The prisoner kept his eyes forward, an odd sense of fearlessness dancing behind them. That alone intrigued Damien, and he motioned for the guards to escort the man to a seat by the large bay window that overlooked the High-Rise Sector. They did as they were told, handcuffing the man's hands behind his back and securing his ankles to the legs of the chair. Clearly this man had left a dangerous impression on the guards.

Damien hid a smile and rounded his desk to sit across from the prisoner. He nodded for the guards to leave them, and after a moment of hesitation they did, pulling the office door closed behind them.

"It's Sam, correct?" Damien asked the man across from him.

Sam said nothing but kept his eyes on Damien.

"That was just a formality; of course I know exactly who you are," Damien said.

Again no response.

"Samuel Miller, older brother to Katherine Miller, son of Stanley and Demi Miller, both deceased—tragic. You were barely sixteen at the time. Your sister was several years younger. You had other family to go live with—an aunt, I believe. But instead you fled the city. Why?"

"Clearly you haven't met my aunt," Sam said.

"Truth is, I never really liked any of my aunts either. Would you like something to drink?" Damien asked.

Sam shook his head and Damien shrugged. "Suit yourself." Damien reached for a pitcher on the small table beside his chair and poured himself a glass. The water was cool against his lips and he let the silence linger as he sipped at the liquid.

"So, you abandon everything you know, risk death beyond the walls of the city, simply because you don't like your aunt?" Damien asked.

Sam kept his mouth shut, his eyes moving from Damien to the wall on his left.

"I only seek to understand what would drive a young man such as yourself into the life you have chosen. You don't really gain anything from refusing to answer," Damien said.

"And what do I gain from answering?" Sam asked.

Damien smiled. "You're smart and resourceful; I'm starting to understand how you have survived on your own this long."

"I have never been alone."

"Of course; you've had your sister."

"I have more than that."

Damien set his glass down and laced his fingers together in his lap. "Yes, tell me about the rebel group. I'm fascinated by the ideas you've all latched on to so tightly."

"Ask all you want. I'm not telling you anything about my people."

Damien chuckled. "Your people. Well, I wasn't aware you were a different species than the rest of us. Is that some kind of transformation that takes place once you leave these walls?"

It was Sam's turn to smile. "No, that transformation happens right here, under your nose."

Damien felt his left eye twitch and the humor fell from his face. "Why is it that you rebels still harbor such attitude even in dire circumstances? That pretty girl—oh, what was her name?—Larkin, I believe. She was relentless in her belief that she would be saved. In the end, it turned out that all of her faith was for nothing."

Damien watched for his words to edge themselves under Sam's skin, but as with the other rebels he'd encountered, his words didn't have the effect he'd hoped for. Sam's face remained fearless, his eyes hopeful. Breaking the spirit of these people was impossible. Or at least it had been until now.

Damien's smile returned. "As a man of moral integrity, I am actually impressed by your ability to believe so effortlessly. I think it a humbling quality. Unfortunately it is also a disease that has plagued humanity for far too long. See, unlike the Authority members who have come before me, I do not intend to eliminate your people; in fact, I don't think eradication would do us any good. Change is what we need—scientific, evolutionary change."

"Whatever you're hoping to get out of me, you might as well give up now. I'll never talk," Sam said.

"Don't be so certain," Damien said.

"Do your worst," Sam said, his eyes fueled with fire.

Damien paused and then let out a loud cackle. Sam looked a bit shaken by Damien's reaction and his resolve appeared to waver for a moment.

"Why does everyone assume that violence is the only way to solve a problem? It just proves how far our society has fallen from the ideals of true intelligence. Torture is completely barbaric, my boy. As I mentioned, I don't want to eliminate; I want to change." Damien leaned forward and placed his hand on Sam's knee. Sam flinched at the man's touch, and power coursed through Damien's veins. "You should be honored for the role you're about to play in history. You'll never understand how the change you're about to undergo will impact the world, but rest assured that after today, nothing will ever be the same."

"I don't know what you're talking about," Sam said. Hard as he was trying, he looked mentally shaken. The door opened behind him and three men in long white coats, followed by the CityWatch guards who had escorted Sam in, filled the room.

Damien cocked his head slightly to the left and surveyed Sam's face. For the first time he saw something new lighting the boy's eyes. Fear.

Damien patted Sam's knee. "Don't worry, Sam. You and I are going to change the world."

21

Jesse had agreed to help without hesitation. Remko had found him in the same spot he'd been in the night before. The kid had lit a small fire, rolled out a sleeping mat, and was roasting something he'd hunted that filled the tunnel with a delicious smell. Jesse was right; he really was good on his own.

Remko had discovered before going to search for Jesse that Wire and Kate were not on foot. The keys for the main camp vehicle were missing, which made sense. In Kate's condition it was pretty unlikely that the two rogue agents would attempt Sam's rescue without transport help. When he'd mentioned this to Jesse, the archer's face had lit up and he confessed that he had his own mode of transportation. Remko had radioed back to camp, where Ramses was waiting for an update, that he and Jesse would check back in when they could, and the two of them were off.

Jesse led him aboveground through an overgrown subway exit and a couple of miles west through thickening stands of trees. He explained that once he'd discovered the Seer camp, he'd moved his transportation so that it would be close when he needed it. "There it is," he said as they approached a tall bush. Remko couldn't imagine what Jesse had stored inside the tiny hiding place, and when Jesse rolled a motorcycle out of the single, tall bush, Remko was shocked.

The bike was ancient, made of rusted parts, a large black leather seat, steel handlebars, and an old-fashioned electric push motor that didn't give Remko confidence. "Where did you find this thing?" he asked.

"It was my grandfather's," Jesse said. "He kept it hidden from the Authority, and after he died, I found it."

"And it works?" Remko asked.

"Don't be rude; she has feelings and won't start if you insult her."

"Right—that's comforting."

"I keep her plugged into a portable battery-operated charger, so she's got plenty of juice."

"Let me guess: the battery charger was your grandfather's too?"

"He was into the classics."

Jesse pushed the small silver button near the handlebars and the motor roared to life. The kid beamed with satisfaction and Remko wished he'd apologized to Carrington before he'd left. Looking at the small rusted contraption, he worried he'd die before he'd get the chance. He and Carrington had hardly spoken at all since their confrontation the night before. Then he'd woken to hear that Wire and Kate were missing, and with their several-hour head start, Remko hadn't had much time for lounging around.

He'd found her before heading off to seek out Jesse, told her what was happening, and promised they'd talk when he got back. She had given him her bravest smile, the one that still made his heart melt, and he wanted to stop rushing, yank her into his arms, and beg for her forgiveness. But he didn't have time, and his anger was proving to be pretty stubborn. Instead, he'd given her hand a tight squeeze, brushed his fingers along the top of Elise's head, and left.

"You ready?" Jesse said.

"Do I have a choice?" Remko said.

"Oh, come on. I'm a good driver."

Remko swallowed away his misgivings and climbed on the back of the bike. He would probably feel more secure if he were the one driving. Putting his life in the hands of someone else wasn't a strength of his.

"Hold on, and careful of your calves there by those pipes; they get hot," Jesse said. He was either terrible at putting people at ease or was making Remko nervous for the fun of it.

The bike launched forward and Remko wrapped his arms around Jesse's waist. The sun was already high in the sky, which meant half the day was gone. If they were going to find Wire and Kate before dark, they were going to need to hurry. Remko had mentioned to Jesse while they'd made the trek to his hidden motorcycle that Wire and Kate's only objective must be to locate and free Sam. That meant they were probably headed back to the place where they had lost him. The prison was on the north side of the city, but there was more than one way to get there.

Remko knew Kate was impatient, so he figured they would take the shortest route, but with Wire working alongside her, they would also want a route where they faced the smallest possibility of detection. Remko had narrowed their options down to two. They had a 50 percent chance of finding the runaways, but also a 50 percent chance of being unsuccessful. Remko hoped the odds would fall in his favor for once, but that was the thing with odds. They were fickle and did not necessarily align with the desired outcome.

Remko directed Jesse to drive the bike south. There was a tunnel entrance in that direction that their team had used many times, and Remko knew Wire was familiar with it. It would lead them under the city wall and toward the prison. If Remko had planned this rescue mission, that's the path he would have suggested using. He was hoping that he and Wire were thinking alike.

The travel time was slower on the bike than it would have been in one of the Seers' regular vehicles, partly because it was older than most of the things still running in the city and partly because it was carrying more weight than it was designed to. Remko held on to Jesse as he maneuvered through the forest, keeping them hidden. The one advantage this piece of scrap metal had was that it was small. Remko couldn't help but wonder whether, if Wire was given all the necessary parts, he could build the camp a couple of these motorized devices for short scouting trips.

Jesse slowed the bike to a crawl and then to a stop. He set his feet down on either side to keep the bike standing and Remko climbed off. They both saw it—up ahead a black CityWatch vehicle was parked just beyond the edge of the trees. It was different than most, a much older version that still operated mostly on wheels. Large and square. More clunky, but better for transporting.

They both moved behind thick trunks to keep themselves concealed. They were pretty far away, but if they could see the vehicle, then it was logical to think that the CityWatch guards would also be able to spot them.

Jesse pulled a pair of small binoculars from deep inside his quiver and peered through them. After a long moment, he handed them to Remko, who did the same.

"Two soldiers. Looks like they may have people in the back of their vehicle, but I can't make them out," Jesse said.

Remko looked through the magnifying lenses and searched for signs of life. Jesse was right: two black-clad guards stood beside the car, and there was movement inside, but it could be anyone. Another guard even. It was too hard to tell from this distance.

"We need to get closer," Remko said. Jesse agreed and carefully guided his motorcycle along until he found a place where he could store it while they investigated further.

The two sneaked forward, crouching from tree to tree, moving among the foliage silently, until they were only a couple of dozen yards away. Jesse tossed Remko his binoculars again and Remko peeked out from behind his cover to get a closer look.

There were at least two people sitting in the back of the vehicle. Neither of them wore black, so they must be prisoners. From here Remko could hear the muffled voices of the two CityWatch guards. One of them was puffing smoke into the air; the other leaned against the rear of the van using his free hand to elaborate as he told his partner some story. In his other hand he cradled a long-range rifle.

They were definitely transporting someone important; the CityWatch only used that kind of weaponry for Authority security transportation and extremely dangerous prisoners.

"Are those your people?" Jesse whispered.

Remko couldn't be sure; this angle made it hard to make out who was being held in the back.

He handed the binoculars back to Jesse and thought through their options. They could rush in; they had the upper hand because the guards wouldn't see them coming, and they were evenly matched—two on two, Jesse with his bow and Remko with a sidearm tucked into the tight strap around his calf. Then again, something could go wrong. They could risk their necks only to find the people secured in the van weren't prisoners at all.

"What do you wanna do, boss?" Jesse asked.

A small cry came from the back of the van—a child's cry—and one of the soldiers turned around and slammed his fist against the steel doors. "Pipe him down in there!" the guard yelled.

That was enough for Remko. He glanced at Jesse. "I'll move right, you go left. Once you're in range, pull one of the guards' attention; I'll deal with the other. And if you find keys, grab them."

Jesse nodded and snaked off toward the left. Remko followed his own plan, working his way right, staying out of sight as he closed the distance between himself and the van. The smoking guard tossed his cigarette on the ground and mashed it with his heel. A pretty good sign they planned to leave soon. Remko reached the closest spot he could without being completely exposed and crouched down to wait.

The seconds dripped on and Remko started to worry that Jesse may have run into more guards roaming the forest. Finally something snapped in the distance and both guards tensed.

"You hear that?" the nonsmoking guard said.

"Yeah, probably just an animal," the other replied.

The sound came again and both guards glanced at one another. The smoking guard motioned for his partner to go check it out, and with his gun raised, the second guard moved toward the diversion.

Remko waited, watching the smoking guard as the other slowly disappeared from sight. The guard left with the truck didn't seem very concerned with the noise and carelessly let his weapon swing from the strap draped over his shoulder.

He yanked another cigarette from his coat pocket and used both hands to light it. Remko seized the moment.

He moved swiftly, with ease, and the guard had barely registered Remko as a threat before he was standing in front of him, gun raised. The guard moved for his own weapon and Remko cocked his firearm. The guard paused in motion, his eyes cut to slits.

"Take your weapon and place it on the ground," Remko said. The man reluctantly did as he was told and lowered his gun to the dirt. In one swift motion the guard yanked out another weapon, a small military standard that was strapped to his ankle, and sent a shot toward Remko.

Remko ducked, but it wasn't necessary. The guard missed high, and the bullet cracked deep into a tree behind him. But the action was enough to cause Remko pause and alarm, giving the soldier the distraction he needed to run. Remko heard a small yelp to his left and hoped it was coming from the second guard, not Jesse.

Remko dashed after the man who had just shot at him. Remko's familiar and currently friendly companion, anger, pulsed violently through his veins as he pursued his attacker. Partly because the man had shot at him and partly because a soldier should never run away from a fight. Remko's legs pumped under him, his face flushed and dripping with sweat.

The guard glanced back, a look of fear washing over his face, and he aimed his tiny pistol to fire at Remko again.

Remko cut right to avoid the shot and pushed himself

even faster. He was gaining on the runaway when another
CityWatch vehicle drove over the top of the hill in front
of them. Remko slid to a stop while the guard continued
to run, waving his hands frantically over his head. The sun
reflected off the van's black surface, and through the front
windshield Remko could make out two more CityWatch
guards, their faces focused on him.

Remko spun on his heels and headed back toward the
trees. He hadn't realized how far he'd traveled away from
the original CityWatch vehicle, and fear prickled his skin.
He could hear the engine humming louder as the second
vehicle came closer and he dug deep for the energy to propel him onward. The wind picked up dirt from all around
him and kicked it into dust clouds that Remko could taste.
He felt the vehicle behind him. It was too close.

He dove headfirst to his left, rolled once, pushed himself
back up onto his feet, and pumped forward. The low buzz
from the engine revved as the chase vehicle tried to make
the quick turn, but Remko knew he'd given himself a couple
seconds of space. The trees were getting closer, the original
CityWatch transport sitting only a couple of yards off.

"Jesse!" Remko yelled.

After only a beat, the archer stepped from the woods
and registered Remko's predicament. Without hesitation he
raised his bow and aimed it directly over Remko's shoulder.
If there was ever a time to trust this boy, it was now. Remko
felt the air divide as arrows sailed past Remko's right ear,
one and then another. Jesse's face twisted in frustration and

Remko gathered that he'd missed his target. Jesse aimed his bow once more and with a deep breath let another arrow fly. Remko heard it hit something behind him and glanced back to see that Jesse had hit the vehicle's right front tire, causing it to deflate.

The vehicle chasing him spun to a stop, facing away. Remko reached the first van and Jesse tossed him something that shimmered in the sunlight. Keys. Remko turned to unlock the driver's-side door.

"Freeze!" someone shouted, halting Remko.

A new guard stood a couple feet away, breathing heavy from pursuit, gun raised with its barrel aimed directly at Remko's head. The guard's partner stumbled out of the disabled van and reached for his weapon as well, but Jesse was already moving. More fluidly than seemed possible, another arrow left Jesse's bow and hit the rifle in the stumbling guard's hands. He cried out and dropped the weapon, pulling his partner's attention and giving Remko a chance to duck for cover.

The first guard fired a shot intended for Jesse, but the boy had already moved. "Get your gun!" the soldier yelled.

Remko stayed low and close to the first van as he moved down the side and toward the rear of the vehicle. He saw the stumbling guard's rifle still lying in the dirt and moved for it. He looked up and saw yet another CityWatch van headed their way.

They needed to get out of here. Remko looked around for Jesse but didn't see him.

"Looks like we've got reinforcements coming," one guard said.

Remko could hear footsteps moving toward the back of the van and considered making a mad dash back into the trees, but it was too late. A soft metallic click popped near his ear and he went still.

"Don't move," the soldier said.

From the corner of his eye Remko could see the gun pointed at his skull and the guard holding it. Remko lifted his arms, the CityWatch rifle in his left hand. The other guard rounded the back of the van from the other side and moved forward to snatch the rifle away, as well as the keys dangling from Remko's raised right fist.

"Where's the archer?" the second guard asked.

Remko said nothing.

"Find him," the guard behind Remko said. The other guard nodded and looped the rifle through the strap over his shoulder before moving to sweep the perimeter. Remko felt his hands being yanked, one by one, behind his back, where the soldier clasped them tightly together.

"Let's go," he said, and pushed Remko forward. He led Remko away from the original CityWatch vehicle and toward the one with the flat tire. "Your archer friend is going to pay for damaging Authority property."

The third official vehicle slowed as it approached the scene; it pulled over and the guard holding Remko sent a wave of good faith. Had Remko been alone with just the guard working to restrain him, overpowering him may have been possible, but there was no way to know how many soldiers occupied the third CityWatch transportation unit.

The final vehicle pulled to a stop, its windows deeply tinted, the sun making it impossible to count the number of new enemies. The second guard, the one who had been searching for Jesse, reappeared empty-handed. "He must have gone deep into the woods, but the perimeter is secu—" The guard's words were cut short as his body convulsed, his eyes rolled back, and he crumpled to the ground.

Remko glanced up to see Wire slowly stepping down from the driver's side of the newest CityWatch van, a weapon of his own invention smoking from its latest electric shock pulse. The guard behind Remko moved his gun to aim it at Wire.

Another weapon clicked a couple of feet away. Kate hung out of the passenger-side door of the CityWatch van, her gun directed toward the guard. "I wouldn't do that if I were you," she said. Remko felt the tension in his neck release as a smile spread across his face. The soldier stood frozen as Remko stepped away and toward Wire and Kate.

Wire walked over to the guard. "Put it down nice and easy."

The guard did as he was told and Wire strapped the man's hands behind his back in cuffs. Kate sliced the plastic restraints that bound Remko's wrists. He noticed the bandage on her calf was bloody. Her face was pale and shimmering with moisture. He could feel the heat from her body as he stood beside her. She wavered a step and he reached out to steady her.

"You all right?" Remko asked.

In typical Kate fashion, she shrugged him off and nodded, even though it was clearly a lie. Remko gave her shoulder a squeeze and moved toward the guard passed out on the ground. He pulled the rifle from the man's shoulder and snatched the keys from his pocket.

"What are you doing out here?" Wire asked. The boy had bound the conscious guard's wrists and ankles and deposited him on the ground behind his disabled vehicle.

"Coming after you," Remko said. He could see the shame in Wire's face and tried to keep the frustration out of his voice, especially since he and Kate had just saved his skin. "I would have thought you'd be at the south tunnel by now."

"We figured you'd search for us there, so we went east instead. But the tunnel's entrance was heavily guarded; there was no way we could get through, so we were headed to see if the south was the same," Wire said. He glanced over his shoulder at Kate, who was now sitting in the passenger seat. "She's not doing well, though."

"Of course she's not; she was shot yesterday," Remko said.

Remko could read Wire's emotions like a book. He knew taking Kate from camp had been a mistake, but he also loved her, and she was determined to get her brother back. If anyone understood taking risks for love, it was Remko.

Someone cried out in pain and Remko and Wire spun around to see a third guard crumpling backward, an arrow sticking through the top of his foot. It was the guard Remko had chased, the smoker with terrible aim. Remko looked up and saw Jesse perched on top of the original CityWatch van. Wire saw him as well and the expression of remorse on his face vanished.

"You brought him?" Wire asked.

Remko didn't say anything as Jesse dropped down from the van's roof. He ran toward the man he'd just hobbled, secured him with restraints, and retrieved his arrow.

"I still don't trust him," Wire said.

"Well, I do," Remko replied. "No one else would come with me to find you two. Except him."

Wire glanced back at the archer and exhaled.

Remko placed his hand on Wire's shoulder. "We need him."

Wire held Remko's gaze and Remko dropped his hand, pointing to the unconscious guard at their feet. "Let's restrain him before he wakes up."

Wire nodded, and Remko moved toward the van that still held prisoners. He unlocked the back doors and carefully opened them. A small voice whimpered as Remko peered inside. There were only two prisoners, a young girl probably in her midteens and a small boy who couldn't have been older than four or five. They resembled each other and Remko guessed that they were most likely siblings.

For a moment Remko longed for Sam. He was much better at these interactions than Remko.

"Hello," Remko said.

The boy held tightly to his sister and she cleared her throat. "Hi."

Remko reached his hand inside. "Come on; I'll get you out of here."

The girl hesitated but then reached out and let Remko assist her and the small boy from the van.

As Remko examined her face and her perfectly golden hair that fell in soft curls around her unblemished skin and diamond-blue eyes, he couldn't shake the feeling that she reminded him of someone. The little boy beside her looked vaguely familiar as well, with shaggy blond hair and matching blue eyes.

"Are you both all right?" Remko asked.

The girl nodded. "Thank you."

"I'm Remko. This is Wire, that's Jesse, and Kate is the girl in the van."

"My name is Eleanor, and this is my brother Willis."

"Eleanor?" Jesse said. "I knew you looked familiar."

Eleanor's face crumpled in confusion. "I'm sorry; do we know each other?"

"No, but most boys in my Choosing Ceremony group would recognize you," Jesse said. "You're Eleanor Lane, Enderson Lane's daughter."

Her cheeks flushed red and she drilled her eyes into the ground.

"As in Authority member Enderson Lane?" Wire asked.

That's why she looked familiar. Suspicion filled Remko's chest. "What were you doing locked in the back of a CityWatch vehicle?"

She shook her head but didn't answer and Remko looked at his team members, whose faces held the same worried expression.

"We should go," Jesse said.

Remko nodded and they all started back toward the van where Kate sat.

"Please, you can't leave us here," Eleanor said. "My father was sending us away to the Genesis Compound. If you leave us here, they'll find us and bring us there."

Remko looked at Eleanor. Tears were gathering in her eyes and she looked terrified.

"What is the Genesis Compound?" Wire asked.

"A testing facility out toward the mountains." She paused to swallow, her eyes falling away from Wire's face. "They change people there."

Wire looked at Remko.

Remko took a step toward Eleanor. "You know about the facility?"

She nodded. "My father said that the transition has started. Please, we won't be any trouble, and we'll help at the Seer camp however we can."

"You know who we are?" Remko asked.

"You're the famous rebels; everyone knows who you are."

Remko had just turned to Wire to discuss what they

should do when a soft thud clunked behind them. They turned to see Kate on the ground beside the van.

"Kate!" Wire called. They rushed over and found her passed out, her breathing ragged and short.

"Oh no! Kate!" Wire said and pulled her head into his lap. "Toss me that water canteen."

Jesse grabbed it and handed it to Wire, who gently splashed water over Kate's heated face. "Kate, come on." He looked to Remko. "We have to get her back. Help me get her in the van."

"I'll do it," Jesse said, stepping in to lift the bottom half of Kate's body. He and Wire carried her around the side as Remko yanked open the back doors, and then they lifted her inside and laid her down carefully. Wire climbed in after her and set to work on her again.

Remko motioned for Jesse to help him as he dragged all three CityWatch guards into the back of the van with the deflated tire and shut them in. These vans all had trackers; eventually someone would come looking for them.

Jesse headed off toward the trees, tossing Remko a look over his shoulder. "I can't leave my bike. I'll meet you back at camp."

"Remko!" Wire shouted from the vehicle. Remko raced back to the driver's side of their stolen van and saw Eleanor and Willis standing there. The girl's eyes pleaded with him to take them, and guilt tugged at his heartstrings. Authority kids or not, they were just kids. He waved them over and they both ran to jump up into the passenger side of the van.

Remko climbed in and glimpsed Wire in the rearview mirror. He was giving Remko an uneasy look. Remko cranked the vehicle to life. "We don't leave people behind," he said, twisting the wheel and pulling the van away from the other two vehicles, his foot heavy on the accelerator. "We just don't."

22 Carrington tucked Elise in her crib and
slowly made her way back out into the
commotion of camp. Remko had been gone
a couple of hours, and like always when
he was away her heart moved at a constant
accelerated rate. She knew worrying for
him did nobody any good, but it was impossible to avoid.
It didn't help that there was a thick tension wedging its way
between them. After he'd left last night, she'd distracted
herself with tending to Elise, endlessly driving away tears
and thoughts of Remko stewing alone in the darkness of the
tunnels.

Eventually her fight had given way to exhaustion and she'd
been surprised how easily sleep had found her. She'd dreamed
of her field. When she'd woken, Aaron's sweet reminders of
who she was, of her faith, and of their Father still rang in her
ears. Remko had been snoring softly beside her and she'd lov-
ingly watched him sleep for a long while before forcing herself
to rise when Elise had stirred in her bed.

Carrington would have never guessed how painful
the struggle was watching someone she loved miss the
truth that was so clear. Worse still was knowing there was
nothing she could do but wait for him to find his way.

Haunting questions of doubt filled her head even now as she stood outside their tent.

What if he never knows the truth? What if he never believes? What if he insists on leaving? Would she follow him? Could she let him go? Would it be right? He was her husband, the father of her daughter; could she face the world without him? Would she want to? Fear made her hands tremble and she practiced seeing her fear and letting it go. It flickered for a moment and then returned with full force. Letting go was so simple and yet so difficult. She had been talking about it with Selena Carson only a couple of mornings ago. The way Selena's daughter Arianna had spoken about fear had been the same way Larkin had come to speak about it toward the end.

Carrington remembered sitting with Larkin under a row of trees long before the Seers had been forced to move down into the subway tunnels. The sun had been warm, but it was cool under the shadow of the branches. It was the first time Carrington had been without Elise since her birth, and she was struggling to enjoy herself.

Larkin noticed, as Larkin usually did, and she chuckled at Carrington's anxiety. Carrington playfully shoved her.

"You'll understand this one day," Carrington said.

"Hopefully not," Larkin teased. Carrington shot her a threatening look and Larkin innocently shrugged.

"What? If having a baby makes you crazy, then it's not for me."

"I'm not crazy. I'm just worried," Carrington said.

"About what?"

"I don't know. What if something happens to her while I'm gone?"

Larkin gave her one of those knowing smiles she'd been using lately. As if she understood something about the world that everyone else hadn't quite figured out yet. She grabbed Carrington's hand and held it close.

"I'm just afraid, that's all," Carrington said.

Still holding Carrington's hand, Larkin leaned her head back against a tree trunk and closed her eyes. "Let it go, my dear."

"Easy for you to say. You aren't a crazy baby owner."

Larkin softly laughed. It made Carrington smile.

A seriousness settled into Larkin's tone that Carrington had also come to recognize. "You could still let it go, you know," she said.

"I don't know how," Carrington replied.

Larkin opened her eyes, lifting her head, and looked at Carrington. She smiled. "Practice."

A wisp of wind swirled between them and she continued. "Fear is real; we know this, but it only has the power we give to it. Take away its power and what is it? Let go of your fear; don't resist it or fight against it. Don't shove it down or pretend it doesn't exist. See what you are afraid of and trust that your faith and your Father are bigger. All that is supposed to happen will happen. You are afraid for Elise because you don't know what will happen to her while you are gone, but trust that your Father does."

Larkin laid her head back against the tree. "The more you practice surrendering and trusting, the easier it will become."

Carrington knew Larkin's words were true, but it was too hard not to tease her. "Oh, wise one, how did I become so fortunate to sit in your shadow?"

Larkin jabbed Carrington's side and both girls broke into giggles.

"Carrington." A voice yanked her out of her memory and back to the camp beneath the earth, where her fear was very real and Larkin was very dead. She turned to see Neil Stone standing behind her, his face white as flour and a tremor jostling his fingers.

"Neil, what's—?" Carrington started.

"Shh, there isn't much time. Take Elise and get out of here," Neil said.

Carrington was shocked by the state of the man and thought to call out for Connor. "What are you talking about?"

He glanced over his shoulder as if expecting something to be chasing him and then looked back, eyes wide. "I'm sorry. You've always been so kind to me, even when I was at odds with Remko. I just have to protect my son. . . ." He paused as if he couldn't form the words he needed. "You have to leave before . . ."

Again he trailed off and Carrington started to become afraid. "Neil, what is going on? Talk to me," Carrington urged.

Someone screamed from deep within the camp and Neil's eyes glazed over. "It's too late," he whispered, and Carrington couldn't find sense through the panic exploding in her brain. Another scream erupted and Neil grabbed her shoulders.

"I'm so sorry. Run!"

His eyes pleaded with her for another moment before he turned and raced into camp. Carrington moved a couple steps to follow him, but she couldn't leave Elise. More screams echoed around her, and she could make out angry shouts and panicked pleas.

Carrington turned and rushed into her tent. Elise was sound asleep and she swept the baby up, waking her. Elise fussed in her arms and Carrington hushed the child as she grabbed a bag and threw as much as she could inside. Her heart thundered against her rib cage. She yanked the bag closed and over her shoulder before fleeing the tent. She stumbled forward into camp but then came to a halt, a gasp escaping her lips.

Ahead of her, the camp was flooded with CityWatch soldiers in black uniforms. They were ripping through tents, tearing people out and throwing them to the ground. Men, women, and children begged for help and mercy but only received violence.

Many were fighting back, but the CityWatch had come prepared and the people before her could do little to stop them. Carrington ducked behind a nearby tent and searched for any way to help those around her. Women and children cried as they were bound and loaded into the backs of trucks. Guards shouted commands and profanity at those who resisted. One man managed to get loose and head-butted the guard escorting him. The guard cried out in pain and another soldier turned and snatched the Seer before he could get away. The second soldier held the man as the first injured guard pounded him over the head with a black stick.

The woman beside them yelled for them to stop and another guard sent his open palm flying across her face, silencing her. Tears gathered in Carrington's eyes and she felt like she might be sick. These were the people they had rescued, people she had brought here.

Someone tapped her shoulder and a hand suffocated her scream. She turned around and saw a group of faces she knew. Ramses, with his hand over her mouth and a finger to his lips. Lesley, their twins, Selena and both her girls, Connor, several other Seer women and children. Relief flooded Carrington's body and she let out the breath she'd been holding as Ramses released her.

"We have to move quickly," Ramses whispered and Carrington nodded. Guilt ate away at the lining of her stomach; they were leaving behind others to be taken, but they would risk all their lives and the lives of their children if they were to rush out there and try to save them.

Carrington followed as Ramses led the group forward. They carefully sneaked behind the tents that were still standing but could hear guards beginning to work their way through, toward the back of camp. The women did their best to keep the children silent, and every time Elise moved in Carrington's arms, she held her breath and prayed she wouldn't start crying.

They reached the end of the row of tents and the protection their cover provided. Ramses peered around the edge of the fabric, as did Carrington. Most of the guards were working their way through the tents, finding the few stragglers who had hidden themselves beneath benches or under cots. Others were rummaging through the camp's bins, taking what they wanted and making a mess of everything else.

There was an exit shaft with an ascending flight of stairs across the camp, directly in front of them. If they could make it across without being seen, they might have a chance to run for it. But making it across would be impossible with the number of men in black uniforms headed their direction, and it wouldn't be long before the soldiers wading from tent to tent were upon them. They were running out of time.

"Find every last one," a soldier yelled. "Burn this place to the ground if you need to. No one gets away."

Carrington could see the panic in Ramses's face, the fear collecting in Lesley's and the other women's eyes. Selena recognized the trouble they were in and pulled her daughters close to her chest. Nina and Kane clung to Lesley for dear life. Carrington looked down on the tiny face of her own daughter and scraped her brain for a way out.

She felt a presence beside her and saw Selena's face. The woman's eyes were filled with certainty and resolve; her face soft, collecting tears. Carrington opened her mouth to try for a comforting word, but Selena spoke first.

"Promise me that my girls will know of Aaron's Father the way that Arianna did," Selena said, her voice barely louder than a whisper.

Carrington didn't register what was happening until it was too late. She reached out to grab hold of Selena's sleeve, but the woman was already out of reach. She ran back up behind the row of tents, a couple of them occupied by CityWatch soldiers. She moved quickly and covertly. Both of her girls tried to rush after her, but Carrington grabbed Rayna, and Lesley reached out to hold back Lucy. Lucy cried out and a guard swung around in their direction.

"Who's there?" he called. "No use hiding, we'll find you either way."

He started toward the tent they were hiding behind, the rest of the guards still several tents away. Selena was out of sight now, having moved between two tents.

The guard moved toward them slowly and the entire group clustered tightly together and held their breath.

"Stop!" someone yelled.

The guard, nearly to their tent, turned to see what commotion was happening behind him. His radio crackled. "All units report back to armored cars; we have a runner."

The guard spun on his heels and took off in a sprint back toward the front of camp, as did all of the other soldiers who had been moving closer.

Ramses recognized their opportunity and motioned for people to move forward. Quickly, but only two or three at a time, the group crossed the gap to the side service shaft. Nearly everyone was across when the first shot rang out across the tunnel, followed by screams echoing through the air.

"Don't let her get away," shouted a guard.

"Be alert; she's armed," a radio buzzed.

"If you have a shot, take it," a heavy voice echoed.

Another shot bounced through the air.

"Mom!" Lucy shouted. A single guard snapped his head around toward Lucy's voice just in time to see the last group crossing the gap. Ramses had to yank Lucy off her feet and toward the service exit.

"Mom!" she cried again, tears streaming down her face, her arms and legs thrashing out against Ramses's hold. Rayna cried as Carrington dragged her up the creaking stairs with Ramses and the last few of their group stepping into the shaft.

"We have more runners at the other end of the camp," came an angry shout.

Ramses pulled Lucy inside the square room that held only a single staircase and slammed the door shut. He ripped down the manual emergency lock and hurried everyone up the stairs two at a time.

From the tunnel they heard a final shot, followed by more screams and then pounding on the door below. Guards were trying to get in. Carrington pulled Rayna up onto her free hip, willing herself to move faster.

She pushed out thoughts of Selena, of what might have happened to her. She ignored the crying baby in her arms and the weeping girl on her hip. She battled through the pain in her injured ankle and moved. She tried to do as Larkin had taught her and face the fear collecting in her mind, but all she could see were images of the small children around her bloody and dead, so she buried her fear instead of letting it go.

And she prayed—prayed that they would all make it somewhere safe and alive.

/ / /

Chaos swirled around Neil's head as the camp fell to ashes at his feet. The sight of it rocked his core more than he'd thought it would, but he pushed away the madness as he searched the captors for Corbin. Shouts from Seers and guards filled his ears; the smell of smoke filled his nostrils. He heard a guard say that some had escaped down toward the end of camp, and he hoped Carrington was among them. He'd never wanted harm to come to any of them; he'd only done what he'd thought necessary to protect his son.

He heard Corbin's familiar cry and saw him being handled without care through the smoke a couple feet ahead. He rushed forward and grasped for his son. A large guard yanked Neil away and shoved him backward.

"That's my son. I was promised no harm would come to him," Neil said.

The oaf of a guard glanced back to another man dressed in black who was clearly the one in charge. The oaf moved aside as the lead soldier stepped forward.

"So you're the snitch," the guard said, and his words grated at the inside of Neil's chest.

"Please—I upheld my end of the deal. I gave you the Seer camp location. Now give me my son," Neil said.

"Except not all were captured," the guard said.

"So?"

"The deal was the location and *all* the Seers."

Neil shook his head. "Only a few got away—" he started.

"Your leader, Remko, isn't even here, and his wife and daughter were among those who escaped. According to my orders they were the most important."

Neil heard Corbin whimper, still being held roughly by the CityWatch guard, and he moved forward. The lead guard blocked his path. Neil's desperation clawed at him. He had done all of this for Corbin. It couldn't all be for nothing.

"What do you want me to do?" Neil asked.

The head guard took a moment to think before addressing Neil. "The wife and daughter are necessary for capturing Remko. Get them."

Carrington and Elise. Neil could barely think through the panic in his chest. They were with a group, long gone; how was he supposed to find them? "How . . . ?"

The head guard shrugged. "You seem like a smart man.

I'm sure you'll figure it out. You bring us the woman and the girl, and we'll give you your son back."

Neil hesitated, knowing the second he left they could harm Corbin, but what choice did he really have? "If you harm my son—"

"Don't worry. Hurry now," the guard said. "They can't have gotten that far."

Neil nodded and tried to control the impulses raging inside his body. Find Carrington and Elise to trade for Corbin. That was his only choice.

23

Remko climbed out of the transport and placed the keys in his pocket. During the drive back, Wire had been able to rouse Kate and give her what he had left of the painkillers and antibiotics, so she was able to limp beside Wire as they exited the van. Eleanor and Willis had sat mostly silent the entire ride, Willis never letting go of his sister's hand, Eleanor's eyes fixed out the window. Remko longed to understand more of what she knew about the Genesis Compound. He tried asking her during the drive but she'd said very little.

"I don't have many answers," she'd said. "There have been rumors for a while. Rumors that the Authority was getting ready to transition the community toward a new era, make it a better place. People started calling it Genesis because it promises to be a new start. I wasn't even aware that we needed a new start. I was planning for my Choosing Ceremony, worrying about dresses and dance steps. I never would have thought . . ."

Emotion had choked out the rest of her words and Remko hadn't pushed any further. He could only imagine what was going on in her mind. Her father forcing her away to be imprisoned and tested and perhaps changed into something they still didn't understand. The sense of betrayal she must feel at being tossed aside by her own flesh and blood.

A couple miles from camp Eleanor had spoken again. "My father said that the transition had started, that I should be honored to be a part of human history."

"What is the transition?" Remko had asked.

"I don't know, but he looked genuinely surprised when I wasn't thrilled." She'd turned to look at Remko. "This isn't his fault, you know. Damien Gold brainwashed him." Then she'd turned back to the window. "He was always a good father."

Remko had spent the rest of the drive compiling ideas of how to break into the Genesis Compound and set the prisoners inside free. Set them free and then leave.

It hadn't taken long for Remko to realize after speaking with Jesse that he couldn't stay here and fight this battle any longer. He was tired. This wasn't his war. Aaron and his Father's way may have given hope and a false sense of freedom to some, but it had only brought Remko fear and suffering.

He'd given all he had, worked and fought harder than all the rest combined; but he was done sacrificing his happiness and risking the lives of those he loved on the promises of a man he wasn't convinced was sane.

He knew Carrington would take some persuading, but he hoped her commitment to him would outweigh her commitment to Aaron. He had followed her; now he would be asking her to follow him.

Jesse drove up alongside with his motorcycle and parked it by the van. Remko waited as the archer fiddled with a small piece under the seat and gave him a curious look when he finally walked over to join the rest, the piece in his hand, as they made the walk back to camp.

"What? The motor on that thing won't work without this piece. You guys don't fully trust me; well, the feeling is mutual," Jesse said.

The tunnels were dark and cold as the group walked toward camp. Remko kept his eyes on Eleanor and Willis, both of them searching the tunnel with curiosity. He noticed how quiet it was and wondered what Lesley had come up with to keep all the children distracted long enough for so much silence. A strong scent drifted through Remko's nostrils: something burning.

The moment recognition of the smell registered in his mind, he knew something was wrong. He picked up his pace, fear prickling its way over his skin.

"Remko," Wire called out, but Remko ignored him. He felt his legs go from jogging to running as he caught a glimpse of firelight in the distance.

"Is that smoke?" Jesse asked from behind, but Remko ignored them all. He tuned everything out and tore forward. The closer he got, the more panicked he felt.

Smothering ash was floating through the air, falling like snow; the smell of wood and cloth and food being incinerated assaulted his senses as he reached the center of the empty camp. Trash was strewn about everywhere; tent contents he recognized were spilled out over the concrete floor. The entire place looked as if it had been ransacked by thieves. The shock of the sight caused Remko to pause. He didn't know where to look or what to look at.

"Oh no," Jesse said, catching up to Remko.

More hurried steps echoed through the tunnel behind him as the others ran to catch up. Everything Remko had come to know—all they had worked for, all they had gathered and built—sat destroyed before him. As if it were nothing. The only thing missing was people. Remko hurried through camp yanking still-standing tents open and looking inside. Nothing.

Carrington.

Remko took off toward his tent, ignoring the carnage on either side of him as he ran. "Carrington!" he yelled. The panic in his chest pulsed like electric shocks. "Carrington!"

The tent was still standing, barely, its left side caved in. He pushed his way inside to find his and Carrington's bed torn apart. It had been ripped nearly in half. The misshapen crib that had cradled Elise while she slept was scattered in pieces. Anything that had made this humble room a home had been violated. Remko dropped to his knees and searched through the wreckage, looking for clues, begging to find them. His desperation made his hands shake. She wasn't here.

He flew out of the tent and into the ones around him. "Carrington!"

Tent after tent pulled apart like cotton, bits strewn about in chaos.

Tent after tent, empty.

A shrill scream of terror echoed across the stone ceiling. Remko ignored it in his urgency to find Carrington even though he knew she wasn't here. Nobody was here.

"Remko," Jesse yelled.

He swept around and saw Eleanor trembling, her eyes fixed on something near her feet. Remko rushed over and nearly collapsed to his knees when he caught sight of them. Bodies. A row of them, cold, still, left lying on the ground like garbage.

Remko swallowed the bile rising in his throat and stepped forward. The beat of his heart slowed as he searched each face. Sorrow and relief barraged his skull. None of the faces were Carrington's, but each one belonged to someone he knew.

Selena Carson lay among them, her graying lips slightly parted, her eyes closed.

There were only six bodies here, which meant everyone else had been taken. Remko looked around. The mutilation surrounding him was personal and had been done with cruel intent. Intended, just like the row of bodies, to serve as a message.

Only the Authority could have done this, which meant they had his wife and daughter. The weight of it pulled Remko to his knees. He couldn't register anything through the fog collecting in his mind. He struggled to breathe as the air around his face thinned, his head pounding and nausea rolling through his stomach.

They were all gone, all taken, which would probably soon mean all dead.

/ / /

Carrington pulled Elise closer to her chest to block the strong wind blowing through the trees. The sun was gone, the stars and moon out overhead, and the temperature had dropped significantly.

They had run for hours, maneuvering through the forest, dodging groupings of nearly destroyed homes, trying to stay hidden, stopping to let people rest for only a minute in an old school building, the name Whitmore Middle School still etched into the stone sign standing several feet from the front entrance. They tried to be mindful of their tracks, tried to stay clustered as a group, tried to stay silent. They considered circling back to see if anyone else had been left behind, but it was too much of a risk. What if the CityWatch was still there, or what if they had left someone behind to wait for others? With all the children and only two men, they couldn't possibly fight. If they were caught by soldiers they would all be lost.

Terror wreaked havoc on her mind as she imagined Remko returning to camp without any idea of what he would find. Was he there now, collapsed under the weight of the idea that she and Elise were dead? Or had he been

captured the second he walked into camp? Had he even
made it back to camp at all? Would they ever find each
other again? How could they?

She worked to keep herself together. To search for the
light at the end of the tunnel, to see through the impending fear. To stay strong for Elise and for Selena's girls.
After Lucy had stopped crying a few hours ago, she had
fallen completely quiet. She hadn't said a word to anyone.
Carrington's heart ached for the pain she must be facing,
for all the pain she would face. Girls her age were supposed
to be dreaming of dances and dresses, enjoying their practicing lessons and giggling with their friends. Not watching
their sisters die and their fathers be imprisoned and their
mothers ripped away from them forever.

Larkin had told her that everything that was supposed
to happen would happen. Carrington didn't understand
how this was supposed to happen. How could it be that
these two girls were supposed to be in such pain? Why was
their camp supposed to be violated? How were they now
supposed to survive out here without supplies and with the
weight of the world on their shoulders?

"Understanding is a tricky thing," a voice said.

Carrington turned and saw Aaron move out from
behind a nearby tree. The spike of fear that had shot
through her chest eased and she resisted the urge to collapse into his arms. The sight of him released a wave of
sealed emotion. The sorrow and pain and panic she'd been
holding at bay rushed through her like water, drenching

every cell. Tears burst from her eyes and poured down her cheeks. She felt her knees tremble, and before she could stop herself, she sank down into the cold dirt.

She could feel the moisture from the ground seeping through the fabric of her pants and chilling the bones in her kneecaps. The wind raked through her hair and swept it wildly across her face, spirals of air targeting her bare neck and making every inch of her body shiver. The elements themselves attacked, just as the world did, just as her emotions and her mind could.

All at once she lost every ounce of strength she had ever possessed. All the power she'd felt, the love and confidence from being self-assured in truth and faith, vanished. It was just her alone against the darkness with the wind threatening to crush what little remained of her spirit. She wept because she couldn't remember how to stand or how to face her fear. She wept because day after day the world spit at her and called her names and tricked her into thinking she could handle it. She wept because she felt lied to. She had been so sure following Aaron would lead her to freedom, but all she had known was pain and loss. She wept for Arianna, and Selena, and Dodson, and Helms, and Larkin. Most of all, she wept for herself.

A hand rested against her shoulder and warmth spread out across her skin. She looked up through tear-filled eyes and saw Aaron kneeling beside her, his face illuminated against the darkness of the sky. Tears rolled down his cheeks, but love filled his eyes. He was recognizing her pain, sharing in it, but it didn't cause his body to ache or his brightness to falter.

"Let it go," he said.

"I don't know how," Carrington said.

"Yes, you do. You have done this before. In the field with your Father, with our Father."

"I'm afraid."

"Of what?"

"Of losing this war and losing everyone fighting it with me."

"You forget who you are."

"I can't hear my song anymore. All I hear and see is covered in fear and doubt."

"Do you have faith?"

"Yes."

"In what?"

Carrington didn't know what to say. What had she placed her faith in? Remko? Herself? Their ability to fight an opposition that was larger, stronger, and faster than they were? Was that what this was about—winning? Finally triumphing over the Authority for all the years they'd made her feel worthless? Taking up her sword that had been forged from all the pain, fear, worry, and anger she'd held on to because it was her right? Then, once the enemy was bleeding out on the floor before her, would she find peace and freedom?

Carrington knew the answers; she had been down this dark road before. She heard the voices of those who'd come before her, of Arianna and Larkin, telling her freedom wasn't something you fought for. True freedom, freedom from the pain that latched itself to your memories, was only obtained by surrender.

"Yes—surrender," Aaron said. "Let it go."

Carrington recalled Larkin's words. "By trusting. By having faith in perfect love, in my Father."

Aaron smiled. "You can't lose this war, because your Father has already won. This isn't a battle of skin and bones, flesh and blood. This is about your faith, about your identity. When you discover who you truly are, you discover there is no war left to fight at all."

Tears filled her eyes again and she sniffed. "I'll just keep forgetting."

Aaron smiled sadly. "Maybe, but some people never see at all. Help them see, Carrington; help them surrender."

She nodded and Aaron leaned forward and placed a kiss on her forehead.

Her eyes snapped open. She was sitting at the base of a thick tree. The darkness was quiet; bodies were scattered around her in slumber, smoke rising from small pits where fires had been lit an hour earlier. Elise was breathing steadily against her chest, completely asleep.

They had stopped for the night, and she had fallen asleep. There was no Aaron; she had only dreamed of him. Fear rained down over her but she laid her head back, replaying Aaron's words over and over in her head.

"When you know who you truly are, you realize there is no war left to fight at all," she whispered.

Then she let it go.

She pictured the field, recalled the identity that was hers, and let it go. The rain of dread eased and after several minutes Carrington was surprised to feel no fear at all.

24

Remko wasn't sure how long he had been kneeling. Time passed slowly through fog. It could have been only a couple of minutes, but the torment playing inside his brain made it feel like an eternity.

The others moved about; he heard Wire asking Jesse for help with Kate, heard Eleanor comforting her baby brother, but Remko didn't move. He knew he needed to. He should be racing after the CityWatch, tracking their tire marks, trying to catch up with them, doing something—anything but kneeling. Yet he stayed in place. Maybe it was the weight of it, the certainty that he felt in his gut that no matter how quickly he moved or how perfectly he tracked, there wasn't any possible way he could reach them in time.

He had lost them. The only things of value in his life, the two people who kept him striving, fighting, hoping, wishing for more; he had lost them. They'd slipped through his fingers, been taken out from underneath him when he wasn't looking. By monsters.

The longer Remko knelt there beside the row of stiffening corpses that he used to call friends, the stronger his anger grew. It acted as a shield, protecting him from the fear of being utterly alone. Because that's what he would become without them. Alone. He'd learned earlier on in life to be good on his own. Much like Jesse. Then Carrington had changed his reality, offering the idea of not having to face life by himself. So they had been two, and then they'd become three, and Remko had become so engrossed and attached to the idea of being more than one that he'd forgotten how to be alone.

He blinked and exhaled. He hadn't even realized he was holding his breath. He looked around and stood. He couldn't be alone. He needed Carrington, needed his daughter, to make him whole. He refused to go back. Then all of this would have been for nothing. He started in the direction of their transportation, half a mile outside the camp's borders.

"Remko," Wire called.

"We have to go after them," Remko said.

"Go after them? Go after who?" Wire asked.

Remko kept walking as he shouted over his shoulder. "They took my family."

"Remko, stop!" Wire yelled. "We can't just go after them."

Remko spun around. "Of course we can. We go after everyone else."

"Yes, as a full team, but Kate can't walk, and we have a child now," Wire said, pointing to Willis, who was hiding halfway behind his sister's dress.

Remko glanced around. Wire was right. "Then we split up," he said. "Jesse, you—"

"No, Remko, we can't afford to split up anymore," Wire said.

"That's funny; this morning you had no problem splitting up," Remko barked.

Wire looked taken aback. "Are you blaming me for this?"

"I would have been here!" Remko shouted.

The tunnel fell silent. Remko's face burned with anger and the heat spread down his back. He stormed toward Wire. "I would have been here to protect them, but I was chasing after the two of you because you thought abandoning the group to go after your family was the better move. Looks like you were right."

Wire didn't respond and sheepishly kept his eyes on the ground.

"He's right," Kate said. She was sitting on an overturned bin beside Wire. "We did abandon the group. So go ahead—leave. Everyone here is used to being left."

A twinge of guilt slivered into Remko's gut but his anger crushed it to dust. Nothing mattered as much as getting Carrington and Elise back. He wouldn't be held responsible for Wire or Kate's emotional baggage or the pain they'd suffered before.

"What are you going to do?" Kate asked. "Take on the entire CityWatch alone?"

"He won't be alone," Jesse said. He was standing behind Remko, his arms crossed over his chest. He gave Remko a single nod and Remko turned to leave again.

"You're really going to leave us here?" Wire asked. "After everything?"

"My family needs me," Remko said without slowing his pace.

"I thought we were your family!"

Remko slowed and Jesse looked at him for direction.

Wire continued, "That's what this was, right? A family. Become a Seer, become part of the group. Standing against the Authority, following Aaron's way."

At the sound of Aaron's name something boiled over in Remko's stomach. "And where is he now?" he exploded, spinning back around. His words echoed off the stone. "Our great and powerful leader, who is always conveniently absent when we actually need him." Remko turned away from anyone specifically and just started yelling at the darkness. "Such a mighty and noble call to be a Seer; you'd think you could be bothered to show up sometimes!"

Remko could feel the monster inside him taking over. "Where are you, Aaron, follower of the Father's way? Where are you? Where is He? We're yelling about abandoning one another, but the truth is we've all been abandoned by you!" Remko spit the words out like acid into the open air. "How are you any good to us now? Where is your power? All I see is death and destruction for the purpose of a call that has only brought us suffering, and for what? You aren't even here! You are never here!"

Something snapped behind them, and they all turned to see Aaron walking from the shadows. His face held the same expression of peace that it always did, as if he hadn't just been the subject of Remko's rant. For a second Remko felt a stab of shame. He should have kept his mouth shut, but his anger monster felt differently. This was the man who had been the source of all his suffering, who had caused all his pain. The man who paraded around telling stories to children and letting Remko fight all his battles. The man who had won Remko's wife's loyalty so deeply that he had to wonder if she would follow her own husband.

A violent shudder streaked through his body and he balled his fists at his sides. Aaron stood there with his smug contentment as if their world and everyone they loved hadn't just been ripped away from them. Remko fought the urge to rush toward the man, his better sense still controlling his actions. But the monster was strong, inching its way over his control.

Aaron held Remko's gaze and no one said anything. Remko hardened his look, letting his fury leak through his expression. He wanted Aaron to see, to know that this suffering around them was his doing.

Aaron didn't flinch or pull away. He just met Remko's eyes with understanding, his mind tricks in full effect so that Remko began to recoil, began to defuse.

Remko dropped his eyes first, and the monster screeched in agony and shame. What kind of man was he, if he couldn't even stand against one enemy?

No wonder you are failing to measure up.

No.

No wonder your family would willingly follow another.

Stop it.

No wonder you are shrouded in shame and guilt.

Shut up.

You called yourself a soldier once, but you've turned in your honor and strength for submissive weakness.

No.

You aren't a man anymore; you're just a puppet.

No, I'm not.

Prove it.

Something snapped in Remko's mind. The last drop of right and wrong evaporated and all he could feel was his ego. His sense of pride, the warrior strength that he had sacrificed in the name of peace, the anger he had kept at bay in order to appear in control. One by one the cage doors flew open and dark, violent intention filled every corner of his being.

His feet were moving. As if his body had become a single unit acting out of pure instinct, disconnected from his conscience. Swiftly he covered the distance between himself and Aaron, only dimly aware of the scream tearing from his throat.

"Remko," people yelled, but he blocked them out. Jesse tried to move between him and the target, but Remko sidestepped him enough to have a clear shot at Aaron. He reached the man, grabbed him by the collar of his shirt, and ripped the gun from where it was tucked into the back of his pants. He placed the end of it against Aaron's temple.

"Remko! Remko, stop!" Kate screamed. Willis cried at his sister's side while Wire and Jesse moved to rip Remko away.

Still holding on to Aaron, Remko turned and waved his gun for them to back off. He aimed it at both of their heads, and each one slowly stepped away. "Stay back," he warned.

"Come on, man, you don't want to do this," Jesse said.

"Remko, think about what you're doing," Wire pleaded.

They're just trying to prove you're weak. Are you weak, little boy?

"I said stay back!" Remko yelled.

Aaron raised his hand slightly to motion toward Wire and Jesse. "It's all right."

Remko snapped his head back toward his prisoner, blood pounding in his ears. Anger pulsed from every pore. He drilled Aaron with a hateful stare and waited for the man to respond.

Nothing. His eyes remained filled with a startling calmness. As if he weren't afraid of the gun aimed at his forehead. As if he believed the bullets loaded inside weren't even a threat.

He's mocking you.

A tremor ran down Remko's back. "All of this," he whispered, his voice shaking with rage, "all of this is your fault."

Aaron's expression didn't change. He didn't waver or flinch or respond.

"Give me a reason not to pull this trigger."

Still Aaron said nothing. He kept his eyes on Remko's, fearless.

He's playing with you.

"Defend yourself!"

"Resistance only creates suffering," Aaron said softly.

His words washed over Remko like a wind and he nearly released the man, but his anger fought back, blocking out the power that came with Aaron's words.

Are you going to let him play you for a fool?

Remko cocked the weapon, the sound echoing through the still tunnel.

"Remko, please—" Wire tried again.

"Shut up!" Remko yelled.

Don't forget who this man is. He took everything from you. He used you as a tool to fight his battle while he hid away to protect himself. He is the enemy.

"Look through your fear and anger," Aaron said. "See who you truly are beyond it. You don't have to be afraid."

This is who you truly are—a man, a soldier.

"Let it go. Listen to a different voice. A voice that calls your true name," Aaron said.

Don't listen to him and his constant lies.

"The power inside you gives you the strength to walk through the fear. Surrender to it."

He wants you to give in to your fear, to be weak so he can be in control.

"No," Remko said. He was done surrendering.

"You can be free of this—" Aaron started.

"Enough! I am do . . . do . . . done," Remko said. His stutter came back with full force. It only added to the fuel racing through his body.

Pull the trigger; end this.

Remko's hand trembled slightly. He wanted to see fear in the man inches from him, but Aaron's eyes still remained calm.

He doesn't believe you'll do it.

Remko would if it would end this suffering. If it would free him from the lies that Aaron had sold and he had bought. But he wanted Aaron to know he would, wanted him to feel some of the fear he had placed in Remko.

"I will not surr . . . surrender to you anymore. You used me, ris . . . ris . . . risked my life, my family's lives. You say the power gives me stre . . . stre . . . strength, but I have strength. I don't need yours," Remko said. "You said we wou . . . would be free, but we are more imprisoned than ever."

Aaron's expression stayed solid. Remko resisted the urge to pummel the man, his anger soaring to new heights.

"Admit it! Admit you lied to us," Remko said. "Ad . . . admit there is no freedom."

Aaron said nothing.

Remko pressed the muzzle of his gun harder against Aaron's temple. "Admit it!"

"There is freedom," Aaron said, "but only in surrender."

Remko let out a vicious scream as his anger took over

his arm and his finger pulled the trigger on the weapon in his hand.

"No!" Wire yelled, and a part of Remko registered movement, but the majority of his focus was on the trigger his finger had just pulled. The world slowed, the seconds inched forward as Remko waited for the gun chamber to release a steel bullet and echo its disposal with blaring clarity.

But nothing came. The gun only clicked, as if there were no bullets at all. He pulled the trigger again. Once, twice, three more times—with no reaction. Aaron's eyes still held their eerie confidence and Remko was suddenly struck with a different kind of fear. Something he hadn't experienced before. A fear that came from awe and understanding. Aaron was as he said, filled with a power beyond comprehension.

Before Remko's mind could register another thought, shame poured over him like tar. It coated every inch of his skin and hung heavy around his shoulders. What had he just tried to do? He saw the gun in his hand, the end of it forced against Aaron's forehead. His hands shook and his throat tightened. Had he . . . ? His mind was unable to comprehend what his anger had fueled. What kind of man . . . ?

His thoughts were broken by the tugging of arms as the others dragged him down and away from Aaron. His instincts told him to fight, but his body had gone numb, and he let himself be pulled to the ground.

You could have been freed, you could have ended this, but you were too weak!

Pathetic. You deserve to suffer.

Shame pounded inside his head as the voices dispensed more ridicule.

Failure is all you are. All you're good for.

You were a fool to think you could be anything more.

His body numb, his shame vengeful, and his will utterly broken, Remko let the darkness creeping into his mind rapture him.

Voices drifted in like soft, far-off noise that he hardly heard.

"We have to secure him."

"Help me move him."

"This is impossible."

"The gun was fully loaded."

"That doesn't make sense."

Remko blocked out the voices completely. He wanted to be alone in his suffering and shame. He wanted to give in to the darkness closing in, wanted to let go of the will to fight.

He might die like this—all those around him might die—but he couldn't care anymore. He wouldn't. Aaron had told him to let go, to surrender. So he would.

He let go of the will to live and surrendered to the darkness around him.

25

Remko had been lying in his darkness for a while. Time had no value to him. He knew it was passing, or at least he suspected it was. Then again, the world could have ended while he was deep in his own sludge. It wouldn't matter to him anyway. A small part of him, somewhere deep within, itched to be awakened, to come back to the land of the living, to reconnect and remember that technically he was still breathing. But according to his wife, who was dead or dying, living was more than breathing. She had said as much the last time they had spoken. When he'd let his tone cut like razors and he'd questioned everything they'd built their fragile life on. When he'd been angry that she would choose anyone over him, when he'd felt certain he deserved more consideration than she was giving him.

Now such entitlements felt frivolous. His rights, his needs, his wants. The anger that had driven him to kill, to end the life of a man he'd felt loyalty to only weeks before. Then again, he hadn't killed anyone. Aaron was walking, breathing, unscarred, unharmed. Remko was a shell of a man, fading away, locked in his own defeat and suffering, and Aaron was unshaken.

Through the haze of the last few hours, Remko knew a couple of things had happened for sure. Jesse and Wire had restrained him after he'd tried to blow Aaron's brains out, and they had moved him to one of the only standing tents. There had been soft conversations about what to do with him. Angry whispers and fearful discussions.

They should take him with them. They should kill him. They should leave him for dead. He had tried to shoot Aaron with a loaded gun. A loaded gun that had proven useless. He was losing his mind, but they couldn't just leave him. He had lost everything. So had they, and none of them had tried to kill anyone. Where would they go, what would they do? Maybe north, or over the mountains to the west? Without the Seers, what were they now?

On and on their mumbling broke through in spurts and Remko shut it out. He wanted to yell: *What does it matter anymore? We're all as good as dead anyway.* But he didn't. He didn't say anything. They asked him questions, but he couldn't get the words forming in his brain to pass his lips, or he didn't care enough to actually try. It was hard to tell through the fog.

He knew that eventually they had left him alone in the tent, bound and slouched in a far corner. They'd left him and then the battering self-hate had come. A violent wind, rushing over his flesh and chilling his bones.

He had failed everyone. Carrington and Elise, who were probably turning cold from lifelessness or clinging to the false hope that Remko would storm in and save them, would never be saved because he couldn't. He never really had been able to. It had all been a lie he'd fed himself.

You're enough. You're strong enough, capable enough, called to this, chosen for this. Powerful enough. Fearless enough. Remko almost laughed thinking about it now, a chuckle tickling the inside of his mouth and quickly turning to sorrow. How could he have ever been so foolish?

At some point another presence had entered the tent, different from the others, and he'd known it was Aaron. Walking, breathing, not-dead Aaron. How long had it been since Remko had tried to put four bullets into this man's skull? Certainly not long enough for Aaron to forget. He feared Aaron's wrath. A sense of self-preservation made Remko want to move. To recoil as the man sat down beside him. He had somehow stopped bullets from exiting a fully functional, fully loaded weapon. He could probably call down lightning or fire to end Remko's misery.

Remko should be cowering in fear, begging for forgiveness, crying out for mercy. But the haze was thick, crippling. He didn't move; what was the point? If Aaron did strike him down with righteous vengeance, it would be the least Remko deserved.

But Aaron hadn't inflicted painful revenge. He hadn't even spoken. He'd only sat with Remko for a long time, or at least it felt long, his presence barely snaking through the darkness and pulling at Remko's heart. Wisps and whispers trying to convince Remko he was missing a critical piece of this puzzle. That there was more, that this wasn't the end but rather the beginning. Remko snuffed out each attempt. He was too tired to search for Aaron's truth, or Aaron's Father's truth. Maybe it was all real, the path and the freedom, but Remko didn't want to find it. He didn't deserve to.

Eventually Aaron left, taking with him any warmth Remko felt, and the darkness deepened.

Time passed, and Remko moved between dense stupor and silence to chasing off nightmares and memories. A catalogue of failures and mistakes that he would silence only to find more darkness.

He couldn't tell how long it had been when someone entered the tent again. Weeks, days, or only hours.

It was Wire and Jesse, and Remko wondered if they had finally come to a verdict on what to do with him and were here to carry out their sentencing. They rushed to him and tried to lift him from the ground.

"We have to move," Wire said.

Remko was pulled onto his feet.

"More soldiers are headed this way," Jesse said.

Remko pulled out of their hold. And they both stopped.

Wire glanced at Jesse and moved to re-grasp Remko's arm, but Remko sidestepped him and sat back against the corner.

He wasn't going with them. He couldn't fight anymore, wouldn't struggle for freedom that he could never earn. He would rather be taken and serve the sentence he was destined for anyway. They would all end up paying for their rebellion, and he was too weak and exhausted to prolong the inevitable.

"Remko, what are you doing?" Wire asked.

Jesse dropped down and clasped both of Remko's shoulders. "Listen, I get it; you are numb, checked out, whatever, but they will find you and kill you if you stay here."

Remko raised his head to return Jesse's look. "Let them," he said, his voice cracking and dry. How long had it been since he'd had water or food?

"This is crazy," Wire said. "Remko, you can't just give up."

Someone else poked a head into the tent. Kate. "We have to go now," she said.

"Remko, please," Jesse said. "We need you, man."

Remko shook his head and yanked away from Jesse. "Leave me."

"We can't—" Jesse started.

"Leave me!"

Wire just stood back, shaking his head. "He's lost it."

"Leave him," Kate said.

"We can't just—" Jesse fought.

"We have no choice," Wire said.

The three stood looking down at Remko as he hung his head between his shoulders and felt dark, raw sorrow finally push its way through the heavy fog. Tears slid down his face, dripped from his chin. Pain gripped him as if it had wrapped itself around his heart and was squeezing. Eventually the others left and he was alone again with his pain.

Again time lurched forward, but how much wasn't measurable. They did come, as Wire and Jesse had said they would, two large men dressed in black, surprised to find a man bound inside a tent. They dragged him out, threw him in the back of a CityWatch vehicle, and drove him away from camp. They tried to ask him questions, but Remko kept quiet, not because he was being stubborn or defensive but because he had nothing to say. He felt as if he were nothing at all.

/ / /

Carrington saw their approach from the south. Over the last several days, Ramses had been using a device that Wire had programmed to watch for activity and monitor radio communication. Two days ago, they had stumbled upon an old barn, tucked inside a heavy covering of trees. It was rotting away from time but at least had given them a roof and some shelter from the harsh winds that found them at night. They knew they couldn't stay here long, but the children needed to rest, so they had spent the last forty-eight hours hunting, scavenging, and collecting what they could, searching for their next move.

A couple of hours earlier Ramses had picked up a radio frequency that he couldn't make out. They were pretty certain it wasn't CityWatch from the type of codes they were using, and a surge of hope had poured through the small group. It could be Remko and the others.

The thought gave people energy, but Carrington couldn't ignore the worry blossoming in her chest. Something was wrong, though she couldn't place her finger on it. The feeling had been following her for days, like a bad omen or a disturbing dream she couldn't shake. She practiced remembering who she was and what Aaron had told her, and that alleviated the fear for a time, but it always returned. It wasn't fear for herself or those around her; it was fear for something or someone else, and as the small group approached on the horizon, Carrington felt certain for the first time that the fear was for Remko. She didn't know how, but she knew he wouldn't be with them.

Her fears were confirmed as Wire, Kate, Jesse, and a teenage girl and small boy whom Carrington didn't recognize approached.

No Remko.

Her heart burst, dropping into her gut and releasing the sorrow that had been building for days.

Others rushed to greet them while Carrington escaped behind a decaying stone wall that barely hid her. Tears streamed from her eyes, her breath impossible to catch and keep steady. She clasped her hands over her mouth to hide her sobs and slid to her knees.

Her mind begged her to consider that she might be over-reacting, that she shouldn't be jumping to such drastic conclusions, but her heart knew the truth. Had known for days.

Suddenly the overwhelming reality of it all felt like too much to bear. She couldn't do any of this without him. The fear became more real than it had ever been. She felt as if physical hands were shaking her until it hurt.

She swallowed her pain and wiped her face as footsteps

approached the wall that hid her. The steps rounded the corner and she glanced up to see Jesse. His face was mournful and she moved to stand.

"Don't," he said and took a couple steps to cross in front of her. He slid down the wall on her right side. She readjusted on the cold cement floor, her back pressed against the stone next to him.

They sat in silence for a little while, the warm breeze drying Carrington's tears. Jesse yanked a long piece of grass that was sprouting up between the cement blocks and twirled it between his fingers.

"How did you find us?" Carrington asked.

"Wire picked up the radio frequency that Ramses was sending out, or at least I think he did. I don't really understand how any of that works," Jesse said.

They fell quiet again, neither of them wanting to go where the next question would lead.

Carrington finally worked up the courage to ask, her mind desperate to know. "Is he dead?" She choked it out through barely controlled emotions and waited for Jesse to say yes.

"No," he said.

Carrington turned to look at him.

"Or he wasn't when we left him," Jesse said.

"Left him?"

Jesse was quiet for a long time and Carrington fought the urge to grab his neck and shake answers from him.

"I think assuming you and Elise were dead was what

finally pushed him over the edge," Jesse said. "The thought of losing you is what made him pull the trigger."

Dread exploded in Carrington's gut. "What?"

"He tried to shoot Aaron."

Her fear and worry shifted and the conflicting emotions inside her felt like sharp pieces of glass scraping across her mind. Jesse quickly replayed the story of Remko snapping and shooting Aaron with intent to kill. How the gun hadn't worked, how they'd tried to bring him but he wouldn't come, how the CityWatch guards had most likely found him and how his current status was uncertain. Every word that fell from Jesse's mouth increased the shock and despair swirling inside her. How could she not have seen how close Remko was to breaking?

After retelling the events of earlier, Jesse fell into deep contemplation. For long minutes there was nothing but wind and the faint voices of those on the other side of the wall. Carrington couldn't even cry at this point; all she could do was wonder where it had all gone so terribly wrong.

The blame was hard to escape. Remko had followed her into this life, trusted Aaron because he'd loved her, and now she had killed him.

"This is real, isn't it?" Jesse asked.

His words stirred her from her thoughts. "What do you mean?"

"Aaron, his way. This call, the song you hear—it's all real."

Carrington didn't respond. Jesse didn't need her to; he

was working it through out loud, but he already knew the answer in his heart.

"I tested that gun; it should have worked," Jesse said.

Again Carrington stayed quiet as Jesse processed.

"Who is he?" Jesse asked.

"If he were here, he'd say he was just a man," Carrington said.

Jesse chuckled under his breath and Carrington felt a fresh rush of tears. What was she supposed to do now? Should they go after him, try to save him from the Authority—the same Authority from whom he had saved so many? Would anyone go? Would Wire and Kate tell people what he had done? How could he come back from that? But then, he wouldn't have to figure it out. She knew—like she'd known he wasn't with Wire's group—that Remko wasn't coming back at all.

"I just didn't think it was actually real," Jesse said, breaking the silence.

Carrington turned to see him looking off to the west, watching the sun as it began its descent from the sky. She placed her hand on his shoulder and he glanced at her, surprised, as if he had forgotten she was there. His eyes were filled with worry, his face haunted by whatever was happening in his mind. He looked as if he wanted to say something but instead dropped his eyes and the silence returned.

Carrington wanted to tell him it would be all right, but she couldn't get the words to form in her mouth because she wasn't even sure they were true.

26

The room was a sterile white. The walls, the floor, every inch was clean and shimmering white. Remko sat alone on the only object in the room, a hard steel chair that was bolted to the floor. His hands were bound behind his back while his ankles were tied to the chair's legs. The guards who had led him into this room had taken extra precautions to ensure his restraints were inescapable. Remko had considered telling them there was no need, but he'd remained silent and let them work.

After retrieving him from the camp, they'd tried asking him questions, pumping him for the location of any other Seer members, searching for clues as to why he'd been bound, why he'd been left behind, why he wasn't fighting back, but Remko had shut them out and remained in his black hole. Eventually they had given up, and the rest of the journey had been conducted in silence.

He wasn't sure how long he'd been sitting inside the perfectly white room—minutes, hours, or days—when the door slid open behind him. Footsteps echoed off the walls as two guards, carrying another steel chair, appeared and placed the object in front of Remko, facing him.

They left without a word and another moment passed before a softer set of footsteps glided by Remko's left side. Remko didn't raise his eyes but saw someone sit in the chair before him. The newcomer crossed his legs and Remko knew from the colorful material that made up the man's clothes that he was now in the presence of an Authority member.

"They told me you were being very quiet; I see they weren't exaggerating," the man said.

Remko didn't recognize his voice, which meant this man had to be Damien Gold, the new Authority President. The black hole surrounding Remko's mind threatened to crack. How many Seer executions could be attributed to the man sitting inches from him?

"I must be honest; I assumed you would be quite different. From the way people talk about you, I expected more fight," Damien said.

Remko kept his eyes trained on the man's shoes. A small part of his brain began to pulse back to life. Maybe this man had Carrington and Elise; maybe they were alive and being held close by. Maybe he should still be fighting for them. The buzzing in his mind returned but only to remind Remko how useless he was. Even if Carrington and Elise were still alive, an idea that went against every impulse in his body, he wouldn't be able to do anything to save them. He never really had been able to. All his faith had been a lie. He knew that now. It would be better to die and hope that there was someplace beyond this life where they could all be united together again.

"To tell you the truth, I thought this was going to be much more difficult, but it seems as though something has already broken your spirit, so the transition should happen quite nicely," Damien said.

Remko looked up to meet Damien's eyes for the first time. The man was younger than Remko had expected, but his eyes were exactly as he'd pictured: cold, dark, mechanical. This man would be responsible for his death and would never lose a moment's sleep over it.

Damien gave Remko a small smile and casually folded his hands in his lap. He held Remko's gaze, his face calm as if he were already sure of how this would end. Remko had once longed for the certainty he saw in Damien's face; now he only wished for it all to be over.

"I have been waiting for some time to finally meet you," Damien said. "You have become somewhat of a hero among certain groups. People believe you can save them."

"They're wrong," Remko said.

"Of course they are, but that's the problem with humanity. People need to believe that the impossible is possible. That somewhere over the horizon there is freedom."

"I don't believe in freedom," Remko said.

Damien gave Remko a curious look that dissolved into a chuckle. "Then what have you been fighting for?"

Remko couldn't answer, because the truth was he didn't know.

"I actually believe the two of us are more alike than you think. I'm guessing you no longer believe in freedom because your search for the freedom you so desperately desired has failed you. I too once wondered about freedom, but I learned that the question isn't whether or not freedom exists; no, the better question, my friend, is whether or not freedom is necessary."

Damien stood and began to pace. "See, Remko, what I am trying to do is show people that freedom does not have to be a choice. When you eliminate the desire for choice— the human default that says I should be able to choose my own path, that my will should be able to lead—then you eliminate the need for freedom. Without freedom, you have peace and order—true order, not governed by fear and law but rather by people's biochemical makeup."

Damien stopped pacing and fixed Remko again with his intense gaze. "At some point in the evolutionary process, man began to define his truest inner parts as the soul, that imaginary part of the human mind that gives us the inclination to stand against the pack, against the larger group, in order to assert our own dominance. Instead of serving the pack and the greater whole, we serve ourselves. In this we find rebellion, and as long as the option to rebel exists, humanity can never reach its full capacity. Something or someone always gets in the way of progress. But what if we remove the idea of freedom and the soul altogether?"

Damien moved back to his seat and sat on the edge, his knees nearly scraping against Remko's. "How is such a thing possible, you are probably wondering. With science. By removing the memories that convince us we have rights, by changing the neural networks that we associate with freedom, we can physically rewrite the way human minds react to situations so that when faced with a choice to rebel and fight for freedom, they won't."

"That's what this is?" Remko asked. He realized for the first time that he wasn't in the Authority City, as he had assumed; he was in the facility hidden in the valley, the Genesis Compound, where they were experimenting on people. Changing their brains, taking away their souls. The itching that struggled to wake Remko's mind surged again deep inside the dark fog.

"This," Damien said, spreading his arms out wide, "is Genesis. A new beginning. A proper beginning."

"You can't take away a person's ability to choose freedom," Remko said.

Damien sat back in his chair. "Can't we? Have you not lost your freedom? Have you not realized freedom was a myth to begin with? An idea that your soul created that you can't actually achieve? Think of those who have suffered for the sake of your supposed freedom. In the name of your rebellion. Have any of you found it?"

The itching began to die off as memories of failures crashed back against Remko's mind.

"Are you happy that your soul created a false idea that led you through so much pain?" Damien asked.

Remko swallowed and dropped his eyes to the white floor. The truth in Damien's words resonated within his chest.

"Wouldn't it have been better to never believe the lie at all?"

Yes, Remko wanted to say.

Damien leaned forward again, propping his elbows on his knees and dropping his voice. "I can take it away; I can save you from your self-inflicted misery. Aaron may have offered you freedom from the Authority and its laws, but I'm not offering you a fairy tale."

Remko peered back up at Damien's cold stare.

"What I'm offering actually exists. I'm offering you a way to never need the idea of choice or freedom again."

Remko couldn't ignore the pull toward Damien's offer. Not that he actually had a choice; he was bound to a chair in a highly secure facility. He knew he would probably need to accept what Damien was offering or accept his own death.

"If it helps," Damien said, "you won't remember any of this. The people you fought for, the false ideas you carried—all of it will be gone. You'll only know peace. Would you like to see?"

Remko stared straight ahead as Damien stood and walked over to the door. He heard the man lightly knock and heard the door slide open. More footsteps joined Damien's as the man reappeared in Remko's view with a familiar face. Sam.

The boy stood unharmed, gazing through Remko rather than at him. His face was at ease, his eyes clear. He looked at Damien as if awaiting instruction.

Damien motioned for Sam to sit in the free chair and Sam did.

"Sam, I would like you to meet Remko," Damien said.

Sam nodded and extended his hand. Remko glanced at his friend's fingers and then back at his face. No sign of familiarity registered in Sam's eyes. It was as if he'd never seen Remko's face before this moment. The itching started again.

"Sam," Remko said. "Sam, don't you know me?"

Sam squinted curiously and looked up at Damien. "Should I know him?"

Remko couldn't believe what he was seeing.

Damien cleared his throat. "Look closely, Sam. You tell me—do you know him?"

Sam turned his gaze back to Remko and searched his face. A moment of silence lingered as Sam surveyed Remko's features and then huffed. "Sorry, man. If we've met, I don't remember." He chuckled and offered Remko an apologetic smile.

Remko didn't know how to react.

"That's fine, Sam; you can go," Damien said.

Sam nodded and stood, walking toward the exit.

Damien waited until the door was closed and Sam was gone before sitting back down across from Remko. The itch in Remko's brain had grown; it didn't seem possible that Sam could just forget everything they had faced together.

At first Remko sensed anger, and a twinge of it crawled its way through the darkness that still held most of his mind in a numb state. How could they do that to Sam? Take away his memories, change the way he saw the world? But quickly the anger turned to envy. Damien was offering to do the same for him. To help Remko forget the pain and loss. To forget the failure.

Would he be able to do the same in death? Or would his fears just follow him into whatever lay beyond? If freedom really was a lie, then wouldn't it be better to just forget he needed freedom at all?

"Don't worry, Remko; I intend to erase your pain and help you walk into the future of humanity," Damien said, "but before we get started, I do have to ask about something. Aaron. How do we locate him?"

Remko looked up to find Damien's cold stare boring into his skull.

"We have asked others, of course. Neil—you remember him, the one who gave up your camp? He has proven to be little to no use on the subject."

So Neil was the reason the camp had been invaded. Remko should have guessed.

"Although he's going to be very helpful with building a new city," Damien said.

A new city? What exactly were Damien's plans? The itching intensified for a moment before the majority of Remko's mind, the part that was past caring, shut out his curiosity. What did it matter? He wouldn't remember this anyway; soon he would be free from this reality and its torments.

"What can you tell me about Aaron?" Damien asked again.

Remko refocused his mind on Aaron. The man who couldn't be killed. The man who insisted that freedom was within reach. The man who had led them all astray.

"Aaron won't be a problem," Remko said.

"Oh? And why is that?" Damien asked.

"Because Aaron needs freedom to exist in order to lead people out of the city. Take away the need for freedom and you ruin the man's charade."

Damien looked at Remko for a long second before a smile played over his lips. "Just as I said, you and I aren't that different at all."

27

Carrington sat up from the mat where she had been sleeping. The sky was dark around her, still and silent. Sweat made her top cling to her skin and her hair stick to the sides of her face. The air around her head felt thick and thin at the same time, and she struggled to breathe. Something was wrong.

She'd gone to bed early. The day had been exhausting. Word of what Remko had done—or tried to do—to Aaron had spread, and people had been looking at her differently. As if she had been the one pulling the trigger that hadn't released a bullet. They talked to her with pity in their voices as if afraid that saying the wrong thing would send her off the edge.

Wire and Kate would hardly look at her, whether from anger or shame she couldn't be sure. Jesse was the only person who spoke to her like she was still human, but he mostly kept to himself. Lost in thought, putting distance between him and the group as they traveled.

Ramses was desperately trying to remain focused. The news of Remko's actions and capture had hit him harder than he was letting on. Lesley walked around like a mouse searching for cheese, frantic to make sure everyone was okay, trying to keep everything in order.

When they'd finally decided to stop for the night, Carrington had taken her leave with Elise. No one was saying anything to her, but she knew they were all thinking about her; she could hear their thoughts screaming.

Carrington glanced around. She'd been having a nightmare—at least she thought she had. She couldn't remember, but there was a slight shake in her fingers and her heart was racing. Something had been happening in the depths of her mind that had stirred her awake. She clamped her eyes shut and focused on getting air in and out of her lungs. One inhale and one exhale at a time. She felt a soothing sensation begin to erase the panic. It had just been a nightmare.

She turned to search for the soft touch of Elise's skin. The warm and comforting contact that helped Carrington find strength in all the darkness of the life around her. Her hand felt the spot where Elise should have been and found nothing. It was hard to see in the dark, but the baby must have rolled. Panic opened in her chest and she carefully rummaged through the assortment of blankets they were using as a bed. Nothing.

The panic rose through her chest and detonated in her mind. "Elise," she said, then called louder. "Elise!"

Someone stirred to her left. Lesley. "Carrington?" Lesley asked through the sleepy fog in her voice.

"Elise! Elise!" Carrington shot up and yanked the blankets clear of the space on the ground they had claimed.

"Carrington, what is it?" Lesley asked. She was also

standing now, and Carrington registered the movement of several others around them. Her fear and panic threatened to make her head explode as she searched madly around her.

"Elise—where is Elise?" Carrington asked.

"Elise?" Lesley asked, worry creeping into her words. "I don't—"

"Elise!" Carrington yelled.

"Oh no, no, no," Lesley whispered and started moving about camp, asking people if they had seen the baby.

Jesse stumbled into Carrington's sights as she pulled away from those trying to help, her mind focused only on finding her daughter. A familiar sense of loss filled her gut and she ignored the tears moistening her face. It was the same feeling she'd had when Remko hadn't shown up with the others, the same way she'd felt when Larkin had been captured. It was the same dread that let her know, before the reality hit, that nothing was going to be the same.

Elise had been by her side when she'd fallen asleep. She wasn't even four months old; she couldn't have left on her own. The thought made the panic rage into anger and she felt heat spread down her back. The entire camp was stirring now, people asking what had happened, some up and searching.

"Help!" someone called from the night, and several others moved toward the cry. Everything seemed to move quickly yet caught up in slow motion all at once. Carrington stared at the empty pile of blankets where

Elise should have been and tried to see past the blaring proof that was in front of her. Elise couldn't be missing. Carrington couldn't survive that.

"Get him close to the fire," Ramses said.

Carrington saw her brother-in-law materialize out of the dark shadows, Wire on the opposite side of the body they were carrying. The body was slumped forward, head hanging toward the ground, feet dragging through the dirt, creating lines behind them. Ramses carefully lowered the figure and the firelight caught its face. Connor. He was pale even in the dim light. Lesley moved forward to help, but Carrington just stared. She too was caught in slow motion; the world halted in a haze that she couldn't get through.

The top left corner of Connor's shirt was soaked through with blood and he had sustained a massive wound to his forehead. He was unconscious, but his shoulders convulsed as the group tried to rouse him. The flames in the fire to his right flickered up into the darkness and Carrington watched them dance, such a brilliant contrast against the night. Fear and panic were pounding on the steel door that her mind had forged to protect her from the truth. The sound echoed through the nothingness filling her brain and she felt tears drip off her chin.

She should be shouting like a crazy woman, rushing around, screaming into the sky, demanding that the universe give her back all she had lost. Refusing to believe what was standing in front of her, having a mental break of a different kind, instead of standing like a statue, lost to sorrow.

"Connor," Ramses said, splashing water over the man's face. "Connor, come on; wake up."

Kate and Jesse had joined the group by the fire, the rest of the camp gathering around just outside the ring of light the fire cast.

"I can't locate the source of bleeding—something's lodged in his shoulder or chest, I can't tell," Wire said, ripping away the portion of Connor's shirt that was stained.

"Come on, Connor," Ramses said, splashing more water over Connor's face.

Connor gasped and his eyes fluttered open. A moment of relief filled the group, and then the night was filled with Connor's groans. His hand moved to his chest, his body lurching in pain as Wire dug around to locate what was causing all the blood.

"Hold him," Wire said to Ramses, who clamped down on Connor as Wire worked.

Connor cried out in pain, his face glistening with sweat. He mumbled something no one could make out.

"What?" Ramses asked.

"Connor, I need you to tell me how to get this out," Wire said. There was desperation in his tone that he was struggling to hide.

Connor spoke again. "Elise . . ."

The sound of her daughter's name snapped Carrington out of her daze and she rushed toward Connor, pushed her way through, and dropped to her knees to look him in the eye. "What about Elise?" she asked.

Connor's eyes were drooping, his consciousness slipping.

"Connor," Carrington said, taking both of his shoulders in her hands and shaking. "Tell me what you know about Elise."

"He's losing too much blood," Wire said.

A fresh wave of tears rocked Carrington's body. The fog that her mind had instinctively placed over her was gone and only her violent panic and terror remained. "Tell me about my daughter!"

"Carrington," Ramses said, gripping her arms, but she shrugged him off and clasped Connor's face in her hands. She moved herself so that they were only inches apart.

"Connor, talk to me," she begged.

His eyes opened and he saw her face. Tears filled his eyes and Carrington thought she might combust. He moved his lips, speaking softly but audibly.

"He took her. I tried to stop them."

"Who?" Carrington asked. "Who took her?"

"Neil."

Shock hit her like a brick straight across the face, her head ringing from impact. "No—he was taken . . ." She shook her head, her thoughts drifting away.

"Neil," Connor said again before gasping in pain.

"I'm going after them," Jesse said.

"I'll go with you," Kate said.

"You're still injured; you need to stay."

"You can't go alone."

Carrington glanced up to meet Jesse's gaze and he nodded toward her.

"Stay in camp," Jesse said to Kate before turning and vanishing into the night.

"Found something. Hold him," Wire said.

Connor's screams pierced the sky, rattling Carrington's bones, and Ramses ripped her away as he moved in to secure the patient. Connor's cries lasted a couple of long moments before he fell completely silent, having passed out from the pain. Wire dug his fingers into the spot on Connor's chest and yanked out the broken end of a dagger. More blood gushed from the wound and Lesley was there with a wadded cloth. They all worked, trying to save the man's life, and Carrington again was trapped in slow motion. Her mind tried to wrap itself around Connor's words.

Neil.

Impossible.

Why?

He took her.

He took Elise. Her Elise. While she was sound asleep beside the baby, he had taken her. A man she had trusted, cared for. Connor must be mistaken. He must be confused. How could Neil have escaped, and how could he have found them? And why? It didn't make sense; he'd been taken with the others. Hadn't he? Her brain couldn't make sense of it, couldn't rationalize why he would do such a thing. What would he gain? She had come to know him.

He had warned them, saved them. He wouldn't . . . but then maybe she'd never known him at all.

"Carrington," a voice said beside her, followed by a gentle touch. She turned to see that Kate had moved to her side. Her face was empathetic, filled with sorrow, which was unusual for Kate. The girl was always so strong and if not strong then angry. That was the way she processed emotions. But standing beside Carrington now, she looked like a lost child. The sight brought a comfort Carrington wasn't expecting and a sob broke from her mouth. She tried to hold her weeping at bay, but she was out of strength. Out of fight.

She folded forward and down onto her knees, tears rocking her whole body. Kate slid down beside her and folded her into her chest as Carrington cried out into the night. The camp fell away, the fire, the bleeding body, and the rest of her people. All that existed were the arms around her and the anguish of her tears.

/ / /

They called them holding rooms, which made sense since they served only one purpose: to hold their prisoners. After finishing his talk with Damien, Remko had been escorted through a long white hallway into another white room that held a single steel medical chair with long, pale restraining straps. Remko didn't fight as they secured him to the chair and administered a rather painful injection into his lower back.

Then they escorted him to his own holding room, where a bowl of hot soup and a single glass of water had been placed on the small desk inside the space.

The room was plain. A bed, a desk, a nightstand, a chair. No windows, light-gray walls, starched white sheets. Nothing felt comforting or warm, but Remko had long ago abandoned warmth and comfort. He spent the first few hours thinking about what warmth and comfort felt like and found he could hardly remember.

There had been a time with Carrington early on, after they had been married, when fighting against the Authority had felt more like a game than like a prison. He had been comfortable then. Even with the little they'd had, even with the constant running and planning, they had been comfortable. Warm. Nights had been for sleeping and days for surgical attacks that could win them their war.

He couldn't place the exact moment when that had changed. It threatened to drive him mad, as he sat against the single bed in his new room, that he couldn't remember when the world had changed. When the fun had ceased and there had only been danger and when looking at the woman he loved had filled him with worry instead of peace. Maybe it had been after Elise's birth. After the risks became higher than he'd imagined. He should have felt guilty for bringing an innocent life into a world of torment, but he didn't know then what he knew now.

Remko tried to remember the details of the baby's face. Her nose and eyes and fingers. The longer he thought about her, the less he could see. Damien had warned him that the transition was different for everyone, that it could be painful. He'd been told he would start to forget things that weren't deemed necessary to the transformation. Was this forgetfulness the injection, or was it his mind shutting out the things that would only cause him pain? Remko didn't know.

Time didn't exist in the holding rooms because he had no way of tracking it. Each moment simply melted into the next. Sometimes his head was filled with thoughts of his past, of what he would never have again, of what he didn't want to have anymore. Other times his mind was strangely void and dark, filled with the haze that he had become so familiar with.

They brought him a second tray of food, so maybe a day had passed, or maybe they fed the inmates twice a day. He couldn't be sure. He stretched out on the single cot and waited for his memories to vanish.

He tested himself, tried to recall events from his past, and each time he remembered what was supposed to be erased from his mind, he worried that the injection wasn't working. That was his only salvation anymore. That he would be able to forget and have a different future.

After food was brought to him a third time, things started to change. His numb state broke, and waves of emotions crashed against him. All at once and then nothing, as if someone were flipping a switch, on and off again. At first he'd just focused on breathing through the raging sea of panic, fear, worry, sorrow, excitement. He'd focused on its passing, his fingers shaking, his heart thundering, his skin shivering. And finally it would, and he'd go back to being numb, staring at the walls, waiting for the memories to fade.

But when they brought him food for the fourth time, Remko felt his mind starting to break. He could feel the injection scurrying through his body. Like black beetles racing to devour what was his, their little legs itching across his brain as they moved, their teeth gnawing at his mind, their bodies burrowing into the deepest places of his consciousness. It was impossible to hear anything other than the *tap, tap, tap* of their spindly legs.

Remko wanted them out. He scraped at his scalp, pacing, trying to recall and focus on memories that would distract him. Carrington, Elise. Dodson, his former boss. Helms, his former partner, murdered by the Authority. Their faces clear but paired with the *tap, tap* of the demons living inside his brain. Food came a fifth time. Were they feeding him twice a day or once? How long had he been locked in this stone box? He tried to count the minutes between food deliveries, but the itching of memory-erasing insects made it impossible to keep his focus.

He sat on the edge of the bed, his knee bouncing with the constant tapping of his left foot. His palms moist, his head throbbing.

"Wow," a voice came.

Remko's head snapped up so quickly that a sliver of pain coursed down his neck. His eyes met a figure lingering in the corner of the room. The body leaned back against the wall, one ankle crossed over the other, his arms folded across his chest. A familiar ease filled his face, a face Remko could have drawn from memory.

Remko stopped breathing.

Impossible.

"You look terrible," Helms said.

Remko couldn't make his lips move. His body felt like stone, frozen except for his itching mind and the twitch that pulled at his cheek. His friend's dark skin was illuminated by the light-gray walls, his brown eyes filled with life, his smile wide and familiar.

"The silent treatment, really?" Helms asked. He chuckled and shook his head. The sound was so comforting that Remko could feel tears collecting in his eyes.

"Should have known without me you'd become a big wuss," Helms said.

"You're dead," Remko said so quietly it hardly came out as words.

"Wow," Helms said, his eyes growing mockingly large. "That was a terrible comeback."

Remko felt a laugh leave his throat even though his eyes were full of sorrow. He knew he was hallucinating; somewhere in his mind he understood that this couldn't be real. But seeing Helms standing only a few feet away, his chest rising and falling with each breath, his face bright and alive, his voice the same, his jokes the same, everything as it had been, Remko couldn't chase off the hope that this was really happening.

Or maybe Remko was dead too, and that's why he could see his old friend so clearly.

"You aren't dead," Helms said, pushing himself off the wall. "You are stupid, though." Helms took a couple steps and stood tall in the center of the room. He looked around and nodded. "This place could use some color."

"What are you doing here?" Remko asked.

"You tell me, buddy; you're the one imagining me."

Suddenly the familiar pain of loss filled Remko's chest. He *was* imagining him. Helms was dead. It was as if Remko's mind had turned against him and was forcing him to suffer while the little monsters in his head ate away at his brain. He didn't want to see Helms's face, didn't want to imagine the laughs they'd had or the times they'd shared. He wanted to forget it all—the pain, the sorrow, the memories. That's why he was here. Fury exploded in his body; he wanted Helms out.

Remko dropped his eyes to the floor. "Leave me alone."

"When have I ever done what you've told me to?" Helms said with a snort.

Remko could feel his hands vibrating at his sides. Panic gripped his heart and made him feel like he was suffocating. He couldn't be stuck with Helms for hours, tormented by what could never be.

"Just get out," Remko said again, louder.

"Whoa, don't get mad at me," Helms said and moved close enough that Remko could hear him breathing. "You chose this, remember?"

Remko stood to push Helms back, but found his friend was no longer there. Remko searched the room and was alone once again. His breath came in short, hurried gasps, the shaking in his hands now making its way through his entire body.

The insects were back at work, digging their way deeper into his mind, their gnawing inescapable.

He stopped resisting them. He wanted the memories gone, and if the insects couldn't rid him of his pain, then he wanted to die.

28

Damien waited as the Scientist watched the screen displaying their newest subject. Nerves prickled his skin, but he ignored the sensation. Finding Remko hadn't gone exactly as they'd predicted, but they'd found him all the same. Damien wanted the Scientist to be proud of all they'd accomplished. The Genesis injection was working. They had dozens of cases now where the proper neural networks had been erased and the new ones built. Sam was a shining example of progress and success.

So why the nerves? Why the worry that he would still fail? Had he not succeeded already?

Damien kept these thoughts to himself. But what he needed was for the Scientist to acknowledge the work he had done here. To recognize that Damien had been the right choice of leader for this new civilization. Damien knew requiring praise was a sign of weakness, that if the Scientist knew the thoughts spinning through his head he would be furious. That didn't stop him from longing for his mentor's approval; it only stopped him from expressing that desire.

The Scientist carefully turned around to face Damien. "How long until the transition is complete?"

"The results have varied from subject to subject, but we believe based on the rate of his progression that within the next forty-eight hours he should be ready for testing."

"And are we prepared for that?"

Damien nodded, a smirk on his face. "We have what we need."

"Good." The Scientist glanced over his shoulder at the screen where Remko was continuing to mumble to himself. The Seer was transitioning nicely, Damien thought as the Scientist dropped his eyes from the screen and headed toward the door.

"Things are progressing well," Damien said. He knew he was fishing, but he didn't care. He deserved a little acknowledgment.

The Scientist turned back around, his face devoid of emotion. Damien suddenly wished he'd kept his mouth shut, and from the coldness in the Scientist's face, clearly he did too.

"Keep me posted on his progress. For your sake I hope this goes as well as you've foolishly assumed it will," the Scientist said.

Without another word, the teacher left Damien alone to stew on his own inadequacies.

/ / /

The food was bland; it tasted exactly the same each time, as if they had made a large-enough amount to cover a week's worth of meals, sloshed a helping into a bowl, and reheated it right before bringing it to him. He stopped tasting it after the seventh time it was offered. He simply shoveled it down because he was supposed to.

He wasn't sure if the injection was working or if it was merely the time trapped in this plain, dull room that was blurring his memories. He thought about being a child, running and playing with his brother. He couldn't picture his brother's face anymore and as he scooped a spoonful of soup into his mouth, he was struck with an odd sensation. Did he even have a brother?

The question rattled him somewhere deep in his core. He remembered being full of energy, laughing, rolling through the small patch of grass they'd used as a front yard. He even felt like a presence should be with him in his memories, but suddenly he couldn't remember what that presence was. A sister? A brother? His parents?

Did he have parents? Of course he did—how else could he be here—but who were they? Names, faces, and events were replaced with static inside his head. Then, slowly but somehow all at once, they turned to black. Blotted out, as if he'd imagined them or dreamed them.

Remko pushed back from the desk and felt a rush of rage course through his chest. He grabbed the bowl and slung it toward the opposite wall. It cracked against the stone and echoed through the room, soup splattering on the wall and running in lines down its surface.

He couldn't catch his breath. He didn't know where he came from. They were stealing his memories.

You chose this.

Helms's words filled the space around his head and Remko spun around to see if the ghost was there to haunt him again. But no one was there. He took several long, deep breaths and found himself staring at the bits of food sliding down the wall across the room.

He had asked for this. He had asked for this.

He closed his eyes and tried to ignore the blank moments of his past that were calling for his attention.

He had asked for this; he wanted to forget the pain, to shove it out.

Even with the knowledge that he wanted this, he still felt as if he were being robbed.

Suddenly the weight of it all felt too heavy to carry. Exhaustion overwhelmed his senses, and he took several steps toward the single bed before him. He laid himself down and yanked the starched sheet up over his head. The room was dimly lit anyway, so the sheet, though thin, blocked out enough light to make Remko feel like the darkness in his mind had seeped out into the world around him. He barely had time to wonder if sleep would find him before it did.

/ / /

He woke quickly, as if he had only just closed his eyes. Wind rustled across his face and a chill filled his bones. He reached for the sheet to wrap it tighter around his shoulders but found nothing.

Remko sat up and let the scene before him register in his mind. He was outside, no longer in his holding cell. Tall, golden grass swayed on all sides of him, high enough that from his seated position he couldn't see over it. The sun was present, but the field was still cool, the ground under Remko's hands chilled as if a deep winter's snow had just melted, leaving behind its cold in the depths of the earth.

The sky was blue, white puffy clouds hung here and there, birds sang, and the wind swirled to a perfectly harmonious melody.

Remko wondered why he didn't feel panicked at waking up in this strange place, but he didn't. In fact, the opposite of panic softly coursed under his skin. Rest, peace, comfort—feelings he had long forgotten.

He stood and turned in a slow circle to take in the rest of the field, but that was all it was. A gold field that stretched in every direction.

He caught sight of a man walking toward him, the stranger's steps calm, his hands stretched out on both sides, the grass sweeping through his fingers. He grew closer, close enough for Remko to make out his face clearly. He had kind, deep-blue eyes and a bright smile; there was a look of something familiar on the man's face. He was familiar altogether, actually, but something was blocking Remko's recollection of him.

A name slipped through the cracks in his brain. *Aaron.*

But it drifted off as soon as it entered. Was it Aaron? Did Remko know an Aaron? The insides of Remko's skull felt fuzzy and he searched through the haze for something concrete, but everything felt foreign.

"Hello, Remko," the man said.

He knew Remko's name; they must know each other.

"I'm sorry; I can't—" Remko faltered.

"I know; don't worry about it," the man said. "My name is Aaron."

Again Remko felt a twinge of familiarity that lasted only a couple of seconds before evaporating into nothing. An ache pulsed in the front of his skull.

"Do we know each other?" Remko asked.

Aaron smiled. "Not really."

Remko felt an ease wash over him. He hadn't forgotten this man; he'd never known him. "Where am I?" Remko asked.

"My Father's field," Aaron said.

"Do I know your Father?"

"Part of you does."

Remko gave Aaron a puzzled look. "So I have forgotten Him?"

Aaron chuckled and nodded. "Life is a series of remembering and forgetting."

Remko didn't understand the man's words but felt the painful pulse return to his brain. "Maybe if I could see Him, then I would remember. Is He here?"

"Always. He never leaves."

Remko glanced around the field, but the only two people were him and the strange man before him. "I don't understand," Remko said.

"It's a different kind of sight. Something you have long forgotten."

"Why are you talking to me in riddles?"

"I'm speaking to you in truth; you only hear riddles because you don't believe."

"Don't believe what?"

"In who you are."

Remko felt the pulse increase. He rubbed his fingers across his forehead to try and ease the building pressure. A single question filled his mind and Remko couldn't think of anything else.

Who am I?

A man named Remko, a soldier, a member of the Authority's society, a servant of that society. He tried to remember what else, struggled to see past the simple things that lay before him. Surely he was more than that? But nothing came. Only those facts were found.

Remko shook his head, annoyed. What else was needed? Why was he letting himself become unraveled at the small words of a man he knew nothing about? And where was this Father of his, and how was he supposed to know Him if He was nowhere to be found?

"I know who I am," Remko said.

"No, you know who they want you to believe you are. But the truth has been lost to the fog," Aaron said.

"And you know me better than I do?"

"I know you are afraid, that fear and failure haunt you. I know you long to be free but only see freedom in escaping what you fear instead of surrendering to it."

Remko felt the soft vibration of knowing buzz at the back of his brain. In the darkest part of his mind. A sense that he might have heard these words before. The emotions that Aaron spoke of slid into his chest. Fear and worry, followed by a deep need to be rid of them. The ache in his forehead increased.

It all felt like madness. To be certain of who he was but lost all at once. The pulse intensified and his entire face felt as if it were on fire. A wild wind whipped across his shoulders and ruffled the ends of his hair. It was both warm and chilled together. The pain in his head didn't ease, and he shut his eyes, taking deep breaths through the discomfort.

Surrender.

The voice seemed to come from the air itself, tickling at the insides of his ears and causing the pounding pain to spike. Remko cried out in agony and dropped his forehead into his hands. He dug his fingernails into his hairline, hoping a different sense of pain would distract him from the torment raging inside his skull.

Surrender.

Another throb of pain exploded behind his eyes and Remko dropped to his knees. Through the darkness in his mind pictures started to form. Through a dirty lens, muffled and unclear and yanking at emotions he didn't understand. A beautiful girl with long golden hair, swinging a sweet child in her arms, the child's hair black as night, both smiling and laughing, their faces fuzzy but their memory enough to bring tears to Remko's eyes. But he couldn't place them; his heart knew them but his mind did not. Why couldn't he see them clearly?

Surrender and see.

"I don't know how," Remko whispered to the wind.

A hand lightly touched his shoulder and through the all-encompassing ache, he opened his eyes to see Aaron squatting down beside him.

"You do know; let it go. Remember who you are, who your Father calls you to be. Then you will have no fear; then you will see," Aaron said.

Remko hung his head and cried out against the pain again. He didn't understand how what this man was saying could be true: a place without fear, a place where he could see.

A very familiar sense of anger blossomed and he shrugged away from Aaron's touch. This man was a stranger, the people dancing in his mind were strangers, this Father of his was absent *and* a stranger. Remko knew who he was; he did see clearly, and he wouldn't be tricked by this mental game. He clamped his eyes shut and closed out everything but the truth he knew.

For the first time, the throbbing torment eased slightly. Remko let go of the notion that Aaron had spoken of, he disregarded the images, disregarded the whispering wind. He pushed it all from his mind and as he did, the pain began to lessen.

He felt several pairs of hands grab him and his eyes snapped open. He was no longer surrounded by tall grass but rather inside a familiar gray room. Two men dressed in white coats were bracing him down on a single bed as another moved to drive a thin needle into his shoulder. The sight made Remko pull back, but the men restraining him were strong and they held on.

"We need you to calm down, Remko; we are only here to help," the man with the needle said.

There was a soft pinch on his shoulder and then, almost instantly, a weary feeling flooded his body.

"This will help you sleep," someone said, but Remko was already fading into darkness.

His mind thought of the field, of the man that he had met there, but hard as he tried, he couldn't remember the man's name. In fact, the more darkness that crept into his mind from the drug, the less he could remember about the field. And within seconds he couldn't remember what he had been thinking about to begin with.

There was more he should be remembering, he thought, something he should be fighting, but he was done with fighting. He tried to remember why he was in this room, tried to remember where he had come from, but all that came was who he was now. A soldier, in the Authority

Army, his purpose to serve. Nothing else mattered or existed.

With a final exhale, Remko let go of the fight and gave in to the only truth he needed.

/ / /

Remko woke with a start. His eyes snapped open and he found a plain ceiling hovering overhead. The place around him was familiar, which he should have expected, but for some reason he had been wondering whether he might wake up somewhere else. He excused the thought and sat up. Food had been served—soup. He enjoyed soup. He moved from his bed to the small desk and sat down to eat. The soup tasted warm and comforting against his tongue. There was a glass of water, the liquid cool as it slid down his throat.

He was nearly finished when the door behind him opened. An average-size man walked in, his face familiar, and Remko was relieved to see his chief commander.

"President Gold, sir," Remko said, standing to greet the man.

"Remko, how are you feeling?" Damien asked.

Remko thought the question odd. "Fine, sir."

"That's good. I heard you had a hard night. Nightmares, I was told."

Remko gave the man a curious look. "I don't think so; I feel fine."

Damien smiled and nodded toward the chair near Remko. Remko moved and pulled the chair around for Damien to sit.

"I'm glad to hear it. Now, I'm going to ask you some questions, and I need you to be honest with me."

Again, an odd question. Remko would never lie to his chief commander. He nodded.

"Does the name Carrington Hale mean anything to you?" Damien asked.

"No, sir."

"What about the name Aaron?"

Remko shook his head. "No, sir."

"Are you sure? Think very carefully."

Remko did, searching the back of his mind. Maybe he was supposed to know them, but he didn't. "I don't know anybody by those names."

Damien paused for a long second, his eyes working over Remko's face. Then a smile broke across his lips and he stood. "Sounds like you may be ready. Let's test your progress, shall we?"

29

Remko was led through a maze of white hallways and into a larger room devoid of furniture. He was asked to stand in the center of the room and wait. Damien walked to the opposite side of the room where another door was located and knocked on it. Remko glanced around the space to see that several men, clad all in black, stood in groups in each corner. They were armed, standing guard and watching. He assumed they must be here because Damien was present. It was crucial for the future of their society that he be kept unharmed.

After a moment, the door Damien had knocked on opened and another guard walked through, carrying an infant. The child in the man's arms was sucking on the blanket she was wrapped in, her eyes moving about the room in wonder. She was so small; thick black hair covered her tiny head and framed her fair face.

They walked over to Remko and Remko noticed the apprehension on the guard's face. He glanced at Remko and seemed to wait for him to have some sort of reaction, but Remko couldn't understand why. He was just a man holding a child.

Remko could feel tension filling the room. The rest of the guards shifted, poised to move if necessary, their eyes trained on Remko and the tiny baby. Remko thought the scene strange and he looked to Damien for some sort of clarity. Damien's face was the only one that remained calm, and at the sight of his comfort, Remko eased.

"Remko, I would like to introduce you to Elise," Damien said, motioning to the small girl.

Remko wasn't sure what the purpose of any of this was, but he smiled and hid his confusion.

"Would you like to hold her?" Damien asked.

Remko was taken aback and he knew it showed on his face. The baby whined a bit in Damien's arms and Remko shook his head.

"I'm fine," Remko said.

"No, here, I insist," Damien said, handing Elise over.

Worry rushed through Remko, but he extended his arms to hold the child that was being shoved at him. She complained a bit as she was transferred, and Remko nervously tried to settle her in his arms. She stopped fussing and looked at Remko with large blue eyes. They were beautiful, much like the child herself, full of innocence and something else that Remko couldn't place. She looked at Remko with wonder, reaching up and grabbing the ends of his hair with her tiny hand, and he felt a smile sneak across his face.

"She is beautiful," Remko said, glancing up at the guard. "Is she yours?"

Several of the other guards in one corner whispered to each other and Remko thought maybe he had said the wrong thing. He wished he'd kept his mouth shut. He felt uncomfortable. She was just a baby, and yet he had nearly let himself be taken with her.

He handed her back to the guard and forced himself not to ask what this was all about. He'd thought Damien had mentioned he would be tested, but this surely couldn't be what he was referring to.

Damien took the child and she fussed as he handed her back to Jesse.

"Excellent," Damien said. "I was about to grab some lunch; would you like to join me?"

Remko was confused but worked to hide it. He knew that the chief commander only made decisions that were for the greater good, so any confusion must be unnecessary. He nodded toward Damien and gave Elise a final glance before turning to leave.

"You did very well today, very well indeed," Damien said. Though Remko couldn't imagine what Damien was referring to, he felt a sense of pride and was thankful for the recognition.

They were nearly to the door when the baby started to cry behind them. The sound was soft at first, and Remko could hear the guard trying to calm her, but it grew in volume, and soon the child was screaming. Damien paused to motion to a group of soldiers in the corner to assist with the child as the noise bounced off the walls around them.

Something itched inside Remko's brain as the child's cries tore at his heart. At first he felt ashamed that he wanted the noise to cease. Babies cried; that was just part of their growing process, but something about hearing this particular baby cry, something about the aching in her tiny voice caused Remko to pause.

Damien walked out the door, but Remko stood, his hands on the doorframe, his feet stuck to the ground. Why was it that he felt he couldn't leave the poor child? Why did all of his cells feel as if their only purpose should be to protect that baby? Damien turned around and looked at Remko.

"Remko, are you coming?" he asked.

A war broke out in Remko's mind. One part needed to follow his commander; the other needed to save that baby. Suddenly a heavy pulse exploded against his skull. He cried out and grabbed the front of his head as pain pounded like a hammer on his brain. His mind flashed with images—a beautiful woman carrying the baby in her arms, the baby playing with Remko's hair and rubbing her small hands across his forehead and nose. The woman dancing in circles with the girl tucked safely in her arms, the woman looking up at Remko, a smile lighting her face.

"Remko, what is wrong?" Damien asked, but Remko could hardly hear him through the new noises filling his head. Laughter, sweet and full, a woman's voice telling him she was pregnant, that she loved him, asking him to run away with her, to leave this place. Memory after memory burst through the thick black wall that his mind had built, and with a final pulse of images, Remko broke free from the illusion.

"Elise," he whispered. Without another word or thought, he spun around and rushed for the child. The whole room moved at once. Guards from every corner ran to catch Remko before he could reach the baby. The man holding Elise moved away, back through the opposite door, the baby wailing in his arms.

Anger ravaged Remko's body and he fought against those trying to hold him. He screamed, letting his fists fly toward the enemy. He connected with the guard closest to him, sending him stumbling backward, but another guard was already closing in. Remko swung again and missed.

"Do not let him get free!" Damien yelled as the guards surrounded Remko.

He was completely outnumbered, and he knew there was no way he was getting through to go after Elise, but that didn't stop him from fighting.

He glanced around the room and came to a halt as his eyes fell on a hooded boy in the corner. He recognized him and something in him knew the boy would help, but the guards overwhelmed him and quickly gained control of his body.

The archer. A friend and ally.

"Help!" Remko yelled at the hooded boy. "Please—Elise!" But the archer stood still in the corner, his face emotionless.

Confusion racked Remko's mind. *Jesse. My friend. What is he doing here? Why won't he help?*

The guards contained him and dragged him back down the maze of hallways into another small room. He recognized it from somewhere, a single medical chair sitting in the center. He screamed and fought, images of Elise haunting every movement.

Damien went with them. "Hold him down," he said.

There was a doctor in the room who looked confused to see Remko again and Damien shouted at him. "Prepare another injection dose!"

The doctor still looked bewildered and Damien had no patience. "Now!"

The doctor stumbled to comply as Remko was taken to the ground. The guards didn't even try to get him in the chair; they simply pushed him to the floor and secured him as another painful injection was driven into his lower back.

Afterward, they pulled him up and escorted him back to his holding cell. Tears moistened his cheeks. His anger still flowed like blood, fast and steady through his veins.

They threw him into his cell and yanked the door shut before Remko could even stumble back to his feet. He rushed to the door and pounded against it with his fists. "Elise, Elise!" Remko's voice cracked with the emotions crashing through his chest. He continued to hammer on the steel door with all his might, ignoring the pain in his hands, ignoring the blood he was leaving behind.

"Elise!" They had her, his daughter, the baby he had

forgotten, the responsibility he had been given and abandoned. They had her and he had no idea what they would do with her.

The minutes dragged on and his pounding slowed, his body sinking lower to the ground from the weight of this ultimate failure. He reached the ground, snot and tears mingled on his face, blood matted to his fists. He had done this to her; he had given her away.

Her cries echoed in his head as he slid to the ground and curled up at the base of the door. His brain ached with the reality of what he had done and somehow, through the endless assault of pain, Remko fell asleep.

/ / /

Damien watched as the Scientist was escorted into the room. The screens before them showed each room as the inmates were given the third meal of the day. Remko's room was skipped as the man had finally passed out from exhaustion from pounding against his cell door.

"What happened?" the Scientist asked. His voice was low and it came out in a growl.

Damien collected his thoughts and again found himself perplexed. What had happened? Everything had gone as it was supposed to, as flawlessly as it had with other patients. How could Remko's mind have broken through?

"Do I need to repeat myself?" the Scientist asked, his voice louder.

"We aren't sure exactly—" Damien started.

"Has any other patient displayed such behavior?" the Scientist asked the man in the white coat to his right, ignoring Damien completely. That was never a good sign. A small whimper came from behind them, and Damien glanced at the small child cradled in a guard's arms. It had taken them quite a while to get the child quiet. The sight of her pink little face caused rage to spring up in Damien's chest. Remko had showed perfect transformation scores until that brat had screamed her heart out. Why?

Damien turned his attention back to the Scientist, who was murmuring quietly with the doctor beside him. This was another failure on Damien's rap sheet, and the Scientist did not handle failure lightly. Damien felt sick at the way worry rolled around inside his gut. So many patients had made the transformation perfectly and were now serving the greater purpose as planned, but each time one person fell from the higher state—which hadn't happened in weeks with the exception of Remko—Damien felt as if he were being brutalized by the Scientist's judgment.

He needed to speak with the Scientist alone, reassure him that he was still suited to bring the revolution into fruition. Assure him that this was Damien's purpose.

The Scientist's voice ripped Damien from his own mental panic. "What of the child?"

A doctor standing nearby stepped forward. "She'll be given the injection as discussed."

"Very well; see that it's done," the Scientist said, nodding to the doctor.

Damien spoke quickly. "I'll see that everything—"

"You have done enough," the Scientist snapped.

Damien felt as if he'd been socked across the chin and nearly stumbled backward.

"What of the Seer camp traitor, Neil?" the doctor asked the Scientist. "He is demanding his son be returned to him."

"He was never getting his son back. Administer the injection to them both immediately," the Scientist said.

The Scientist's eye fell on Damien's face for a long moment and he understood, without words, that he was running out of chances. A rush of heat rippled up his back and his heart began to race.

The Scientist left without another word.

/ / /

Jesse met the Scientist as he left the control room. Still shaken by what he had just witnessed, Jesse knew the old man would already be on edge, so he'd have to choose his words carefully.

The Scientist let the heavy door close behind him, sealing Jesse inside the long white hallway alone with the man. The Scientist looked up at the archer, his face expressionless. They stood for a long moment this way before the Scientist spoke.

"Where have you been?"

"You seem displeased with the results of the trial," Jesse said.

"Don't try and change the subject, boy. I asked you a question."

"I was with them."

"The Seers? Why?"

Jesse considered his answer. "You have always told me that discovery is one of our greatest tools. It is clear that a war is being waged here, and I needed to see for myself what we were fighting against."

"And you abandon me in order to do so?"

"You asked for my loyalty. I needed to be able to give it to you without hesitation. I needed to make sure I was on the right side."

The Scientist searched Jesse's face. "And what have you concluded?"

"I came back, didn't I?"

"And you expect that to be enough for me?"

Jesse wasn't surprised by the Scientist's reaction. The man was one of the few people in his life who had ever taken an interest in Jesse's well-being. Now he felt betrayed, and for that Jesse couldn't blame him.

The story Jesse had told Remko and the Seers wasn't a complete lie; fooling people was always better accomplished when it was mostly truth. Jesse's biological father really had been a miserable drunk, and his grandfather really had been the only one around to tend to him as a child. The old man had taken a part-time job working as a groundskeeper for the Scientist's estate, and Jesse had spent afternoons working the land with him. He'd met the Scientist then, and after his grandfather had passed when Jesse was only eleven, the Scientist had taken Jesse in.

The Scientist had shown Jesse the truth of the poison running through the human bloodstream, explained and helped Jesse understand how the world needed to change and how certain people were called to act out roles that would better humanity.

Jesse had been called, he'd realized quickly. Once a lost boy who believed there was no place for him in this world, he eventually saw that he belonged and furthermore was an essential part of the evolution that was coming.

But old habits lingered, and Jesse had started to question his place. He knew now that had been a mistake. "In truth, there were moments I considered not returning. Their way of life is simple but effective. They really believe Aaron can lead them toward a better life. But I watched that unbridled faith drive a man to try and kill one of his own. I knew then that I would be coming back to you; it was just a matter of leaving at the right time. You taught me to never waste an opportunity for strategy. I wanted to ensure their trust in case it was needed later."

Jesse gave the Scientist an opportunity to respond, but the man just stared at Jesse, waiting to see how the boy would continue.

"Their entire belief system is frail and will be easily broken by the work you are doing here. I see that now."

The Scientist nodded. "I have always known this, and I thought it was something you knew as well."

"Are we not men of science? Is it not our responsibility to question all things we come face-to-face with? That was all I was doing," Jesse said.

The Scientist took a moment to consider Jesse's words. "Yes, we are men of science, but we are still men. I need to know I can trust you for what is to come."

"Understood. I assure you I can regain that trust."

"Time will tell," the Scientist said.

Jesse felt a sense of relief. "What would you like me to do now? Should I reinsert myself among the Seers?"

"No, Remko is still the key, and we have him now. The others will crumble without him. For now, I want you close. I will need you soon enough."

Jesse nodded and followed as the Scientist started down the hall and toward the exit. Jesse matched him in stride and walked beside him as they left the compound.

"I'm sorry if my exploration made you feel abandoned," Jesse said, "but now I can commit without question. This is the right side to be on."

The Scientist gave as much of a smile as was possible for him and nodded. "Yes, it is."

/ / /

Remko opened his eyes. A cloudy sky hung overhead, and a chill sat in the air. It smelled like rain, even though the ground around him was dry. Tall grass encircled him where he lay.

"Even with the dark clouds, this place is perfect," a voice to his right said.

Remko turned his head to see Helms lying beside him. The man had his arms folded behind his head and was using his palms as a pillow. A long piece of grass shot from his mouth as his eyes gazed upward. Seeing him reminded Remko of the events of the last few hours. He had lost Elise.

"How did we get here?" Remko asked.

"This is where the heart comes," Helms stated simply, "when it's lost."

Tears collected in Remko's eyes, and he couldn't stop them from slipping down the sides of his face. The breeze fluttered past the two friends as they lay there, the air drying Remko's tears as it caressed his cheeks.

"Are you lost?" Remko asked.

Helms chuckled, a familiar sound that Remko missed, and pulled the long grass from his lips. "No, I'm here for you."

"So I'm lost?"

"Surely you know that by now."

Remko was silent for a long moment. "How do I find my way back?"

"You aren't going to like what I say."

Remko knew what would come out of his friend's mouth next.

"It doesn't make sense; I can't see how surrendering will save me," Remko said.

Helms twisted around so he was propped up on his arm. "That's because you have no faith. You are seeing with the eyes in your skull. You have to believe, my brother."

Remko pushed himself up from the ground into a sitting position. "I don't know how to do that."

"Again, you aren't going to like what I have to say."

Let it go.

Remko glanced around but knew he wouldn't find anyone else. It was the voice in the wind. He looked at Helms, who was smiling ear to ear, his face filled with peace. Remko stood as a crack of thunder crashed against the sky. He strode forward, wondering how far he would have to run to get away from this agony.

Helms couldn't understand what was building in Remko. All the fear, all the failure he had to be held accountable for. Abruptly the sky overhead opened up and started to pour. Heavy sheets of rain soaked Remko to his core and threatened to wash him off his feet. He turned to see if Helms was okay but couldn't see anything through the downpour. In every direction there was only rain, thick enough to make Remko feel as if he were trapped inside another prison.

Something moved in the rainy haze to his right and a soft laugh broke through the pounding drops. The figure moved, small in size but with power, and Remko found himself chasing after whatever was splitting the sheets of rain as it ran. More laughter, sweet and innocent, reached his ears. He pushed forward with more strength. The creature had disappeared, but something deep inside Remko's gut was desperate to find it.

Another peal of laughter came from his left and Remko pushed in its direction. He ran for several minutes, changing his course to follow the giggles gliding through the air. The rain began to ease and Remko pushed back the hair that was dripping into his eyes. He pulled up to a stop to catch his breath and searched for what he had been chasing.

Several yards ahead he saw him. A boy with black hair, blue eyes, and a familiar face. Remko knew him but wasn't sure how. The boy was climbing up a tree, each branch shaking under his weight.

Remko started for the tree, a nervous twitch setting into his bones. The little boy was climbing too high, but he didn't seem to be stopping anytime soon. The branches got thinner as the boy ascended, but he didn't even seem to notice. He was going to fall.

Remko's jog turned into a full-throttle run. The boy reached the top, his face bright with joy, not a shred of concern for his safety. How could he be so foolish?

"Hey," Remko called, but the boy didn't look his way. "Stop—you'll fall!"

The boy finally glanced at Remko and laughed, shaking his head. He looked down and with a small gasp, he jumped.

Remko felt his heart stop as he watched the boy fall from the tree toward the hard ground. He pumped his legs as hard as he could manage but knew he wasn't going to reach the base of the tree in time to catch him.

"No!" Remko screamed as the boy plummeted into the grass and out of sight. He stopped. Surely the boy had hit the ground and was dead. Remko couldn't find the air he needed to fill his lungs, and his chest ached.

Familiar laughter drifted up from the spot where the boy must have landed and Remko stood in disbelief. He couldn't have survived. Remko took a cautious step forward and saw the grass ruffle just ahead. After a few seconds the boy stepped into Remko's line of sight. Remko felt disbelieving shock smash against his vision. The boy saw Remko and rushed toward him while Remko felt himself instinctively take a step back.

"Hello," the boy said as he approached.

Remko just stared at the boy, unsure of what to say. How was he walking?

"Do you want to try?" the boy asked, pointing to the tree.

Remko realized he was asking if Remko wanted to jump.

"Don't be scared; He'll catch you," the boy said.

"Who?"

The little boy laughed. "Don't you know?"

With a jolt Remko suddenly knew who the boy was. The realization caused him to stumble backward another step. It was him. The little boy was him.

The boy watched Remko with a puzzled look.

The weight of it all—the loss of his family, the fear clutching at his heart, this place filled with confusion, his worry, his self-hatred—suddenly all of it was too much. Remko dropped to his knees and he wept.

Lost to self-pity, he didn't notice the rain stopping, didn't notice the young boy moving toward him, didn't see the way the sun filled the sky. But he felt a tiny hand on his cheek and he raised his head to face himself. The child's eyes shone with the freedom that Remko longed for.

"Don't be afraid; our Father is here. You can trust Him if you want to jump. He never lets me fall," the boy said. The wind whipped around the child and he smiled. "I have to go."

He slipped away and back into the grass, his laughter sailing back to Remko even after he had disappeared.

30

The field around Remko danced in the warm sun. The dark clouds were gone, the rain only a memory now. Time was moving forward, Remko assumed, but maybe there was no time in this place. The boy had been gone for a while, leaving Remko kneeling on the wet ground, the place on his cheek still warm where the boy's hand had been. His words played on repeat in Remko's mind.

You can jump if you want to.

He'll catch you.

Our Father.

Even in the field Remko felt the familiar gnawing of the tiny monsters coming for his memories. Damien had reinjected him and it would only be a matter of time before he started to forget it all again. He had so longed to forget. He had been convinced the only way to survive the pain was to be rid of it. But the words of his smaller self, the way he'd jumped from the top of that tree without hesitation or fear, were causing him to question what he thought he knew.

The words of Helms were burrowing into his mind as well.

That's because you have no faith.

You are seeing with the eyes in your skull.
You have to believe, my brother.

Was that all there was to it—belief? So many around
him had found peace and freedom, and he'd thought he
was heading down the same path, but looking back he
wondered if he had missed something. Overlooked what
was right in front of him.

His logic tried to talk him back from the edge of the
imaginary cliff he was considering leaping off. Of course
belief was not all there was to it. They were fighting a war,
and he was a soldier. He needed to protect those around
him; he was responsible for their well-being. The path
Aaron had sent them on was a lie, filled with dangers that
only tormented him. Helms spoke of faith, but why was
faith necessary in war? Faith was only a distraction.

Remko knew his own arguments by heart, found the
language familiar, but something was different this time.
Somewhere his resolve, his faith in his own wisdom, had
snapped. He had lost everything following his way of
thinking. He had nothing left. He was drained of power
and strength. He would become just a flesh suit, unable
to remember who he had been because his memories were
again being taken from him. What did he have left to
defend? What was he fighting for anymore?

"You could stop fighting," a voice said. Remko glanced
up from the ground he'd been memorizing and saw Aaron
standing several feet ahead of him. Rushes of memories
hurled themselves at Remko and he took a deep breath to

settle himself. The last time he remembered being with this man, he'd tried to kill him. Shame and guilt heaved themselves on top of Remko's head like boulders, crashing one after the other against his feeble stability.

"Because I've lost?" Remko asked.

Aaron moved forward, his eyes warm and fixed on Remko's. "No, because there was never a war to begin with."

Remko let out a laugh that was mixed with a sob and shook his head. "Is that your attempt to make me feel better for what I've done to—" Remko couldn't finish his sentence. Aaron's eyes never left Remko's, but Remko couldn't look at the man any longer. His guilt was slicing him open and threatening to overwhelm him. He should say he was sorry, but the words felt like sand in his mouth. How do you apologize for trying to kill someone? Again Remko went back to staring at the ground.

Aaron closed the distance between them and sat down beside Remko. They sat in silence for a long while, the sun warm on their backs, the wind still.

Aaron spoke first. "Anger is a powerful emotion, one that I have experienced plenty of myself."

"I have a hard time imagining you angry," Remko said.

"I am just a man; I have felt all the things you do. I've just learned to surrender them to my Father."

Remko felt the new tug in his heart at the word *Father*. "And now you feel nothing?"

Aaron chuckled. "Of course I feel. I feel fully, all the

time. I just walk through what I feel without hesitation or fear, because I know who I am."

"All I know about myself is that I've failed everybody, especially you."

"What if I told you that you couldn't fail? That all the outcomes of your choices are just steps on a necessary path to get you here?" Aaron said.

"How could that be possible? I have clearly not lived up to the standards set for me."

"Set for you by whom? Yourself, your ego, the world around us that tries to mark us all and place us in chains?"

Remko glanced up at Aaron. "What else is there?"

Aaron smiled, a sparkle in his eyes. "A different standard. One that calls you by your true name, which says you are blameless, perfect, that your only purpose is to take the journey."

"So people can't mess up?"

"Of course they can, by the standards of this physical world, and they judge themselves and others; they are filled with self-hate and fear that they'll never really be enough."

Remko connected with Aaron's words and felt heat rush to his face.

"But the great news is, my friend, that this isn't the true standard. You can be free from all of that if you want," Aaron said.

"I just don't know if I can believe that," Remko said.

"Yes, well, belief is everything."

The sun worked its way across Remko's skin and its

heat filled his bones. He thought of what it might be like to be truly free. To be fearless, filled with certainty. Was it possible? Could that life really be his? His heart rammed against the inside of his rib cage. A deep longing sprang up from his core and he realized he'd never wanted anything else as much as he wanted the belief Aaron spoke of. But his past transgressions pounded back at the ringing of truth and reminded him that he wasn't worth it. Not after all he'd done. The longing died down to only a small vibration in his gut, dampened by his shame. Such things weren't possible for people like him.

The wind that had been still moments before now violently whipped across the field and over Remko. It tore at his shirt and the ends of his hair. It was mostly warm, paired with the sun, but chilled in spots as it ripped across Remko's skin. It shook him inside, under his flesh, past the shame and blame calling him unfit, past the monsters eating away at his memories. It drove into the darkest parts of his fear and exploded. Light filled Remko's chest, flooded through his skin and out into the field. An intense heat caused Remko's breath to catch in his throat. His heart seemed to pause and then speed forward, its beat coursing through his body.

He felt fear at the sudden appearance of such power; he wanted to run from it, hide from it. Because it saw. Nothing was hidden from this light.

Remko felt overcome with joy. He wanted to laugh and cry all at once as the light and wind continued to sail around him. He heard a soft chuckle and looked over to see Aaron lying back in the grass, letting the wind wash over him. A soft giggle filled the air on his other side, and Remko turned toward the sound to see that the small boy was back, twirling with the light and laughing against the sky.

Suddenly Remko felt as if the wind was lifting him from the ground. The light itself was holding him, wrapping him in warmth. Tears drained from his eyes and he began to shake. Sobs racked his shoulders as the wind and light pulled him close.

A voice boomed through Remko's consciousness. *I call you mine, son of the Father. Fearless, blameless. Know who I am and therefore who you are.*

Remko opened his mouth to respond but was so captured by the light that he couldn't find words. Awestruck, he wept as the words flowed through him.

I call you mine, son of the Father. Fearless, blameless. Listen to your true name and know.

Dark memories filled Remko's mind. The prison the night Helms was killed, how Remko couldn't save him, couldn't make it in time. The image played like a fatal blow, but the light holding him close pushed into the memory and washed it clean. Remko cried out as the light filled him with peace where there had been pain. He saw Larkin's face, singing hymns of joy before being executed. Again the light rushed in and made the picture whole, filled now only with warmth. Over and over, memory to memory, the wind and light wiped the slate clean, replacing Remko's guilt and shame with a peace that caused him to tremble with joy and awe.

Love. That's what it was. A love that rescued his mind and broke him from his self-hatred. A love designed specifically for him, to hold him and cast out his fear.

The wind danced in a frenzy of motion and the light spread out so wide that all Remko could see was love. He felt joy spilling through his skin, out of his mouth and into the air. Laughter and peace rocking him free.

Freedom—at last he was feeling true freedom.

I call you mine, son of the Father. I call you fearless, blameless, loved.

Remko's laugh turned into a full bellow. His sides ached from the motion, his mind rumbling with the new sensation of freedom. How long had he wandered away from what he could have touched? How long had he searched for freedom within his limited version of reality, a false freedom he could find by defeating his enemies, when true freedom existed here, in his heart? He laughed instead of feeling shame for what he could have claimed as another failure.

For the first time, he believed. He believed in the way of Aaron, in his true self, in his Father. Joy bubbled to the surface as the wind died down to a calm breeze, softly tugging at his heart. The sunlight bathed him in its gentle touch.

A fresh set of tears slid down Remko's cheeks. "I surrender," he whispered. "I believe and I surrender." The light expanded in him once more and he felt the face of his Father smiling.

I call you mine, son of the Father.

Remko smiled and breathed in his new truth, the truth that had always been within him but that he'd finally opened his eyes to see. A hand clapped his shoulder and Aaron was there, his face threatening to split open from his smile.

"Ha!" he said, slapping Remko's back. "Welcome to the family, Seer."

Remko chuckled and Aaron joined in. Within moments the two were lying back in the grass, clutching their sides, laughter echoing from their mouths.

Remko wasn't sure how long he lay there, filled with joy, but it consumed him wholly so that he didn't notice when Aaron's laughter drifted off, didn't notice when the field faded; he just rested in the truth that he was created for.

/ / /

He woke in his holding cell. His first instinct was to be filled with fear, and it started to come. He felt it creeping along, up his chest, through his mind. Then he recognized where letting himself be filled with fear would lead him, and he closed his eyes, searching for the words of his identity.

They came with roaring clarity. *I call you mine. What shall you fear?*

Remko smiled and walked through the fear that threatened him to find it was nothing compared to the truth pulsing through his veins. His true power.

Remko sat up. Nothing had changed around him, but everything had changed within him.

The daggers came, the world trying to sling its hurtful reality at Remko's mind. And a few stuck. Elise was still in the hands of the Authority, his own flesh and blood captured by his former regime. And if Elise was here, it was safe to assume so was Carrington. The people he loved more than anything.

Panic filled his chest and he struggled to find the peace within the light that had held him close. How could he walk through this fear? He wished for the field, for the wind and the light, for Aaron, for the small boy. It was easy to be free of fear in that place, but how would he find it here?

I call you mine, son of the Father. What shall you fear?

The doorknob twisted and a guard walked in. Smith. Remko's mind instinctively flashed to Smith shooting Dodson dead. Anger welled up inside his chest and he stood.

Smith carried in a tray of food and set it on the desk. He glanced at Remko, and Remko saw sorrow lining the man's eyes. The light that Remko now carried flared against his anger and he felt the fury ease.

Was this man not also a son of the Father? Was he not also trapped, just as Remko had been, in the duty of this world's standards? Were they not just the same? Something different bloomed inside Remko's heart. Compassion.

Smith quickly peered over Remko's shoulder to the highest corner of the wall, where a camera was placed to monitor all of Remko's movements. Remko sensed that if that camera weren't there Smith would have something to say to him, but he was trapped with the eyes of the Authority watching.

Remko took a step toward Smith, who inched backward. Remko loosened his face and let the compassion filling his heart seep into his eyes. He took several more steps until he was close enough to Smith to place his hand gently on the man's shoulder. Smith tensed, ready to react if needed, and Remko kept his touch warm.

Smith's eyes darted from Remko to the camera, and back to Remko. Remko broke the silence. "I forgive you, my brother."

Shock filled Smith's face and softly turned to sorrow.

"There is freedom from this pain. I know that now," Remko said. "I hold nothing against you."

Tears rimmed the inside of Smith's eyes and he swallowed to contain his emotions. He held Remko's eyes for only a moment longer before turning and closing the door behind him as he left the room.

Silence engulfed the cell and Remko stayed standing by the door, thinking about the moment that had just passed. He smiled, feeling the joy of truth buzzing inside his head. The little monsters were no longer gnawing away at him;

his fear was no longer filling him with panic. The light had squashed them both. Remko walked to the desk where Smith had set his food and sat to eat, filled with too much joy to care that it was once again soup.

31 The day flew by. Remko was alone in his cell but not alone in his spirit. He spent the day listening to the voice of truth, searching for new truths he felt he was discovering every minute. It was like opening a box filled with notes, each one holding a different secret to the universe, a box he had always possessed but had forgotten about. New truths brought new fears, new daggers, but Remko practiced remembering who he was and walking through them in faith and belief. Faith that his Father was bigger, joy that he was called His son.

Food was brought to him several more times, and he waited for the insects that had been planted in his mind to begin eating away again, but they didn't. He knew Damien must be watching him. Eventually he would see that the injection wasn't working and most likely Remko would be injected again. He walked through that fear and trained his eyes to look for the light when he felt like the darkness was closing in. Thoughts of Elise and Carrington stayed with him always; he trusted that they too were called by the Father. He was learning that trust was part of faith.

He understood what Aaron had meant when he said there was no war to fight because the war had already been won; all they needed to do was surrender and accept their true nature. Child of the King. Remko chuckled—that made him a prince. What did a prince fear? Was his Father not the greatest King of all? Who was more powerful, more beautiful than He? As His son, was Remko not unlimited in what he could do, the access he could have?

Again Remko laughed and wondered if moving mountains was a real thing. He spent hours in this place of joy, imagining limitlessness. Resting in the power the light brought him. He hardly noticed Smith enter when he did.

The lieutenant rushed over and pulled Remko from his waking dream. "Come with me," he said.

He spoke in hushed tones and Remko glanced up at the camera in the corner.

"I disabled it for the moment, but they'll realize soon enough, so we have to go," Smith said.

Remko stood and followed Smith out through the door of his prison. He marveled that despite the locked door, the only prison that had truly contained him was the one he had erected himself.

Smith moved quickly down the hallway, and Remko saw rooms on either side, more prisoners behind locked doors, just as Remko had been moments before. He couldn't help but wonder if they were prisoners locked in their own minds, as he had been.

His eyes scanned their faces as they moved and fell on a man he knew.

Neil.

Remko stopped. The man looked disheveled, broken, pale, as if he hadn't eaten in days and was withering away to dust. Remko glanced at the other rooms on either side and saw more faces he recognized. Kal on one side, Ian Carson on the other. All men from his past, all trapped, being injected and conformed to the will of one sick man. All trapped in prisons of their own making as well—ones they could be free from.

"We should let them out," Remko said, coming to a stop.

Smith turned to Remko and shook his head. "We don't have time. Our window is small and we need to get you out of here."

But how could he leave them?

Another thought fell like a stone in Remko's mind. "Elise."

"She isn't here anymore; they took her into the city, and before you ask, Carrington was never here. They never caught her."

Remko's heart seized. His daughter, his precious little girl, was in the city out of reach, but his wife, the woman who had loved him even when he was lost to darkness, was out there somewhere away from the cruel hands of the Authority. The reality of it weighed heavy on his back and he searched for the light.

"Remko, we have to go now," Smith said.

"Why?" Remko asked. "Why do this? Why risk it?"

Smith paused and exhaled. "Because you know something the rest of us don't. I've seen Damien's plan. The people are going to need someone who can show them what you know."

Remko was taken aback but felt the light balloon anew in his chest.

Go, be a true Seer. I will lead you, and they will see.

He would, he would show them all.

Let all who come, come.

/ / /

"What do you mean, he's gone?" Damien yelled. He ripped the man from the chair that sat in front of the patient-monitoring console. Damien pounded on the keys and flipped from patient to patient. Remko's room came onto the screen, empty, the door ajar. It was impossible. How could he have gotten out?

"Someone fed us with a loop, gave him enough time to get out before we realized he was gone. We're watching so many participants," the man said.

"And that's an excuse for why you let him slip through your fingers?" Damien screamed.

The man said nothing and kept his eyes on the floor.

"Who could have done this?" Damien asked.

The man gulped. "It had to be someone with access. Only a handful of people can get into this room."

Damien turned to the guard standing by. "Gather everyone who has access to this room and find out who did this!"

The guard nodded and left.

Damien ran his fingers through his hair and tried to calm his breathing. If the Scientist found out about this . . . He couldn't finish that thought without a tremor passing through his fingers. The Scientist would see this as failure, Damien's failure, and people didn't fail the Scientist without paying consequences.

Damien let out a frustrated growl and swept his hands across the top of the desk in front of him. The contents crashed to the floor, bringing the room to a complete standstill.

What had happened? Things had started off so well with Remko; the injection had worked. How had that stupid child broken all that Damien had built? How had the second injection had no effect? Everyone else was showing perfect results.

Damien knew the Scientist would care more about Remko than the others. There were still other members of the Seers out there. Jesse had reported their most recent position, but of course they had been gone, as Damien expected.

Remko was the key. If for some reason he was above being affected by the Genesis injection, it meant uncertainty ahead, and that was unacceptable. Remko had to be apprehended.

Damien's future depended on it.

/ / /

Jesse entered the stuffy office the Scientist called home. He thought the place smelled like dust and old age so he usually avoided it at all costs. But he was trying to win back favor, so he ignored the stench.

Jesse knew Remko had escaped from the Genesis Compound several hours earlier. He understood what kind of trouble this would mean for Damien. Jesse had never had a problem with the Authority President, but he was surprised by the man's failure. It seemed the task ahead required more than Damien had to give. Especially after all that Jesse had witnessed. There was no denying the strange power that existed within the Seer group. He himself had watched a flesh-and-bone man stop bullets.

He'd known then that there was more to this story than even they understood. Jesse couldn't ignore the itching questions that haunted his dreams. If Aaron was what he said, the son of a Father with that kind of power, what were they actually fighting against? And now with Remko's escape, it was hard to know what the future would bring.

Jesse thought of Elise. Something about the way the girl looked into his eyes, as if she understood him, was unnerving. And he'd worried about what her fate would be after her purpose was fulfilled. He hadn't planned on worrying about it, but somehow it had happened. She was asleep and being monitored even now. Never to be left unguarded.

If Remko was free, his people would come for her, and she couldn't be taken. She was different somehow. The Scientist had taught Jesse to listen to his instincts, to determine which ones were for the bigger purpose and which were unfortunate side effects of being trapped in a lower level of existence. Right now his instincts were warning him against letting Elise be rescued.

The Scientist was staring out the window into the street below, and Jesse waited for him to speak.

"Thank you for coming," the Scientist said.

"Is everything all right?" Jesse asked.

"No, but it will be." The Scientist turned to face Jesse. "We just need to dispose of the fat."

"How can I help?" Jesse asked.

"There's going to be a change in leadership within the city. I have mistakenly placed my hopes in the wrong man, a mistake I take full responsibility for and one that I will solve," the Scientist said.

Damien, Jesse thought.

"The time has come for you to win back my trust."

Jesse waited as the Scientist thought through his next statement. Whatever the Scientist asked, Jesse would do.

"We have much to discuss, but first let's discuss the child. I was told there were complications with her injections."

Jesse had known this topic would arise. "Not complications really; rather, nothing happened."

"Explain."

"After giving her the proper dose for her size and age, we ran a neural scan, as we have done with the other children, and we found nothing irregular. As if she hadn't been injected at all."

The Scientist thought through Jesse's words. "And you injected her a second time?"

Jesse nodded. "The results were the same."

"That seems highly improbable."

"All of the doctors attending her are stunned."

The Scientist thought another moment. "Well, if she cannot be injected, then we will need to dispose of her."

Jesse had assumed as much, but he was not willing to let that happen. "Actually, I propose we hold off on that. The injections may still work if we tweak the solution, and she could become very helpful as we track down the remaining Seers."

The Scientist glanced over at Jesse and met his eyes. He held them, as if time were suspended, and Jesse waited. "You will tend to her?" the Scientist asked finally.

"Of course, and when she shows no further use of any kind, I will dispose of her myself," Jesse said.

The Scientist nodded and Jesse felt a rush of relief. Elise would be spared, at least for now. Jesse didn't know why exactly, but he felt the child was immensely important. He was actually beginning to believe that she might be the key to everything.

"I have always had big plans for you," the Scientist said. "We need to start executing those plans immediately." He looked at Jesse sternly. "I have already been let down once by you; I will not tolerate it a second time."

Jesse felt a swirl of fear move through his gut but kept it from showing on his face. The future was unclear. What would become of the Seers was still to be determined. And Elise's purpose was in question. But he was certain of one thing.

Jesse returned the Scientist's gaze with as much intensity as he could manage. "You won't have to."

/ / /

The sun was setting behind the mountains when Remko and Smith finally stopped for a break. They'd escaped the Genesis Compound with little trouble. Smith had known exactly where to lead Remko so they wouldn't be detected until they were miles away. Once out, they'd headed north as the light inside Remko called him forward. He listened, as Carrington had listened when they had first left the Authority City all those months ago. He'd wondered then how she could be so sure of where she was going, but now he understood.

The truth was he'd always known where to go, what road to take, what path to travel, but he'd covered up the light that lived inside with the shadow of fear and self-hate. Now that the light was pulsing freely, following it was natural and simple.

Smith had very little to say, but Remko could hear his mind working. Making the choice to break Remko out meant that Smith could never return to the life he'd known before. But Remko wasn't worried, because there was now truth inside Smith, and Remko would do all he could to help the man discover it.

Wasn't that what they were called to? To see each other just as they saw themselves? To know that they were all the same, with the same light living inside them all, just waiting to be discovered? The only option was to respond to the light with pure love, even if a person hadn't discovered it yet. *There is no war,* Remko thought, and it brought a smile to his face. Even in the ominous gloom of his current situation he still felt joy. Because he knew it would all be different now.

Remko glanced back at Smith, and the man nodded, offering him water from a canteen at his waist. Remko accepted the gift and let the cool liquid touch his lips. A warm wind, even in the cold night, softly shuffled around Remko. He closed his eyes and breathed the air into his lungs. It filled him with energy and made his flesh buzz. His Father was close and leading him.

The thought nearly brought Remko to his knees again. He wondered if he would ever get used to the overwhelming wave of emotion that came from knowing his true identity. He hoped not.

Smith used his binoculars to survey the land ahead while they still had some fading light. He paused, looking through the scopes, and handed them to Remko. "I think I see something."

Remko took the binoculars and looked for what Smith had seen. He smiled. A fire, small in the distance. A camp. Hopefully Carrington's camp. A heavy dose of sorrow and fear dropped into his gut. How could he possibly beg her forgiveness for abandoning her, for not being there to protect their daughter, for all his failings?

As the questions banged against the inside of his head, they threatened to cover the light that had moments ago been so vibrant. Another gush of wind swirled around them and Remko listened for truth. This was the journey of remembering and forgetting. Smith nodded for Remko to lead on and he did, even with a small tremor in his steps. It was hard to hear truth over the pulse of his blood.

By the time they made it to the outskirts of the camp, the sky was lit only with shining stars. A figure noticed them approaching and alerted the rest of the group; the sentry probably thought they were a threat. Remko and Smith approached carefully, their arms raised until they were bathed in enough light that those in the camp could make them out. For a long moment no one moved.

Remko scanned their faces. Wire, Kate, Ramses, Lesley, Eleanor, others he knew, all of them too shocked to move. But he didn't see Carrington. Panic started to blossom in his chest until a small woman walked out from behind the crowd, her green eyes damp and red, her face shadowed by exhaustion.

Remko's eyes filled with tears and he took a step toward her. Carrington broke the stillness as if she had been finally set free and rushed toward him. She was up in his arms, sobs already shaking her shoulders, his hands clasping her close, arms holding her tightly and soaking in her warmth.

They said nothing; there was nothing they could really say in this moment. Remko only wanted to hold her, to feel her breath and heartbeat, to kiss away her tears.

Carrington pulled back to look at Remko's face. She placed both hands on his cheeks and held his eyes with her own, her tears glimmering in the starlight. He leaned down and kissed her, aware that everyone around was watching, but not caring. He'd been certain she was lost to him, certain he'd never feel her again. Yet here she was, wrapped in his arms.

He released her mouth, and through labored breaths she spoke.

"Elise—" she tried but couldn't continue as another wave of tears engulfed her.

"I know," Remko said. "She's alive and we'll get her back. We will get her back."

Carrington nodded and laid her forehead against Remko's chest. He looked up to see the faces of people he loved dearly waiting for him to say something. There was so much hurt in their eyes—hurt he'd caused, pain that needed mending. It was almost impossible to feel the light inside through the guilt and shame, but he heard the voice and felt an ease fill his bones.

I call you mine, son of the Father. What shall you fear?

Kate stepped forward, her eyes fixed on Smith, her mouth a straight line. "What is he doing here?"

Remko hadn't even thought about how Smith's presence would look to the others. Smith was their enemy, he'd been a large part of capturing Sam, and they were not to blame for feeling afraid.

"Please," Remko said. "He is the reason I'm here."

"It's some sort of trap," Ramses said from behind Kate. Remko felt another tug of joy at seeing his brother and took a step forward before noticing the pain in Ramses's face.

Remko stopped. Much healing needed to be done before they trusted him again. He hadn't anticipated how much that would sting.

He swallowed and held Ramses's eyes. "It's not a trap. I trust him." He knew his words probably meant very little, but it was enough to make both Kate and Ramses stay where they were. No one was charging anyone yet. That was a start.

"And Sam?" Wire braved.

Remko could feel the change in Kate as much as he saw it. His heart broke with her and again he had to stop himself from moving forward to comfort her.

Smith spoke before Remko could. "Sam isn't what you remember. Damien has made him into something else. Damien plans to make us all into something else."

Remko saw Kate's eyes flood with tears and before she could respond, another figure walked into camp from the darkness. Aaron.

His eyes found Remko's and the rest of the camp turned to see him. He walked straight for Remko and Carrington. He stopped beside them and placed his hand on Carrington's arm, his eyes filled with empathy. She gave him a tired smile and he squeezed her arm. Then he turned to Remko and the overwhelming sense of the Father within him shook Remko to the core. The guilt, shame, and fear that had inched up Remko's back fell away.

Aaron smiled, his eyes filled with contagious joy, and Remko followed suit. A soft chuckle left Aaron's mouth and the two men embraced as brothers for the first time. Remko felt his own laughter bubbling as he patted Aaron's back.

"Welcome home, brother," Aaron said. And home was exactly where Remko felt he was. The two men released each other and Remko turned to the rest of the group.

"Where do we go from here?" Wire asked. The boy's eyes were filled with tears and Remko again found himself practicing letting go of his shame.

"We do things differently now," Remko said. "We stop fighting them, because that is only bringing us suffering. Now we learn to be true Seers, and then we show them, not by our actions but by our choices. We will be what we are called to be: brothers and sisters of the light, truly awake. We will show them by our faith, and we will let the awakening begin, with us."

Remko saw the hesitation in people's faces, but he knew they would see as he did with time. He turned to Aaron. "Thank you."

Aaron smiled and squeezed Remko's shoulder. He stepped to welcome Smith as the camp watched.

"It's good to have you here," Aaron said and extended his hand toward Smith. Slowly Smith reached out and accepted.

"Let all who come, come," Aaron said and turned to the group. "The days ahead will be dark, but we are filled with light, so there is nothing to fear."

"Damien's plans are terrible," Smith said.

Aaron smiled sadly. "Yes. Thankfully we follow a different plan."

"I have heard you are powerful; can you not just stop this?" Smith asked.

The rest of the group stayed quiet. They had all had the same thought before. Remko watched as Aaron looked at the faces surrounding him, a somber expression in his eyes.

"My role is to lead you to power. I can't save you. I never could. But a time is coming when someone can. We have done what we can here, and now we will leave for a season."

"Leave?" Kate asked.

"Where will we go?" Ramses asked.

"There is a city where others like you live. A place you will be safe as we prepare for what comes next."

"What!" Kate said.

"Then why did we stay here all this time?" Wire asked.

"All that has happened was necessary for what is to come," Aaron replied.

"We can't leave. I won't go without her," Carrington said and the rest of the group fell silent.

Aaron turned his gaze to Carrington, then moved to her and grabbed her hands with his own. Tears glistened in his eyes. "Elise is more powerful than you know, and she is where she has been called to be."

Tears rolled down Carrington's cheeks. "She is a baby— my baby!"

Remko shook his head. Aaron couldn't possibly be suggesting they leave their daughter? As if in response to Remko's disbelief, Aaron reached out one hand and placed it on Remko's shoulder.

The moment he did, a strong wind swirled through the group, lapping at Remko's hair and easing his fear.

What shall you fear?

Remko closed his eyes and let the wind rustle against his worry and pain. Carrington cried out in sorrow beside him, and he opened his eyes to see the wind wrapping itself around her as well. He saw all the members of the group being affected by the truth he now knew. The rush of love and strength fought against their fears.

Remko looked to Aaron, who was etched in a glowing light, assuring Remko of what he already knew. Aaron was not merely a man, not even anything they could really comprehend, but he was their guiding force, and he knew the wind better than any of them.

And then, almost as soon as it fell upon them, the wind left, leaving behind the spirit of freedom it had carried. The entire group rose as one, each person seeing truth clearly and understanding their journey was just beginning.

Silence surrounded them as they breathed together. Long moments that were filled with both pain and light, but the light was stronger. Remko pulled Carrington close and felt her sorrow melt into his own. "Now we have to practice trust," Remko whispered to her.

Carrington squeezed his side and fresh tears soaked through his shirt.

"We have to trust that something bigger than us will hold Elise close. The power we've both experienced will protect her. We have to remind each other to have faith, and listen for the truth, and trust."

Carrington softly turned in Remko's arms so she was facing him. Their eyes connected. She placed her hand on the side of Remko's face and the heat from her skin spread down his neck.

With tears still wet on her cheeks she spoke. "You're going to have to remind me often." Emotion caused her voice to crack and she swallowed. "Because I won't be able to remember on my own."

Remko nodded. "I will."

"We will all remind each other," Aaron said beside them.

Remko shared a moment of knowing with Aaron before looking across the group and seeing knowing in them as well.

He knew everything would be different now. There was much they needed to hear, many moments of fear and suffering to come, but they would practice faith; they would trust in a power bigger than their own. They would walk the path of the light, the wind as their source, Aaron as their guide, the truth as their anchor.

They had been chosen, and they had been called. Now they would move toward their final awakening.

ACKNOWLEDGMENTS

When I sit down and think of all the people who helped shape this novel, the list becomes almost overwhelming. How did I get lucky enough to have so many inspirational people in my life? The kind who listen, love, give advice, laugh, cry, and hold me up when the sky feels like it's falling down around me. Their constant encouragement and support are the reasons this novel, or any novel I write, gets finished.

To Tyndale, the greatest publisher in the world. I hope you know how fortunate I feel to get to work with your team every day. To Jeremy, my editor, and the copyediting team at Tyndale, thank you for making this manuscript shine.

To Whitney and Esther, the two beautiful women who I know are always fighting for me. Thank you for being so enthusiastic and dedicated. Seriously, you two are like superheroes.

To the Blue Monkeys, who never seem to doubt me. Kelsey and Stephanie, your friendship has become a necessary part of my life. Even across the distance that separates us, I always know you have my back and I lean on that truth more than you know.

To Katy, one of the world's greatest women and my dearest friend, thank you. The time you spent walking this path with me, and the way you loved this story and helped it grow, is inspiring.

To my family. My siblings for making me laugh and keeping me humble. My mom for being a beautiful rock of encouragement and a nonjudgmental place of love to run to when the world sends its doubts. My dad for continuing to seek truth and in doing so inspiring me to do the same, and for encouraging me to step into my fear rather than run from it. Thank you all. I love you more than I could say.

To my stellar husband. Doing life with you is my favorite thing. Thanks for never kicking me out when I get "story-crazed," for listening to me talk myself in circles, for taking me to eat chips and salsa when I need inspiration, and for picking up all the other pieces of my life so I can just write. I could never do this without you. I love you.

But most importantly, to my Father. The One writing my story. Let your words be my words as I seek love first. Let your thoughts be my thoughts as I learn to walk through fear, and let your way be my way every time I sit down to write. May every word be a reflection of truth, of love, and of you.

Thank you all,
Rachelle

ABOUT THE AUTHOR

The oldest daughter of *New York Times* bestselling author Ted Dekker, Rachelle Dekker was inspired early on to discover truth through storytelling. *The Choosing* was her critically acclaimed debut novel. Rachelle graduated with a degree in communications and spent several years in marketing and corporate recruiting before making the transition to write full-time. She lives in Nashville with her husband, Daniel, and their diva cat, Blair. Visit her online at www.rachelledekker.com.

DISCUSSION QUESTIONS

1. Authority President Damien Gold says, "Fear is a powerful sedative for rebellion." What does he mean by this? Do you agree with him?

2. What are the effects of fear in Remko's life? How does it affect his ability to lead and make decisions?

3. In chapter 7, Carrington reflects, "Faith was an impenetrable wall, not because it shut the fear out but because it invited the fear in." Can you think of an example of this from your own life—where faith meant acknowledging your fear and trusting God anyway? Later, in chapter 12, Larkin tells Carrington to accept and surrender her fear. What does it look like to surrender your fear to God?

4. Are there times when fear can be a valuable instinct? When does it go from helpful to harmful? How can you avoid letting fear become debilitating?

5. In chapter 5, Remko admits that he's following Aaron more because Carrington believes and he's seen the effect it's had on her rather than because he fully believes himself. How does that complicate things for him? Have you ever experienced something similar in your own life?

6. Also in chapter 5, Aaron tells Remko, "You enslave yourself with expectations." What does this look like in Remko's life? Can you think of a time when you enslaved yourself with expectations? What was the outcome?

7. Why does Carrington decide not to reach out to her mother? (See chapter 8.) Did you agree with her decision? How should we discern when to share our beliefs with others and when not to? Have you ever struggled to trust God with the salvation of your loved ones?

8. In chapter 26, Remko wonders, "If freedom really was a lie, then wouldn't it be better to just forget he needed freedom at all?" What would you say in response to his doubts? Can you think of a situation in your own life where it was important to know the truth even if that truth was hard?

9. In chapter 27, Remko wrestles with guilt over bringing a child into such an uncertain world. Should he feel guilty? Why or why not? How can we reassure ourselves

and others when worries about the dangers and uncertainties in this world start to creep in?

10. After Remko encourages Carrington to "trust that something bigger than us will hold Elise close" at the end of the book, she tells him, "You're going to have to remind me often. Because I won't be able to remember on my own." Throughout the Bible, God encourages his people to remember his acts of faithfulness in the past. Why is this important? How can we remind others to trust God's faithful character, the way Remko reminds Carrington?

11. Were you surprised by the identities of those who betrayed Remko and the Seers? In each case, what was the motivation behind the betrayal? In your opinion, can betrayals like that ever be justified?

12. What do you predict will happen for Carrington, Remko, and the rest of the Seers in the next—and final—book of the series?

JOIN RACHELLE ON THE JOURNEY

Visit www.rachelledekker.com